# BRAHMA HATHYA

T.V. MAHALINGAM

# BRAHMA HATHYA

First published by Westland Books, a division of Nasadiya Technologies Private Limited, in 2024

No. 269/2B, First Floor, 'Irai Arul', Vimalraj Street, Nethaji Nagar, Alapakkam Main Road, Maduravoyal, Chennai 600095

Westland and the Westland logo are the trademarks of Nasadiya Technologies Private Limited, or its affiliates.



ISBN: 9789357769273

10 9 8 7 6 5 4 3 2 1

This is a work of fiction. Names, characters, organisations, places, events and incidents are either products of the author's imagination or used fictitiously.



Typeset by SÜRYA, New Delhi

Printed at Nutech Print Services, India

*Dedicated to Mahadeva and Mahamaya,*
*the Soul of the Universe*

# CONTENTS

Disclaimer:
This map and its locations are entirely fictional, drawing inspiration from the Ancient Indian civilization.

# 1. After Time

The shepherd boy woke up just before dawn like he always did: cold, stiff and with only one thought gnawing at the back of his foggy mind.

*Was the jogi alive?*

The room was dark and freezing—like the bottom of a still, icy lake. Slowly, he peeled away the layers of smelly wool that he used to cover himself with every night and carefully placed his feet on the floor. Immediately, he winced and pulled them back. The fire had sputtered out in the night and the stone floor was hard and cold.

*Was the jogi alive?*

In the dark, he groped for his socks under the blankets. He slipped them on and wiggled his toes to get the blood rushing back again. He tiptoed across the room for he did not want to wake up his grandfather, who lay motionless on his cot, either dead or in deep sleep.

He unslung his sheepskin cloak from the hook on the wall and wrapped it around himself. The cloak felt cold but he knew that, in a few moments, it would feel warm and comforting—much like the memory of his dead mother's embrace.

He picked up his heavy bamboo staff, the backpack he had packed the night before and paused for a moment at the door, gathering his courage. He slipped on his battered wooden slippers, took a deep breath and cracked open the door just a little.

The morning breeze rolling down the mountains tore into him—instantly numbing his face, drying his lips and paralysing his fingers.

Behind him, grandpa stirred. 'Get out, boy,' the old man moaned, his voice thick with sleep.

The boy stepped outside the warm sanctuary of his stone home and pulled the door shut.

As he stumbled along in the dark, he realised that it had snowed heavily the night before. The path was slippery and his heavy wooden sandals made progress tough. He stood for a while to catch his breath, pulled his cloak a little tighter around his frail shoulders and looked around. He had seen the same view every morning of his life and yet, something about its brutal majesty always filled him with awe and wonder.

The sun was yet to show its face but he could see the massive silhouette of the mountain they called Kedar towering above his little home. Grandpa always said that Kedar was the oldest mountain in the world—older than the world itself and even older than the eternal one.

Most of the time, the boy did not believe in these stories. But looking at the gigantic outline of the peak in the dark, the story felt true. The mountain sat there, large and looming—watching over the boy, his house, his village, and the gurgling Mandakini River. Kedar dwarfed the snow-clad peaks around it and the little temple at its base. In fact, Kedar made everything around it look miniscule, insignificant.

Instinctively, the boy folded his hands, closed his eyes and said a silent prayer to the eternal mountain. A stiff breeze blew down the mountain, like a cruel cold blessing. The boy pulled his cloak tighter around him and his thoughts wandered back to the man who sat alone in that dank, icy cave high up in the mountain: half-naked and unprotected.

*Was the jogi alive?*

Halfway up the mountain trail, the shepherd boy again took a moment to catch his breath. It was almost dawn but the sun was still playing hide and seek. Furiously massaging his frozen, numb fingers, the boy wondered how the sun rose in the flatlands. *Did it suddenly jump out from behind a clump of trees?*

His grandfather had worked in the flatlands, tilling the land, for a few years in his younger days. He did not have good things to say about the people who lived below the mountains.

'Fat, silver-obsessed folk, always scurrying around like ants,' grandpa would grumble.

The boy himself had never left the village. His short life, for as long as he could remember it, had followed a mind-numbing routine that was driven by the sun. Wake up at dawn, walk up the mountain, feed the jogi, graze the sheep, cook food for his grandfather and himself, eat before the sun set and go to sleep as the stars come out.

On some evenings, the shepherd boy went to the temple dedicated to the god of the mountain, the one the villagers called Kedarnath. He seldom prayed. He just liked sitting in the warm womb of the temple and seeing the occasional pilgrims who came from the flatlands.

Unlike the people in his village, the flatlanders spoke in a thousand tongues. And dressed in a thousand different ways. Some spoke in the slippery language of the gods that only the priest in the temple understood, others spoke in the coarser tongues of the lands farther in the south. Some of them were tall, sword carriers with drying wounds on their bodies. Others were small, plump men dressed in fine silks who carried purses on their hips that jingled with silver and gold. The temple priest would brighten up when the men in silks turned up.

And then, there were those who came in tattered clothes, shivering in the cold. They would gaze at the lord of the mountain from outside the temple. The boy never understood why they never went inside.

In the nights, once the temple doors had closed, he would go back home, light a fire and often dream of life in the flatlands: kings, queens, chariots, mountains of gold and great battles.

A stiff icy breeze cut through his early morning daydream. He turned back and looked at the temple at the base of the mountain. From here, it looked just like a pebble, one you could pick up and toss.

He knew he wasn't far from his destination now. He gathered up his backpack which was tied to his stout bamboo stick and started walking up the mountain.

Up above, in a cold cave that only wild animals stalked, sat the half-naked jogi.

*Was the jogi alive?*

Nobody in the village quite knew how the jogi had come to live in the cave—or, for that matter, who he was.

Everybody in the village had a theory though, which they discussed usually around a warm smoky fire in the village square as snowflakes swirled and danced around them.

'Jogis can fly, you know,' the ironsmith loved to say, always flapping his muscled arms dramatically. The gathered children tittered nervously whenever he did that, for it made the ironsmith with his soot-covered face and round belly look like a giant black bat.

'One dark night, I saw a light streaking across the night sky,' the butcher began his story, each time with the same line. 'A few days later, the jogi was found in the cave. Maybe he came from another world riding on a bolt of lightning,' said the butcher, blowing out perfectly round smoke rings.

Most villagers privately scoffed at this story but kept their scepticism to themselves. The butcher had a hot temper and carried a big hammer. In fact, on various occasions, the butcher had seen flying horses with pale, luminous wings, heard gandharvas singing melancholic songs in the afternoon and had, once, even seen the eternal one dancing joyously inside a lotus bud. These visions were attributed to the butcher's habit of constantly pulling on his chillum.

'It's a bad omen. May Shiva save us,' the temple priest often told pious worshippers. 'Why would a jogi turn up in the cave of Bhairon, the incarnation the eternal one assumes at the end of all time? Mark my words: death and destruction is coming. Only dharma and good deeds can save us,' he would prophecise, before extending the offerings plate to wide-eyed devotees for them to drop their silver in.

The boy was not sure what to believe in. Nor did he care. All he knew was that the jogi had been a part of his life for as long as he could remember; he could not even recall how many winters ago he had seen the jogi first. And all that mattered to him now was that the jogi was still there. In the cave of Bhairon. A mystery waiting to be solved, in a village where everything was as predictable as the sunrise and sunset.

Seeing the jogi every day in that cave gave his life purpose, even excitement. So, each day the shepherd boy walked to the cave of Bhairon, fed the jogi and then returned to his dull life.

Up ahead, he could see the yawning mouth of the Bhairon cave. Nothing grew inside the cave. Or around it. Neither shrub, nor weed. Not even moss. It was like a cold, barren hole in the face of a mountain teeming with life.

The boy shivered. Just the thought of going inside the cave froze his bones. The snow on the path was thick and scrunched under his wooden slippers. He grabbed his bamboo stick and started walking towards the cave.

*Was the jogi alive?*

The jogi sat there. As always, he was motionless. Like a rock—perfectly still and with no sign of life.

*More like a corpse*, thought the boy.

Crouching down on all fours on the floor of the low cave, the boy studied the jogi closely. The jogi's legs were crossed. His neck was limp, leaving his head slumped backwards. Thick matted locks, layered with dirt, grew from the back of his head like the thick roots of a banyan tree reaching down to the ground.

Big, glassy eyes stared vacantly at the roof of the cave. The jaw was slack, leaving the mouth agape. A small line of ants was slowly marching into the jogi's mouth. A shaggy, wild beard covered most of his face and neck, extending down to his chest.

The woollen rug that the boy had covered the jogi with, had slipped off his shoulders, leaving his torso bare. The once-muscular chest was still broad but by now had wasted away with almost no flesh on it.

Out of sheer habit, the boy placed a finger under the jogi's nostrils. No breath. There was no sign of life. No heaving of the bony ribs, not even the blinking of an eye.

The jogi's unceasing gaze made the boy uneasy. They seemed to peer into infinity with an expression the boy couldn't quite fathom. The elders in the village said it was an expression of bliss. But the boy could never be sure. *Was it really bliss? Or was it pain? Or horror?*

A pool of tears gathered around the rims of the jogi's eyes and spilled down the corners in an unending cascade that drenched his beard. Instinctively, the boy wiped the tears away from the jogi's cheeks with his cloak.

He placed his palm on the icy-cold, bony chest of the jogi. And waited.

At first, silence.

And then: *Doob-doob. Doob-doob. Doob-doob.*

The beat was faint, like a drum beating far away. But it was there.

*The jogi was alive.*

The boy's eyes moved to the jogi's torso. At the right side of his stomach, was the familiar ugly, festering wound that never healed. The wound was the length of his thumb, deep and open. Maggots clung stubbornly to the opening, feasting on the ooze.

Winter after winter, summer after summer, the boy had applied herbs, salves and every kind of balm that the vaidya in the village had suggested but the wound had remained doggedly raw and unhealed.

He felt a wave of pity for the jogi, this man who sat in this cold cave alone, with a river of tears flowing from his eyes and a stubborn, filthy wound that refused to heal.

*It had to be pain, not bliss,* thought the boy.

On the wall of the cave, behind the jogi, was the fearsome

carving of the god after whom the cave was named. A face that belonged to a time when the world would come to an end: a fearsome smile, a garland of skulls around the neck, locks that looked like slithering serpents. The god who came at the end of time to deliver terrible, divine justice: Bhairon.

A bird call broke the boy's thoughts. It would soon be light outside and he still had to graze the sheep. But first he had to clean the jogi's scar and then pour a few drops of honey and water into the jogi's open mouth.

*The jogi was still alive.*

How long he would continue to live, the boy did not know.

## 2. The Lords of Vaishali

A rivulet of sweat snaked down the dark, thick locks of the courtesan and curved down her delicate shoulder. It paused for a moment, hanging on the edge of her shoulder like a pregnant dew drop, before it trickled down the muscular chest of the Lord of Vaishali, who lay next to her, locked in a tight embrace.

The light slumber of Trivikrama Shaurya—king of kings, protector of the virtuous, lord of the sixteen kingdoms, vanquisher of the nishadas, bravest of the brave—was thus broken.

The first thing the groggy eyes of the king saw was a pair of bare, curvy breasts. Who the breasts belonged to, the king could not quite recall but, for a moment, he marvelled at their shape and youthful vigour as they heaved rhythmically in the morning light.

His mouth was parched, his head felt as though a thousand horses had trampled on it, and his breath reeked of *sura*.

*Too much cheap sura*, he thought.

King Trivikrama buried his face between the warm, fragrant breasts of the woman. A heady concoction of champaka essence and jasmine filled his breath. Usually, he loved the sweet fragrance of champaka but just now, he felt sick.

Yet, Trivikrama stayed there, eyes closed, breathing in the overpowering smell of the nauseating perfume. For he knew what would happen once he opened his eyes. Another day would begin—an endless parade of empty rituals and meaningless chatter.

Yet another hollow day without *her*—the love of his life.

*She is gone … leaving me alone.*

Trivikrama felt a stab of pain, a dull familiar clasping ache at the centre of his chest. Grief, he now knew, was not a mental illusion like the wise men of his court had told him. He knew it was a physical experience—a hidden ache in his heart that struck like a wily foe every morning, reminding him of what he had lost. Trivikrama had heard of warriors who lose an arm in battle and yet, years later, wake up with a sensation of freezing cold or burning warmth in their missing fingers.

The loss of a loved one was like that, Trivikrama had come to realise. The person was gone. But their memories remained hidden, lurking in the crevices of the memory of the living, striking at will, inflicting pain. There was no running away from them, no hiding.

Trivikrama pulled away from the woman's chest and, opening his eyes, looked at her face. Memories of the night before flooded back. He had sneaked out in the night, dressed like a commoner—a wealthy merchant, this time—and headed alone, on horseback, towards Nataranga, the bohemian quarters of the city where the courtesans lived and gamblers lost all their money.

He had met her at a newly opened natyashala, the public halls where dancers practised their charms at night.

*What was her name?* He struggled to recall.

She had danced like a tender leaf swaying in the early morning breeze while Trivikrama guzzled goblet after goblet of cheap soma and fell deeply in love with her. Exactly the way he fell in love with a new courtesan every time there was a new moon in the sky.

At the natyashala, an obese singer with a hoarse voice had sung a sad song:

'Live tonight without regret, my friend
Some men fall in love to forget …'

By the end of the night, even though his purse had become empty and his vision had blurred, at least the dancer had been as smitten with him as he had been with her. She had certainly been as drunk as him. They had mounted his horse and headed towards the royal quarters. The rest of the night he did not remember—nor cared to.

Now he extricated himself from her embrace, leaned back on his bedpost and sat quietly for a moment. In the distance, he could faintly hear the voices of a hundred brahmans coming from the royal household, reciting the thousand names of Indra, the god of gods.

It was still the first hour after dawn. There were things to be done—a kingdom to be ruled. Trivikrama picked up the tiny bell lying next to his bed and tinkled it.

Outside the door, the two dwarapalakas proclaimed in one loud voice:

'Hail Trivikrama
King of Kings,
Protector of Sixteen Kingdoms,
The Just one,
The Vanquisher of evil,
Ruler of Vaishali,
Whose walk makes the world tremble,
Make way for him,
Make way for him,
Make way for him.'

Trivikrama smiled at the dancer who was now wide awake and staring at him wide-eyed. Looking at her startled face, he knew that she, too, could not remember what had happened the night before. He kissed her on the cheek, wrapped a silk loincloth around his waist, walked up to the massive, jewel-studded door of his bedroom, and threw it open.

Three men, all of noble birth, were waiting outside.

*The chosen ones.*

Chavuka, his personal physician, a corpulent man with bulging eyes, who forever seemed to be bathed in an ocean of sweat, stood staring at his feet. Next to him stood Brahmadatta, the royal astrologer, with an uncertain smile on his thick lips which waxed and waned every other minute.

And then, there was Jayaveera, the king's friend, wrestling partner, childhood friend and brother-in-law.

*Former brother-in-law*, Trivikrama corrected himself.

With bulging shoulders that could crack an elephant's skull with a single blow and a neatly trimmed beard, Jayaveera looked every bit the senapati of Mithila's formidable army.

'You look tired, my king,' said Jayaveera flatly, his large brown eyes filled with sadness at the plight of his friend. As always, the brown eyes reminded Trivikrama of her. Sometimes, he wished he did not have to face Jayaveera and his brown eyes every morning.

'Just a long night, my friend,' said Trivikrama, trying to smile.

Chavuka, the physician, bowed and handed him a silver vessel brimming with scented water.

*Time for a royal shit.*

Eyes closed, Prince Ajitha Shaurya breathed in slowly and exhaled.

'Slower,' Aacharya Gurukripa whispered in his ear. 'Breathe quietly … like a snake slithering in the grass.'

Ajitha breathed in again, even slower. And exhaled. The chirping of the early morning birds melted away. He could hear his heart thumping noisily, the blood flowing sluggishly through his veins. The tightness in his arms and wrists eased.

The prince inhaled again, this time even slower. His heartbeat was a gentle murmur. All that existed was the solitude within. He opened his eyes slowly and looked at the target at the far end of the archery field.

Five pots, tied with silk threads, hung on five bars placed one behind the other, parallel to each other. Each pot was painted a different colour. The pots swung like pendulums—all in a straight line but criss-crossing each other occasionally.

The prince breathed in, one last time.

'Red,' whispered the aacharya.

Ajitha watched the swinging pots—a moving kaleidoscope

of colours. One moment he saw blue, the next green, then it was black, and then it was the white pot.

*The red pot would come next*, thought the prince. He exhaled slowly and released the arrow. He saw the pot shatter before he heard the twang of the string next to his ear.

*Finally*.

His heart pounded with joy. He could hear the birds chirping again as well as the voices of the praying brahmans coming from the palace.

A smile of victory spread across his face.

'You shattered the wrong pot, my prince!' said Aacharya Gurukripa, stroking his long flowing grey beard. 'You waited too long before releasing the arrow.'

A tightness welled up within the young prince's heart. For the last six weeks, his mornings had been the same. Wake up well before dawn, drink a quart of pungent oil on an empty stomach, do a hundred sit-ups, wrestle with a man twice his size who would pound him into the mud, and practice fencing with the best swordsman in all Vaishali, who would stab at his chest with a blunt sword, day after day. And then, when he could barely breathe, shoot at a bunch of swinging pots. He had improved at every task, including that of keeping his vomit down after downing the oil, but shooting at the correct pot was still beyond him.

Right now, Ajitha wanted to break his bow and every arrow in his quiver over his knee. But he knew better. Aacharya Gurukripa would not approve.

'Anger is like a wild elephant, Ajitha. It tramples everything along its path and when there is nothing left to destroy, it consumes its own caretaker,' said Gurukripa, as if reading the young prince's mind.

Ajitha looked up at the reddish sky of the dawn and tried to master his emotions.

'Once more, Gurudev?' he asked.

Aacharya Gurukripa opened his mouth to reply just as the sound of a gong ringing thrice came from the palace. The king was awake. Court would begin in an hour. It was time for the prince to get ready for his royal duties.

'Once more, Gurudev?' Prince Ajitha repeated.

*The boy is as stubborn as a mule*, Gurukripa thought.

He smiled and nodded his head. His gooseberry green eyes twinkled in approval.

The prince picked up an arrow from his quiver, placed it on the bow and pulled the string right up to his ear.

'Breathe in slowly, Prince Ajitha,' said the aacharya.

The bow-legged man entered Mithila from the western gate, soon after sunrise. Despite his tattered clothes and unwashed body, the guards welcomed him, bowing low with folded hands. The tuft on the back of his head and the thread around his chest were sufficient to ensure a respectful welcome.

One of the guards asked the man his name and where he was from.

'Divyakshu Sarma, Brahman, Soumyapur,' said the bow-legged man. The guard scribbled the details on a parchment and waved the brahman ahead, even as he stared at the incredible bend of his bowlegs.

Up ahead, just before the inner gate, five spearmen, a vaidya and a scribe waited next to a sandpit. The vaidya, dressed in a spotless white dhoti with a silk angavastram draped around his shoulders, saluted the brahman.

'Welcome to Mithila, sire,' said the vaidya, who had a few leaves of tulsi tucked behind his ear, a practice followed by all healers in the kingdom. 'Now please stand in the middle of the sandpit and raise your hands above your head.'

Divyakshu Sarma did as he was told. The vaidya stood at the edge of the sandpit and circled it, his eyes studying every inch of the brahman's skin. When he was done with the inspection, he stepped into the sandpit and asked Divyakshu to raise his neck. The vaidya stepped closer, so close he could smell the sweat off the brahman's body. For what seemed to Divyakshu like a very long time, the vaidya stared at a pus-filled boil on the brahman's neck, distaste written all over his face. When he was done with this inspection, the vaidya stepped out of the sandpit.

'He is fine,' screamed the vaidya, even as the scribe wrote it down. 'Just a small boil on the neck. It looks like a heat boil.' The vaidya stepped forward and offered Divyakshu a bowl of water with neem leaves floating in it. 'Welcome to Mithila,' repeated the vaidya.

Divyakshu gulped down the water despite its bitter taste. Then, heaving a sigh of relief, he started walking towards the unguarded inner gate pointed to by the vaidya, and into the city.

Divyakshu Sarma was exhausted. He had not known tiredness like this before. For thirty days and thirty nights, he had walked the sunbaked, dusty plains till his calloused feet had bled. Sleep had played hide and seek, more hide than seek. Hunger had gnawed at his insides. Every limb in his bony body had begged for a warm bath and a soft bed. But Sarma had kept walking, until he had seen the gates of Vaishali.

Since he was a boy, Sarma had dreamt of seeing Vaishali's sprawling palaces and temples, its noisy markets where rubies and diamonds were sold like boiled sweets, its fabled gardens that smelled of parijata and nagachampa blossoms, and its placid blue lakes on whose shores children splashed around in the afternoons.

But, right now, as he dragged his stiff, calloused feet along, Sarma felt blind to the charms of the greatest city in the sixteen kingdoms. All around him, the people of this glorious city were going about their lives—ignorant of what was coming their way.

*Like goats being led to slaughter.*

Only he, the man called Divyakshu Sarma, knew better.

The fair-skinned women of pale eyes and smooth skin, carried by servants in palanquins, did not know. The coarse horse traders from faraway lands—haggling for more pieces of silver—did not know. Nor did the pompous priests who extracted payments in gold and silver know what fate had in store for them.

*Only I know. A man from nowhere, whom nobody recognises, knows.*

And he was going to tell the king of Mithila all about it.

Freshly barbered, bathed, and perfumed with an extra layer of sandalwood paste on his body and cloves in his mouth to mask the smell of sura on his breath, King Trivikrama hummed a melody softly as he walked towards the Queen Mother's quarters at the northern end of the palace.

Behind him, a train of nobles followed. It was the same pack everyday: Chavuka the physician, Bramhadatta the astrologer, two of the king's personal guards and a servant who carried a tray with lime juice and a handful of jasmine flowers.

*The king is in a good mood*, Chavuka thought, smiling. He had sneaked a glance at the woman in the king's bedroom earlier in the morning. She was young, firm-bodied and beautiful. *I, too, would be jumping with joy if I had bedded her.*

As the group entered the hall of the thousand pillars, the king slowed his pace, as was his habit. The hall with its stone pillars, each as tall as a pine tree, dazzled any one, be it a commoner or royalty. Visiting kings and queens often asked for a walk down the hall, and depending on the size or influence of their kingdoms, a tour down the hall was granted or denied.

Each pillar had the likeness of a ruler of Vaishali carved on it. Right at the beginning of the hall was the image of Sudheendra the Magnificent, the founder of Vaishali, who had established the city thousands of years ago. Then came the likeness of his brother, Rudraveera the Fierce—a giant of a man, with broad shoulders that could carry a battle axe and eyes that resembled coal pits. He stared down menacingly at everyone marching down the hall.

Then came the likeness of Sumukha the Gentle, the only king in the hall who was sniffing a rose. While Sumukha had brought peace and prosperity to the kingdom unlike the earlier kings and had even commissioned the building of the palace they were walking in—he was rumoured to have spent more time with handsome soldiers than with women, in activities of pleasure.

Staring at Sumukha's half-closed eyes and full lips, Chavuka felt a strange stirring in his loins. *The man had his charms*, thought the physician, who favoured both masculine jawed women and chubby men in his bedchamber.

They walked past king after king, with their fancy titles and ornate sculptures, till they reached the last pillar in the hall—the one just outside the chambers of the Queen Mother.

King Trivikrama paused, looking up at the sculpture of

his late father, Simhamukha the Great. For forty-six years, Simhamukha had ruled Vaishali—some said with the love of a benevolent father, others said with the ferocity of a despot. But no one disagreed that, at the end of his reign—the longest of any monarch in the history of the kingdom—Vaishali had become the most powerful kingdom on earth.

As always, Trivikrama marvelled at the statue of his father. A tall man with a strong muscular body, a thick mane of hair that flowed under his crown down to his shoulders and a shaggy beard that resembled a burning forest fire. Simhamukha—the sacker of cities, the burner of forests and the last king to perform the Ashwamedha yagya—had the face of a proud lion and hence the name Simhamukha.

The physician cleared his throat, breaking the spell that the king always got into while staring at his father's image. The servant extended the glass of lime juice. Trivikrama gulped it down, enjoying the tartness of the lime and the sweetness of the honey. He turned away from the carved pillar and walked towards the massive doorway at the end of the hall that was covered with silk curtains.

'Is it time?' asked King Trivikrama.

The astrologer stepped ahead of the train, making a big pretense of studying the charts.

The king already knew the answer. But tradition was tradition, however tiresome it might be.

'Yes, sire. The hour of Rahu is not yet here. It is an auspicious hour to meet near and dear ones,' said the astrologer, folding his charts and flashing a nervous smile. The king noticed that the astrologer's pupils were almost milky white. He was practically blind and yet, each day, he pretended to study the charts.

*What a joke!*

'Where is my dear brother?' asked the king.

Even as he said this, he heard the sound of running feet from the far end of the hall.

His brother, Ajitha, was late as usual. And, he was the one running across the thousand pillared hall. Two soldiers were running behind him, struggling to catch up. One of them was carrying the prince's footwear.

The king smiled. The sight of his brother always made him beam.

'Vikrama …' Prince Ajitha began, stopped himself and then, added with a smile, 'Your Highness!'

'My dear Ajitha, please don't run. You are a prince, not a messenger boy,' replied Trivikrama with a smile and embraced his brother, who faintly smelled of sweat and mud. 'And wear your slippers, will you? You don't want to upset our mother this early in the morning. Shall we go in?' he said before ringing the bronze bell outside the queen's quarters.

The Queen Mother did not look up when her sons entered the room. She sat cross-legged over a wooden mat on the floor of the anteroom, scribbling furiously on a piece of parchment. Once she was done filling up one parchment, she would place it carefully over a growing pile on her side. Then, she would dip her quill into the earthen ink pot and start scribbling again on a fresh parchment.

What she scribbled from dawn till dusk, no one knew. Comfort was a stranger to the queen's chambers. The polished floor was bare and there were no cushions, chairs or curtains. No paintings adorned the walls, the old sculptures of buxom dancers and merry musicians had been removed. The red floor, which had not been plastered for a few years, had developed cracks which crisscrossed like spiderwebs across the room.

Trivikrama had heard rumours that the Queen Mother personally swept the floor. But he did not know if that was actually true, nor did anybody else, for, except the queen's trusted servant—a eunuch called Nila—nobody was allowed inside the room.

Queen Madhusmita, the widow of the late emperor Simhamukha, lived like a pauper—much to the chagrin of her sons. But no one questioned the queen. Because Madhusmita never answered any question. For twelve years, the queen had not uttered a word, not even to her sons.

Whenever she wanted to say something, or make a rare grant to a temple in some obscure corner of the kingdom, or even give a word of advice to her sons, she would write it down on a piece of parchment and pass it on to them.

Her sons went to meet her every morning, right before they got on with their courtly duties. As custom demanded, they would prostrate themselves at her feet and seek her blessings. If they sought counsel, the queen would write it down.

The queen's shadow and guard, Nila the eunuch, tall as a palm tree and thick as a palace pillar, stood like a statue carved out of stone, mute and staring at the familiar scene with dead, empty eyes. Nila stood behind the Queen Mother, towering over her. Nila's beefy arms were folded just below her massive breasts and she looked at the princes with dark, kohl-lined eyes that seldom blinked and never missed a thing.

No man or woman, other than her sons and Nila, had entered the queen's antechamber since that night of the great treachery, eighteen summers ago, when Trivikrama had been a mere boy of six and Ajitha had been a toddler, when blood, common and noble, had flowed in Mithila.

Both brothers had grown up listening to whispered tales of how their late father had been betrayed by those closest to him, of how the young queen, mother of two small children, had wreaked a terrible and swift vengeance on those who had widowed her, of how she had ruled the kingdom till her firstborn, Trivikrama, had come of age and been crowned king twelve summers ago.

Maharani Madhusmita never spoke of that night, nor did she let anybody else speak of it in her presence. Nobles, who had carelessly wagged their tongues about the happenings of that night, had been banished from the court; a balladeer, who had sung of that night on the streets of Vaishali, had been given a hundred lashes; an amateur court historian, who had been careless enough to chronicle the events of that night, had lost his thumbs.

Soon after her son's coronation, like common widows, Madhusmita had shaved her head, given up wearing silk and stopped attending court. Since that day, she was seldom seen and never heard. All she did was scribble in her scrolls. Nobody knew what happened to the scrolls afterwards.

Trivikrama and Ajitha waited patiently, listening to the sound of the queen's feather quill scraping on the parchment. After what seemed like an eternity, the queen stopped, looked up at her sons and smiled.

She picked up the scroll she had been writing on, dropped it on the pile of scrolls lying next to her and stood up. Her sons walked up and touched their mother's feet. She placed a palm on each of their heads and blessed them.

'Mother, how long will this go on?' asked Trivikrama, as he rose. 'You are the queen of the greatest empire in the world, yet you live like a mendicant. You shun palace food; you don't allow flowers inside your chambers. You don't allow slaves to tend to you or to clean your chambers. Why do you punish yourself for a cruel card played by fate so long ago?'

The queen did not answer. Instead, she smiled and pointed to his right shoulder, where the dancer from the night before had sunk her perfect pearly teeth, leaving behind a purple mark of passion.

Trivikrama fingered the mark nervously. His father, the late king, had been the first king to devote himself to the love of a single woman. Every king in the illustrious line before his father had prided himself on the size of his harem—be it a harem of women, men or even boys. But not Simhamukha—the man had loved only one woman, Queen Madhusmita, till the day he died.

Trivikrama could see that his brother, Ajitha, was struggling to keep a smile off his reddening face. The queen sat down again, picked up a parchment, dipped her quill into a pot filled with scarlet ink and started scribbling. When she was done, she handed the parchment to Trivikrama without looking up.

*A wise king does not spill blood or seed in vain/ For blood and seed are what life is made of.*

—the scroll read, in blood-red ink.

And so, the dowager queen of Mithila dismissed the most powerful man in the sixteen kingdoms.

A gong struck at a distance. It was time for court. Trivikrama and Ajitha bowed to their mother and took her leave. In the hall of a thousand pillars, Trivikrama's band of followers were waiting, but he ignored them and continued walking. His good mood had soured.

As they walked towards the assembly room, Trivikrama paused before a room that he had not entered in eight weeks. The doors were bolted and locked. A heavy lock hung outside. He stared at it and felt a clenching feeling inside his chest.

*I miss you every day, every waking moment.*

Suddenly, he felt thirsty. He gestured to Chavuka, who snapped his fingers at the servant. The tumbler with lime juice was produced again. Trivikrama held it for a moment, resisting the desire to fling it against the wall and see it shatter into a hundred pieces. He knew lime juice wouldn't quench his thirst, only sura would.

But there was court to attend, an empire to be ruled. Trivikrama took a sip and kept walking.

## 3. Run or Die

She ran as fast as her tired little legs could carry her. She did not know where she was running to, or how far she had already run.

All she knew was that she had to keep on running. Run for her life. And not look back.

The thick, vengeful rain that lashed her face—blinding her—did not matter. Her bleeding feet did not matter. Her burning breath which felt like the anger of a jealous god did not matter. Nor did the leaves and the thorny branches of the trees matter, as they slapped against her bare arms relentlessly, leaving a thousand little cuts on her pale, mottled skin.

'Run to the river,' her mother had screamed, right before choking on her own blood.

The girl had run and not looked back.

Suddenly, she felt like she was flying, like she was a spider gliding on a warm summer breeze. She felt as though she had sprouted wings, something she had always dreamt of.

Maybe she would fly away. Fly over the wet, cloying

forest; above the dark clouds that were pouring rain. Maybe, just maybe, she would fly away from them—the ones who had come when the night had been the darkest and snatched away everything and everyone she loved.

And then, she landed—hard. The breath went out of her and everything became dark.

A steady whisper pulled her out from her warm, comforting abyss.

*Run to the river. Run to the river.*

Her eyes fluttered open. She was on the forest floor, with her face in a puddle of water. Her mouth tasted like burnt charcoal.

For a moment, she could not recall where she was. Then it came back to her: the pitch-dark night, the shrill screeching of a bird, the men who had come noiselessly, the screams that had followed, and her flight into the jungle.

She wanted to go back to sleep but she knew better.

*Run to the river.*

They would still be searching for her. She raised her face from the damp, muddy forest floor and listened, like the hunted animal she had become.

The rain had stopped. The jungle was quiet. And in the distance, she could hear the calming sound of flowing water. She used her frail arms to hoist herself upright. Every bit of her body screamed with pain.

She dragged herself towards the sound of the water.

Up above her, a bird of prey circled the grey sky with keen, hungry eyes.

Gajendra looked forward to Budhwara, the fourth day of the week. He was born on a Budhwara, thirty-two years ago. His son and sole heir to his fortunes—despite his toad-like face—had stuck his head out of his mother's womb on a Budhwara. And, twelve monsoons ago, after his father's passing, Gajendra had become the gopa—the collector of taxes of 18 villages—by King Trivikrama's decree on a Budhwara.

Budhwara was his lucky day. So, as his father had done in his time, every fourth Budhwara, Gajendra dressed in his finest silks and headed out to collect the king's dues along with his band of armed men.

Sukrama, the servant who tended to his cows and horses, led the way, carrying the banner of Mithila. Two glum soldiers bearing spears, who had ridden down from the nearest garrison six kosas away, came next. Not that they were of any use. Everyone paid their taxes, even though a few ungrateful tillers wore long faces as they deposited their meagre bag of grain.

Then came Gajendra himself, mounted on a fat horse that had never broken into a gallop in its life. Behind Gajendra was a cart drawn by two bullocks, driven by Sukrama's idiot brother, the drum beater who rarely understood anything.

That day, as this party wound its way up to the first village, Gajendra realised that it had rained the night before. The ground was slushy and his overfed horse seemed to be struggling to find its footing.

On both sides of the road, the lush forest was greener and quieter than usual. The screeching monkeys, who usually taunted them along the way, were missing today. The trees, beaten and whipped by the heavy rain, drooped down looking sullen.

Gajendra reached out and touched the hilt of the dagger he carried on his hip. It felt cold and failed to reassure him. Up ahead, the two soldiers were chattering away about the flavoured boar meat they had eaten the night before. Sukrama, though, seemed to be throwing wary glances at the woods.

Gajendra knew that their first stop, an agrahara—the village where brahmans lived—was just a few gallops away. On most days, Gajendra hated visiting the agrahara but today he could not wait to get there. It was the only village that paid no gold or grain to the king's coffers, unless you counted blessings as currency.

Then, there were the rules. Gajendra had to dismount from his horse each time he addressed a brahman. Most of the brahmans did not bother even looking at him and all of them kept him at an arm's length, as though he were a leper with sores and boils. They even offered him water in a clay tumbler which he was sure they discarded as soon as he was on his way. But, at this moment, Gajendra wanted to get to the agrahara, and far away from this brooding jungle, as fast as he could.

As the party turned a corner, Gajendra saw the stone arch that marked the beginning of the agrahara. From a distance, something about it looked unusual. But Gajendra could not quite figure out what looked different about it today.

'Announce us,' said Gajendra, turning to the cart driver, who stared at him with glazed, moronic eyes.

'Announce us, you idiot,' Gajendra snapped.

Comprehension dawned on the cart driver. He stopped the bullock cart and got down. He tied his drum around his neck and started banging on it with his palms.

The hollow thump-thump of the drum echoed down the forest. But in the very next moment, Gajendra noticed that up ahead, Sukrama and the soldiers carrying the banner were frozen in their tracks. All of them were staring at the arch. Without warning, Sukrama dropped the royal banner, turned around and started running away from the arch.

'What is it?' yelled Gajendra.

Sukrama did not reply. He ran past him, wide-eyed and wobbly-footed.

Gajendra saw one of the soldiers stagger down from the horse, get down on his fours and retch. The other soldier continued to stare at the arch, mouth wide open. Gajendra kicked his horse on the belly and galloped towards the arch. When he got under it, he looked up and his blood ran cold.

On the stone arch was a new kind of decoration. A neat line of heads of men, women and children. The heads were smiling—a gruesome smile of bared teeth and bloody gums.

Their lips were missing.

By the time the girl reached the river, it was dusk. The forest threw long shadows and the branches of the trees resembled the fingers of wrinkled old men.

Her mouth felt hot and she felt dizzy.

'Run to the river … run to the river,' she repeated the words like a mantra over the roaring sound of the river, which seemed to get louder with every step she took.

She sank her face in the fast-flowing water and drank it in big gulps, making loud lapping sounds just like the cows and sheep in her village did. The cold water felt like a blessing from the gods. She washed her face and arms, wincing as the water stung when it touched the countless cuts on her bare skin.

When she'd had her fill, she looked up and saw something that filled her with wonder. A few paces away from where she lay, the mighty river seemed to disappear. One moment the river was there, pearl green and fast-flowing, and the next it wasn't. Instead, in its place, rose milky white mist.

*Is it magic?* the girl wondered as she walked towards the mist.

The roar of the river was now deafening, drowning out the sound of her footsteps and the birdcalls from the forest. When she got to the rocky edge where the river seemed to disappear, she lay down on the ground and peered over the edge.

The girl watched the scene with wonder. The river was leaping down a cliff so high that it made her dizzy. Below her was an iridescent sea of foam and mist that blew skywards lifted by a breeze blowing up the mountain.

She opened her mouth and let the spray of fine mist wash over her tongue and throat. For a moment, she forgot about the jungle, her flight and those who were pursuing her.

That is when she heard the screech of the falcon—shrill and triumphant.

*They were nearby.*

She jumped to her feet and looked at the thicket around the river. The shadows in the woods were alive—moving around like earthworms under wet soil.

One by one, the shadows stepped into the dying light. They were not shadows anymore but forms from a nightmare, just like those from the night before. Naked above the waist, they were thin, scrawny, hairless skeletons of skin and bone. All of them stared at her, wordlessly.

A man on a black horse, darker than a moonless night, stepped out of the woods. He was just like them: skin and bone. But, unlike the others, he wore a helmet that covered most of his face. On his shoulder perched a fiendish-looking falcon.

The man on the horse advanced towards the girl, taking his time, while the others stayed back at the edge of the woods.

She crept back to the edge of the cliff. She could hear her heart pound over the roar of the plunging water.

'Child,' said the man on the black horse, in a voice that sounded like the hiss of a coiled cobra. 'Look at me.'

She looked at him. He sat on the horse, staring at her. Behind the helmet, his browless eyes, like simmering coals, bored into her.

In a slow, deliberate manner, his hands moved taking off the helmet. She stared, in a trance, as the helmet came off and the face revealed itself. She screamed. And then screamed some more, till her voice became that of her mother's.

'Ardhamukha!' she screamed in her mother's voice and threw herself off the face of the mountain, into the foam and rocky death below.

## 4. The Brahman

The long blade of grass twitched at first, like a worm being poked with a stick. Slowly, very slowly, it levitated upwards, like smoke wafting from an incense stick, before bursting into flames and floating down as black cinders on the marble floor of the great hall of justice.

Most of the assembly gasped. Others slapped the marble pillars next to them or their thighs in high excitement and appreciation.

'Black magic!' screamed a panicked voice from the back of the great hall. A pretty dancer pretended to swoon, largely to get the eyes of the nobles on her.

Trivikrama scratched his chin with a jewelled forefinger and nodded to his treasurer, who tossed a coin into the outstretched palms of the magician.

For four hours, seated on his hard stone throne, the king had heard his subjects complain relentlessly about corrupt tax collectors, thieving courtesans, the increasing adulteration of soma in the Sumeru province, rising prices of horses across the realm and a strange disease that was afflicting the groins of men in faraway villages. Some stated their grievances in petulant voices, other beat their breasts till they turned a deep shade of red. A few, as always, to demonstrate the depth of their sadness, pretended to faint.

Trivikrama heard them out patiently and dispensed subjective justice. The corrupt tax collector would lose a finger or three, depending on how much he had stolen. Wax was poured and the royal stamp pressed onto a decree to regulate the adulteration of soma—a cause His Majesty deeply felt for.

A vaidya was dispatched to the village to probe the outbreak that was giving villagers hideous sores in unmentionable places, though Trivikrama privately wondered about the health of the courtesan in that village. But decorum prevented him from voicing his thoughts.

After the litany of complaints, the magician was a welcome change. He had pretended to be a petitioner—a farmer who had lost his produce to a mysterious pestilence—to get past the gatekeepers of the hall of justice. He had even shown them the blade of grass as evidence. Once inside, he had gone on to demonstrate his trick without a word.

Pocketing his gold coin, the magician bowed low and retreated from the hall, but not before flashing a smug, triumphant smile at the doorkeepers.

'Next, my king,' yelled one of the doorkeepers, in a strident voice that could have shaken the bones of gods in the heavens. 'Divyakshu Sarma, son of Devakshu Sarma, from the village of Soumyapur in the province of Rajagriha. His complaint … a shortage of dharmshalas in his region.'

The king sighed. The brahman who entered the room was scrawny and dark-skinned. His dhoti looked like it had all the dust of Mithila on it. His angavastram, with which he had covered his bare chest, was tattered. His feet were bare and calloused.

*Yet another brahman looking for alms*, thought the king.

'How can I help you, noble one?' said the king, greeting the brahman with the customary folded palms. The brahman bowed to the king—a bow not quite low enough to honour a king. When he raised his hands to greet the king, a gentle murmur rippled across the room. The brahman had a vakra, a deformity. On his left hand, sticking out of his thumb was a finger. It was fully formed, just smaller and darker than the rest of his fingers.

The brahman seemed to be aware of the stares and hushed whispers rippling through the court. He waited for it to die down, while staring intently at the king, as though he was carefully choosing his next words. His right hand continued to count his prayer beads.

'Tonight, king of kings, four hours after the sun sets, look up at the sky,' said the brahman and paused. 'The gates of hell will be thrown open tonight. Death and disorder will descend on Mithila.'

Silence hung over the court like a noose around a condemned man's neck. Everyone knew the king hated soothsayers and oracles, especially the ones who predicted dark days or doom in the future. Even the court astrologer—once an important man in the reign of Simhamukha—knew that a happy prediction was rewarded with a gold coin and a really gloomy one with a trip to the desert provinces.

Trivikrama stared at the brahman for a while, stone-faced. The brahman met his gaze and held it, even as the prayer beads continued to move in his hand. Someone coughed nervously.

'Fine way to beg for alms from your king, brahman,' the king said, slapping his thigh and bursting into laughter.

Chavuka, the astrologer, joined in with a nervous titter. Then, Jayaveera laughed his deep booming laugh. Yet another noble joined him. And then, yet another joined in. Before long the whole assembly echoed with the raucous laughter of a hundred men—some of them slapped the pillars in glee while others clapped the backs of the men next to them.

Divyakshu Sarma continued to stand in the middle of the court, in his tattered clothes, staring at the king. The king waved a lazy hand at the treasurer, who tossed the brahman a silver coin.

The brahman did not raise his hand to catch the coin, which hit his chest and rolled on the floor.

The raucous laughter continued, as the king slapped the stone throne he sat on and guffawed till tears rolled down his eyes. The brahman turned around and started walking down the long hall, past the gatekeepers, with the sound of the ringing laughter in his ears.

The only ones not laughing in the great hall were Prince Ajitha and Aacharya Gurukripa, who were staring at the disappearing brahman with identical looks of sympathy and worry on their faces.

## 5. The Gates of Hell

'Your lips taste like … mmm,' mumbled Trivikrama, nibbling on the courtesan's lips.

'Like?' she asked, pushing him away playfully with her long, bejewelled fingers.

'Like a pomegranate pearl,' he said, trying to kiss her again.

She held him at arm's distance, her eyes gleaming, teasing, in the dark room lit only by an oil lamp on the bedside.

'A raw one or a ripe one?' she asked.

He wasn't in the mood for games. He pulled her closer with one strong arm and started devouring her lips, while his other arm circled around her waist, holding her in a wrestler's embrace.

'Ripe and juicy … so succulent, I want to stay in this bed and nibble on them till we grow old and bow legged,' Trivikrama whispered, breathless, as he rained kisses down her long neck and cheeks, which smelled of sweet jasmine.

'That's all? When, handsome stranger, will you ride me like one of the horses you sell?' she mocked.

Tonight, he was pretending to be Sumitra, a wealthy horse trader from Tamralipti, the port town at the edge of the Purva Samudra, where ships bearing stallions, muslin and fine silks came to dock from across the world. The courtesan was new to Mithila and fresh as a lotus bud, or so the crier outside her parlour was telling wealthy passersby. Trivikrama knew she was new to the city; he had visited every natyashala in the city, including the ones that did not pay taxes to the treasury, and he hadn't eyed this thick-thighed beauty before.

As for her floral freshness, he wasn't entirely sure. She had a practised feel to her, like a seasoned mare that knew when to throw a rider off her back. But she was fun nevertheless. Most courtesans were, especially the older ones who knew the intricacies of their craft. They may no longer have the slender hips of the younger ones but they knew how to make their lips taste like exotic fruits or how to make their patrons shed a joyous tear or two. There was also an enchanting tattoo of a scorpion curling around her navel.

When they were done, she lay next to him, drawing slow,

gentle circles across his chest with her shapely fingernails. He closed his eyes and listened to the faint sounds from the street that filtered in through the open window. The clop-clopping noise of the horses' feet as they hit the roads, the raucous singing of a drunkard and the soft, undignified moaning of a man in the throes of absolute pleasure from a room nearby.

'Did I sound like that?' he asked her, opening his eyes.

'No,' she said. 'You sounded like a … horse.'

He was getting a little tired of the horse jokes.

'So, what brings you to Mithila?' he asked.

'Gold,' she said. 'What else? Plus, I hear your king is unmarried. Maybe I will marry him,' she said, chuckling at her own joke.

'Maybe you will,' he said, smiling at her. 'What else have you heard about him?'

'That he is as strong as a bull and drinks an ocean of soma every night. The courtesans say he has the appetite of a wild horse,' she said pinching his nipple and laughing as he winced.

'To hell with the king,' he said with a smile, a little flattered, and got off the bed.

'You could lose your head for saying something like that,' she said, feigning concern, her eyes staring hungrily at his pouch of gold lying on the table beside them.

'Unlikely, my love,' he said as he tied his dhoti around his waist. He picked up the jingling pouch, smiled at her, and removed one coin from it. He dropped the rest of the pouch beside her.

'That's for saying good things about our king,' he said and left the room, as she stared after him.

The stable boy of the natyashala was waiting for him outside, holding the reins of his horse.

'Fine horse,' said the boy. Trivikrama threw him the only coin he had and rode away into the night.

It was a cool, dark amavasya night. The breeze from the Netra river dried the sweat on his skin as his horse trotted at a brisk pace. Around him, his subjects were drinking, gambling, whoring and cursing. The steady beat of drums, cymbals and jingling anklets streamed out from the natyashalas. Men drunk on wine, cheap and exotic, were vomiting into gutters. Courtesans stood in their balconies making eyes and pouting at passersby. *In all, a good night in the greatest city of the world*, Trivikrama thought, tugging at the reins of his galloping horse.

He heard it before his eyes could see it. It sounded like a serpent's angry hiss, followed by the deep booming sound of thunder. Without warning, his horse bucked backwards. It took all his riding skills to keep himself from falling as the beast reared up on its front legs.

All around him, men and women ran helter-skelter. A woman stood in the middle of the road, staring at the skies, her eyes as wide as full moons. A trembling hand pointed towards the heavens. Trivikrama followed the line of her gaze.

In the dark, moonless sky, a fiery serpent streaked across the sky, writhing about with a burning head, a long, curving tail and a feral smile that radiated evil. It looked like a flaming gash, a scar on the face of the heavens, like something that gorged on blood and guts.

*The gates of hell*, thought Trivikrama.

At that moment, the face of the thin, bow-legged brahman with calloused feet and tattered clothes flashed through his mind.

# 6. Agni Varsha

The shepherd boy was falling through the bright blue sky. He flipped midair like a tossed coin and tore through a puffy white cloud, enjoying its cottony embrace as it caressed his skin. Below him, he could see the mighty mountains which looked like tiny pebbles topped with powdered sugar; the frozen lakes resembling emeralds gleaming in the morning sun.

He flew past a circling falcon, which looked at him with startled eyes, before diving after him. The bird plunged towards him, squawking angrily, before giving up on the chase.

He continued falling, faster and faster, gaining momentum—like a raindrop from the heavens. The breeze buffeted his face and pinned his arms up as if he were a rag doll. The mountains rushing by grew bigger and bigger. They were no longer pebbles and looked like sharp pointy claws jutting out of the earth instead. The temple of Kedar was there too, a small stubborn speck at the foot of a peak.

Without warning, the skies turned gloomy and foreboding. The fluffy white clouds disappeared. In their place were dark monstrous spectres that roared and flashed in the darkness. Blue bolts of lightning singed the darkness around him.

The boy stifled a scream. He was hurtling face down towards the icy mountain, when he spotted a small form walking on it. A man, all alone, was stumbling up the cliff. He suddenly looked up and his eyes met the boy's, for just a moment.

*It was the jogi.*

The jogi's eyes were no longer vacant but deep, dark pits of fire. His matted locks had turned into a mass of curling, slithering snakes—each one of which was hissing and spitting venom.

The shepherd boy woke up from his nightmare, screaming. Yet, he couldn't hear his own voice. His scream was drowned out by a noise louder than the sound of a thousand thunderclaps.

Across the ill-lit room, his grandfather was sitting up on his bed, eyes bulging with fear. The boy jumped off his bed, unmindful of the cold floor and of the blast of bone-chilling wind that hit him when he threw open the door of his house.

Up above, the night sky was alive—roaring, sizzling and burning. Fireballs screamed across the purple night sky, one after the other, leaving white angry clouds of steam as they burnt the cold night air.

'Agnivarsha,' yelled his grandfather. A rain of fire.

Suddenly, the earth started shaking, while the fireballs kept getting louder and closer.

Trivikrama bounded through the cramped tunnel, a flaming torch in his hand. The wavering flame conjured eerie, long shadows that danced and swayed on the walls of the tunnel. He could no longer hear the screams of his panic-stricken subjects, just the echo of his ragged breath and heavy footfalls bouncing off the narrow walls.

Night after night, ever since he had discovered the tunnel eight years ago, he had used this bare passage to sneak out for his nightly excursions. It was wide enough to accommodate just one man but long enough that it connected the king's bedroom to an old, dilapidated mansion in the pleasure district in the heart of Vaishali.

He often wondered which of his predecessors had built this secret passage. Had it been Sumukha the Gentle, the rose-sniffing emperor, the one who had surrounded himself with cherubic young men? Or had it been Suryakrupa the Glorious, Trivikrama's great grandfather, who had left behind a hundred bastards, most of whom had inherited his light brown eyes and his insatiable appetite for procreation?

Right now, none of that mattered. Trivikrama had to get to his chambers before the nobles and his dear brother—who undoubtedly would be in a state of high distress—broke down his bedroom door only to find the king's bed empty.

He doubled his pace as he saw the familiar sight of a grey stone door, with the carving of the royal sigil of the flying eagle, at the end of the passage. Pausing at the door to catch his breath, he planted the sputtering torch into a hole on the wall. Grabbing the stony wings of the eagle, he turned it around till it had turned a full circle.

The door opened with a low, squeaky groan and Trivikrama entered the small chamber at the back of his bedroom. He could hear a torrent of muffled voices from beyond the bedroom door.

'... break it open?' enquired the court astrologer.

'What if his highness is undressed?' asked the royal physician.

'Won't be the first time we have seen him naked,' said the astrologer, trying to keep his voice low.

'Where is the prince? I can't find him either.'

'We have to do something. The sky is falling, and neither the king nor the prince is here,' said a booming gruff voice, which Trivikrama knew belonged to the head of the royal guards, who had been kicked by a horse in the face a few years ago and was now hard of hearing.

Trivikrama had heard enough and he quickly stepped into his dark bedroom. He walked to the door quietly and was about to turn the doorknob, when he heard the rustle of silk behind him.

Out of sheer reflex, he reached for the dagger on his hip.

'Brother, put that away,' said Prince Ajitha in a low voice, turning up the wick of the lamp kept on the bedside. 'I have been waiting for you for a while.'

'How did you get in?' asked Trivikrama, trying to mask the surprise in his voice.

'Did I ask you how you got out, Vikrama? Or where you go every night?' the prince asked, flashing a knowing smile.

'Do you know?'

'Yes, I do.'

'Since when?'

'It's been a long, long time now, brother,' said the prince.

'Fine! Let us talk to the men waiting outside first. Some of them have their ears to the door, of that I am certain,' said the king, before he turned the knob and threw the door open.

## 7. Wooami

The air reeked of smouldering iron and spoilt duck eggs. The icy breeze billowing down the snow-clad mountains did little to quell the nauseating stench, which enveloped the village like an invisible cloak of fear. The villagers sat in small huddles around dying fires, teeth chattering in the morning cold, praying for the sun to rise over the stony mountains.

Even in the dark, they could make out the scars in the sky that the fireballs had left in their wake. They stared nervously at the long plumes of white smoke stretching across the dark skies like the skeletal fingers of a phantom. Some villagers muttered mantras under their breaths, begging the gods for the long night of terror to end. Some, like the butcher, sat around the fire, taking deep drags from a shared chillum, stoking fear and conspiracy theories with their tall tales.

'Those fireballs were vimanas,' said the butcher, in a low voice, staring resolutely at the simmering embers. 'None of you believed me when I told you about that rakshasa riding on a bolt of lightning. You mocked and laughed—blaming it all on this,' he said, shaking his smoking chillum at the sky, before taking a deep drag.

'Now, you see!' he continued, as he exhaled a puff of the sweet-smelling smoke. He held his chillum out for anybody who was interested in a drag.

The temple priest hesitated for a moment, and then took the chillum with shivering hands, carefully avoiding touching the butcher's fingers.

*Usually, he would not be spotted even sitting under the same tree as the lowborn butcher but when stars start tumbling out of the sky, even the gods would understand if he shared a chillum with the butcher. After all, adversity knows no sin*, the priest thought, sucking on the chillum.

The sweet warmth of the smoke filtering into his chest felt comforting. 'Shambho,' he said, taking the name of the lord of the mountains. 'The gods are sending us a message. The era of Kali—when the virtuous suffer and evil thrives—is upon us. I don't think the fireballs were vimanas with rakshasas riding on them. They were falling stars—an omen that we need to do a prayaschitta yagya, to repent for our evil ways,' said the priest.

The butcher held his tongue with a sullen silence. The priest locked his eyes with the bloodshot eyes of the butcher and, seeing no resistance, deemed it safe to continue.

'Why else would this particular star pass over our village?' he said, pointing at the long tendrils of smoke above them, passing the chillum back to the butcher. 'Why did this happen of all days on an auspicious amavasya day ...'

The butcher plucked the chillum from the brahman's hands, placed it on his lips and stared at the heavens; the beauty of what he saw drowned out the droll commentary of the pompous priest. The first rays of the sun were yet to shine upon the mountains, but somewhere else in this beautiful world, Ushas, the goddess of the morning, had opened her beautiful eyes.

The cobalt blue sky, which had given birth to the night of terror, was now turning to the colour of a cool stream. The plumes of smoke above them no longer resembled the eerie pale hand of a demon, but streams of white milk, flowing off the hand of Shiva, the lord who did not distinguish between him or the brahman. A tear ran down the butcher's cheek.

It was at that moment that the butcher saw a silhouette approaching them from the distance. A man, his back bent with age, was stumbling towards their huddle. He carried a stick with which he was tapping the ground to get a sense of the lay of the land.

'H-has anyone seen my grandson?' asked the old shepherd, as he came near.

The shepherd boy dragged himself up the slippery mountain path, tripping and falling on the fresh snow underneath his feet. The air was foul with the stench of acrid smoke, which was getting stronger with each passing step. In the sky above him, long fingers of pale smoke were tracing the path of the fireballs which were heading right towards the cave of Bhairon.

*Was the jogi alive?* wondered the boy.

Or had the rain of fire finally snuffed out a stubborn life that had refused to be extinguished in the harsh mountain cold, or from a wound festering with worms or at the hands of cruel fate?

The boy's stomach churned and he fought the urge to retch. He paused for a moment, leaning on his heavy bamboo staff to catch his breath. He tried not to inhale the smoke that clung around him like a ghostly veil.

He looked up and saw a familiar shape—a gigantic boulder twice the size of the temple in the village. Beyond the boulder, the path curved and narrowed sharply at the edge of the bottomless precipice before turning upwards towards the cave of Bhairon. Not until he crossed that boulder, would he know if the fireballs had turned the cave into a tomb for the jogi.

He quelled the serpentine ball of fear that was crawling in his guts and fought the urge to run faster towards the cave. Years of walking on the mountain's trails had taught him that darkness and ice were treacherous foes. One false step, one twist of the ankle and he would be rolling down the mountain like a pebble, his bones turning into powder.

The boy lengthened his stride instead, till he reached the boulder, turned around its wide circumference and looked up for the first sighting of the cave.

His blood ran cold.

Trails of smoke streaked over the cave of Bhairon. The fireballs had missed the cave. But seated at the gaping mouth of the cave was a mountain cat—a kind the boy had never seen before. On his climbs, he had seen mountain cats on many occasions—ones with white fleece and thin bellies, slightly bigger than dogs but smaller than wolves. They were usually shy of men and preyed on sheep.

Not this one.

This mountain cat looked like a hunter of men. It sat outside the cave on its haunches, mouth agape, eyes glimmering in the dark like fireflies on a dark night. Warm vapour puffed out of its broad mouth, which was full of sharp teeth. Its fleece was streaked with long lines of yellow and black.

A mountain cat of this kind hadn't been spotted in these mountains for years. The boy took a step back, keeping his eyes peeled on the cat, hoping that it would not notice his presence. A pebble moved under his foot. The mountain cat turned its head languidly and their eyes met.

*Don't run.*

He kept looking into the cat's eyes, just like village elders had told him to, and tightened the grip on his bamboo staff. His heart was beating like a drum and his knees felt like they were made of butter.

*Don't run. Don't show your back.*

The cat continued to stare at him for what felt like an eternity. Then it stood up, turned away and left—just like that. The boy waited for a few moments before he collapsed on his knees, tears of relief stinging his eyes.

*Or were they tears of sorrow? The jogi is dead.*

The jogi lay on the floor of the cave, facedown, a human scarecrow of skin, bones and hair. The boy stared at the shrivelled form on the floor, not wanting to touch it, not wanting to disturb its final repose.

*Let him rest once and for all.*

In the confines of the cave, the only sound he could hear was the echo of his own laboured breathing. Waves of grief crashed into his heart for the fate of a man he had never ever spoken to, whose name he did not even know.

In the end, it was not the cruel cold of the mountains that

had claimed the life of the jogi, thought the boy. Nor was it disease, nor a grievous wound that had claimed the last breath of this orphaned man. What had ultimately got the jogi was a hungry mountain cat!

The boy smiled at the thought, bemused, before guilt strangled it. He held the jogi by his shoulders and turned the body around tenderly.

*No blood.*

All of a sudden, a cry escaped from the boy's mouth. He stared at the face of the jogi. The large eyes were wide open, as always, staring into nothingness.

And then, they blinked—once. For the first time, in the many years that the boy had known the jogi, the eyes were not just staring at him unblinkingly. The boy cupped the jogi's head in his palms and rested it on his shoulder.

'What … who are you?' the boy asked the jogi.

The jogi's eyes looked at the boy with an expression the boy couldn't quite fathom. Then, his parched lips moved.

'Wooame …' mumbled the jogi.

The boy leaned closer, till his ears almost touched the jogi's lips.

'Woomai,' said the jogi again.

*Is it a mantra? Is that his name?*

The lips began to move again, this time with what seemed to the boy as superhuman effort.

'Who am I?' said the jogi before slipping back into darkness and oblivion.

# 8. The Message

Trivikrama sucked on a plum noisily, savouring its sweet ripeness. He spat the seed out that flew in a lazy curve and landed on a polished bronze bowl, clattering noisily, before ricocheting off the bowl and hitting the floor. A servant tiptoed across the room, picked it up and put it back in the bowl. Ajitha looked at the king with a look of disapproval—the brown, judgmental eyes similar to their mother's, the king thought.

Trivikrama smiled back at his brother, then pursed his lips in mock hurt. They were seated in the small council room—the princes on their high chairs. Bramhadatta, the royal astrologer, and a gaggle of priests, who claimed to be fortune tellers of various abilities, sat at the other end of the room.

The priests studied astrological charts, gravely debating the position of celestial bodies like Rahu and Ketu, nodding to each other. One of the priests kept tossing a handful of small seashells on another chart, before coming up with his prophecies in hushed tones.

Another priest, with a hairy sagging chest and uneven teeth, sat quietly, staring at the high ceiling, as though waiting for Rahu or Ketu to themselves appear on the marble roof. Bramhadatta, the royal astrologer, sat amid the priests, on a small stool, pretending to study a fat tome, occasionally throwing nervous glances and weak smiles at the king.

'Maybe I should toss him a plum just to make him feel better?' chuckled Trivikrama. 'Or will a seed do?'

'Keep your voice low, brother,' Ajitha whispered. 'They are brahmans.'

'Incompetent brahmans … that's what they are. Wasn't it

their duty, their only duty, to predict that a fire storm or that dhumketu or whatever that was would descend on us?' said Trivikrama, spitting each word out.

Ajitha was sure the priests heard the king but without exception, all of them pretended to be lost in study and in contemplation of the charts. The one staring at the ceiling blinked furiously a couple of times but that was all he did.

'Nobody can predict how the gods and the heavens will behave,' said Ajitha, keeping his voice low.

'Add courtesans to that list. You have much to learn about that, brother,' said Trivikrama.

'It was you who laughed at the brahman,' said Ajitha gravely.

'And I don't feel one bit guilty about it. I am a kshatriya, a warrior. I know how to fornicate and fight. Rahu, Ketu, skies spitting fire ... that's their job,' said the king loudly, wagging a finger angrily at the astrologers.

Before Ajitha could retort, the door of the council room swung open and Jayaveera strode in with long graceful steps. Trivikrama's face lit up, for Jayaveera was just the man he had wanted to see. They were childhood friends—as much as a victorious prince and a vanquished prince could be. Jayaveera bowed low to the king, his long curly locks swinging like vines in the breeze.

'Give me some good news, old friend. Have you found that brahman yet?'

Jayaveera shook his head and said, 'No, my king. But I am sure we will before the sun sets over the Netra.'

'What do you know about him?' asked Trivikrama.

'Just that he had come all the way from a village called Soumyapur. That's what he told the doorkeepers.'

'Where is this village?'

'Up north. Ten days away by horseback. A month's walk.'

'He looked like he had walked here. Didn't he?' asked Ajitha.

Jayaveera nodded and tried his best not to smile as the king loudly sucked on a plum.

'I hope you find him fast. Till then, I am stuck with this bunch of old tricksters,' said Trivikrama, before he spat the seed out. This time, the seed landed right in the middle of the bowl and stayed there.

Vishnupada stared at the steaming mountain of rice resting on the banana leaf in front of his only son. The nine-year-old boy scooped out a fistful of rice from the peak of the mountain and spread it around the base with his plump fingers. A large spoonful of piping hot ghee was poured into the newly formed crater in the mound of rice, followed by a ladle of piping hot curry made of lentil and ground coconut. The boy mashed the rice and curry with his palms, rolled a wet morsel which he gobbled down with one quick swallow.

*The boy has the appetite of a pregnant elephant*, thought Vishnupada.

'Krishna, keep eating rice like this and that belly of yours will explode like a volcano,' Vishnupada said with venom. 'And your brains will shrivel to the size of a peanut.'

The boy tore his eyes away from the food, and looked at Vishnupada with doe eyes and a mouth stuffed with half-chewed rice. Across the room, Vishnupada's wife, who was standing behind a pillar, which did nothing to hide her wide girth, threw daggers at him with her eyes but otherwise kept quiet.

'Shall I tell them how much you used to eat when you were a boy, Vishnu?' came the quavering voice of the boy's grandmother from the bedroom inside. Vishnupada, one of the richest, sharpest vaisyas in the whole of Mithila, knew it was time to make a quick exit. His aged mother, may Krishna bless her, had been bed-ridden for the last six summers, but illness hadn't blunted her sharp tongue.

'Shall I, Vishnu?' challenged the irate grandmother from inside the room.

His son was now smiling, his fat cheeks rippling as he slowly chewed the rice. Vishnupada grunted loudly, got up, picked up his turban, put it on his head and went into the courtyard of his house.

*These women will make the boy as dull as a doorknob.*

In the courtyard, white swans swam languidly across the pond, cleaving elegant trails on the water. The sweet smell of jasmine and the sight of blood-red chrysanthemum blooms did little to calm his frayed nerves.

He stared at his house, a palatial mansion, made of the finest teak and sandalwood from the forests of the south. A hundred-year-old house that had stood the test of time and fortune.

*All of this would eventually go to the boy and stay with him, but only if he would be sharp. After all, Mahalakshmi, the goddess of wealth, walked away from gluttons and dimwits. If only women understood that!*

Over a hundred years, empires had risen and fallen, kings had ruled and died, armies had shed blood, learned brahmans had written wise treatises and become paupers, but Vishnupada's family—a spider web of distant cousins, uncles, nephews and brothers—had prevailed and thrived. In Mithila, they sold spices and sandalwood obtained from the forests in the southern plain; in Rajagriha, they dispatched men deep into the bowels of the earth to dig up iron and copper; from Kausambi to Gandhara, every time a courtesan bedded a noble or a commoner, his family made silver or gold.

*And how had they done all that? Not by gobbling down mountains of rice and becoming thick-skulled like coconuts,* Vishnupada thought bitterly, *but by remaining sharp.*

The sound of drumbeats from the street disturbed Vishnupada's pensive musings. Absently, he plucked a rose petal and chewed on it as he walked towards the outer gate of his house.

Outside, a small crowd of people were assembled next to the public fountain. In the middle of the crowd, the town crier sat on an elephant, banging loudly a drum made of buffalo hide. The elephant seemed to dislike the sound and so it kept shaking its head, willing the noise to stop.

As soon as a gaggle of people had assembled around him, the town crier stopped the feral banging.

'Citizens of Mithila,' he screamed in a voice that made a baby wail in a house nearby. 'A brahman from a village called Soumyapur in Rajagriha had predicted the fire in the sky last night. Anyone, who can produce him in the king's court or share his whereabouts will be duly rewarded with a hundred gold coins and an audience with the king. By the order of King Trivikrama, ruler of the sixteen kingdoms, king of kings—'

The town crier droned on, but Vishnupada did not wait to hear anymore. Nor did he see the crowd melt away, or the elephant walk past his house, with chains and bells jingling around its neck. In his mind, all he saw was the reward—a chance to make some gold—but more importantly, an opportunity to meet the king.

He turned around and walked past his burping son, who

was still plundering the mountain of rice at a fast pace, and rang the bell hanging in his courtyard thrice.

The swans in the pool flapped their white wings, alarmed at the sound. Shortly, a dozen of his servants converged in the courtyard.

'Drop whatever you are doing! I need you to find a brahman,' shouted Vishnupada. 'The one who finds him gets five gold coins and three bags of rice.'

*Goddess Mahalakshmi loves a good bargain*, thought Vishnupada smiling.

The pigeon had flown three days straight, pausing only to fill its belly with seeds and worms or to have the occasional drink of water. In the nights, it rested on leafy trees so tall that even marauding monkeys balked at climbing them. The pigeon had started its flight from the cold mountains where streams gurgled to life and thick forests made sure that sunlight seldom touched the wet earth. It had flown over lush green valleys, where few men had ever set foot, where marshes crawled with strange reptiles. It had flown over verdant farms where women toiled over blazing hot rocky mountains, where black bears prowled, and over barren lands where not a blade of grass grew, where kingdoms were no more than mere villages.

Eventually, the pigeon's tired wings flapped over the placid waters of the Netra river, which curled her mighty arms around the greatest city in the world—Mithila. She knew her destination was almost there, that soon she would be fed green seeds and loving hands would caress her wings. With one last burst of vigour, she defied the scorching afternoon heat and swooped down over the tall walls of the city, into the crowded squares dotted with tall palms, and into a terrace on the highest tower in Mithila that housed the royal aviary.

'Come, come, my love,' said the birdman, making cooing sounds. 'Have a peck,' he said offering her a fistful of seeds, as she sat on his long dark sleeve streaked with white patches of pigeon shit. He stroked her back with the affection of a doting mother, before checking on the little piece of parchment tied to her feet with thin threads.

'Red and white threads,' said the birdman to the young boy next to him, who envied the reception the pigeon had got. 'Tell me, boy, where has it come from?'

'Blue and white threads are from the Sumeru province. Green and white are from the Vakra province. Red and white are from …' the boy's voice trailed off.

The birdman rolled his eyes and waited patiently. When no further answer came, he clouted the boy on his head with his closed fist.

'Rajagriha, dunce, Rajagriha … from up in the mountains,' said the birdman. 'How are you going to be a birdman if you can't even remember your threads? Red and white is Rajagriha. Repeat this ten times, boy … till it gets into your skull.'

The boy started parroting the lines while the birdman set down the pigeon on a high stool. He gently began untying the threads from her leg. When he was done, the parchment covered in dried lambskin fell on the stool.

'Boy, run along now. You know who to give this to,' said the birdman. 'Hope you can run better than you can remember things.'

The boy had light feet. He skipped down the spiralling stairs of the tall tower which housed the aviary, three at a time, dodging other boys who were either rushing up or down the stairs. By the time, the birdman had placed the pigeon back into her cage and given her a bowl of water, the boy had reached the bottom of the stairwell. He skipped into the long hall where sixteen message-men sat next to wooden tables overflowing with messages from every part of the realm. Each message-man wore a unique turban representing a particular province of the kingdom.

The boy paused for a moment. He was supposed to give the message to the message-man who took care of the messages received from Rajagriha.

*The colour of Rajagriha is …*, the boy racked his brains and then it came to him. *Red and white.*

He walked up to the man wearing the red and white turban, who stared at the boy with sharp eyes.

'Rajagriha?' enquired the boy.

'What do you think, idiot?' said the message-man, with a scowl. 'Drop the message in the bowl and be gone.'

The boy dropped the message into a wooden bowl on the table, which was already brimming with parchments. Then, he ran back up the stairs like the wind.

❧

Trivikrama paced up and down the ivory chamber like a caged lion. *More like a lion in heat*, thought Chavuka, wondering if a concoction made of cooling herbs would calm him down.

It was the hour of the king's afternoon siesta, but the king was anything but restful. The afternoon heat of Mithila was stifling and the king's muscular upper body and chest was covered in a thin film of sweat which made his wheatish skin glisten like polished bronze. The slaves, frantically waving fans made of peacock feathers, hardly managed to lessen the sultry heat of the room.

The king was in an exceptionally filthy mood. Usually a man of large appetites, Trivikrama had pecked at and played with his food during the afternoon feast, even waving away his favourite dish of charred lamb marinated in seven spices and glazed with honey. After lunch, he had turned down an invitation to play a round of dice with his brother, who had then left to practise archery in the burning afternoon sun.

Now, the king was pacing restlessly in the ivory chamber, lost in thought. He was blind to the elegance of the room, which was adorned with white, silk curtains and had polished tusks of elephants killed in royal hunts mounted on the walls. Occasionally, he stopped at the window that overlooked the courtyard of the royal quarters and stared at the horizon, biting his lip. Chavuka and the royal astrologer, Bramhadatta, sat in the room staring at each other, stewing in the heat and the uncomfortable silence.

Eventually, Chavuka coughed discreetly.

'Sire, would you care for a small dose of soma? If taken in small quantities, even in the afternoon, it is known to aid digestion and … calm the restless mind,' said the physician, who wouldn't have minded a little intoxication himself to take his mind off the sweat and the stifling heat.

The king did not reply but continued to stare at the horizon, with a glazed expression on his face.

'Tell me, Chavuka, do you believe in omens?' Trivikrama asked eventually, without turning around to look at the physician.

Chavuka coughed again and weighed his words carefully. The king wasn't a superstitious ruler. Unlike some of his predecessors who had lived their lives based on the dictates of the panchang, the astrological calendar, Trivikrama was a man of strong impulses and indomitable will. He woke up much after the brahma muhurta, the hour before dawn prescribed by scriptures as the best time for waking up. He ate as he pleased and slept when he pleased. Of course, he consulted astrologers before waging a war with a neighbour, or before donating cows and land to temples, but for Trivikrama, the stars were a lazy afterthought.

'Yes, Your Majesty, I do,' said Chavuka, hesitantly. 'But men, especially great men, carve the lines of their own fate.'

The king turned around and examined the physician with piercing eyes. 'So, am I a great man? Or should I be worried about the fire we saw in the sky last night?'

A knock on the door interrupted what would have been a long and uncomfortable monologue from the physician extolling the king's greatness.

Jayaveera entered the room. By the look on his face, Trivikrama knew he came bearing bad news.

'What is it?' asked the king.

'I have bad news, my king.'

'I can see that from the sweat on your brow. What is it?'

'We have received a message from Rajagriha. An agrahara of brahmans has been … attacked,' said Jayaveera with hesitation.

'How many survivors?'

'None. Not even women and children were spared,' said Jayaveera, ashen-faced.

'Something tells me there is more,' said the king.

'A tax collector found their heads hanging from an arch at the entry of the village … badly desecrated.'

'What do you mean desecrated?'

'Their lips had been cut off.'

The king stared at Jayaveera and then at the astrologer and the physician; both brahmans were shaking their heads in shock.

'Who would do something as *vile* as that?' Trivikrama demanded.

'It's worse, my king' said Jayaveera. 'This happened in a village called Soumyapur—the village, where the brahman we are looking for, is from.'

# 9. The Wound

Even in the dark depths of oblivion, the jogi could smell it—the nauseating stench of rotting flesh. But it was much later, when the darkness had receded, that he realised that the stench of decay came from his own body—from a raw opening in his torso which refused to heal. It was the odour that finally woke him up.

When the Jogi's eyes finally fluttered open, he saw a crone sitting next to him, staring at him with curious eyes. Her skin was pale, the colour of curdled milk. Wrinkles criss-crossed her face like fissures on parched earth and a bulbous nose rose out of this strange landscape.

The jogi lay on a stone slab, swaddled in blankets like a newborn.

In the next moment, the old woman got up and placed her cold fingers, gnarled and deformed by age, on his forehead.

'The fever is breaking,' she said softly. 'He will live.'

'Thank god,' said a boyish voice.

The jogi turned his head slowly, following the voice. A boy stood in the corner of the room, smiling. Something about him seemed familiar.

*What was it? Was it his voice?*

'Who are you?' he asked. His voice sounded unfamiliar, like a stranger's from another life.

'I-I am Jeeva ... don't you recognise me?' asked the boy, with a tone in his voice that the man could not recognise.

*Was it disappointment? Hurt?*

'What's my name?' asked the man.

The old woman and boy exchanged a glance but said nothing.

'Sleep,' said the old woman, patting the jogi on his head, before pouring a few drops of poppy juice into his mouth. 'You need it.'

He drifted off again. Darkness, his old companion, soon held him in a tight embrace.

The jogi dreamt of a seed, buried deep under the moist earth. A green sprout arose from it, fresh and tender. It tore its way through the dark soil, fighting its way towards sunlight and freedom. The sprout wiggled and pushed its way upwards. But then, it was no longer a sprout but something else, something with more life, more animation. Something that crawled and wriggled. Something *without* eyes, ears or teeth—a worm, a maggot. And then, there were two of them. The twins writhed and crawled in the dark wet soil, hungry and gnawing.

He felt their hunger, burning and all consuming. They began to eat the soggy soil, first in little bites and then whole clumps of it. Only now, it wasn't the soil that they were feasting on anymore. What they craved for was red, raw, bloody, juicy and alive. They were *inside* him, feasting on his insides, devouring him bit by bit. And it hurt. The pain came in waves, throbbing and searing.

He screamed.

The crone, who was tossing and turning in the cot across

the room, heard the man from the cave moan feebly. *Probably one of his nightmares*, she thought.

On the floor beside her, Jeeva, the shepherd boy, was fast asleep on his makeshift bed of hay. She turned the wick of the lantern up and waddled up to the jogi lying on the stone slab. His eyes were half open and his pupils were rolling upwards, like a man possessed or one who was in the grips of a nightmare so terrible that it burned through all sanity. The woollen blanket had fallen away from his body. His hands, had they not been bound down with thin strips of cloth to the edge of the stone slab, would have torn at the wound on his stomach.

She brought the lantern closer to the wound and examined it in the yellow light. In all her years of healing people with ghastly tumours, raging fevers, pus-filled abscesses and demonic dreams, she had never seen a wound on his stomach.

She had thrown at it everything she had mastered over the years—soothing salves crushed from neem leaves and turmeric paste, caustic potions that burnt through the skin before sealing the wound shut—but none of it had worked. She had even burnt a small cloth doused with the oil of camphor over the wound, after having drugged the man with a strong dose of poppy extract. But the maggots had come back stubbornly and the wound had remained open, mocking her.

*Was it because of a curse? Was this karmic retribution for some unspeakable deed? Who was this man?*

She had asked herself these questions over and over for the last two days, ever since the shepherd boy had dragged this man into her house. The villagers usually avoided her, except when a loved one was dying or when their pain had become unbearable. Even then, they sneaked into her house only in the dead of the night with their faces fully covered.

In their heads, full of dread and superstition, she was only one thing: a witch. One who had swallowed her husband's life as a child, who could now cure people miraculously. When they saw her jars of healing herbs, they imagined them filled with dark magic cursed by the gods. When they overheard her prayers to Bhadrakali, the goddess of the night, they imagined incantations to the demonic forces.

The boy, still young, clearly had fewer inhibitions. The villagers did not want anything to do with a man in a cave with an ugly wound. The boy knew only she could help.

She stared at the man, the one the boy referred to as the jogi, and again wondered who he was. In his fevered ramblings, he had given a few hints. For a man who couldn't remember his own name, he spoke many tongues fluently. He had spoken in Sanskrit, the old language of the gods, which was now spoken only by priests and kings. And, he had spoken in Kusha, the language spoken by the common folk of Mithila. He had also spoken in two other tongues that she could not place, only one of which had sounded familiar to her.

*Who spoke so many tongues?* she wondered. *Was he a trader, who had travelled to faraway lands in the search of profitable friendships, where he had learnt to speak so many languages? Was he a learned brahman who had walked across kingdoms preaching his dharma? Was he, like the shepherd boy believed, a jogi who had come to the mountains to get away from the madness of the plains to perform penance?*

*Brahmans or jogis usually don't have a wound crawling with worms. What terrible deeds had he done to deserve this kind of misery?* she thought. *Was he a Kshatriya, a warrior?*

She examined the bony chest and scarecrow-like arms and legs. Maggots and ill health had stripped away all his flesh.

*Even if he had once been a warrior, there was no way he would be able to wield a sword or ride a horse ever again,* she thought. *If the goddess of night was kind, maybe, just maybe, he would be able to walk again.*

Three weeks later, as the days in the mountains slowly started becoming shorter and snow started getting thicker, Jeeva walked up to the temple of Kedar at the base of the mountain. He wore a toothy smile on his face, one beaming with pride.

On Jeeva's shoulder rested the arm of the jogi, who walked slowly a step behind. He leaned heavily on a bamboo staff and took small unsteady steps, as if he were a child just learning to walk. His back was bent and his brow drenched in sweat. Tied around his waist was a sash, which was soaking wet from the bleeding wound on the right side of his stomach. Each step seemed to come with superhuman effort.

But the man kept walking.

He still did not know who he was or where he was going. But unknown to him, the same fate that had thrown him into a dark cave on a mountain, was taking him towards his destiny, one step at a time.

## 10. A Feast for Brahmans

The rituals began well before dawn. The brahmans sat in circles around the hundred and eight homa kundas—sacrificial fires of burning wood and dried cow dung cakes—chanting the vedas in a nasal singsong tone. They fed the raging fires with offerings of ghee, puffed rice, barley and sesame seeds. Smoke rose in great columns from the fires and, driven by the morning breeze, blew across the city, leaving children with runny noses and watering eyes.

Three days before the Navagraha Mahayagya at Mithila had begun, brahmans had started swarming in from every province of Mithila. They flocked in hundreds representing the ninety-six vedashalas of the kingdom—six schools of scripture and learning for each of the sixteen provinces. Some of the brahmans were worshippers of Varuna, others of Rudra and a few were followers of Vishnu, but all of them also worshipped the old gods of the Vedas—Agni, the god of fire, Vayu, the god of the wind and Ushas, the goddess of the mornings.

Special pavilions made of wood and cloth had been erected on the banks of the Netra at the king's orders. An army of slaves and water carriers had ferried water in mud pots from the river to the great open hall where the yagya was taking place. The brahmans had, of course, prepared their own food. For a week, town criers had gone around the city canvassing the public, especially wealthy merchants, to donate liberally for the yagya. King Trivikrama himself had offered five thousand cows, made grants of whole villages to the vedashalas and had even made an offering of his own weight in gold.

The head priest of a vedashala from Mithila, who happened to be standing next to the king when he was getting himself weighed on a balance, swore he had heard His Majesty make an unkind remark. The king had apparently joked about the growing waistlines of the brahmans and of his relief that gold was not being given away from the royal coffers by *their* weights. But the priest knew better than to spread such things about. Kings were kings after all, and this king had a temper.

By the time the yagya came to an end, it was well past noon and the scorching sun had sucked all the energy out of the priests. They were now eagerly looking forward to the cool sanctuary of the shaded pavilions and to the highlight of the day: a nine-course feast. Rows of banana leaves were laid out, as volunteers—brahman women from the city—served mounds of finely steamed rice topped with dollops of aromatic ghee, curries made of sweet potatoes, melons, turnips and lentils. Large servings of flavoured milk and yogurt were served in little bowls made of areca leaves.

By the time the feast came to an end, the quiet hubbub of contented priests talking to each other was only matched by the slurping sounds as they scooped up the wet mixtures of rice and curd with their palms.

When it was all over, four brahmans—all of them wizened and old enough to remember the reign of King Dhruvasena, the grandfather of King Trivikrama—retired to a tent in a quiet corner of the pavilion. Inside the tent, Aacharya Gurukripa sat on a small wooden stool, waiting for them.

*Here come the most learned men of Mithila*, thought Gurukripa to himself. *Or are they just the most powerful men?*

He stood up with folded hands and gestured to the brahmans to take their seats. They took their time, shuffling around the room slowly, like sleepy tortoises, before easing themselves into their seats.

'Tambula?' Gurukripa asked them, gesturing towards a silver plate laden with betel leaves, areca nuts, rose essence and slaked lime. All four nodded their heads in approval. The aacharya picked up a small bell next to him and shook it once. A servant answered its gentle tinkle, entered the tent and saluted the priests with folded hands.

He squatted next to the table and was about to start making the tambula, when one of the brahmans—the oldest amongst the four and the head of the Vaishali Vaishnava vedashala—raised his hand to stop the servant.

'Aacharya, is he a brahman?' asked the old priest, pointing a knobbly finger at the servant. His words came out in a lisp from his toothless mouth.

'Yes, he is,' said Gurukripa.

The aacharya nodded to the boy, who began cracking betel nuts with the nutcracker.

'I was told you wanted to meet me. How can I be of service, learned ones?' enquired Gurukripa, even though he knew exactly what this conversation would be about.

'Well, Aacharya Gurukripa,' began the head priest of Sumeru vedashala, a relatively younger man with an enormous belly and a weak chin. 'The omens are good. The Mahayagya has happened without any obstructions. The nine celestial beings have been propitiated. The king need not worry about the agnivarsha anymore. We are very grateful for his continued patronage ... for the causes of dharma. However, there are some worries ... concerns about some recent happenings to our clan—'

'What clan would that be?' cut in Gurukripa, who wanted this conversation to be as short and uncomfortable as possible for his guests. The priest had chosen his words gingerly, which clearly meant he was uneasy.

'Brahmans!' this time it was the old, toothless brahman who spoke. His tone was curt and direct, almost angry. 'We, the brahmans of Mithila, are worried about the senseless slaughter of our people that happened in the village of Rajagriha ... and wonder if justice will ever be served. We are also curious about the fate of the brahman from Soumyapur, I forget his name ...' he said, looking directly at Gurukripa.

'Divyakshu Sarma. That is his name, learned one,' said Gurukripa, 'Let me assure you, the search for him is on, in all earnest. His Majesty, himself, has taken a great interest in the investigation of the … incident in Soumyapur. Rewards have also been announced—'

'Yet, even two weeks later, we don't know who slaughtered entire families of defenceless brahmans. And their faces were defiled … even women and children were not spared … what kind of an animal does that?' said the old man, his voice rising.

Aacharya Gurukripa did not reply. Instead, he kept quiet and looked at the brahmans in the room one by one, with an expression no one could fathom. The silence of the powerful speaks infinitely louder than their words. The aacharya had learnt that art of studied silence from kings and queens.

He let the silence sink, like a drop of blood in clear water. The only sound in the room was that of the crisp cracking of areca nuts. Eventually, the boy had the tambulas ready and he looked at Gurukripa, who waved his hand, gesturing to his guests. The boy walked around the room, offering the tambulas. The brahmans picked up the offerings of folded betel leaves, laced with slaked lime, rose essence and packed with pieces of areca nuts, put them in their mouths and started chewing.

'You are right, sires,' Gurukripa said, in a quiet voice. 'As a brahman, as one of you, I understand your pain. Let me talk to His Majesty about your concerns. If there is nothing else …' saying that he got up.

The brahmans knew the audience was over. One by one, they took their leave, each greeting Gurukripa with folded palms. All except the toothless old man, who waited for the others to leave before he turned around and addressed the royal guru.

'Aacharya Gurukripa, did I tell you that I knew your father?'

'No, sire. I did not know that,' said Gurukripa, a little surprised.

'A very wise man, your father. He once told me an interesting story. Would you like me narrate it to you?' said the old priest. 'It's a short one, I promise you.'

Gurukripa knew that he would have to listen to the story whether he wanted to or not. So, he nodded at the old priest.

'A long time ago, an asura king performed great austerities to please Lord Shiva. He went without food and water for years, stood on burning coals and even lopped off his arms as sacrifice. Pleased, Shiva appeared and granted the asura two boons—anything his heart desired. "Give me indestructible arms and legs stronger than mountains" was the first boon that the asura asked for. "Give me enough wealth that Kubera, the god of wealth, has to beg and borrow from me"—that was the second one. Shiva granted them both and I think you know what happened afterwards,' said the priest.

'Yes, I do, learned one,' said Gurukripa, who had heard a thousand stories like this before. 'The asura became powerful and arrogant. He raised an army and started tormenting all beings, humans, animals and even the gods themselves. The question is: how does the asura's story end?'

The brahman smiled at Gurukripa before continuing, 'Well, the asura had all the gold in the world. He had the might of a thousand elephants. But what he had failed to ask for was intellect. Eventually, the gods created a being so small that no mortal eye could see it. A being capable of inducing fever and pain. The being made its way into the asura's head and caused a fever that drove him mad and wasted him from inside. He died a man with strong arms and legs, surrounded by all the wealth … but with a shrivelled brain—ranting and raving,' said the old priest, and paused to gather his breath. 'Like your father told me once, the brahman may not have the strength of a thousand elephants or the wealth of Kubera, but he is the brain of the society. Without the brahman, all is lost, meaningless,' saying that the old priest left, bowing himself out of the tent.

Gurukripa walked down the hall of a thousand pillars taking his time, savouring the cool comfort of the hall. The effort of organising the yagya and the feast in peak summer had robbed him of his usual vigour. The conversations with the brahmans had done little to improve his outlook. He dreaded the upcoming meeting with his one-time disciple and now the Lord of Mithila, King Trivikrama.

He had to inform the king about how upset the brahmans were, and the king wasn't in the mood for bad news these days. For three weeks, he hadn't been his usual self—sullen in court, snappy with the nobles and distant from most of his daily delights. Just yesterday, he had snubbed a poet who had recited a long poem extolling the virtues of the king in open court. A few verses into the poem, the king had yawned loudly, stretched out his arms, before ending the recital by saying: 'I am told Dheevara has not slept for a few days. Perhaps, this poem might be of more help to him.' Dheevara was the king's favourite stallion. The poet had left the court ashen-faced, almost in tears. Later, Gurukripa had arranged for a purse of silver to be delivered to the distraught poet's house.

The Queen Mother had also not helped—her refusal to grant the king an audience for over two weeks had further soured his disposition. The king, a lover of dice and chaturanga, had lost several games in a row to his friend Jayaveera, someone he usually defeated even after having a few glasses of soma. *Well, that's the only pleasure he allows himself these days,* thought Gurukripa glumly. Lots of soma, sometimes even a few glasses of it in the afternoon.

He wondered what bothered the king more. Was it the talk of the agnivarsha that was boding ill for him? Or was it the fact that the brahman who had predicted it had just vanished like vapour? Or was it the wanton slaughter of a village of brahmans soon after that troubled the king? Nobody ever asked His Majesty what he was thinking, and kings usually didn't go around sharing their burdens.

Outside the king's chamber, he saw Chavuka, the royal physician, and hailed him.

'How's the king's disposition?' asked Gurukripa.

'Darker than the monsoon clouds,' said the portly vaidya, rolling his eyes. 'After all, it's not often that kings get to see skies raining fire and brahmans getting chopped up like lambs,' he said gloomily, as he shuffled away.

Gurukripa entered the room and found the king reclining on a pair of pillows, staring at a chaturanga board intently. The king reached out for a gaja piece, almost moved it, before changing his mind and moving his ashva.

'Bad move, brother,' said Ajitha grinning. 'There rolls your mantri's head.'

Trivikrama stared at the board for a moment, before reaching for his glass of soma and downing a mouthful. A small trickle of the pale fluid ran down the corner of his mouth and dripped onto his chest. He looked up, saw Gurukripa and rose from his seat unsteadily to welcome him. The king's face looked gaunt; his eyes had sunk deep into their sockets.

'How did the feast go, Aacharya?' asked Trivikrama.

'It is done. The cowsheds are empty and the deeds for the lands you have bestowed are being signed and waxed even as we speak, Trivikrama,' said Gurukripa, addressing him by his name, something he did rarely and only when none of the other nobles were around.

'And yet, Aacharya-ji, you don't smile,' said Ajitha. 'Why?'

*The young boy misses nothing.*

'I met the heads of the four vedashalas. They are … unhappy,' said Gurukripa.

'About *what*?' demanded the king. 'Do they want more cows? More lands? It is always about that, isn't it? More and more and more.'

'It is about the killings that have happened in Soumyapur. They are unhappy with the … slow speed at which the wheels of justice are moving, if I may say so,' replied Gurukripa.

'So am I, Aacharya-ji,' the king said. 'What more can I do? I have sent riders and scouts in every direction. I have announced rewards of gold for anybody who knows anything. I have doubled the reward—twice. Yet, here I am sitting and playing chaturanga with my brother, no wiser than I was three weeks ago about what happened. What *do* I do?' said the king, bitterly. He snapped a finger and a servant refilled his glass.

Gurukripa wanted to politely remind the king that only drunkards, men of ill repute and degenerate gamblers drank soma before it was dark. But this wasn't an opportune time for such a reminder.

The king gulped down half the glass and eyed the chaturanga board with sullen eyes.

'So, what did you tell the *holy* men?'

'I told them that the king is taking personal interest in the matter.'

'Did they seem satisfied?' asked Trivikrama.

'Pacified may be the word. For now.'

'For how long?'

'Not for long, my king.'

'Bah!' said the king, gulping down the rest of his glass and tossing it to the floor, causing a loud clatter. 'What can these priests do? What can they *do*? March on Mithila with an army of the cows that I have given them? Refuse to name my unborn child? What can *they* do?'

Gurukripa knew exactly what the brahmans could do. They could preach at temples, marriages, naming ceremonies and thread ceremonies about how Kali Yuga was upon the world, how the rain of fire had been a sign of things to come. They could gossip about a king, who was not able to protect the followers of dharma and how he had led his people into dark times. They could predict poor rains, pestilence and disease—and if, for even one season, the gods decided not to be kind to the people of Mithila, those predictions could become true. Seeing all this, farmers and merchants could begin brooding on how the previous kings were better and start seeing evil in the shadows, believing in things that did not exist. Belief was everything—be it in the rulers or the gods. If that was lost, everything else crumbled.

But the wise aacharya kept his thoughts to himself. He knew that an inebriated man loved only one voice—his own.

'Brother,' said Ajitha, trying to break the uncomfortable silence. 'I suggest you send a messenger to each one of them personally. Perhaps tell them that you are doing all you can and will punish the perpetrators in the harshest possible manner. Will that help, Aacharya-ji?'

'Yes, my prince. That should help. Nothing works like a personal message from the king. It will flatter them and buy us some more time,' said Gurukripa.

'That's done then,' said the king, sheepish at his outburst. 'Now Aacharya-ji, since you don't drink soma, would you care to join us for a game of chaturanga or dice?' Saying that, he snapped his fingers and his glass was refilled again.

❧

The painter deposited the thick sheaf of palm leaves on the table gently, as though he was putting a newborn to sleep. His large black eyes had lashes that drooped like branches of palm trees.

*Why do painters always look so morose?* thought Jayaveera, as he picked up the first palm leaf and stared at the face on it.

'Too fair,' he told the painter.

He picked the next leaf.

'This one is close but I would make the face thinner. That brahman looked tired ... as though he had eaten only boiled nuts all his life,' said Jayaveera.

'There are more versions, sire,' said the painter.

'Ah, this one is better,' said Jayaveera picking up another. 'Can you include his appendage in the painting?'

'Is the sire suggesting that I draw a thumb on the brahman's face?' asked the painter.

The painter's sarcasm was not lost on Jayaveera, who fixed him with a glare that could have withered flowers. Ignoring the rhetorical question, he asked the painter, 'Now, can you ask the students in your shala to make a hundred paintings like this? Exactly like this one. I don't want him to look fairer or darker, or his nose to be longer or his cheeks to be bigger. And can I have these paintings in three days? We are sending a fresh bunch of riders to the countryside tomorrow,' said Jayaveera, dismissing the painter with a lazy wave of his hand.

The painter nodded his head, picked up the painting that Jayaveera had chosen and bowed low before leaving the room.

Alone for the first time since the morning, Jayaveera stared at the sunken eyes of the brahman peering back at him from the remaining paintings the painter had left on his desk.

*Wretched brahman, where are you?*

For three weeks, the thought of the brahman with the eleven fingers had occupied Jayaveera's every waking hour. Chitralekha, his youngest wife, had even claimed that he had mumbled the brahman's name in deep sleep. Jayaveera had dispatched parties of scouts, spies and riders in every direction from Mithila. He had even arranged for search parties to scour the trade routes to Rajagriha, which teemed with grain merchants and horse traders.

Within the city, he had got the guards to check every dharmshala, vedashala and brothel. Twice a day, he would go to meet the dandanayaka of Mithila, who controlled an army of spies that kept an eye on everybody from petty criminals to thieving tax collectors. Yet, the brahman was nowhere to be found. He had vanished, like a ghoul at dawn.

Jayaveera had also sent soldiers to the village the brahman hailed from, Soumyapur, and they came back with nothing. There was no one there to talk to. The village was now just a row of empty houses, with empty pots and pans, bags of rice that would never be cooked and bare walls that would never echo with laughter again. Even worse, since the agrahara did not pay any taxes, there were no records of the people who had lived there.

*Where could he go?*

Jayaveera knew that time was short. The daily audiences with the king were becoming increasingly shorter and more tempestuous. They were friends and were also related by marriage, but friendships with kings can be fickle—they curdle quicker than milk left out in the summer. Falling out of favour with the king had its consequences—a temporary exile to one of the distant provinces would be one of the better options. Jayaveera did not want to mull on the what the other consequences could be.

His pensive thoughts were interrupted by a gentle knock on the door. His servant entered carrying a small wooden box.

'Sire, a snack from home,' said the servant.

Jayaveera was in no mood to fill his belly. But his marriage with Chitralekha was still young and she was enthusiastic about fattening him. She liked him full of vigour when he came home and these days, he was falling short.

'Leave it here,' said Jayaveera.

He opened the box. Inside it, was a small copper container, wrapped in cloth. It was still warm.

*What was it today? Flavoured peacock meat?* he thought, as his mouth filled with saliva. He eagerly unwrapped the cloth and opened the vessel.

Something juicy was floating in a pool of red gravy. It was not peacock's meat. A hand—cleanly severed at the wrist, with a stump of bone and flesh sticking out of it—was afloat in a pool of blood.

The hand had six fingers.

It was well after dusk that Nila, the eunuch, entered the Queen Mother's chamber. The oil lamps had been lit and the corners of the room were bathed in their pale-yellow light. The other eunuchs had been dismissed for the day.

Queen Madhusmita sat alone, cross-legged on the floor, in the middle of the bare room, a brass lamp next to her. She was furiously scribbling away on a parchment. The flickering flame of the lamp accentuated her austere features—her high cheekbones were as sharp as daggers, her once soft cheeks now looked like hollow bowls, like dried-up lakes. Looking at her now, nobody could have guessed that not very long ago, Madhusmita had been considered one of the most beautiful women in kingdoms near and far, a beauty that had inspired poets to write ballads.

Nila waited while the queen went about her unchanging routine: Madhusmita would dip her quill into an inkpot filled with blood red ink, scribble on a piece of parchment and then drop it on the floor next to her.

Ever since Nila had joined the service of the queen, twelve summers ago, she had seen the queen wake up before the sun had risen in the horizon only to start writing in her scrolls. She would keep at it until the last of the lamps had flickered out in the dead of the night. She paused her writing only twice every day, once when her sons came to visit her for their daily audience and once to eat a saltless lunch of warm rice gruel and boiled vegetables.

Eventually, the queen looked up and smiled at Nila, who greeted her with folded hands.

'Maharani, it has begun,' Nila said, gravely.

Madhusmita picked up a parchment and scribbled one word on it: *Where?*

'A village called Soumyapur,' said Nila.

Madhusmita stared at Nila for a long time, lost in thought. At long last, she rested her quill back in the inkpot, waved a hand and dismissed Nila.

Madhusmita sat staring at the quivering flame of the brass lamp for a few moments. The brass lamp was engraved with the royal emblem of Mithila—the head of a roaring lion. The wick of the lamp snaked out from the mouth of the lion, making the flame look like a fiery tongue.

A gust of warm wind blew into the room, ruffling the curtains, making them dance and sway like banshees in the dark.

Madhusmita cupped her palm and shielded the flame, which twitched and quivered because of the breeze. But the breeze was strong. The flame fought for its life valiantly before sputtering out. The lion's face on the lamp now had a burnt tongue.

*A storm is coming*, she thought. *Nothing can stop it.*

She got up from the floor, picked up her parchments which the breeze had scattered all around the room. One after the other, Madhusmita gathered them meticulously, before dumping them in a wicker basket.

She carried the basket into her bedroom which was conspicuous by its emptiness, just like her life. The wooden mat, on which she slept, lay on the floor with a thin folded sheet of cotton at its head which served as a pillow.

Madhusmita opened a door at the rear of the room and entered a storeroom, which smelled of dust and disuse. The queen placed the basket she was carrying inside the room and turned to head back. As she closed the heavy wooden door of the storeroom, she gave one final glance to the contents of the room, like she did every day.

*This is all that remains of my life.*

As far as her eye could see, in neat rows and columns, wicker baskets stuffed with parchments were lined up, wall to wall.

# 11. Ajiva

'Can't you remember anything?' asked Jeeva, toying with a pebble in his palm. 'Where you lived, who your parents were, the names of your friends … anything at all?'

The jogi did not answer and continued to stare blankly at the dark flowing waters of the Mandakini. Above them, a thousand stars dotted the night sky and the bright moon was just a sliver short of a full moon. The snow was yet to fall but the breeze blowing down the mountain was so biting that despite the fire crackling next to them, both the jogi and Jeeva had pulled the collars of their woollen cloaks to cover their necks.

'Maya says you speak several tongues. You even speak the tongue of kings and brahmans. Were you … are you a king?' Jeeva soldiered on.

The question seemed to amuse the jogi who stroked his flowing unkempt beard which now reached his navel.

'Do I look like one, Jeeva?' the jogi asked, a smile slowly spreading across his full lips. Jeeva liked it when the jogi smiled, which was rare, even rarer than the sound of his deep voice.

Jeeva tossed the pebble into the river. He could not see how far it had skipped along the surface of the water before drowning, but he wished he could have seen the fate of that stone. Yet another mystery, like the jogi.

'So, what *do* you remember? What do you know?' the boy persisted, aware that the man he referred to as the jogi was likely to get a little irritated at his persistent questioning.

The jogi sighed deeply.

'Well, by the mountains we see around us, I know that we are at the edge of the Bharatavarsha, at the foothills of the Himalayas. Few men have ventured beyond these mountains, and even fewer have come back to tell their tale. Below these mountains are the flatlands where kingdoms and men wage war over land and prestige. I know that there are kingdoms called Mithila, Rajagriha, Sumera, Patali but I don't know if I have ever been to any of them. Beyond these kingdoms, further south, where the rivers crisscross the green forests, are lands ruled by mighty kings who worship gods unlike ours. And beyond those lands lie the mighty oceans, the Purva Samudra from where the sun rises and the Apara Samudra where it sets—'

'Have you seen these oceans?' Jeeva cut in, unable to contain his curiosity.

'I don't know,' said the jogi. 'Maybe I have, maybe I haven't. Maybe all of what I am saying is nothing more than an imaginary story in my head.'

The boy and the jogi sat quietly, listening to the soothing sound of the gurgling river.

'Do you see that star?' the jogi asked, pointing to a twinkling star in the sky. The boy looked at it and nodded. 'For some reason, I know the name of that star. It is called Dhruva. I know someone told me that if I followed that star every night, I could reach the edge of Bharatavarsha—where the hills are white with snow, where mother Ganga was born as a stream—the Himalayas,' the jogi paused and stoked the dying fire with a small log. A few embers hissed angrily.

'Can you remember who told you that story?' the boy asked hesitantly, because he already knew the answer.

The jogi shook his head, his dark eyes glued to the fire.

'No,' he said. 'But it was someone who loved me. That I know.'

A breeze blew down the mountain—bitterly cold and angry. The boy placed his palm on the jogi's hand, who continued to stare at the fire.

'Let's go home,' said Jeeva, getting up. 'It is getting colder. The snow will start swirling anytime now.'

The jogi nodded, slowly got up and started walking down the moonlit path to the village. The boy suddenly whipped around, looked at the jogi and smiled.

'You got up without using your staff,' said Jeeva. 'Everyone told me you will not live. Maya told me that you may not ever walk. And yet, just a month later, you are alive and walking without a staff.'

*Yet, the wound still does not heal*, thought the jogi touching the sash around his waist, which forever remained soaked in his blood.

'I don't think you are a *jogi*,' said Jeeva. 'I think we should think of a new name for you. Something I can call you.'

The man gave it some thought before he answered, 'Since you found me, I think you should be the one to name me.'

'No, I can't think of any name,' said Jeeva. 'Why don't you? Please ...'

The man looked up at the stars for a moment, weighing his options.

'Ajiva ... you are Jeeva, so I will be Ajiva. Do you like that?' he asked. The boy smiled and clapped his hands in approval.

'What does it mean, though?' asked Jeeva.

'I don't know,' said Ajiva.

It was a lie. For the first time since he had woken up from the darkness, he had lied. He knew Jeeva was the word for life in Sanskrit. Ajiva was the opposite—lifeless—something that was never born or something that could never die.

How Ajiva knew what his name meant he had no clue.

Outside, the dark night was quiet as the snow fell slow and thick. The old woman, Maya stared into the darkness, listening to Ajiva toss and turn on the stone slab. The shepherd boy had gone back to his grandfather's house.

'Sleep is not your friend, is it?' she finally asked.

'No,' replied Ajiva.

'Is it the nightmares?'

'Yes.'

'What do you see?'

'I don't remember when I wake up.'

'Do you want to?'

Ajiva did not answer. The snow continued to fall noiselessly.

The midnight hour was half past when they sat facing each other. Maya was drawing a shape on the floor with a powder as fine as sand, only it was black in colour. She drew a triangle first and then another triangle around it. She did this again and again, until Ajiva lost count of the triangles. She drew each figure carefully, taking her time. There was a practised ease with which she drew the figures, as though she had done this a thousand times before.

Eventually, she drew the figure of a man in the heart of the first triangle—a stick figure with a circular head and straight lines for arms and legs, like how children drew men in the sand. Time passed slowly as she drew, like dew drops slipping down a blade of grass.

When she was eventually done, she placed an earthen vessel brimming with water over the drawing and looked up at Ajiva. In a strange tongue, she started muttering incantations under her breath, before extending a hand towards him.

Ajiva placed his palm over hers, which felt cold, soft and fleshless. Without warning, she picked up a blade lying on the floor and slashed at his palm. His skin tore open, as if it were made of the same material as a dry leaf, and a small trickle of blood burst out of his palm. Ajiva bit his lip to stop himself from crying out. She turned his palm over gently and allowed drops of blood to plop into the water.

Maya's mumblings became faster, more fervent. Her breath turned ragged and the black pupils of her eyes rolled upwards, making her eyes look like round hollow eggs.

Ajiva watched mesmerised as drops of his blood dripped into the water—hypnotised, like a snake swaying to the tune of the charmer. Drop after drop fell into the vessel, and the water started to turn red. His eyelids began to feel heavier and his body lighter.

And then, he saw the seed. The seed from his dreams. Green and tender. A shoot emerging from it, fighting its way up to break through the dirty soil. It was a tender shoot no more but a worm right now, hungry and young. And then, there were two of them. Just like the ones he had seen in his dreams earlier. He could feel their hunger, all-consuming and burning, in the pit of his stomach.

All of a sudden, they were no longer worms. They were serpents, two of them, with dark eyes and sharp fangs. They coiled around and writhed against each other, savouring the pleasure of the other's soft scaly skin. Still entwined, their mouths agape, they began to rise. And then, they froze and turned into stone. The final image was of two cobras, curled around each other, carved into stone.

Ajiva's eyes opened. The room was dark. He was still sitting on the floor. A small stream of blood was flowing out from his right palm, which was resting on his lap.

Maya sat across from him, staring at him with curious eyes.

'Do you remember now?' she asked.

'Yes.'

'So, do I,' she said. 'I saw your dream too.'

'What does it mean?' asked Ajiva.

'It was your dream. You tell me,' she said.

'I don't know, I don't know anything,' he repeated, anger and frustration creeping into his voice. 'Do you know what it means?'

The witch touched his bleeding palm with her index finger. Using his blood as paint, she traced the figure of two snakes curled around each other on the floor. She used her nail and slashed at the heads of the snake figures. Their mouths were wide open now.

'I have lived in the mountains all my life,' she said. 'I know very little about the flatlands or of kings and their kingdoms. But I know that once upon a time, this was a symbol of men and women who lived in the forests and shunned the cities. A breed of people who studied the stars and healed the sick. They did not believe in gods or demons, or that prayer or penance could better their fate. Their children did not till the farms nor did the parents work for gold or silver. They lived in the jungles, along with beasts and birds, hunting like them and living like them, one with nature. Some called them heretics; others branded them as impractical hermits.'

'Where are they now?' asked Ajiva.

'Perhaps still hiding in the jungle, perhaps nowhere,' said Maya, as she wiped the floor clean. 'A few years ago, people began to see lesser and lesser of these simple folk. Their symbol, the twin serpents, once seen carved on many temple walls and city gates, has all but disappeared.'

'What were these people called?'

'Ajiva ... I was curious to know why you chose that particular name,' she said, smiling revealing a few crooked, rotting teeth. 'Now, I know. These people were called the Ajivika.'

The steady stream of pilgrims going to the temple of Kedar became thicker as the days went by. In a month's time, snow and ice would bury the mountain path they were taking and the trees would grow bald as their leaves fell off. The summer, an unusually long and warm one this time, would end and the flow of pilgrims would end with it too.

A few villagers would even move to villages located in the foothills below, where the winters were more bearable and the snow did not fall from the skies. Cousins, brothers and friends would welcome them with warm hugs and host them, while the earth turned hard and cold above in the mountains.

Jeeva had no friends, cousins or brothers. If he did, he had never met them. He did not remember the face of his parents. All he had was his grandfather and, now Ajiva, a new friend, who seemed to be getting restless with every passing day. In their daily walks and in conversations on the banks of the Mandakini, over pebble-throwing, Ajiva spoke of going to the flatlands, finding out who he really was and searching for the Ajivika, whoever they were.

*Why does he have to go?* thought Jeeva as he stared at his grandfather, who was stirring a pot of lamb broth.

The old man turned around and offered the boy a bowl of the steaming broth. The boy held the warm bowl with both hands and stared at the shredded pieces of meat floating on top of the broth.

'So, how is your jogi?' the old man enquired, pouring himself some of the broth.

'He is not a jogi,' said the boy. 'His name is Ajiva.'

'Oh!' exclaimed the old man. 'So, he remembers his name now?'

'No, not fully,' said Jeeva. 'I named him ... actually, he named himself.'

'After you?' said the old man, looking confused. He lifted the bowl to his toothless mouth and began slurping down the broth. Some of the thick broth flowed down the sides of his mouth and onto his clothes.

'What does he want to do now? How long will he stay with that witch?' continued the old man.

'He wants to go to the flatlands and find out who he really is,' said Jeeva, with a tinge of sadness in his voice.

'Oh,' said the old man, looking keenly at his grandson with his pale eyes and then, turning away. Both drank their broth silently, without looking at each other again. One mourned the impending departure of a friend, the other mulled over the strange maps of love between human hearts called relationships.

Ajiva was sitting outside Maya's house, staring at the white mists on the crest of the mountain, when he heard the tapping sound of a cane. Jeeva's grandfather was walking towards him, coming down the path from the village that led to Maya's house. When their eyes met, the old man stopped.

'Is the … she there?' the old man asked, hesitantly, trying to keep his voice down.

'No, she has gone to collect herbs,' said Ajiva, greeting the old man with folded hands. 'She will be back soon.'

'Shambo!' exclaimed the old man, looking relieved. 'I came to meet you.'

'Me?' asked Ajiva.

'I am told you are leaving soon. For the flatlands,' said the old man.

Ajiva nodded.

'Where to? Any province in particular? Or are you a wanderer?' asked the old man.

'I really don't know,' said Ajiva. 'Why do you ask?'

'Because the thought of your departure is making my grandson—that boy who took care of you like a sparrow takes care of its young ones—sad,' said the old man, his voice shaking. 'I have a request.'

*Please don't ask me to stay.*

'Take him with you,' said the old man, tears lining his old eyes. 'I have lived out most of my years. I have lived them well. People born after me—sons, daughters, brothers—have left me, much before their time. This boy is the only one remaining. I want him to see the world, even the flatlands, which I think are god's vision of hell on earth … full of disease and dirt. But the boy has dreams, though he doesn't tell me about them, of shining palaces and magical cities. He doesn't know better. But he deserves to see for himself. I don't want him to live and die just as another shepherd in the mountains, grazing the sheep, summer after summer, winter after winter.'

The old man paused, gathering his strength. 'So, will you take him?' he asked.

'Yes, I shall,' said Ajiva.

'One last thing,' said the old man. 'Promise me, you will watch out for him. Be the father he has never had. Make sure he comes back to this village, to our house, to offer a ball of rice for my soul on the day of my passing.'

'I promise,' said Ajiva. 'But who will take care of you?'

The old man smiled. 'The same person who takes care of all of us,' said the old man, pointing a finger towards the heavens. 'We are all dew drops basking in the warm morning sun, shining in the light, revelling in our own reflected beauty. Little do we realise that the sun is really burning the dew drop alive. I am tired of being the dew drop,' said the old man.

The old man looked up and saw Maya returning with a bag full of herbs. Without a word of farewell, he turned around and walked as fast as his legs could carry him. As he crossed the witch, he spat on the ground.

'Charming old man,' said Maya, eyeing Ajiva. 'What did he say?'

'He said goodbye,' said Ajiva.

They left two days later, just as the sun peeped out from behind the mountains. Jeeva was lugging a sheepskin satchel on his back, which was packed with a few clothes, dried strips of meat and a few fruits for the road. Ajiva had nothing but the clothes he wore and a stout bamboo staff.

Earlier, Jeeva's grandfather had hugged him at their doorstep and kissed his cheeks in farewell. As Jeeva and Ajiva stood outside Maya's porch, the old witch stepped out with two jars carved from wood.

'That's the salve for your wound,' she said to Ajiva, handing him a jar. 'It will reduce the pain but the wound itself ...' she trailed off.

Ajiva took the jar and handed it to the boy, who put it in his satchel.

'And this one ...' she said, handing the second jar, which was much smaller, to the boy, '... is for something else. If you ever find yourself overwhelmed by the forces of darkness, this will give you strength. Why! Even courage. Use it well,' she said.

Ajiva looked at the witch curiously. 'What is it?' he asked.

The witch tapped the jar with a long, dirty fingernail.

'Just use it sparingly,' she said. 'Goodbye, children. May the goddess of the night always keep the skies above you blue and fill your path with friends and adventure.'

## 12. The Elders of Urba

The three elders of the Urba tribe squatted in a circle, devouring raw mangoes, chatting about the fate of the girl that the river goddess had delivered to them. They sucked on the green mangoes loudly, savouring the soft pulp, licking the sticky sap that flowed freely down their fingers and forearms. Occasionally, they made funny faces as the sourness of the unripe fruit hit the back of their throats. Naked toddlers ran around them, sprawling and squealing in the dirt, hurling pebbles at each other.

They had found her three weeks ago, half dead, floating down the river. Fish had nibbled at her thin arms and legs.

Scars, small and large, ran across her frail body. Yet, she had been breathing. For a week she did not open her eyes, and when she finally did, she rambled incoherently and screamed while she slept.

'A fine wife she will make once she bleeds,' said the one-eyed elder, adjusting his loincloth.

'Don't you have enough wives already?' snapped another elder. 'This one will take many more summers to bleed. When she does, we will see who makes her his wife … till then, we will have one more mouth to feed.'

'If she lives …' said the third elder, looking at the house where the girl was fast asleep.

The elders of the Urba tribe continued to argue as the sun slowly travelled across the sky, while their women foraged in the jungle for honey, berries and roots. The hunt had gone well the day before, and the wild boar's meat was now marinating in a paste of the black spice that grew freely in the mountains. The young hunters were now in their bamboo houses, making love to their wives or squabbling with them, while the elders sat around killing time, waiting for the feast in the evening where the boar would be roasted over an open fire.

'I think we should give her back to the river goddess,' said the one-eyed elder.

The other two continued to suck on their mangoes, mulling over the proposition.

'She is frail, so she can't work. She is going to take years to bleed, so …' the one-eyed elder continued. 'The skies have been raining fire. Mountain cats are growing in number … and there are fewer fish in the river these days. The yellow fever killed half our kind last summer. It is time to please the river goddess,' said the one-eyed elder.

'I agree,' said the other elder. 'A sacrifice!'

They looked at the third elder, who nodded his head slowly.

'Why not? I am tired of boar meat,' he said.

It was late in the evening when the girl woke up from her dark slumber and started rambling aloud, repeating the one word she knew, again and again. The girl realised that a strange-looking woman was bathing her. The woman had long earlobes that almost touched her shoulders, which were weighed down with heavy earrings made of polished black stones. Streaks of red and black paint covered her face. An emotion—maybe, fear—tiptoed into the girl's feverish mind, though she didn't know why.

The woman with the sagging earlobes gave the girl a tumbler with something to drink. It tasted bitter, as though it were made of raw grass. The drink flowed down to her belly, filling her with warmth and peace—something she had not felt in a while now. She thought of her mother, of her soft hands, her smile and the fragrance of her skin. It felt like another lifetime.

The woman lifted the cup to her mouth and the girl took one more sip. She felt light, as though she were a feather. The woman lifted the girl in her arms and walked out of the hut they were in.

A strange crowd was waiting there; most of them were naked. There were three old men, wearing loincloths. A few kids of her own age were looking at her, smiling. She smiled at them. Her eyelids felt heavy.

One of the old men stepped forward and pinched the flesh on her arms.

'Soft,' he said, smiling.

From the corner of her drooping eyes, she saw a bonfire. A young boy was poking it with a stick. A shower of sparks flew upwards.

All she wanted to do was sleep and dream—of her village, of her mother, to hear her bedtime stories.

The old man wearing the loincloth started muttering something that sounded like a prayer, in a tongue she could not understand. He touched her throat with his finger and raised his other hand towards the dark blood-red sky.

Someone gave him a knife, which he kissed.

The girl closed her eyes.

And then, it happened. She heard the sound of an arrow piercing through the air. The arrow had struck the one-eyed elder's throat, spraying the girl's face with blood. Her eyes fluttered open.

Around her, men and women had started screaming. Arrows were swishing past her. One of the old men in a loin cloth was staggering like a drunkard, holding his stomach. He stumbled and fell into the bonfire, screaming, as his hair caught on fire.

The girl did not care. She just wanted to sleep.

The last thing she saw in the yellow light of the fires burning all around her, before succumbing to sleep, was a fluttering flag with a triumphant eagle on it—the banner of Mithila.

# 13. Chaturanga

It started as a whisper among the brahmans of Mithila—a story of dubious origins that few believed entirely. Despite that, it spread like forest fire on a hot summer day. Like all juicy tales, everyone knew how the story had begun but no one knew how it ended. So, the storytellers embellished it with the spice of their own imaginations and served it up to their eager listeners.

The story began thus: Divyakshu, a brahman with a deformed hand from a village called Soumyapur, was humiliated by the king for making a dark prophecy—one that came true. This much everybody agreed on. But the rest of the story took twists and turns, depending on the mood and style of the fable tellers.

Some said the drunken king had hurled insults at the brahman, others said he had thrown a gold coin which had struck the brahman on his forehead. Another storyteller said that as the brahman's blood had dripped on the floor of the court, jackals, dogs and other beasts of ill omen had howled on the streets of Mithila. A few listeners wondered how jackals could have howled in a city they hadn't been seen or heard in for generations.

A learned brahman, a prolific composer of popular stories, hymns and poems, was telling tales of black rain drenching crops in the hinterlands, turning the soil crimson. Swarms of locusts, as per him, had laid waste to orchards.

Before long, it was not just the brahmans who were gossiping. In the crowded grain markets and gambling houses of Mithila, traders and swordsmen began betting on the fate of the brahman. Some wagered silver on the fact that he was alive and hiding in the mountains to escape the wrath of a petulant king. Others believed that the brahman was languishing in the dark depths of a dungeon that King Trivikrama had thrown him into.

And then, a more sinister story began to be told.

'Say that again,' said Aacharya Gurukripa, shaking his head in disbelief when he heard it for the first time. The informer, who worked as an usher at a prominent natyashala in the city, stared at the aacharya squeamishly.

'They are saying that … pardon me, Aacharya-ji … that the king killed the brahman,' said the informant. '… and then, sliced his hand off and had it pickled.'

Distaste clearly showed on Gurukripa's face as he picked up a coin and tossed it to the informant who grabbed it with both palms. 'Keep me informed about every rumour, however … vile it might be,' he added, and waved the informant away.

The informant, however, stood rooted to the ground.

'Sire …' he began hesitantly, his eyes glued to the ground. 'Is it true?'

'Of course not!' snapped Gurukripa. 'Why would the king want to pickle someone's hand, least of all, a brahman's hand? Go now,' he said, dismissing the informant, who bowed low and walked away.

*How had they found out about the hand?*

The royal procession slowly snaked its way through the streets of Mithila. First came the water carriers who sprinkled water on the sizzling roads to keep the dust from blinding the onlookers. Behind the water carriers came the drummers who pounded on the leather with all their might, announcing to all and sundry that royalty was around the corner.

And then came the king's guard: archers who could shoot the beak off a parrot, swordsmen with curved blades that dazzled in the afternoon sun and mace bearers with shoulders bulging like prize bulls. A fleet of nimble-footed boys were tasked with distributing baskets of yellow gandhapushpa flowers all along the route to onlookers, who tossed them at the king as he went past.

Trivikrama sat on a trundling elephant, smiling and waving to the cheering crowds. He waved a lazy arm at the little boys and girls who sat on top of their parents' shoulders just to get a glimpse of him. For over an hour, he had been waving his hand. The novelty was now wearing off and his shoulders were hurting. The crown, made of solid gold and encrusted with jewels, which he wore only during public appearances, weighed on his head as if a heavy oak pillar from the palace had been placed on it. Lines of sweat trickled down his back, despite the shade of the umbrella held by a servant seated behind him.

Then, he saw the two beauties—full-breasted, fair-skinned, long-limbed with strings of parijata flowers adorning their long, dark tresses. One of them was leaning over her balcony, tossing flowers at him, when her upper garment slipped revealing more of her shapely breasts. The petals did not reach him but her gaze did. She covered her exposed breasts quickly, but not entirely. Her friend caught the king's gaze, and started laughing, giddy with excitement.

It was in that moment that Trivikrama wished he wasn't a king but just another man who had been stung by a scorpion called infatuation. That he could just jump off this lumbering, swaying elephant, walk into that woman's house and make sweaty passionate love to her, and maybe even to her friend.

*Would they smile and giggle if I weren't a king?*

He removed a string of pearls from his neck and flung it

at the woman in the balcony. She squealed and grabbed it, pressing it to her bosom. The elephant walked past the house while Trivikrama continued to wave at her.

'Easy, brother, easy,' yelled Ajitha, who had trotted up to him on his horse from the rear of the procession. 'People are watching,' he screamed above the din of the drummers.

Trivikrama smiled at his brother, and pretending that he had not heard him, kept waving at the woman. He turned his head back one last time to look at her, before the elephant rounded the corner. Up ahead, the royal courtyard loomed, with its raised ramparts and gates manned by guards. The flag of Mithila was aloft.

Trivikrama heaved a sigh of relief. He couldn't wait to get back to his chamber, take a bath, smear his burning back and arms with cool sandalwood paste and down a glass of soma. The proceedings of the morning had dulled his spirits. After his ablutions and an hour of horse riding, he had gone to meet his mother, who had blessed him with her usual silence and a smile.

Then had come the biggest chore of the day: a visit to the Mahadeva temple that his father had built, followed by the opening of a new dharmshala and a bathing tank for the brahmins visiting Mithila. Normally, the king wouldn't have needed to grace such a minor function with his presence. But, as his dear brother loved reminding him these days—it's not normal when the skies burn like a haystack and the deformed paws of missing brahmans are delivered in cooking vessels.

The dharmshala opening was a peace offering, a gesture to the brahmans that the king was their protector and, more importantly, their benefactor. Even kings have to stoop to conquer, Aacharya Gurukripa loved reminding him. At the inauguration, Trivikrama had announced a seemingly spontaneous grant of thirty more villages to the vedashalas of Mithila. The brahmans had smiled politely at the gesture.

'They are still not pleased, brother,' Ajitha had whispered to him at the inauguration.

'Perhaps, I should throw in a few lashes for each of these daylight robbers,' Trivikrama had whispered back with gritted teeth, before throwing in a donation of a hundred cows.

At the footsteps of the royal courtyard, Aacharya Gurukripa was waiting. The elephant kneeled on the ground and Trivikrama jumped off it.

'My dear king,' said the aacharya. 'Someone in the royal council has been talking.'

'One of you …' began Trivikrama, toying with the iron tumbler next to him, brimming with asava, the sour wine of wood apple, '… has failed me. One of you has opened his mouth in places he shouldn't have.'

One by one, he looked at the faces of the five men in the ivory room. Ajitha was leaning back on his tall chair beside him, trying hard to maintain a straight face. If there was one fault with his dear brother, it was the inability to mask his true feelings. Right now, Ajitha was amused—Trivikrama was not sure if it was his rising fury or the petrified looks of the other men in the room that so tickled his younger brother's sense of humour.

Aacharya Gurukripa looked like he always did—an island of calm surrounded by choppy seas. The old brahman looked back at his old disciple, with neither a smile nor a frown, just an expression of casual curiosity.

Chavuka's chubby jowls, which reminded Trivikrama of a

milch cow's udder, were undulating up and down, bathed in sweat. The physician met the king's angry stare for a moment, before looking away. The royal astrologer, Bramhadatta, looked like a condemned prisoner awaiting his executioner. His narrow eyes darted from side to side while his pink tongue made nervous little excursions over his dry lips. He eyed the others around the table tremulously, almost as though he was hoping for one of them to confess their guilt and end his misery.

At the far end of the table sat Jayaveera, his friend from boyhood days, the brother of his wife, and his commander-in-chief. Jayaveera's hawkish dark eyes met Trivikrama's sharp gaze and held it. Perhaps for a moment too long.

*Is he really my friend? Or have the old family feuds turned his head?*

'Jayaveera, my friend,' said Trivikrama. 'The manservant who gave you the vessel with the severed hand. Did he open it before he gave it to you?'

'No, my king, he wouldn't dare,' said Jayaveera. 'Nor did I tell him what was inside the vessel, once I saw it. I came to you as soon as I could … I spoke to no one. If you recall, I wanted to talk to you alone. But you insisted that I talk about it in front of everyone assembled, which was all of us.'

'Yes, I recall,' said Trivikrama, considering the argument for a moment. 'How was it delivered to your chambers?'

'That's still a mystery,' said Jayaveera. 'My manservant thought the person who delivered it was someone new employed by my wife. He had never seen him before. He just assumed the courier was bringing my evening snack.'

'And did you try hunting for this mysterious deliverer of chopped hands?'

'Yes, my king, but to no avail.'

The king swirled the wine in his glass for a while, before taking a small sip.

'For weeks, I have been patient. Most of you have failed me in one way or the other,' said Trivikrama. 'From here on, failure, unintentional or otherwise, will not be tolerated. In fact, it shall be punished. To begin with, I intend to find out who spoke out of turn. In the next few days, impress me with your deeds … else, there will be consequences. Henceforth, the price of sloth will be paid in blood,' said Trivikrama and dismissed most of the council, except for his brother and Aacharya Gurukripa.

'So, who do you think it is, Aacharya-ji?' asked Ajitha, when they were alone.

'I am not sure. Both Chavuka and Bramhadatta are brahmans. And, I have been told the rumour started amongst the brahmans. Yet, neither of them has the courage to carry tales from the royal council to the outside world … at least not intentionally.'

'So, you think it's Jayaveera?' asked Trivikrama.

'His friendship and his kinship to His Majesty apart, he has been unusually unsuccessful in tracing the brahman. Also, why was the brahman's hand delivered to him and not to anyone else?' said Gurukripa, staring at the intricate patterns on the roof, which was carved with the royal sigil of Mithila.

'So, you do suspect him?' asked Trivikrama again.

'Maybe this whole thing was just an innocuous slip of the tongue—drunken men talking in a tavern or loose pillow talk with a courtesan. But if that was not the case, Jayaveera would be the one I would keep an eye on, Your Majesty. Kings, unlike commoners, have no true friends,' replied Gurukripa.

Trivikrama sighed aloud and, for some reason, he thought of the buxom woman in the balcony who had smiled at him earlier in the day. He really wished Jayaveera was not the one who had broken his trust, at least not intentionally. If he had, there would be several thorns to pluck out.

*But why would he even do it?*

'Let's assume that it is him,' said Trivikrama. 'If that's the case, what do we do about the search for the missing brahman? Should Jayaveera still lead it?' asked the king.

'No, brother,' said Ajitha. 'Perhaps, we need to find someone else ... someone who would do so discreetly, without Jayaveera finding out.'

The silence in the room was stifling, even more than the afternoon heat. Guards marched outside the room, stray pigeons cooed from the dark holes in the ramparts, horses neighed in the distance and somewhere beyond the palace, temple bells rang.

'I might know just the person for it, Your Majesty,' said Gurukripa.

'Does he suspect me?'

'Are you doing something that's worth suspecting?'

'If I said no, would you believe me?'

'Not entirely.'

'Why?'

'Because that's the nature of the world. Big fish eat small fish. The lion kills the deer. And, most men dream of becoming king ... especially those who were kings once upon a time,' said Aacharya Gurukripa, smiling.

'Do you?' asked Jayaveera.

'I am a brahman. My ancestors were priests and cooks before they started serving kings.'

'You evade my question. Do you want to be king? After all, like you said, Aacharya-ji, that's the nature of the world.'

'Kings wear crowns and live in fear. I desire neither.'

'So, what do you desire?'

'The welfare of Mithila.'

'Don't we all?' said Jayaveera, smirking. 'So, why did you want to meet me in the middle of the night?'

'To understand what your game is,' said Gurukripa.

'Have you, Aacharya-ji?'

'Not yet, but I will ... soon, Jayaveera,' said Gurukripa. 'Mithila is a game of chaturanga. You have your coins and I have mine.'

'Yes, Aacharya-ji. Just like you have your spies and I have mine.'

## 14. The Pillar of Devprayag

It was four mornings since they had last seen snow. Jeeva was already missing the clear air of the mountains and the sight of grey peaks with puffy clouds smothering the summits. As they walked, it seemed to get warmer with every passing step. The trees became shorter and thicker. Now the Mandakini was no longer a cool, blue gurgling stream but a wide, roaring angry river which tossed boulders around as though they were mere pebbles.

Villages with smoking chimneys kept popping up like mushrooms. He could see men and women labouring on small vegetable patches under the sun. Occasionally, they encountered groups of pilgrims who were going in the other direction, up the mountains, to the temples of Shiva. The young walked while the old were perched on mules or rested on palanquins that sweating porters carried on their shoulders. Occasionally, they crossed bands of soldiers on horses, with their gleaming breastplates, swords, spears and flags that flapped in the wind.

Ajiva spoke very little and walked fast with long strides. Sometimes, he would stop in the path, waiting for Jeeva to catch up, then point towards a shrub and say something like, 'Eat it's seeds and you won't see the sun rise tomorrow.' Or, he would pluck the leaves of a plant, mash them between his fingers and smell them before saying, 'Ah! Leaves from heaven.' And yes, the leaves smelled divine and they tasted even better when chewed on.

*Yet, he can't remember his real name or his past life*, thought Jeeva.

They walked all day long, till their calf muscles turned to stone and their backs became stiff. At dusk, they would bathe in the river and find rest either in the courtyard of a temple or under the open skies in the company of mendicants and mongrels. Jeeva would collect twigs and dry firewood, while Ajiva cooked over a roaring fire. Some days, other passersby joined in and offered them warm curries they had cooked over the fires. On other days, they lived off the land—fruits if they found them or fish if they happened to be close to a stream. At night, while the boy slept, Ajiva stayed awake and kept the fire alive.

'Tigers … big mountain cats with yellow fleece. The plains and forests are full of them,' said Ajiva. 'They hunt while we sleep.'

Jeeva had seen this cat only once, that too in the mountains. But he did not tell Ajiva about the day he had seen the cat, the day fire had rained from the sky and Ajiva had come back to life.

It was on the afternoon of the eighth day, when the sun was high up in the sky, that Jeeva saw a sight he would remember for the rest of his life. Warm air and sluggish bees hummed lazily around his ears, putting him into a stupor. Just ahead, the mountain path curved sharply, almost plunging down into the valley, where the wide river flowed. The water was now pearl green in colour, like the floor of a lush forest.

Ajiva was standing at the edge of the path, looking at something, lost in his own world as usual. The boy quickened his pace, reached the edge of the mountain path and stood next to Ajiva. Below him, the pearl-green waters of the river curled smoothly, looking like a sickle carved in the valley floor. From the other side of the valley, another river was cutting through the mountains—a dark, muddy river, slow moving but wider.

At one point, the two rivers met and locked each other in a tight embrace—one, a rushing stream of pure green waters from the heavens and the other, an unstoppable sludge from the plains. For a while they resisted, each retaining its own colour and character, before giving up and becoming one calm river, the mighty Ganga.

'Devprayag,' declared Ajiva, pointing to a small piece of land jutting out at the confluence, where the two rivers, Bhagirathi and Alaknanda, were locked in their violent embrace.

At the edge of the land stood a tall pillar, dark and gleaming in the afternoon sun.

'I think … I have been here before,' said Ajiva, and began to walk down the valley.

Jeeva had never seen so many people in his life, at least not together. The crowds, the noise and the stench of the crowd made him nervous. The annual mela at Devprayag was teeming with folk from across the kingdoms and strange beasts that he had not even heard of. Horse traders with almond-coloured skin and thin eyes sold stallions with gleaming, long manes. Stout traders and farmers were haggling over the prices of oxen, who snorted and belched loudly.

A man playing a damroo was making a beast with shaggy black hair—he could stand on two legs but ran on four—dance and jump through hoops on fire. A small crowd of people tossed coins at the beast, which was hopping on its feet clumsily. The beast had the face and teeth of a wolf, sharp claws, and was twice the size of man when it stood up on its hind legs. Ajiva said the beast was called a bear.

'It can take the skin off a man's face with one swipe of its arm,' said Ajiva, with a tinge of sadness. 'Yet, look at its fate ... chained like a pet, dancing to the beat of a drum.'

The fair also had an assortment of strange men. In an enclosure made of bamboo shoots, two giants in loincloths, with swollen bellies and arms as big as tree trunks wrestled in the mud. The red mud clung to their oiled bodies making them look like overripe melons that could burst anytime. Each time one of the wrestlers fell and started tapping the ground in defeat, the crowd roared with joy and threw in a few coins.

And then, there were the dwarfs who wore colourful costumes and sang bawdy songs that Jeeva could not understand but that made the grownups giggle; hunchbacks who swallowed flaming swords; jugglers who tossed knives in the air and even a holy man who lay asleep on a bed of nails. 'A fraud, if I have ever seen one,' said Ajiva, looking at the wonder in Jeeva's eyes for the sleeping man.

From inside a tent, the sound of music and merriment streamed out and Jeeva started walking towards it. Ajiva gripped his shoulder and pulled the boy back. Outside, a man with a twirling moustache and colourful clothes waved a hand which had a ring on each finger, some made of bronze and others made of gold.

'Two pieces of silver for you,' he said, eyeing Ajiva's beard, soot-covered clothes and the stained sash around his waist. 'And six pieces for your son … if you really think he should go in,' he laughed, pointing at Jeeva.

'What's inside? Sounds like fun!' asked Jeeva, as waves of music and laughter streamed out from the tent.

The man's face gleamed with a wicked smile as he flashed a row of shining teeth. 'Take a peek,' he told Ajiva.

Ajiva opened the tent flap and stuck his head inside, a little hesitantly. The tent was full of men holding cups full of medaka, the rice wine which drove men and horses wild with lust. At the centre of the tent, two skimpily clad women on a pedestal were dancing vigorously to the savage thumping of drums. One of the women tugged down the blouse of the other woman, exposing her bare breasts. The crowd roared in approval. A shower of coins rained on the women, who bent down to pick it.

'Come on! This is not for you,' said Ajiva and dragged the boy away from the tent, as the mocking laughter of the tent owner followed them.

Up ahead, they saw a line of men queuing up before a tent. On the roof of the tent, a flag with an eagle sigil flapped in the breeze.

'Food for all,' screamed a soldier. 'From the king of kings, ruler of Mithila, Trivikrama. Eat to your heart's content and bless the great king … come one, come all.'

The two of them stood in the line, along with sadhus, beggars and dwarfs, while a soldier handed them plates made of leaves.

The pillar stood at the edge of the land like a loner—dark and brooding. It rose out of the mud abruptly, without any purpose or preamble. There were no inscriptions of great import carved on its surface, no celebratory plaques or stone tablets anywhere near it, no temples around it. It was just a brown polished pillar, made of brass or iron or some secret alloy that neither the harsh sunlight of the mountains nor rain could rust or dull.

On clear days, some people said, you could see the top of the pillar, on which rested a heavy bowl of stone. But it wasn't an easy story to believe, for only hawks and eagles could fly as high as the top of the pillar. And for reasons best known to these birds of prey, they steered clear of it. From the peaks of the mountains which rose above the valley, the pillar looked like a long sword that the gods had thrust into the ground and forgotten to pull out.

Around the pillar, the two rivers roared past, drowning the babbling of the men who gawked at it with awe and wonder. Up close, men examined the pillar with pursed lips and a hushed silence. The few who dared to touch the pillar immediately drew back their scalded palms, scorched by the heat radiating from it.

Legends about the pillar were plenty, though. Some called it Vajra, the thunderbolt of Indra. Some others speculated that Karthikeya, the son of Shiva, exhausted after vanquishing the forces of evil had thrown his trident into the river and the pillar was what remained of it.

But there was one legend that most people believed in. That an eternal flame had once burned atop the pillar, a flame so hot that it had burned through centuries, without oil or wood or the help of men. The flame had burned since the time of the first men, a time when gods still walked the earth.

And then, the flame had died. Some said it was because Arjuna, the man who had made a god his charioteer, had shot an arrow into the heart of the flame and doused the fire. Some said the flame had died when the last eon, the yuga of kali, had begun. There were those who spoke of dark prophecies: of a man who would one day rekindle the flame with the shot of an arrow and change the course of history. But prophecies were as common as fish in the river.

At the base of the pillar rested the challenge—a bow made of steel and strung with silk. Next to it, lay a quiver of arrows and a bowl of camphor oil. A naga sadhu, his naked body covered in ashes, sat on the bare ground next to the quiver, stoking a fire, day and night. He lit up his chillum and stared contemptuously at the men, women and children who milled around the pillar.

Few archers took up the challenge, for how do you shoot at a target you cannot even see? Those who did, picked up the bow, looked up at the pillar that grew into the skies and gave up.

'Do none of you cowards dare shoot an arrow?' the sadhu asked, taking a drag off his chillum, taunting the gaggle of onlookers, most of whom ignored him.

'You … you!' he said, pointing towards a thin man with a scruffy bamboo stick and a sash around his waist. A rosy cheeked boy stood next to him staring at the pillar. 'You look like you can wield a sword or shoot an arrow. Be a man—'

Ajiva turned back and looked at the sadhu. Something about his dark eyes made the sadhu stop his tirade. The look triggered a memory in the sadhu's mind, something from a long, long time ago, something that chilled his blood. But just as suddenly as it had tapped the corners of his mind, it was gone.

The thin man averted his gaze and walked away with the boy.

'Go on, you worm,' yelled the sadhu at him. 'Crawl back to your wife and boast about seeing a pillar that you did not even dare touch.'

The sun dipped behind the mountains as the sadhu took one more deep puff from his chillum. The river continued to roar in the darkness.

It was a moonless night and the clouds hung low. The naga sadhu slept fitfully, despite the intoxication from the chillum. Even in his sleep, he heard the whining moan of the boulders as the roaring river crushed one against the other. Occasionally, he woke up and thrust a log into the cackling fire next to him. Sleep played hide and seek with him.

It was the sound of a thunderclap that startled him awake. Above him white clouds moved like apparitions against the dark sky.

*Was it going to rain?*

The monsoon had come and gone a few months ago. But who can predict the mood of the hills? He sat up in the dark and realised that the bow next to him was not there. A silhouette moved in the dark, next to the river, away from the pale circle of light that the sputtering fire cast. A thin form with long matted hair and a beard. Perhaps it was another sadhu like him.

'Who's there?' the sadhu barked, to the darkness. His own voice sounded different, hoarse and even afraid. The hair on his neck stood on end.

'Reveal yourself,' he said louder.

The silhouette walked towards the fire with slow measured steps. The stranger in the dark held the bow with a practiced ease and the quiver full of arrows hung from his shoulder.

'Ah,' said the sadhu, when he saw the face. 'It's you. Where's your, son?'

'Asleep,' said Ajiva.

'Came to take a shot when nobody was watching, did you?' said the sadhu, as his courage came back to him.

Ajiva did not reply. Instead, he bent down and picked up a handful of mud from the ground, and then slowly released it from his hand. The wind blew the sand away from the pillar.

'The greatest archers in a thousand years have not been able to shoot an arrow at the summit of this pillar, even during the clearest of days. And you—fool that you are—want to shoot one on a moonless night? You want to shoot it when the breeze blows down from the mountains … either you are stupid or you smoke more chillum than I do. Which one is it?' asked the sadhu.

'What do you think?' asked Ajiva, as he tore a piece of cloth from the sash around his waist, tied it around the arrowhead and dipped it in the pail of camphor oil, before exposing it to fire.

The arrowhead burst into flames. Ajiva stood straight with his legs apart, lowered his bow and set the arrow on the bow string. The flaming tip of the arrow almost touched the ground. With his head down, he pulled the string up to his ear and closed his eyes for a moment.

The sadhu watched transfixed. Every sinew in the thin man's body was taut, like the string on the bow, waiting for release. And then, suddenly, the man's body swung upwards, his heels thrust into the ground, the arrowhead pointed skywards. Little flecks of flame fell off the arrowhead, towards the man's wide-open eyes. He was looking up at something that the sadhu could not see—something beyond the low clouds.

The man released the arrow. The twang of the string sounded like a clap of thunder rolling off a barren valley. The sadhu got to his feet and watched the flaming arrow shoot skywards into the darkness. It raced past the clouds, a point of light in the darkness—like a shooting star—before it disappeared across the skies.

The thin man slumped to the ground, clutching his waist. The sash had untied and the wound was exposed.

The naga sadhu looked up at the sky again. 'You missed,' he said. 'And yet, I have never seen any man shoot an arrow the way you did tonight … who are you?'

'I am Ajiva. Beyond that … I don't know,' said the thin man.

The three of them sat gazing into the fire, while the boy narrated the strange story of the man he called Ajiva. The naga sadhu listened, rarely offering a comment. When the tale was told, he tossed a log into the fire, unmindful of the sparks that flew out and grazed his naked body.

'When I was a younger man,' the sadhu began. 'I used to be a merchant of spices, chasing profit and gold. I had a wife, children and even a mistress. Then, a war came, kings fought and strangers slaughtered each other for pride, for cows and for land. When it was over, all those who I'd loved were gone … my wife, children and even the mistress,' said the sadhu.

'That was a lifetime ago. Feels like another birth. Now, I sit here at the confluence of these two rivers, raving and ranting, cursing people, hoping for a prophecy to come true … perhaps it never will,' said the naked sadhu. 'That symbol you see in your dreams,' he continued, handing Ajiva a twig. 'Draw it for me.'

Ajiva drew the two lines on the sand, which curled against each other, like two mating snakes.

'I haven't seen this in recent years,' said the sadhu. 'But back in my days of travel, I used to see this carved on stones at the entrance of villages around the city of Kampilya, the old capital of the Panchalas. Going there might give you some clues.'

As the night lengthened, the sadhu kept speaking to them like they were long lost friends. He spoke about the strange beasts he had encountered in the mountains, narrated legends of old and even told a few stories from his old life.

'So, what is this legend of the pillar? What if Ajiva had set it on fire today?' asked the boy.

The sadhu uttered a bitter, belly laugh. 'Well, he hasn't, has he? Shouldn't we all sleep now?'

The naga sadhu woke up before dawn, as was his habit. He stoked the dying embers of the fire and staggered towards the river. The river water from the mountains was freezing cold. As he entered the river, he bit into his dry lips, drawing blood. He stood for a second, letting his bare legs get used to the icy water, before diving in. He emerged screaming with agony as the freezing water cut through the smog of sleep and sucked the breath from his lungs.

He breathed in lungfuls of air and squatted into the water again, drowning his entire body and his matted locks. Around him, the river was a black flowing mass, swirling and raging. When he emerged from the water, he sniffed the air like a wolf.

Something smelled different. The breeze was blowing down from the mountains, carrying with it something fine and powdery. It swirled and danced even in the darkness.

*Was it snow?*

It couldn't be. Snow rarely fell in Devprayag. And it wasn't even winter. The powder fell on his body. He rubbed it with his wet hands and smelled it.

*Ash. It can't be.*

The sadhu looked up at the pillar. It glowed in the dark. Its tall unending body was no longer a shade of bronze but the colour of molten gold. The sadhu raised his head, and high up above the clouds, he saw the flame that raged and smoked.

The eternal flame that hadn't burned for a thousand years was alive.

*The prophecy had come true. Rivers of blood will flow.*

The sadhu laughed and laughed, till tears flowed down his eyes. He splashed around in the water, screaming and crying till the sun came up above the mountains.

## 15. The Miracle of Kampilya

With every passing day, the crowds swelled. Everybody wanted to see the girl who had lived. The Miracle of Kampilya, they called her. The one who had survived the horrors of the flesh eaters of Urba. Ever since the band of soldiers who had rescued her, had brought her to the walled city at the foothills of the mountains, people had flocked to see her from near and far. Some had walked from nearby villages, while others had come on oxcarts from far away provinces, just for a glimpse of the girl.

Once a great city of warriors and traders, everything in Kampilya was now brown and dank. The roads, unlike those of Mithila, were unpaved, usually covered in a slippery mix of mud and horse dung. Drainages in the city overflowed, whilc mosquitoes and gnats buzzed and feasted on the blood of men and cattle. Traders chose not to stay within the city, choosing to stay in camps outside the walls instead.

On the street outside the public dispensary, men and women waited patiently in long queues under the sweltering midday sun for a glimpse of the girl, who lay in a cot next to a window. An elderly matron who usually cleaned the floors of the dispensary fanned the girl, and a physician put on a great show of tending to the girl's wounds. The crowds stared at her through the open window. Soldiers took turns to narrate the tales of horrors of the Urbas, especially their love for eating human flesh and bedding young girls. A donation box was passed along the queues and non-donors were brusquely asked to move on.

As for the girl herself, she slept for most of the day and seldom spoke. And when she did, she uttered only one word, over and over again.

'Ardhamukha … Ardhamukha … Ardhamukha.'

When the skies grew dark, she would shun sleep and refuse to turn down the lantern in her room. If sleep overcame her, she would toss and turn and claw at her clammy skin until she woke up again. Often, in the dead of the night, she would soil her clothes and scream only one name aloud.

'Ardhamukha … Ardhamukha … Ardhamukha.'

The name and the terror it inspired in the girl spread around the city like a swamp fever. Who was Ardhamukha? Was it a demon who haunted the poor girl? Was it a highway robber? Was it a filthy Urba fiend who had defiled the poor girl? Or, was it the name of a god who had appeared in her dreams before sending a band of soldiers to rescue her?

As her fame spread, so did the gruesome quality of the stories. It was on the morning of the twelfth day of her arrival in the city that things changed. She had stayed awake all night, fighting off sleep, till the sky had turned red at dawn. And then, she had curled up and gone to sleep.

In the morning, the matron let her sleep for a few extra hours, and then tapped her shoulder to wake her up. The crowds had been building up since morning and not many liked to see a sleeping girl. One sleeping girl was no different from the other. They wanted to see a famished-looking girl, mumbling that strange name again and again. That's why they had dropped silver into the donation box.

The girl continued to sleep. The matron dipped her fingers inside a copper bowl brimming with cold water and pressed them to the girl's eyelids.

They fluttered open. She looked at the matron.

'Where's … my mother?' asked the girl, before a strange look of comprehension came in her eyes, and she burst out crying.

The matron dropped the bowl and ran to find the physician.

The girl had spoken.

Vishnupada scowled when he saw the expression on his son's face. The boy's nose was crinkled in distaste, his lips were pursed, making his pale fat cheeks hang like overripe jackfruits. With his small beady eyes, the boy looked like a stuffed piglet.

Unlike his son, Vishnupada loved the scent of the central market of Mithila. He loved the strange concoction of odours in the market: the sweet scent of fresh flowers, the overpowering perfumes that merchants dabbed on their chest and armpits, the choking odour of the sweat of labourers who hauled grain on their bare backs, the stench of rotting vegetables and even the cloying smell of cow, goat and horse dung. For Vishnupada, the richest merchant of Mithila, the smells and sounds of the market were the closest thing to heaven. It was the sweet scent of wealth.

His son's expression was an affront to him and his ancestors who had made their fortunes in this very market. Five generations ago, their family had sold baubles and trinkets on the streets of Mithila, and, now, their caravans crisscrossed the sixteen kingdoms.

From Tamralipti at the edge of Purva Samudra to the wild valleys of Gandhara, caravans of carts drawn by oxen and camels hauled grains, spices, saffron, copper, gold, fly whisks, leather, wool, spices, and even strange beasts and beautiful courtesans to and from faraway lands for the amusement of kings and nobles.

*And this idiot boy makes a face*, thought Vishnupada and smacked his son on the back of his head. The boy started bawling, letting out a long howl that made people around them stop and stare. Vishnupada ignored the boy and the curious glances of people, and kept walking. His son followed reluctantly, dragging his feet.

Up ahead, outside his warehouse, a swarm of people were

basking in the morning sun, talking to each other. Vishnupada adjusted the turban on his head before wading through the crowd to reach the door of his warehouse. Bhima and Anja, his two servants, had set a table and chair for him outside.

Vishnupada sat on the chair, looked at the crowd and flashed an empty smile at nobody in particular. The crowd stopped murmuring and started staring at him.

'Good turnout, master,' said Bhima, bowing obsequiously. Anja began fanning Vishnupada with a fly whisk made of yak tail.

'Where's *my* chair, father?' asked his son, already holding onto his knees.

'Keep standing and keep your mouth shut and ears and eyes open,' snapped Vishnupada.

'Why?' asked the boy, with a sullen expression.

*Indra—please grant me patience*, thought Vishnupada, gritting his teeth. He wanted to smack the boy on the back of his head again, but chose to glare at him instead. If the boy squealed to his mother and grandmother about his father's treatment of him, Vishnupada knew he wouldn't hear the end of it for weeks.

'One more word from you and I will make sure you sleep in the warehouse tonight … on sacks of grain,' hissed Vishnupada, before turning his attention to Bhima. 'Make the announcement.'

Bhima clapped his hands over his head a few times. All eyes turned towards them.

Vishnupada smiled. He liked what was coming.

Bhima cleared his throat before launching into his speech, one he gave year after year.

'Like you all already know, the caravan from Mithila to Kampilya leaves in five days. We are looking for cart drivers, cooks, loaders, water carriers and cleaners. The journey will be thirty-five days long. The journey is long and hard. A vaidya will examine you for health problems, so if you have any, walk away right now. You can opt for payment in silver or grain. Once you have been selected, if you desert the caravan, in the unlikely case of any attack by wild animals or highway robbers, you will not be paid anything. Not one coin of silver. Not one handful of grain,' said Bhima, pausing for effect. 'Any questions?'

There were none.

'Hope you learnt something today,' said Vishnupada to his son, who seemed to be lost in thought, busy chewing on his fingernails.

*God save me*, Vishnupada thought and again smacked the boy on the back of his head.

Her name was Ushas and her parents had chosen to name her after the goddess of dawn, the girl told them. Like Ushas, you have a beautiful smile, her mother liked to tell her. Her father, like her grandfather who lived with them, had been a priest. The fever had taken her grandmother three summers ago.

She remembered that day clearly. Her father and a few other men from the village had carried her grandmother, who seemed fast asleep with her mouth open, on a crude bed made of bamboo poles, while chanting hymns. Her father had led the procession, carrying a pot filled with smouldering coals on his shoulder. She had wanted to join the men. However, Ushas, like the other girls and women in the village, had been forbidden from even watching this procession.

But she had always been curious and light on her feet, like

a cat. So, she had sneaked out of the house and followed the men carrying her grandmother, crouching in bushes, making sure twigs didn't snap under her feet. Either way, they couldn't have heard her, for they were chanting hymns loudly. She watched as the men laid her grandmother's body on a crude platform made of piled wooden logs. Her weeping father circled the platform once and then placed a burning torch at the foot of the woodpile.

The woodpile slowly caught fire and flames started licking at her grandmother's feet. She expected the old lady to wake up screaming but nothing happened. Her grandmother was fast asleep. Hiding behind the bushes, the girl had covered her mouth with her hand to stop herself from screaming out. She had run back through the bushes and cried herself to sleep that night.

Ushas had never wanted to see anybody else die. That's what people called it. Dying. Grandfather always said that dying was just like changing clothes. 'The one who is inside is just changing bodies. Burning the body is like burning old clothes,' he would tell her, looking at her with his sad, droopy eyes, as she sat on his lap. In response, Ushas would tell her grandfather that she did not want anybody else to die, not her mother, or father, or grandfather. She wanted them to keep wearing their old clothes. Grandfather would laugh at that, every time.

But then, all of them had *died*. Except for her.

It had been late in the evening and she had been playing Kings and Queens with her friends. The boys of the village were kings and the girls were queens. The queens were on the run and would hide all over the village while the kings hunted for them. It was her favourite game because she always won. She was fast and silent, like a cat in the woods. Unlike the other girls, she wasn't afraid either. So, she had sneaked away to her favourite hideout, the clump of bushes behind the temple of Agni, where the old anthill stood.

No ants lived there anymore. Empty anthills were where snakes made their homes, her father had told her. But she hadn't cared. Nobody could find her there. The boys and girls would never dare to come near the anthill.

She sat in the bush as the evening darkened, waiting for the call from one of the kings that they had given up trying to find her. Around her, the thicket was alive. Frogs croaked, crickets chirped and birds squawked as they returned home. From the distance, she could hear the excited squeals of the other girls as the boys found their hiding places. She smiled, knowing she would win again.

Suddenly, a silence set in. It was as though the frogs and crickets had all gone to sleep suddenly. And then, she heard a scream. At first, she thought it was one of the girls who had been found by the boys. But this sounded different. It made her heart race faster and the hair on her neck stand. And then, another scream followed and then, another.

*Ma*, that is all she could think about.

She ran out of her hiding place, past the temple and the peepal tree, and abruptly stopped. The village was bathed in a golden glow. Everything was on fire. Flames were eating at the thatched roofs of the houses, the granary at the far end of the village and even the idol of Indra at the centre of the village.

That's when Ushas had seen him—a man on a horse who was holding her mother by her hair. His skin was the colour of night, dark and shining with a black paste. In his thin hand, he gripped a long, thin sword.

Her mother's eyes had met hers from across the distance.

'Run to the river,' her mother had screamed, just before

the man had slashed at her throat with the blade. Blood had gushed out of the open wound.

The girl had run as fast as she could into the woods. And that was the last time she had seen the hamlet she had grown up in—a village called Soumyapur.

'Were these men from the Urba tribe?' asked the physician, handing the girl a bowl of soup. Three guards sat on the floor, staring at her. A fat man, wearing a silk dhoti and string of pearls, was the only one sitting on a chair, with his feet crossed. He was fanning himself with a palmyra leaf fan. The matron was standing behind her, fanning her.

'Don't interrupt the child with your idiotic questions,' snapped Gajendra—scowling at the physician, who apologised immediately. 'Let me ask the questions.'

He paused for a moment, pondering on what to ask the child.

'So, child, I know you have already said this before … but I wasn't here when you did—what's the name of your village?'

'Soumyapur.'

*Thank God!* Gajendra smiled. *That's all that I wanted to hear.*

'And who were these men who attacked your village? Were they those hideous Urba men the soldiers rescued you from?' asked Gajendra.

The physician and the matron exchanged glances.

'N-No,' said Ushas.

'Are you sure?' asked Gajendra.

'Yes. These men … they were ghosts. They came from nowhere. They were … dark … dark like the night,' said the girl.

Gajendra scratched his chin with the tip of the fan. 'Were they black … like this man?' he said, pointing to the physician, whose brows knitted together at the reference.

'N-No,' said Ushas. 'They were thin … as though their bodies had only skin and bones … and their skin was shining and dark.'

'What were they wearing, child?' asked Gajendra.

*The first enlightened question*, thought the physician. *The Urbas chose to be sky clad. They shunned clothes.*

'Black … black clothes,' said Ushas.

Gajendra shook his head, trying to assimilate that information. He extended his hand; three fingers had heavy rings of gold on them. One of the guards handed him a palm leaf tied with a string. He untied the string and unfurled the leaf.

'Do you know this man?' he asked, showing the girl the palm leaf that had the image of a man drawn on it. It was the face of a brahman with a pockmarked face, protruding front teeth and six fingers on one hand.

The girl stared at the image for a while, before shaking her head.

'Is that a yes or a no, girl?'

'No,' said Ushas.

'Now, young one,' said Gajendra, moving closer to her. 'I am going to ask you something. Don't be afraid.'

*Don't do it*, thought the physician.

'Who is Ardhamukha?'

The girl turned pale. The room became deathly quiet. Suddenly, the smell of urine filled the room. And then, she began screaming.

By the time Gajendra stepped out of the dispensary, the crowd outside had become restive. An angry murmur spread when they saw him emerge. He wondered what they were *really* upset about. Was it the fact that they had been sweating under the boiling sun while he had taken his time in questioning the girl? Or were they just envious of his clothes of fine shimmering white silk and the thick chains of gold around his neck?

Either way, he did not care. Today was Budhwara, his lucky day.

*Why else would I have met this girl?* he thought, as the crowd parted to make way for him. A servant locked his palms together and Gajendra placed a foot on them, hoisting himself onto his horse. The fat horse snorted and broke into a lazy trot. The servant jogged alongside.

Gajendra had slept uneasily ever since he had stumbled onto that hideous massacre at Soumyapur, where the mutilated bodies of the brahmans had been displayed like scarecrows in a paddy field. Some nights, he dreamt of having long, boring conversations with brahmans from that godforsaken village, before he would notice that they had started slurring, because their mouths had no lips. Just ghastly mouths with teeth, tongues and gums oozing blood.

Gajendra would have been fine if the dreams had just been that. But business was beginning to suffer. Blood and gold do not mix, his father always said. And how right the old man was! Since that day, his servants had begun to make excuses to leave early as the sun went down. They wanted to return to their homes on the outskirts of Kampilya before dark.

The caravans to Kampilya had started thinning too, as traders began to imagine highway robbers lurking behind every tree in the forests surrounding the city. Of course, there had always been bands of highway robbers prowling the road that connected Kausambi and Kampilya, but they had been few and far between. Grain and saffron had started to pile up in the warehouses of Kampilya and even the soldiers were starting to demand more silver to guard the caravans.

And, then he had heard about the Miracle of Kampilya, as they called the girl these days. At first, she had just been another child that the soldiers had saved from the jungle tribes, but then she had told the physician where she was from.

*The only survivor from Soumyapur*, thought Gajendra. *And she fell right into my lap.*

Gajendra's horse stopped in front of the tallest structure in Kampilya. His servant, breathless and sweaty, crouched on all fours next to the horse. Gajendra stepped on his back and heard the servant's bones creak under his foot, as he dismounted from his horse.

He handed the reins of the horse to the servant and looked up at the tower. It was a tall stone tower with a winding flight of stairs inside its belly. Gajendra did not look forward to the climb. He took a deep breath and walked towards the tower.

The cooing of the pigeons and the smell of their shit welcomed him as he stepped on the terrace on top of the tower. The birdman at the aviary saw him and walked towards him with a big smile.

'Sire, it's been a long time since you graced us with your presence,' said the birdman. His tunic was covered with the white stains of bird shit. His grey, wispy hair was unkempt and resembled a nest. In all, the birdkeeper looked like one of his pigeons.

'Good to see you …' began Gajendra, and realised that he had forgotten the old bird keeper's name. 'I need you to send a message to Mithila.'

'Of course, sire,' said the birdman, opening a huge register. 'Whom to?'

'My cousin, Vishnupada,' said Gajendra. 'Has anybody else come in today with messages to be sent to Mithila?'

'Yes, sire. Just earlier today, the chief of guards of the city came down to send a message,' said the birdman.

'Who did he send it to?' asked Gajendra.

'Sire, as you know, I am not supposed to tell you that … it's against the royal aviary rules …' the birdman trailed off.

Gajendra knew this game. He loosened the strings of the purse tied to his waist and took out a silver coin.

'Perhaps this might help with the rules,' said Gajendra, holding out the coin. The old man took a step closer and relieved Gajendra of the silver.

'It was to Veerabhadra, the Commander-in-Chief of Mithila.'

'Would you know what the message was about?' asked Gajendra.

'Sire, like you know, royal messages come sealed with royal wax,' the birdman said, pursing his lips. 'However, I do recall hearing the chief of guards talking about finding that unfortunate little girl—the Miracle of Kampilya. I believe she is from that agrahara where everyone was killed … the Miracle of Soumyapur, he kept calling her.'

Gajendra thought about what he had just heard. The chief of guards was sending a message to Mithila about the girl. It is the message he, too, wanted to deliver to Mithila. To his cousin, Vishnupada, who in turn would pass it on to the king. They would split the reward and the royal favours. Vishnupada might even show his gratitude by sending him two or three cartloads of copper.

*All of this will happen only if I deliver the message first.*

'This message that the chief of guards wanted sent … has the pigeon flown already?' asked Gajendra.

'Not yet, sire,' said the birdman. 'I was planning to send the bird after having my lunch.'

*Thank God!*

'Tell me,' said Gajendra. 'How often do pigeons get lost on the way?'

The birdman studied Gajendra carefully before he answered.

'Not too often, sire. They don't get lost. But on rare occasions, other birds of prey, like eagles and kites do attack them and sometimes feed on them,' said the birdman.

Gajendra smiled and loosened his purse strings again.

## 16. Avanti

Vishnupada watched as his only son chased a fluffy duck around the courtyard. The duck squawked loudly and wagged its white tail feathers as it waddled away. The boy, chubby-cheeked and red-faced, was gasping for breath as he pursued the duck with as much gusto as he could manage. After a few sedate rounds of the yard, the boy conceded defeat and paused to take a break.

*When I was his age, I could swim across the Netra*, thought Vishnupada. *And this boy can't even catch a duck.*

'Go catch the stupid bird, you idiot, otherwise I will cane your fat behind till it turns blue,' yelled Vishnupada. The boy resumed the chase half-heartedly; the duck was winning easily.

Vishnupada's wife came in carrying a glass of buttermilk. The boy stopped again and eyed the buttermilk. Vishnupada picked up a pebble from the ground and hurled it at the boy. It missed him by a whisker but it caught the boy's attention.

'Did I ask you to stop?' asked Vishnupada.

The boy started wailing. His mother, face red with rage, flung the glass of buttermilk to the ground, shattering it to pieces.

'Fine man you are ... picking on your own son,' she snapped. 'If you have problems in your business, don't take it out on my boy.'

For a moment, Vishnupada thought of walking up to his lawfully wedded wife and planting a hard slap on her cheeks. But an old memory prevented him from doing so. The last time he had slapped her, she had refused to share his bed for a whole month.

For the first few nights, he had gone to visit a new courtesan every night and had, then, recklessly, even boasted about it to his wife. She had continued to ignore him and treated him to cold, long silences. Then, one night, he had come home drunk and had threatened to sleep in the courtyard of the house, hoping to embarrass her into letting him back into their bed. He had woken up the next morning, cold and shivering, asleep on a bench outside his palatial house.

By the end of the first month, he had come to realise that his visits to the natyashalas and drinking houses were not exactly cheap. And silver saved was silver earned. So, he had begged for his wife's forgiveness and peace had been restored in his house again, after a few weeks of silence.

*She is right, he thought. I can't take my anger out on the boy. My problems are my own.*

And problems he had aplenty. The caravan was leaving in three days and his warehouses were brimming with grains and saffron from the mountains. Two days ago, he had hired forty workmen: cooks, waterboys, loaders, cleaners. Their names had been rostered, their identities double-checked and they were even paid an advance in silver.

Earlier this morning, the loading of the oxcarts was supposed to have begun. Vishnupada had dressed in his finest silks and ridden to the market with Bhima who carried the accounts books. When the roster had been opened and names of the workers called out, they were eleven men short. Vishnupada had sent Bhima to enquire about the men who had not turned up.

Bhima had returned, late in the afternoon, bearing bad news. The men, all of them out-of-towners, had taken grievously ill. They had spent most of the silver advanced to them in raiding the gambling dens and devouring stale boar meat. In the morning, they had woken up with upset stomachs and raging fevers. It was unlikely that they would recover in two days, the vaidya attending them had informed Bhima.

Vishnupada had cursed the drunkards and their families. He had even cursed their gods and wished ill on their future generations. Bhima had been dispatched to hire more workers but the chances of getting new workers this late were slim. Only two long caravans had left that morning, taking most of the able-bodied workers with them.

*I must find more workers somehow by tomorrow evening*, Vishnupada thought glumly. His son, in the meantime, had caught the duck and was trying to feed it.

A few minutes later, Bhima entered the courtyard and bowed, before handing over a small, rolled-up message to Vishnupada.

'Have you been able to hire more men?' asked Vishnupada.

Bhima shook his head. 'I have informed every innkeeper, sire. I even took the liberty of telling them that we will pay double the usual price for able-bodied workers. I hope that meets with your approval,' he said.

'Yes,' said Vishnupada, though he really did not relish the thought of paying more silver. 'Where is this from?'

'It's from Kampilya, sire.'

Vishnupada opened the message and his heart raced like a mare in heat. He ran over to his son and kissed the startled boy on his cheeks. Taking long steps, he strode into his house.

'Get me my finest turban,' he yelled out to his wife, as he smeared his arms with the sandalwood paste. 'I am going to meet the king.'

Like all duels, this one, too, began with posturing and shadow play. The fighters circled, sword in one hand and wooden shield in the other, eyes locked and legs spread wide apart. They twirled their swords, trying to get the blood going in their wrists and arms, sizing up each other, waiting for the other to make the first move.

At first sight, they seemed like unlikely opponents. One was a giant—broad-shouldered, thick-necked with muscular arms that resembled thick pillars. His heavy broadsword swooshed as he swung it slowly in the air. The other fighter was built like a boy. Skinny arms and legs stuck out from the fighter's breastplate. But the smaller fighter moved like a spider, light-footed and fast. His long sword blade was silent but swift, like a whip cutting through air.

The warriors wore iron helmets that covered most of their face and mouth. All the audience could see were their unblinking, hawk-like eyes.

'Get on with it,' yelled Trivikrama. He wasn't here to watch fighters move around each other like a pair of mating crabs. He wasn't even sure why Aacharya Gurukripa had wanted him and his brother to watch a duel. Perhaps this was the old man's way of distracting them from the worries of statecraft, from the unfruitful search for the mysterious brahman. Or perhaps it was his way of keeping him from having soma early in the evening.

'Brother, who do you think will win? The giant or the midget?' asked Trivikrama.

Ajitha shrugged and said, 'Too early to say. Let the swords clash first.'

'And Aacharya-ji, who would you wager on?' asked Trivikrama turning to Gurukripa.

'I don't believe in wagers, my king. May the better swordsman win,' said the smiling aacharya as he stroked his greying beard.

In the ring, the fighters circled, crouching closer to the ground. It was a game of patience, each waiting for the other to make the first move. Finally, the giant broke the stalemate. He dug his heels into the red mud and swung his broadsword in a long arc using all the strength of his mighty shoulders. The heavy sword whistled through the air and would have cleaved the boy's skull into two, had he not been quick on his feet.

In a flash, the smaller swordsman raised his shield above his head. The wooden shield rattled loudly when the heavy broadsword landed on it. Under the shield, the boy's body shook from the impact.

The giant grunted and stepped back, yanking off his sword from the boy's shield. A chunk of the shield peeled off along with the broadsword. The fighters started again.

'The swords have clashed. Now tell who is your gold on?' asked Trivikrama, turning to his brother.

'The giant,' said Ajitha.

'Bah,' spat Trivikrama. 'I thought you would choose the boy ... given your love for underdogs. But you chose well, little brother. The giant is going to shatter the boy's shield with one big swing -'

The giant swung his sword again, this time like an executioner with both his hands on the hilt. The shield shattered into pieces, as the full might of the giant's body drove the broadsword in. The smaller fighter threw what remained of the broken shield. The giant spat on the ground.

'This is no contest. Perhaps we should stop it,' said Ajitha.

'No ... it's just getting to be a bit of fun,' said Trivikrama, his eyes peeled on the circling swordsmen.

The boy's attack, when it came, was as furious as it was sudden. The light sword shone in the dying rays of the evening sun as it swished past the giant's shield and slashed at his neck. For a big man, the giant was surprisingly lithe. He jumped back but his opponent's sword was faster, like a cobra shooting through the grass. A gash opened on the giant's neck. A stream of dark blood gushed down from the giant's neck and onto his armour. The giant wiped the wound with the back of his hand.

'Well done, boy,' yelled Trivikrama, slapping his thighs in excitement.

The king's words seemed to infuriate the giant, something Trivikrama had hoped would happen. The giant charged at the boy with his sword and shield, an unstoppable wall of muscle, armour and steel. The boy thrust his sword out, even as he pivoted away from the giant's path. The boy's longsword met the giant's shield with a hollow thump.

The giant yanked at his shield and stepped back, smiling. The boy's sword was now stuck in the giant's shield.

The smaller fighter was now barehanded, without sword or shield.

'Yield and I will let you live,' said the giant, in a voice that rose from his bowels.

The smaller fighter ignored the warning and continued to circle the giant, arms spread out like a wrestler.

'Should we stop the fight?' asked Trivikrama, looking at Gurukripa. 'We know how this will end.'

But Gurukripa seemed to be enamoured by the duel.

'For you, I don't need these,' the giant laughed, and threw off his helmet and shield.

*Bastard. He is putting on a show for us. He still carries his sword against an unarmed opponent*, thought Ajitha, hoping that his brother would call the fight off.

The giant swung the sword towards the boy and missed. The boy was even faster now, lighter without the weight of his shield or sword. He rolled away from the giant. The giant swung again and missed. This time, as the giant's sword hit the ground, the boy kicked at the giant's wrist. Ajitha heard the sickening snap of bone breaking.

'Bravo!' yelled Trivikrama.

The giant dropped his heavy sword and held his wrist with his other hand. The boy was now on the giant's back, his thin sinewy arm locked around the giant's neck, choking him.

The giant clawed the boy's eyes with his other hand, but the waves of pain from his broken wrist were making him dizzy and unsteady on his feet. The giant stumbled around the yard, like a blind bear trying to get a monkey off its back.

The boy continued to strangle the giant's neck. The giant's knees buckled.

'I yield … I yield,' croaked the giant, before slumping to the ground, a giant mass of broken muscle and ego. Trivikrama was on his feet clapping and screaming. The boy finally got off the giant's back.

'Present yourself to the king,' Gurukripa shouted out to the boy.

He walked with small, brisk steps towards the king, knelt on one foot and bowed. The sword was offered to the king with both hands.

'Show your face, warrior,' said Trivikrama.

The fighter placed the sword on the ground and removed the steel helmet. Long, curly locks of dark hair tumbled down the thin shoulders and fell on the armour.

The victor was a girl.

For a few moments, Trivikrama stared at the woman's face. He knew her. The full lips, the delicate chin, the dark locks—and that soft, long neck. They seemed familiar. *Oh, so familiar*, thought Trivikrama.

He had kissed those lips, caressed that neck, buried his face in those lovely curls which were now drenched with sweat. They had been fragrant and soft to the touch. He had kissed those shapely shoulders. But where and when?

She returned his gaze with an almost empty gaze of her own. She held her head erect like the mast of a proud ship. But her mouth, ruby-red lips, told another story. They quivered, as though they were struggling to suppress a smile, a secret and a story too embarrassing to be told in public.

Aacharya Gurukripa cleared his throat. Kings don't gawk at commoners however good-looking they might be, the cough seemed to say. Trivikrama looked at his guru, who was not looking at him but at his younger brother. Ajitha was on his feet, staring at the girl with eyes that seemed to have forgotten the art of blinking. Even in the gloomy light of dusk, Trivikrama could make out that Ajitha's face was flushed, the colour of the morning sun. He thought he could hear his brother's breathing—it sounded like a galloping horse.

*The boy is in love ... for the first time*, thought Trivikrama, smiling.

*Breathe, brother, breathe*, he wanted to tell the boy but held his tongue. He stared at his brother's face and for a moment, he felt envious. Trivikrama had not felt like this—this feeling of all-pervasive, sense-numbing attachment—for years. The unending conquest of courtesans, the dizzying highs of soma, even the thrill of combat was nothing compared to this moment of complete surrender that his brother was experiencing.

*It won't last*, he wanted to tell his brother. Love, like lust, was a drug whose magic wore off with time. But, at its peak, it was supreme sorcery, an ecstasy that seemed like it would last till the end of time. But time was the enemy of love. Time would gnaw at and erode this joyous delusion.

Aacharya Gurukripa coughed again.

*Time, and the discreet coughs of older men*, thought Trivikrama, a little bitter.

The moment was over. Ajitha eased back into his chair, firmly back in the present. He tore his gaze away from the girl and looked right into his brother's eyes.

Trivikrama smiled at him.

*Wouldn't it break his heart if he found out that I have bedded her? But, when did that happen?*

He couldn't ask her right now.

'You make us proud,' said Trivikrama. 'Who are you?'

'Let me answer that, my king,' said Gurukripa, waving a hand at the girl. 'Her name is Avanti. For the past year, she has been your shadow. She has always been a step behind you, watching you and if I might say, guarding you in person. She follows you when you go out on royal processions, on tiger hunts and even when you … feel the need for a late-night excursion alone.'

It came to him, right then. She was the courtesan to

whom he had made love on the day that dhumaketu had burnt across the skies of Mithila. The woman with the scorpion tattoo around her navel. The one who had teased him about his appetite for women.

'Well done, Gurudeva. I like … my shadow,' Trivikrama said. Perhaps with too much enthusiasm in his voice. Gurukripa gave him a quizzical look.

*Does he know I made love to my shadow? Was she supposed to?*

'My king, there is a reason I am presenting her to you today. Avanti is a master of disguise. She can be a courtesan one day, a sorceress the next, and a huntress the day after that. She speaks six tongues, including that of the hill tribes from the south. She is a master of poisons and is trained in the knowledge of healing herbs and potions. And, like you saw, she is an excellent swordsman. How old do you think she is?' asked Gurukripa.

'Remove your armour, warrior,' said Trivikrama. Avanti undid the leather straps on her shoulders, and the breastplate came off.

*The scorpion tattoo is there alright*, thought Trivikrama.

'Sixteen summers old,' said Trivikrama, stealing a glance at Ajitha, who was drinking in every detail of Avanti with his eyes.

'Seventeen,' said Avanti, her eyes dancing with amusement. She knew exactly where the king's roving eyes were focused.

'You forget your manners, child,' Gurukripa chided.

'Seventeen, *my king*,' she said, smiling at him.

*Is she teasing me? Had Aacharya Gurukripa noticed?* thought Trivikrama.

'Let her age not fool you … Avanti has mastered skills that men, warriors and brahmans of noble birth struggle for years to master. She has travelled across every one of the sixteen kingdoms and nobody, except me, is aware of her existence. She will be our spy, the perfect one to track down that brahman from Kampilya. Who would ever think of a woman as a spy?' asked Gurukripa.

Trivikrama pondered on the idea for a moment. The girl was smart. She had got past his defences and had even managed to bed him. If Jayaveera was not aware of her existence, she might just be the perfect spy. But, was she worthy of his trust?

'I vouch for her … on my honour,' said Gurukripa, as though reading the king's thoughts.

Trivikrama turned and directed a long, probing look at Gurukripa, who steadily met his gaze.

'It's settled then,' said Trivikrama. 'Avanti, you will speak only to us. Just the three of us and nobody else. And anything you find out … anything … you will inform us in person. Nobody else should know.'

'My king, I am honoured to serve *you*,' she said, emphasizing on the last word and bowed to take her leave.

'Avanti, I have … a question,' said Ajitha. 'Does your father … or husband approve of you being a spy?'

*Well played, brother*, thought Trivikrama. *What a lovely, roundabout way of asking her if she was already taken! The boy's aim is sharp.*

'I am a free woman, my prince,' she said, looking at Ajitha, who looked like he had just drunk a cask of soma. But, of course, the prince did not drink.

'The sword, bow and arrow are my family,' Avanti said.

'So, you are an archer too?' said Ajitha. 'Perhaps, we should have a contest one of these days.'

*Young love can be devious in its means*, thought Trivikrama.

'It would be an unfair contest, my prince. My duty will

require me to lose. That's something I don't relish,' said Avanti.

Aacharya Gurukripa waved her away before she said something more intemperate. Avanti bowed and left, while the prince watched her leave. For a while the trio sat in silence, each lost in their own contemplations.

'Aacharya-ji, I know you have vouched for this girl and your word is as good as any man's in the sixteen kingdoms,' began Trivikrama, weighing each word carefully. 'But history has taught us that the greatest of men have been fooled by other men and especially by women. What makes you trust her so?'

'That's because she is my daughter,' said Gurukripa, flatly.

Ajitha and Trivikrama resisted the urge to look at each other in surprise. For they knew this was not possible—Gurukripa had sired only one son, a cripple who had died young. And his wife, unable to bear the sorrow of her son's death, had followed him soon after. Since then, he had been a recluse, who lived alone in the royal quarters, shunning everything but his duty to the king and kingdom of Mithila.

*Unless, this girl is his bastard child*, thought Trivikrama. *A mistake he made a long time ago. Even saints can err.*

The thought made Trivikrama smile. He saw Gurukripa's burning eyes on him and his smile evaporated as fast as it had come.

'Well, Aacharya-ji, I need no further assurances,' said Trivikrama, bowing his head towards his teacher. 'I am thirsty. What does a man have to do here to get some soma?' he added, hoping that this would help the awkward moment pass quickly.

Vishnupada waited outside the north gate of the palace, watching people come and go. A procession of guards, servants, cooks, accountants, nobles were entering and exiting through the palace gates. Some rode out on horses, others on chariots and yet others walked, chattering in groups. The guards were marking their names and the hour of their entry and departure in a thick book with pages of palm leaves.

As the red sun slowly dipped behind the ramparts of the palace walls, the guards at the gate changed. Twelve new soldiers arrived. To Vishnupada, they all seemed alike: tall, stout as buffaloes, moustachioed ogres armed with long spears and swords, whose darting eyes viewed everyone with suspicion and malice. The guards stood silently, rarely talking to each other, staring at nothing.

*They are like statues with moving eyes*, Vishnupada thought.

The guards only came to life when someone like Vishnupada tried to enter the palace compound. Earlier in the evening, he had tried to get past the guards with his usual mix of bluster and charm that worked so well in the marketplace. But one ogre of a guard had shooed him away ingloriously, that too in the presence of his servant Bhima.

'I have information about the brahman of Kampilya … and I can share it *only* with the king,' Vishnupada had declared finally, with a haughtiness he reserved only for the porters and loaders in the market. That should do the trick, he had thought. The guards had guffawed until Vishnupada turned red in the face.

'Half of Mithila has information about the brahman, *your highness*,' one of the guards had said mockingly, in between spurts of laughter. 'Some have spotted him in a brothel. Some have dragged men with an extra finger or two here, after soundly thrashing them. Why, the other day, we had a man who claimed he was the brahman! Needless to say, he came here stinking like a bee that had fallen into a vat of soma. We sent him away … but not before making sure his backside looked red like a langur's,' he said. The guffawing doubled and this time, even a few cooks, leaving the palace, joined in.

Vishnupada waited for the cooks to leave and for the laughter to die down, before he loosened the string of the purse tied around his hip, with a great show of ceremony. The guards watched him carefully but did not say a word.

'How about if each of you goes home with two pieces of silver tonight?' Vishnupada asked in a hushed voice.

One guard—clearly, their superintendent—had stepped closer to Vishnupada. He was as tall as a palm tree and half as wide as a horse. He leaned forward and whispered something into Vishnupada's car.

'How about you go back home with both your hands missing?' he had asked, smiling and baring a line of betel juice-stained teeth. 'Or would you like to go home without the fruits hanging from your loins?' he had continued, much to the merriment of the other guards.

*Brutes*, thought Vishnupada and walked away from them with as much dignity as he could muster.

Once it grew dark, there was a change in guard again. It was then that Vishnupada saw a familiar face. A horse trotted out of the palace. On it was a man with a flowing beard, whose body bore the marks of a brahman. He was dressed in white garments, wore a sacred thread of cotton and did not wear any jewels. Yet, he looked like a man who could bear arms. The guards bowed low to the brahman.

*I have seen him before. But where?* thought Vishnupada.

The brahman on the horse had stopped to have a conversation with one of the guards.

Vishnupada waved at a water carrier who had also come out of the palace. 'A silver coin for you if you tell me who that brahman on the horse is,' said Vishnupada.

'That's the rajguru, sire … Aacharya Gurukripa,' said the water carrier, sticking a bony palm under Vishnupada's nose.

Vishnupada tossed him a coin and started walking briskly towards the aacharya. 'Sire … sire!' he screamed, with all the might of his throat. The aacharya and the palace guards turned to look at him. A couple of the guards even drew their swords.

'I know something about what happened at Soumyapur,' said Vishnupada. 'And I will tell it only to the king.'

By the time the merchant of spices and furs had finished his tale, all the lamps in the ivory room had been lit. The white silk curtains billowed and rustled in the evening breeze wafting in from the open windows. A pair of elephant tusks mounted high on one of the walls glowed in the yellow light of the oil-fed lamps.

'Mithila thanks you for your service,' said Trivikrama to Vishnupada. Seated next to him, Ajitha wore the same glazed look he had worn all evening.

'It was my duty as a humble citizen of Mithila, my king,' replied Vishnupada, folding his hands in a namaste and bowing low to the king. 'All I ever wanted in my whole life was to gaze at your magnificent self, nothing else … not even a … reward of gold or silver—'

*Spoken like a true merchant*, thought Gurukripa, trying to suppress a smile, which nevertheless sneaked through.

'You will be amply rewarded for your devotion to the king,' said Gurukripa, as he got up from his seat and escorted the merchant out of the room. As he left the room, the merchant kept bobbing and bowing to the king, like a crane dipping its beak into a pond to catch a fish.

'Sire, I have one more desire,' said Vishnupada to Gurukripa, once they were outside the room. 'I am told that the thousand-pillared hall is a feast for the eyes in the evening, when all the lamps are lit. If it's not a problem, can I take a look at the hall? Even if it is from a distance?'

'Yes, why not?' said Gurukripa, before dispatching the merchant off with two burly guards who were to escort him on a tour of the hall of thousand pillars. He also gave the merchant a note so that the latter could claim his reward of a hundred coins of gold from the treasury.

When Gurukripa made his way back into the ivory room, he saw Trivikrama standing at the window staring at the dark night outside, a glass of soma in his hand. Ajitha was still rooted to his seat and was gazing mutely at the ceiling with an expression Gurukripa could not quite fathom.

'Since my younger brother seems to have taken a monastic vow of silence tonight …' began Trivikrama with a teasing smile, even as Ajitha scowled. 'Aacharya, what do we do about this girl … the Miracle of Kampilya? I think this presents an opportunity. I am thinking we get her here, to Mithila, with a show of pomp and splendour. Perhaps, I could even adopt her under my care to be raised as a part of the royal household. Or, Aacharya-ji, if it meets your approval … you could adopt her as your own ward.'

*I have taught him well*, thought Gurukripa, with a measure of pride. He could imagine the scene—a procession of horse-drawn carts, crowds lining the streets, and the poor, terrified girl in an open chariot, escorted by the royal guards. The day before her arrival in Mithila, drummers would go around the city, announcing the arrival of the Miracle of Kampilya, the brahman girl who had survived the monsters who had butchered her village.

Perhaps they could even arrange for her story to be told at street corners for a few days. Plays could be conducted in the marketplace, balladeers could sing—all at the royal treasury's expense. The crowds would flock to see her when she arrived. And, when the girl reached the palace compound, the king would personally welcome her into his household.

*Women would weep and even the brahmans will be pleased*, thought Gurukripa.

'It sounds like a good idea, my king,' said the aacharya. 'I would be glad to take her into my care.'

'It is done then,' said Trivikrama, clapping his hands. 'I think I can now drink my soma in peace tonight.'

'One thing worries me,' Ajitha piped up.

'Ah! My mute brother speaks ... go ahead, defile my peace!' mocked Trivikrama.

'The merchant said she did not recognise the painting of that brahman, the one with the six fingers, when it was shown to her. Why would that be?' asked Ajitha.

'Have you even seen my statue in the Agni temple, brother?' said Trivikrama. 'Our own dear mother would disown me if she saw that. I am sure the good people of Mithila think they are ruled by the ugliest king in the sixteen kingdoms. That monstrosity was carved by Mithila's best sculptor. I had half a mind to carve his nose out after I saw that hideous piece of sculpture ... The wretched brahman's face was probably drawn by some painter who possibly did it for half a bag of rice ... and he made a few hundred copies, each worse than the other. I am sure the poor girl wouldn't recognise the brahman even if he was her own departed father,' said Trivikrama.

'I am not convinced, brother,' said Ajitha, frowning.

'My prince, the king could be right,' said Aacharya Gurukripa. 'We also need to consider that the poor girl has been through an unspeakable ordeal. Her memory of things might be mixed up. Perhaps she might be in a better condition to remember things when she is here … in better hands.'

'Yes, Aacharya-ji, you could be right,' conceded Ajitha. 'One more thing bothers me—who is this Ardhamukha?'

Silence draped the room like a black shroud. A servant entered with a glass of soma. Trivikrama took a big gulp and waved the servant away.

'Now, that's a good question,' said Trivikrama. 'And why is she so afraid of him? Is he just some figment of her feverish imagination? Or is he a jungle dacoit? If he is the latter, we need to hunt him down before he creates any more trouble. What kind of a name is that anyway?'

'Perhaps, that's not his name … the girl may be describing him,' said the aacharya. 'Ardhamukha means half face.'

'Imagine that … a man with only half a face. Wonder what happened to the rest of it …' mused Ajitha.

A strong gust of wind blew into the room, making the torch flames leap and dance. The shadows in the room bobbed and weaved.

'Perhaps his mother found him terribly ugly … and named him half face,' said the king dourly.

Gurukripa gave the problem some thought, but could come up with no easy answers. The day had been long and tiring. For once, he wanted to take a sip of the soma. But soma and clarity were not friends and right now, he needed clarity.

'My king, as far as I can see, we have two birds to kill. One, we need to find this man, this cruel slayer of women and children, called Ardhamukha. Two, we need to find this brahman, who has just vanished off the face of the earth. Strangely, both the brahman and the girl hail from Soumyapur … and yet the girl doesn't recognise him,' said Gurukripa. 'Soumyapur is up in the mountains and just a night's horse ride from Kampilya. Either way, we are better off if we started by looking for the brahman or even Ardhamukha in Kampilya. I suggest we send Avanti to Kampilya at the earliest. She can begin from there. I will ask her to leave tomorrow at the crack of dawn, if this meets with your approval.'

Trivikrama nodded his head in approval and drained his glass of soma in one big gulp.

'What if I went with Avanti to Kampilya?' said Ajitha.

'Enlighten me, brother,' said Trivikrama, toying with his glass. 'Why would you want to do that? Princes do not escort spies … however beautiful they might be,' said Trivikrama, breaking into a belly laugh.

*The boy is smitten*, thought Gurukripa. *That explains his dazed look all evening.*

'*Brother!*' said Ajitha through gritted teeth, his face reddening. 'What if the Prince of Mithila himself went to receive the Miracle of Kampilya? Just imagine the message it would send to our people, especially to the brahmans? That we care for them, would it not? Also, you first toured the kingdoms when you were fifteen. I am sixteen and I have rarely stepped beyond the walls of Mithila, except maybe on some silly boar hunts and temple visits beyond the river. Don't you think I need to see the lands and rivers that we rule over, meet the people we rule?' said Ajitha.

'The lands and rivers *I rule, brother* … not *we*,' said Trivikrama, a little testily. 'What do you think, Aacharya-ji? Should Ajitha go to Kampilya?'

*Please say yes*, thought Ajitha.

'My prince, royal travel across kingdoms takes time to prepare. Soldiers need to be mustered and posted across highways. Chieftains and governors of kingdoms you will travel through need to be informed in advance. Food, travel routes and places of stay need to be planned and arranged for. All of this takes time … when your brother travelled across four kingdoms, it took us eleven weeks to plan for a two week-long trip. And as of now, we need to get that girl to Mithila at the soonest,' said Gurukripa.

Trivikrama shrugged. 'I would love to send you, brother. But sending you along with Avanti means that we might have to wait at least two to three months, at least—'

'Not if … nobody knows I am a prince,' Ajitha cut him off.

'You want to travel incognito?' Trivikrama asked.

'Yes, as a commoner. Nobody needs to know who I am.'

'Ajitha, my dear brother,' said Trivikrama. 'Commoners shit behind a bush and wash their behinds in the nearest stream, sometimes even using a leaf. Sometimes, those leaves cause rashes. Common folk sit on a horse all day long, till their bottoms turn to stone and they start walking like men who have been kicked between the legs by a horse. The forests are full of thieves and dacoits. Like this half-face pest, Ardhamukha. For them, you are just another boy who can be slaughtered for sport. Then, there are the beasts who don't care about royals or commoners … they just need something to sink their teeth into. Like you said, you have never left the borders of Mithila. You don't know what the world outside is like. And, you are a prince … why put yourself through these perils?'

'I cannot be a boy forever, brother. I am sixteen summers old. I am an archer and a swordsman. It is time I saw the world. Don't you think?' said Ajitha, his hairless jaw tightening in the way it did only when he was angry or upset. 'Give me your approval, brother … please!'

Trivikrama sighed. *This is a lost cause.*

'What do I tell mother?' asked Trivikrama.

'You are the king. Think of something,' said Ajitha, smiling.

*The stupid things the young do for love*, thought Trivikrama.

'Perhaps, there is another way … what if we send the prince and Avanti along with a merchant's caravan leaving from Mithila to Kampilya in the next few days,' said Gurukripa. 'He need not reveal his identity until he gets to Kampilya. There he can produce the royal seal and come back with a procession escorting the poor girl. Caravans are well stocked with food and comforts, and are reasonably well-guarded. That way, my prince, you can be a commoner and yet, be safe.'

Ajitha opened his mouth to protest.

'It's done then, brother!' Trivikrama cut him off. 'You will go with Avanti to Kampilya. You *will* join a caravan and your identity will be kept a secret … except, maybe from the merchant who owns the caravan … just so that he doesn't treat you like a common servant. Aacharya-ji, can you find out when the next caravan to Kampilya leaves from Mithila? Now, if you'll excuse me, it is dark outside and I have a reputation to maintain. If I don't gulp down a few cups of soma, the servants will start gossiping about how the king of Mithila has renounced the world. And we cannot afford that, can we?'

# 17. The Moon Brothers

The crescent moon hung low above the mountains. Fireflies danced in the dark, lighting up the forest floor. A stream gurgled in the distance. Snakes crawled in the underbrush while flying foxes hung upside down from trees, their glowing eyes peeled firmly to the ground, scanning for prey.

The council of moon brothers had assembled in a cave which had once been home to a family of tigers. Now, the men sat on the rocky floor of the cave, that would have been bitterly cold except for the carpet made of tiger hide adorning the floor. Each moon brother wore a necklace around his neck, a simple string with a pendant hanging from it: the hooked talon of a tiger.

Though they called themselves brothers, they were not born of the same womb. And yet, they looked remarkably alike. They had shaved heads, and their bodies and faces were also hairless. Even their brows were bald, shaved clean. And they were all dressed in the colour of the night: a single black garment wrapped around their waist.

They sat around a fire in perfect silence, massaging their numb fingers, occasionally staring at the heart of the burning flame. Deer meat roasted over the fire on a spit.

One of the brothers heard a langur screech in the distance. And, then he heard another. 'An intruder, moon brothers,' he said quickly and picked up his sword that had been resting on the ground. He ducked out of the cave and scanned the dark jungle. Twigs snapped in the darkness. Leaves rustled. A little while later, he saw another moon brother coming up the slope on a horse.

They exchanged smiles as the newcomer stepped into the cave.

'It's only our moon brother, Jwa,' said the other man, escorting his visitor inside.

The moon brother called Jwa smiled at the council. They invited him to squat around the fire. Another moon brother carved a piece of meat and offered it to Jwa, who accepted it eagerly and chewed on the steaming flesh with big, hungry bites.

The other moon brothers smiled at his hunger. While Jwa had his fill, the others waited for him to begin his tale.

'Moon brothers,' he finally said. 'The pillar of Devprayag is on fire.'

A moon brother sitting in the shadows, far away from the fire, spoke up. 'Really, brother?' he asked, his voice silky and soft, like a snake's hiss.

'I saw it with these very eyes, brother,' said Jwa.

The man in the darkness, considered this in silence. The others stared at him, waiting for his pronouncement. He was neither their chieftain nor their king. Yet, he had always led them.

'The moon has waxed and waned. Now, it will turn red,' said the moon brother and walked closer to the fire. 'Our time has come. Find us the man who set the pillar on fire.'

Jwa looked up at the moon brother they called Eka and winced. He had seen Eka's face all his life and yet, in the darkness of the cave, it was still a sight that turned his stomach. A mass of molten tissue, flesh and bone on one side; and a face of perfection on the other.

*Half man, half freak.*

# 18. Ajitha's Adventure

'When lady luck deserts you, your own cock turns into a cobra and bites you in the backside. And when that happens, very few line up to suck the venom out.' Vishnupada remembered his late father saying this in his high-pitched voice, every time he got into trouble. 'However, when things are good ...' his father had continued, '... and lady fortune flashes her pearlies at you, the same cock can piss out a stream of gold, and people will pay to see that miracle.'

Yesterday morning, Vishnupada's cock had threatened to grow fangs and hiss at him. And then the message had come from his cousin in Kampilya. Today, he was ready to fire that shower of gold. He had woken up early in the morning, bathed, smeared his body with sandal paste and perfumes, and worn his favourite silk dhoti, the one with the red border that he had purchased in Kasi.

He had considered making love to his wife in a hurry, who looked especially wholesome, her ample breasts jiggling as she ground the sandalwood paste. But he had abandoned the idea when he realised that if he did that, he would have to bathe again before heading over to the palace complex to collect his reward.

As Vishnupada sat ruminating over all this, Bhima came in with the good news. News that made Vishnupada look towards the skies and thank the gods. Bhima had found replacements for the caravan. What's more, they were cheaper than the men who had fallen ill.

'All they want is two bags of rice and pulses and two coins of silver per person,' said Bhima, displaying his perfectly formed buck teeth which were forever stained with betel juice.

'What? Are you sure? Did you find the only remaining idiots in Mithila?' asked Vishnupada, his eyes as wide as a startled owl.

'Master, they are from Kampilya. They arrived this morning in another caravan and want to get back home at the earliest,' said Bhima. 'We just got lucky.'

*Today, I can fart in the wind and the good folks of Mithila will smell jasmine incense,* Vishnupada thought, and looked up at the sky to thank Lord Vishnu, the patron god of his family.

Up above, he saw a pair of kites flying in lazy circles. He strained his eyes and stared at the birds. Their feathers were brown, except for their heads and breasts, which were as white as the clouds around them. *A good omen.* The mount of Vishnu was flying right above him. *Nothing can go wrong today*, thought Vishnupada, smiling.

'Where are they now?' asked Vishnupada.

'Outside, sire. I knew you would want to meet them,' said Bhima.

'Lead me to them,' said Vishnupada.

'Sire, one thing though … they look a little weird … strange-looking,' said Bhima, following Vishnupada who bounded across the courtyard to meet them.

'They could have heads of horses and tails sticking out of them for all I care. As long as they can work—' said Vishnupada.

Twelve men waited outside, arms crossed across their chests, eyes down, just the way servants were expected to be. They were strange-looking indeed. They were the thinnest men that Vishnupada had ever laid eyes on. Their bodies were strange accumulations of skin and bone. Bones stuck out from their bodies: from their faces, shoulders, hips and chests. It's as though flesh had shunned their bodies or someone had carved the muscle out of their bodies with a knife. Yet, their skin looked healthy: shining, the colour of polished copper.

And then it struck Vishnupada. All of them were balder than newborn babies. Their heads and faces were shaved clean, their chests had no hair, even their skinny legs were smooth and hairless. In some strange way, they all looked the same, as though their god had made them all from one batch of brown clay, covered them with skin and then forgotten to slap on accessories like hair and muscle.

'Sire, I did warn you ...' whispered Bhima into Vishnupada's ear, who was gaping at the men with his mouth open.

'Umm ... are you all related by blood?' asked Vishnupada.

One of the men looked up. Vishnupada couldn't make out if he was fifteen summers old, or fifty.

'No, master,' said the man, in the sing-song twang that the men of Kampilya spoke with.

'Then, why do you all look alike ... as though all of you share a father?' asked Vishnupada.

'Master, great wrongs were committed on our forefathers. As a reminder of the wrongs, they swore never to grow locks of hair or smear their bodies with perfume or adorn their women with flowers, till the wrongs were corrected,' said the man, with downcast eyes. 'We are just following in their footsteps.'

Vishnupada did not want to hear anymore. Everyone in the sixteen kingdoms had a tale of woe going back a thousand years. Someone's temple had been desecrated. Somebody's ancestors had been ill-treated. Someone said their lands had been usurped a hundred years ago. Sometimes, Vishnupada wondered, that if everybody felt persecuted, who was actually doing the persecution? Vishnupada did not care for such tales, all he cared for was good rains, for the feel of silver and gold in his hands and, most of all, the safe movement of his caravans from one kingdom to another.

So, he shook his head, pursed his lips as though he deeply sympathised with the bald man's story and shot him another question.

'So, can you guys lift that rock, one by one? If you can, you are hired,' he declared, pointing at a large boulder that lay at the entrance of his house.

'Along with the boy?' asked the man.

'What boy?' said Vishnupada, turning to look at the rock, on top of which sat his son, peeling a banana. 'Get off it, you idiot!' The boy ran away, rather slowly, the flesh around his chest and hips swinging.

'No, just the rock,' said Vishnupada. 'Get on with it. I have three hundred oxcarts that need to be loaded by tomorrow evening,' he snapped at the men.

Trivikrama stood outside his mother's chamber, at the end of the hall of a thousand pillars, staring at a bare pillar. Unlike the other pillars in the hall, this one was still a work in progress, just a block of stone, yet to be carved and chiselled. After his lifetime, once his body had been cremated, his horses sacrificed, and his ashes scattered in the placid waters of the Netra, some well-paid sculptor would decide his legacy by carving it on that pillar.

Down the hall, Sumukha the Gentle could be seen sniffing a flower—a subtle dig at his effeminate nature and his love for young boys. Further down, Dhruva the Conqueror, who had sacked five out of the sixteen kingdoms in his lifetime, was carved standing with his right foot resting on a crushed skull. Tradition dictated that the statues of kings be sculpted only after their death.

What would the next king—be it his younger brother or his unborn son—be looking at when he stared at this pillar? How would he be carved? Would it be with a cup of soma in his hand, his eyes half closed? Unlikely. Chandradatta, one of his great grandfathers and the first of his line, was reputed to be so fond of soma that he would start his day with a cup and then keep drinking till he couldn't hold a cup anymore. But even that man was sculpted petting a deer on its head, to show his love for preserving the forests around Mithila.

*Perhaps I will be carved patting a courtesan's head, with her face buried in my lap.*

The thought made him chuckle.

'Your Majesty is in fine spirits,' remarked Chavuka. 'I hope the new paste of herbs is helping,' said the physician, fishing for praise.

Trivikrama absently nodded at the old man. He was far from being in good spirits. He had slept fitfully the night before. Strange dreams, most of which he could not remember clearly, had punctuated his sleep. All he could recall was a macabre patchwork of moving images: the pockmarked face of the skinny brahman, his slowly moving prayer beads dripping with dark blood; a severed thumb becoming taller and taller until it stood like a pillar over Mithila; a shooting star that turned into a serpent and then hissed, spat venom and fell into his lap ...

He had woken up before sunrise and lain in his dark bedroom thinking about the strange happenings of the past few weeks. None of it made sense. Questions had shot through his head like arrows. Who was that wretched brahman from Soumyapur? How had he known about the shooting stars? Why did that brahman's whole village get butchered? Why did only the girl survive? What if the brahman was dead? What if he was alive? What if this beast Ardhamukha had kidnapped the brahman? What if he got his hands on the little girl too? What if Jayaveera was no longer his true friend? What if … What if …

By the time the first rays of the sun broke into his bedroom through the curtains, Trivikrama had become tired of the questions, especially of the *what ifs*. Once his morning ablutions were done with, overseen by Chavuka who had remarked on the constitution of his shit, Trivikrama had gone looking for his younger brother. For a change, the prince's attendant had informed him that Ajitha wasn't practising archery or wrestling.

He found Ajitha, sitting at the edge of his window, feet dangling over the ledge, staring at the crimson sky.

'What is it, Ajitha?' asked Trivikrama, placing an arm around the boy's shoulder. The question was a formality, because Trivikrama knew the answer.

The boy turned and looked at him. His eyes were red-rimmed and resembled sunken coal pits.

*First love can be exhausting,* thought Trivikrama.

'You haven't slept, have you?' he asked, smiling.

'Don't mock me, brother,' his brother said, with a sting in his voice.

Trivikrama wanted to tell him that he wasn't jesting, that he understood what his brother was going through; after all, everybody, at some point of time or the other, had felt the cruel sting of love.

'It's the girl, isn't it?' Trivikrama asked. 'She is yours brother. Who doesn't want a prince?'

'Is that all? Should I just tell her I am a prince? And she will … like me?' Ajitha asked him hopefully. 'I saw her look at you.'

*Should I tell him the truth?* Trivikrama wondered.

'Everybody looks at the king ... you know that,' said Trivikrama. 'You have mother's beautiful brown eyes. And as much as I hate to admit it, between us, you are the handsome one. If God was kinder on Mithila, he would have made you the elder one, brother. You would have made a fine king ... a better king.'

Ajitha stared at the brightening sky. 'Do you mean that?' he asked.

'Everything ... the eyes, the good looks, all of it ... except the bit about you being the better ruler,' Trivikrama said teasingly.

The brothers laughed together, till their eyes teared up.

'Do you really have to go, Ajitha?' asked Trivikrama.

Ajitha nodded.

'I can make her your chief of guards you know or your personal spy or whatever else you want ... both of you can stay here in Mithila.'

'No, brother,' Ajitha insisted. 'It's time I went out and saw the world for myself. How long will I shoot arrows at stick figures in the palace?'

Trivikrama had hugged his brother, held him for a while, before leaving him to his brooding. He had to tell his mother about Ajitha's little adventure, and he wasn't looking forward to it.

Trivikrama sighed and turned away from the pillar and walked towards his mother's chambers. The rest of his retinue stayed behind. Up ahead, Nila the eunuch was waiting outside his mother's chamber with her arms crossed, head bowed. Just as the king reached the door, Nila looked up and examined the king with her dark, kohl-lined eyes. For some reason, Nila's eyes reminded Trivikrama of flying foxes in the night: they could see what others couldn't. Just the way she looked at him, Trivikrama could feel his hairs beginning to rise.

'The queen is not in the mood for an audience, my king,' said the eunuch, in her deep, scratchy voice, that sounded like boulders scraping against each other.

Trivikrama felt his jaw tighten, and a wave of scalding anger rise, coil and tighten in his stomach. 'Tell my mother it's something important … something about Prince Ajitha,' said Trivikrama, testily.

The eunuch leaned closer to the king, so close that Trivikrama could smell the cardamom on her breath. 'If this is about Prince Ajitha's trip to Kampilya, he came by earlier in the day. The queen has granted her approval,' said the eunuch, before bowing and retreating noiselessly into the queen's chamber.

Trivikrama stood at the entrance, staring at the flapping curtains.

Sleep had played hide and seek with Ajitha too last night. The dark hours had dragged on, slowly, like water dripping from an earthen pot with a hole in its bottom. His breath had felt ragged, mouth feverish and his heart had thumped against his ribs most of the night.

All he could think of was one name, one face, one body: Avanti.

The curl of her locks as they fell on her shoulders, her sharp eyes that scorned him, her delicate neck, her full lips, the way she handled a sword, the scar that ran down her right shoulder …

How had she got that scar? Did it feel like a scorpion's

sting whenever she bathed and water ran down her back? Were her palms soft to touch? Or were they coarse, having held the rough reins of horses for years? Ajitha had tossed and turned in the darkness, hoping that he would eventually fall asleep, and slip into a dream about her or into a darkness blacker than her tresses.

But sleep had, stubbornly, evaded him. He cursed his own weakness, his feeble mind, his fickle heart.

'You have met her only once. You do not know who she is. Maybe she is cruel and inconsiderate. Maybe she is dull to talk to. Maybe she laughs like a fool. Maybe her breath smells like a horse. Maybe she is fast asleep, while I am putting myself through this torture …' Ajitha had told himself again and again.

He had tried to think of the six-fingered brahman from Soumyapur, the girl in Kampilya and that fiend called Ardhamukha, but in the end all he could think of was this girl who could defeat giants in combat and speak six tongues.

He wanted to talk to her, smell her hair, run his fingers over her scars, kiss her lips … the soft bed, the silk sheets felt treacherous. He had dragged himself away from his bed and slowly opened the door of his bedroom. The hinges on the door creaked, but not too loudly. Ajitha had insisted that they be oiled regularly. He liked his quiet excursions, in the middle of the night.

The palace had been fast asleep. His attendant was snoring, seated on a chair, cushions propped at his back and his sides. Ajitha walked silently out of the room and past the two guards outside his chambers, who were sleeping too. Once he was past them, he doubled his pace and walked towards the hall of thousand pillars.

The lamps had flickered out in the night. Dawn was still

an hour away. His footsteps echoed in the dark. And then, out of nowhere, a familiar figure—with a ramrod straight back, draped in coarse clothes—had emerged holding a lantern, gazing at the pillar depicting his father.

'Mother,' Ajitha exclaimed. 'I did not know that you ever ventured out of your chambers.'

The Queen Mother looked at him, smiled and then waved a hand beckoning him to follow her into her room. In the corner of the anteroom, Nila slept on a wooden mat spread out on the floor.

Madhusmita sat next to her parchments and dipped her quill into her inkpot.

*I thought you slept well unlike your brother*, wrote the queen and passed on the parchment to Ajitha to read.

'Yes, Mother. Usually, I do. But tonight is different,' Ajitha had admitted.

The queen had raised her right hand in enquiry as if asking him to explain.

'I feel strange, Ma,' Ajitha replied. 'I feel like I have a fever, an illness, an all-consuming illness ... one that will kill me, and yet I have never felt more alive ...'

The Queen Mother smiled and wrote deliberately on the parchment.

*Is it the girl?*

'Is there anything you don't know, Ma?' Ajitha had asked in surprise. 'Your seclusion is only a farce.'

At this, Madhusmita's quill had paused and hovered over the parchment for a few moments. After gathering her thoughts, she had written in her neat script, *I know you want to go away Ajitha. You are almost a man and I cannot stop you. But remember, the world outside is very different. It's a cruel place with treacherous men and women. You are born to rule. You can do that right here. Whatever you want can be yours. Very few men born in this world have that power. Soldiers have died in battles just for you to have that power. Blood has been spilt for you. And yet, you want to risk it all. Are you sure about your decision?*

Ajitha had read the parchment and looked up at his mother.

'I don't know if I ever told you this, Mother. I was probably three or four summers old when you took your vow of silence. And since then, for better or worse, Trivikrama has been both my father and my mother. You are like a deity to me, locked away in your sanctum … shrouded in a stony silence,' said Ajitha. 'Ma, I don't even remember your voice anymore … or the lullabies you sang to me … if you ever sang them to me. I hold no anger or ill will against you. I respect you because you are thc one who gave birth to me … But I'm just not sure if I love you anymore.'

Madhusmita's eyes brimmed with tears before they spilled over; she did not wipe them and let them flow down her cheeks.

'Bless me Mother,' said Ajitha. 'I leave tomorrow evening.'

*My blessings are always with you, my son. My vow of penance is for the benefit of you and your brother. I hope you will understand that someday. May the gods always be with you, Ajitha,* she wrote and placed her palm on Ajitha's forehead to bless him.

'Can I hear you speak once, Ma?' Ajitha said. 'Anything, even a word of anger will do. I had hoped at least my hurtful words would get you to say something …'

With a sad look on her face, Madhusmita had shaken her head. She had picked up a parchment and begun writing again. The rolling tears from her eyes had dripped on the parchment and smeared her writing. The only sound that Ajitha heard as farewell was the scratching sound of the quill on parchment as he bowed and left the room.

In the distance, the brahmans had begun chanting their morning prayers. It was almost dawn.

*Today, I will leave Mithila*, thought Ajitha.

Trivikrama did not like the way she looked at him. Avanti's large and alluring, jet-black eyes stared at him—as though she was appraising a slave or a farm animal for purchase. Her eyes roved down, not so politely, from his strong shoulders, down to his broad, hairy chest and onto his stomach, which had bloated a little in the last few weeks. At that moment, he wished he hadn't drunk as much soma or feasted as much as he had in the past few months. Trivikrama felt naked and violated.

Then, there was that cursed smile. Avanti's full red lips curled around the corners, as though she was struggling in her efforts to stop a smile from sneaking through. And, then, she actually smiled. No, it was more of a smirk, one that indicated she knew more about Trivikrama than she should.

Alone with her, in the confines of the ivory room, Trivikrama felt uncomfortable. And the thought made him flush with anger. He was not sure whether he wanted to kiss her or strangle her.

He did not offer Avanti a seat. He wanted her to stand and sweat.

'Can you keep secrets, woman?' he asked, crossing his legs and leaning forward from his ornate perch.

'Yes,' she said. 'Which secret is *my king* talking about?' Her smile widened, revealing a perfect row of pearly teeth.

'Do you find me amusing?' asked Trivikrama testily, his voice a little louder than he thought it would be.

'Does my smile offend my king?'

*She is toying with me. Maybe I should just behead her … maybe ask her to sit on my lap, untie the knot of her blouse and take her right here,* thought Trivikrama.

He wished Gurukripa was here. He would have taught this wildcat a quick lesson on how to speak to kings. But Trivikrama had specifically asked for an audience with the girl alone. His teacher had given him a long, searching look but had, mercifully, held his silence.

'Woman, I need your word. You will never speak about whatever … transpired between us to my brother. Not one word. Not a hint,' said Trivikrama, glaring at her, hoping to scare her.

'Why though, my king?' she asked.

'Aacharya Gurukripa tells me you are a great spy. I am sure you noticed the besotted gaze of my younger brother,' he said.

'Yes, I did,' she said. 'But he is a boy. And I don't bed boys … even if they happen to be princes. I prefer a certain type of man.'

'And I fit?' enquired Trivikrama, smiling, ashamed at himself for having asked the question.

She nodded, smiling, looking right into his eyes.

'Well, Avanti, as tempting as you are,' said Trivikrama. 'I have a proposition for you. I don't know what Aacharya-ji has promised you as a reward for doing what you are going to do. But whatever it is … I shall double it if you bed my brother once during the journey.'

Her eyes widened. Her smile stayed, but it was no longer a teasing one.

'I am a spy, not a common whore,' she said, with some venom. 'I choose who I bed and who I kill … *my king*.'

Trivikrama scratched the back of his neck. 'So, do I have your word?' he asked.

'Yes, you do,' she said.

'Good,' said Trivikrama. 'Now, for your mission. One, you will escort the prince to Kampilya safely. Once there, you will take him to the governor and produce the royal seal, after which the prince will be under his care. Two, you will speak to that girl from Soumyapur, and find out what she knows about what happened at her village and anything she might know about the brahman. Three, you will find out what happened to the brahman. Is he really dead? Or is he being held captive by savages who are removing his hands for sport?'

'What if I find the brahman?'

'Get him back to Mithila … unharmed,' said Trivikrama. 'One more thing. During this period, address all your messages to either me or Aacharya Gurukripa. Nobody else. And lastly, find out whatever you can about this Ardhamukha.'

'What if I find him?' Avanti repeated.

'Get me his head on a platter.'

They walked down the dark, airless tunnel, silently. Trivikrama led the way, holding a blazing torch. Ajitha walked behind him, staring at the walls which seemed to be closing in on them with each passing step. Before they had left Trivikrama's bedroom, Ajitha had carefully folded his silks, removed his jewels and chains of gold and deposited them on his brother's bed in a neat pile. The royal ring bearing the insignia of the twin eagles was handed over to his brother. Ajitha had, then, changed into soft white cottons, draped a thin chain of gold around his neck, and slipped on a band of silver around his index finger. He examined himself in the mirror of polished bronze. He looked wealthy, but not like a royal. Definitely not a prince. The son of a merchant, a wealthy merchant, perhaps.

On his shoulder now, he carried a bag of leather, inside which was a messy bundle of clothes, all made of cotton, not too coarse but not too expensive either. At the bottom of the bag lay a wooden flute. Inside the flute, carefully wrapped and sealed with wax, was a letter from Trivikrama addressed to the commander of the army at Kampilya introducing the prince. Aacharya Gurukripa also planned to dispatch a bird to Kampilya announcing the prince's imminent arrival the day before Ajitha reached the city.

'Just in case you lose the flute,' Trivikrama had said, before opening the door to the secret tunnel from his chamber.

'Someday, I would like to find out who built this godforsaken tunnel,' said Trivikrama, as they walked deeper into it. 'Not that it's without its uses,' he added, chuckling at the memory of the nights he had sneaked out of the royal palace for his nocturnal adventures.

Trivikrama's voice and their footsteps echoed off the tunnel's walls. He occasionally waved his hands to clear the cobwebs that hung from the roof of the tunnel in strange shapes and patterns. Some of the cobwebs caught fire, burned and sizzled as the flame of the torch kissed them. In the pale-yellow light, Ajitha could see black spiders and thick-tailed lizards scampering away from them.

Eventually, they came to a small flight of stone stairs. Trivikrama bounded up, two stairs at a time. Ajitha followed his brother. He could not wait to breathe some fresh air and get out of the tunnel. Trivikrama opened a heavy door, that groaned like a dying horse.

Both brothers blinked furiously, as they struggled to adjust to the bright light streaming in from the high windows. They stood inside an old, dilapidated building with a high roof and wooden walls. Once it had been a royal granary in the age of Chandradatta; later it had become a store for weapons. But, during the reign of their grandfather who had built the royal complex, it had been abandoned and left to rot. It was half a kosa away from the natyashalas of Mithila and just two kosas away from the grain market. No one dared to enter the building even though it was unguarded. People who tampered with royal property often lost a few fingers, sometimes even a hand.

'So, brother, this is it,' said Trivikrama, as he stuck the torch into a peg in the wall. 'Avanti is waiting for you in the grain market … not too far from here. I am sure you will find her. A horse from the royal stables awaits you at the corner of the street.'

Ajitha smiled. And at that moment, his heart was awash with sadness. For he realised that he would be, for the first time in his life, parting ways with the one person who had been his only friend all his life—even if only for a while. The one constant, his north star.

Trivikrama smiled weakly. 'I'm asking you again, are you sure you want to do this, Ajitha?' he asked quietly.

For a moment, doubt seized Ajitha's heart—a fear that grabs men when they take paths unknown, journeys unpredictable and stand at the beginning of roads that few have travelled on before.

Ajitha leaned forward and hugged his brother. They embraced tightly, despite the sweat pouring down their backs, despite the awkwardness that brothers usually feel in showing affection to each other and in defiance of all rules of royal conduct that Aacharya Gurukripa had taught them.

'Goodbye, brother,' whispered Ajitha.

'May Mahadeva, the god of gods, protect you,' said

Trivikrama. 'Trust only him and no one else.'

Ajitha pulled himself away and started walking briskly towards the exit. While turning the door knob and stepping out in the blinding sun of Mithila, he turned back to take one last look at his brother.

Trivikrama, the king of Mithila, was holding the torch and ducking back into the tunnel. In an instant, he was gone.

Ajitha turned back towards the exit. His grand adventure had begun.

She stood out in the crowded grain market like a rock jutting out in the midst of a frothing river. Avanti sat on a dark-skinned horse, straight backed and proud, while a sea of people parted around her.

A few heads turned to stare at her flowing locks, at the bare back that curved so beautifully around the base of her spine and at the ugly, dry scar just above her breasts. A quiver filled with arrows rested on her shoulder. A bow hung from the saddle. Few people dared to gaze into her dark eyes; for despite her striking beauty, there was something fierce about the woman sitting on the horse.

'You are late,' said Avanti, as Ajitha's horse trotted up next to her. 'The caravan would have already started from the grain market.'

Ajitha nodded a weak apology.

'If you are wondering why I am not addressing you as my prince ... well, that's the way it is going to be from here on. From this moment, if anybody asks, you are *just* Ajitha, the son of a grain merchant from Mithila who is on his way to Kampilya,' she said.

'And who are you?'

'I am Avanti … your elder sister. You are escorting me to Kampilya to worship at the temple of Agni there before I get married,' she said.

'Can't you be my wife? Or promised to me in marriage …' said Ajitha feebly. '… or my lover?'

Avanti's only reply was a cold stare. Then, she gently kicked her horse on the side who broke into a trot and started moving away.

Ajitha followed her, smiling broadly.

'And why is my beloved sister bearing arms?' asked Ajitha.

'Because she loves hunting and the jungle is full of beasts … ones that crawl on four feet and those that walk on two. The latter are more dangerous, for they carry spears and shoot arrows dipped in poison. One more thing, unlike my younger brother, I love long silences during a journey. I hope you remember that, Ajitha,' she warned.

A hundred carts stood lined up and loaded. The oxen had been fed and harnessed. A pigeon had been dispatched to Kampilya. All that was left before the caravan could begin its journey was the propitiation of the gods.

Vishnupada watched as the brahman poured *ghee* into the sacrificial fire and recited his prayers, singing praises of Indra, the god of gods. When the verses on Indra were done, the brahman made offerings to Agni, Varuna and Vayu. Vishnupada was tired by now, his eyes watering from the smoke of the sacrificial fire. He wanted the ceremony to get over soon, so that the caravan could leave the city limits while the sun was still high in the sky.

But the brahman, a stickler for custom, kept droning on in his monotonous sing-song voice. After what felt like ages, the brahman picked up an earthen pot, filled with pale soma, and handed it over to Vishnupada, who gratefully accepted it and took a sip.

Vishnupada hated the taste of soma and the dizziness it caused, but who was he to turn down an offering from the gods. He placed the pot on the floor and led the brahman to the first of the carts in the caravan. The brahman smeared a paste of vermillion on the oxen's foreheads, in between their eyes. The beasts shook their heads in protest making the bells around their necks tinkle.

The brahman closed his eyes and muttered another prayer, hands resting on the yoke tying the oxen. When he was done, he opened his eyes and looked up at the sky. He used his palm to protect his eyes from the glare of the blazing sun.

Up above, two birds were flying in slow, lazy circles.

'Ah! A fine omen! Two kites fly above us. This is an appropriate time to begin the journey,' the Brahman declared, with a smile, although he really couldn't make out whether the birds were kites, eagles or vultures.

Vishnupada sat in the first cart and whipped the bulls. They flinched and then the first cart moved. One by one, the carts began to move and the jingling of bells filled the air. The crowds in the market made way for the row of oxcarts and gawked at them as they rolled through the grain market.

Vishnupada couldn't wait to get to the outer gates of Mithila. Once he got there, he would get off, pay the taxes for the goods and then return home for a cooling bath followed by a rubdown of sandalwood paste on his burning back. He was dreaming of his wife's soft hands on his body, when he saw a woman on a horse, bearing arms, come towards him.

Beside her was a boy, whose face seemed familiar. Vishnupada's eyes widened as he recognised the boy as the one who had sat next to Trivikrama that day when he had gone to see the king.

Vishnupada realised, with a start, that the woman was waving at him. He pulled on the reins, and the cart came to a halt. He got off the cart and walked towards the woman on the horse, who also dismounted.

She whispered something into his ears. Hearing what she had to say, Vishnupada felt as if the gods were smiling down on him. Like his father would tell him, if he urinated today, he would likely piss out a shower of gold.

He looked up to the skies to thank the gods and spotted a flock of birds circling above.

The brahman had been wrong.

They were not kites.

They were vultures.

## 19. Ardhamukha

Kampilya was a sore disappointment. Jeeva disliked everything about the city. He hated it, in fact. In his mind, the boy from the mountains had imagined shimmering palaces in the city, tall towers that spiralled into the clouds, fragrant gardens with flowers and fountains, beautiful princesses in palanquins and soldiers with armour that gleamed in the sunlight.

But he found Kampilya flat, filthy, squalid and smelly.

With every passing moment, Jeeva hated Kampilya more—everything about the city disgusted him. The smell of garbage, the sludge from the overflowing drains, the cramped streets, the rabid mongrels that snapped and barked at passersby, the rude crowds that pushed and shoved. Kampilya reminded him of a giant, messy anthill.

*Only anthills don't stink*, he thought glumly. If this was how all big cities were, he wanted no part of it.

On the other hand, Ajiva seemed unmindful of the noise, the malodorous surroundings or the commotion. Strangely, he seemed to be at home in the place. He waded through the crowd in long strides, never asking for directions, not pausing to look one way or the other, as though he knew exactly where he was, where he was going and what he was doing.

'Have you been here before?' asked Jeeva.

'I think so,' said Ajiva, as they walked towards the centre of the city. 'Things seem … familiar.'

There was something different about Ajiva ever since they had left Devprayag. He walked straighter and faster. His speech was more direct and his gaze was less lost. It was as though Ajiva had found his purpose. His reason to live. Things were different at night though. Ajiva's nightmares continued and so did his nocturnal ramblings.

Even the people of Kampilya stared at Ajiva in wonder. His matted hair, flowing beard and the stout stick he carried seemed to make an impression on people and even the rudest of them parted and made way for the stranger. Jeeva struggled to keep pace with him, forever out of breath.

'Slow down. I am out of breath,' Jeeva said, tugging at his companion's arm.

Ajiva apologised and stood still, waiting for the boy to catch his breath.

'What seems familiar?' Jeeva asked.

'I knew that this city would stink even before I entered it.

I know that in the centre of this city there is a ruined palace … one made of brick and stone,' said Ajiva. 'I know that once upon a time, a few hundred years ago, this city was the magnificent capital of the Panchala kingdom. A great beautiful city, with a race of fierce warriors ruling it …' said Ajiva.

'How did it become … this?' asked Jeeva, pointing his hand at a pig who seemed to be enjoying a swim in a drain of vile sludge.

'The same thing that happens to every great kingdom. Fortunes of men and cities rise and fall with time. Great kings die early deaths. Their children squabble. Fools take over. People suffer,' said Ajiva, in a slow, measured manner. 'Once upon a time, this city was ruled by a great king, who married his daughter to five brothers who were all great warriors. Unfortunately, the eldest brother, otherwise a good man, was a fool. He gambled and lost everything, including his wife, in a game of chance to his own cousins. The wife was humiliated—'

'How was she humiliated?'

'You are too young to hear that, Jeeva. You just need to know that the brothers fought a great war with their own cousins. Blood was spilt on both sides. Fathers, brothers, cousins slaughtered each other. Some say all the bloodshed happened because God had willed it that way. It was just a game God was playing. But I think it was because a woman, a good woman, the brave princess of Kampilya was humiliated publicly. Any race or kingdom that ill treats its women eventually pays its price in blood,' said Ajiva.

'Was Kampilya destroyed in this great war?' asked the boy.

'No. It survived that war. But the great war had maimed most of the other old kingdoms who had fought in it. Younger, smaller kingdoms arose from the ashes of the old war. One of them was Mithila—,' said Ajiva. For some reason, Ajiva paused abruptly, as though he was grasping through the fog of his memories for something that was elusive.

Eventually, he continued. 'Fifty years ago, Mithila and Panchala fought a war. Panchala lost. Simhamukha, the king of Mithila, wanted to teach the people of Panchala a lesson. So, he razed the old palace—the pride of Panchala—to the ground and imposed such heavy taxes on the kingdom that it ruined this great city. Kampilya was not just beaten in a war, it was choked and ruined by Mithila,' said Ajiva.

'How do you remember all of this and yet, remember nothing about what happened to you?' asked Jeeva.

'That's a question I ask myself every waking hour.'

'I think you were once a warrior,' said Jeeva. He meant it as a statement and yet, it sounded like a question.

Ajiva stayed mum, staring at the pig which was still rolling in the sludge.

They had not spoken about what had happened at Devprayag since they had left the confluence in the early hours of the morning ten days ago. But Jeeva knew he would always remember the sight he had seen that misty, cold morning. They had been standing at the edge of a cliff, watching the sun rise, its crimson rays turning the waters of the rivers red. At the edge of the confluence, the pillar of Devprayag—the one whose eternal flame had been doused by the great warrior Arjuna and that hadn't burned in a thousand years since then—stood alight and smouldering.

Ajiva had not said a single word that day. Even for a silent man, his silence had been unusual. He had just ignored the boy and walked as fast as he could, as though he was trying to punish his body, wracking it with pain, just so he could remember something from his past.

That evening, when they had taken a dip in the cold waters of the Ganga, Jeeva had noticed that Ajiva's wound had fewer maggots and it looked less livid. Ajiva had noticed it too, and had gingerly fingered the wound, before tying the red sash back on.

'I think you were once a warrior. Probably, a great one,' said the boy now, prodding Ajiva for an answer.

'If that were the case, if I were indeed such a great warrior, why was I sitting in a dark cave for years, oozing blood and pus like a diseased animal?' said Ajiva, a tinge of anger in his voice. Or was it just confusion? 'Who defeated me and left me there to die?' he asked. 'Come, let's not waste any more time here. Let us go take a look at that ruined palace.'

The palace was a ruin alright. Weeds grew out of cracks in the crumbling mud walls. Pigeons cooed from ill-lit crags. Sunlight streaked in from gaping holes in the roof. Vagrants and drunkards slept under the shade of the walls in various states of undress. As they sauntered around in the ruins, their footsteps echoed off the empty walls. Pigeons scattered above them, unhappy with the intrusion.

Despite the disrepair, Jeeva could see that once upon a time this must have been a glorious residence for the great kings of Panchala. The roof was high, as tall as five men standing one on top of another, and the doorways broad. Where the plaster had not peeled off, colourful drawings of lotuses, chariots and birds were still visible.

In the heart of the palace was a courtyard with a green mossy pond and a statue of a woman at its centre that stared at visitors as they passed by. She was the most beautiful woman Jeeva had ever seen. A sari-like garment was wrapped around her body that accentuated her shapely breasts and hips. And yet, there was something fierce about her. Her hair was dishevelled, and her eyes wide-open, as though they would scorch the world with her burning anger. Her full lips were tight, and she held her head high with pride, bordering on arrogance.

'That's the princess of Panchala. The daughter of King Drupada,' said Ajiva. 'Some people called her Panchali.'

They sat down near the pond and marvelled at the princess' statue while lunching on the berries they had plucked from a tree outside the city walls. The day-old berries were more seed than fruit but their hungry stomachs didn't care. Ajiva watched as the boy tried to crack the seeds open with his teeth before giving up. Ajiva passed his share of berries to the boy, who shook his head stubbornly.

'I have lived without food for god knows how long … you know that better than anyone else,' said Ajiva.

'Even more reason for you to eat properly,' said the boy. 'Also, I am not the one with a wound that refuses to heal.'

Ajiva often wondered what it was about the boy that had made him take a liking to an abandoned man in a cave, an orphan that the rest of the world did not care about. Was it because Jeeva himself was one? Or did he just have a kind heart? Or was it some strange twist of fate that he could not understand?

As Ajiva looked at Jeeva staring at the seeds like a hungry rat, he felt a strange clutching in his chest. What was it? Was this what people called love? And if it was, wasn't it worth living and dying for? Then why did kings and soldiers fight for land, cattle and pride instead?

They finished their meagre lunch and said a silent goodbye

to the princess who continued to examine them with her dead, burning eyes. The boy waved at the statue before leaving the ruined palace. If the pond wouldn't have been mossy, the boy would have waded in and hugged her.

Outside the crumbling walls of the palace, they spotted a noisy crowd of men, women and children, queuing up in front of a building. It was an unruly line; squabbles kept breaking out as people tried to edge ahead of each other. A guard waved around a stout staff menacingly, trying to maintain the line and control the crowd. Urchins sold salted buttermilk, spiced mangoes and boiled nuts to the people standing in the queue.

'What are they standing in line for?' Jeeva asked a boy, who was selling spiced mangoes.

'Haven't you heard? The Miracle of Kampilya is here. It's the girl who survived the flesh eaters of Urba. All her people were chopped up, boiled and eaten alive,' said the boy. 'Go see her. Just looking at her is supposed to fetch you good luck … spiced mangoes for you?'

Jeeva shook his head and thanked the boy. Even though he would have loved to taste the spiced mangoes, he couldn't afford them. The seller of mangoes made a face and hurried on.

'I want to see this miracle girl,' Jeeva said.

'You will be disappointed, Jeeva,' said Ajiva. 'She is unlikely to have a pair of horns. Or a halo of light around her head.'

'But she is lucky and you badly need luck,' insisted Jeeva.

'How lucky can she be if everyone she knew was eaten alive?' said Ajiva, dourly.

Jeeva ignored the quip and marched towards the end of the line. Ajiva sighed and followed the boy.

The person standing ahead of them was a tall, thin man. Ajiva noticed that the skin on the man's back resembled earth parched during a harsh summer. Scars, deep and dry, crisscrossed his back. The man wore a heavy turban on his head and most of his face, except one eye, was concealed with a dirty cloth.

Perhaps, the stranger felt their gaze on his back. Perhaps, he was just curious about the new people who had joined the line. The stranger turned around and looked at them. As he did so, the veil covering his face came undone. Jeeva bit his lip to stop himself from screaming.

The man's face was a mess. A horror. Only one eye stared back at Ajiva. The other eye was missing. In its place, a lumpy shapeless blob of flesh and tissue flopped over an empty socket. The man's jaw was mangled—smashed and scooped out. It ended abruptly, halfway at the chin. The lips were missing, instead there was just a gash of a mouth, with a few teeth inside them. Three vertical, deep scars of similar length creased the man's forehead.

It was as though someone had taken the man's face and savagely scooped out most of it. No man could have done this to another man, thought Ajiva. Quickly the man pulled back the cloth over his face and turned away.

Jeeva felt Ajiva's arm on his shoulder. 'A bear,' whispered Ajiva, into his ear. 'That's what bears do. When you encounter one, you hope and pray it kills you.'

The duo stood in silence. Jeeva wondered why any animal would have been that savage. He wondered how people, who saw this poor man's face, usually treated him. He felt guilty about having stared at the man. But that didn't mean he wanted to talk to him either. What if the cloth covering his face slipped again? Jeeva kept his eyes peeled to the ground.

The line inched ahead slowly. The mango-seller came back and tried to get them to buy a slice or two. Up ahead, the line ended outside a window. People peeped inside for a moment before being shooed away by a stout, grouchy guard. Some of the onlookers passed him an extra coin or two to stare at the girl for a little longer. The woman currently in front of the window folded her hands and prayed to the girl, before tossing a flower inside.

'Bah! We came all the way and waited under the sun to see a sleeping girl,' said a small man with protruding teeth, who had just spent a few moments staring through the window.

'I told you,' said Ajiva, smiling at Jeeva's disappointed expression.

'But what if she really is lucky?' replied the boy.

The man with the scarred back was now at the window. He waved his thin hands at Ajiva, inviting him to stand beside him and take a look at the girl. The three of them—the scarred man, Jeeva and Ajiva—squeezed next to each other and peered inside the window.

The girl was fast asleep on a bed. An old woman was standing next to the window, inside the house. She stuck a bowl out at them.

'For the girl,' the old woman said and shook the bowl. Coins already in the bowl clattered loudly. Inside the room, the girl stirred in her bed. Her eyes fluttered open. She looked right into Jeeva's eyes and for some reason, smiled. Then her gaze moved upwards to the others next to him. Ajiva saw as her mouth tightened and she let out a sharp piercing wail.

Jeeva looked up and realised that the scarred man's veil had fallen away. His hideous face had been revealed. The girl was staring at him. Her eyes had widened. Fear, pure and white, had spread across her young face.

'Ardhamukha ... Ardhamukha,' she yelled. The guard with the stout staff ran up and dragged the scarred man away, landing blows on his back with his stick. Ajiva and Jeeva forgot about the girl and started following the guard.

The crowd quickly became incensed. A few men started chucking stones and mud at the scarred man. A woman spat at him. A man stepped out of the line and started kicking the scarred man. A few more joined in.

It was a while before the girl stopped screaming. And then, she slipped back into darkness and oblivion.

Ajiva sat in the dungeon, eyes wide open, seeing nothing. All he could hear was his own breath. Darkness felt comfortable, like a warm familiar bed, an old friend.

His hands were manacled behind his back. A brace around his neck forced his head down. His neck and shoulders felt like they were on fire and the wound on his stomach felt wet. But the pain felt familiar, almost reassuring. Had all those years of living like a corpse in a dark cave made darkness and pain seem like old acquaintances, he wondered. Or was he feeling calm because he knew the boy was now out of harm's way?

Things had happened fast after the girl had started yelling. Guards had rushed in from every direction. At first, they had turned all their attention and anger to the man with the scars. They had kicked and punched him in the stomach, and beaten him with their fists and staffs. They would have killed him, if Jeeva had not come in between him and the guard who was hitting him with a staff. The staff had grazed Jeeva on his shoulder and the boy had gone down in a heap.

What happened afterwards was something Ajiva wasn't quite sure of. Seeing the staff land on the boy, he had felt his world slow down. The noise of the angry mob had receded and become a quiet murmur. The screaming of the girl had died down to almost a whisper. Even the boy had seemed to fall very, very slowly. The screaming faces in the mob were mouthing words that seemed to take a very long time to form in their mouths. It felt as though the earth had stopped spinning.

The next moment, Ajiva had seen his own fist connecting with the guard's chin. Even though the blow seemed to travel in the air as gently as a butterfly, the guard's eyes rolled into their sockets. Spittle burst out from the guard's open mouth and he flew in the air for a moment before crashing to the ground.

*Not to his face,* a voice had spoken in Ajiva's head. *You will kill him.*

So, the next guard who had come forward trying to slash at Ajiva's chest with a sword had got punched in the stomach instead of his face. Ajiva had weaved away from the arc of the shining sword and seen the tip of the sword glint where the sunlight kissed it, as it slashed through the air. The guard seemed to be screaming but Ajiva did not hear a word.

And then, he spotted a guard holding a dagger to Jeeva's throat. Suddenly, the world came back with all its noise and fervour. The girl was still screaming inside the house. The mob was yelling angry expletives and egging the fight on. In the crowd, he even saw the boy who sold mangoes clapping his hands furiously.

Ajiva had stepped back, raising his arms in surrender. Then he had knelt on the ground, slowly putting his hands behind his head. The guard who had been punched in the stomach, straightened and staggered towards Ajiva, like a man drunk on several jugs of soma. The first guard, who had been punched on the chin, slowly got off the ground, dusted himself and tied Ajiva's hands behind his back with a cloth. They kicked, punched and spat on him while he stayed curled up on the ground, face down. The boy started crying loudly and he continued to sob till the guards had taken both of them and the scarred man back to the dungeon.

'Throw these two idiots into separate cells. Chain the tall one. Get me the ugly freak first,' the warden had said.

'What about this brat?' a guard, who was holding Jeeva by his hair, had asked.

'We are not savages. Feed him something and cut him loose,' the warden had said before turning to Jeeva. 'Boy, your father is going to be with us for a while. Go home.' The boy was on his knees, begging and pleading, as Ajiva was dragged away.

In the dark cell, Ajiva counted his breaths. He did not know why. Eventually, the door opened and yellow light streamed in. The guards left the torch they had been carrying outside before entering. Ajiva could only see three silhouettes.

The man with the scars had been dragged in by the two guards. His head was lolling like a broken rag doll's, his feet were trailing behind him and his breath echoed unevenly in the room. They dumped him at the other end of the room like a mound of garbage. Ajiva heard a faint moan.

'Your ugly friend will be dead by tomorrow morning. If he is not, he will pray that he was. As for you, we will come back tomorrow when the rooster crows again,' one of the guards told Ajiva. 'But to be sure, your son will be an orphan by the time the sun sets tomorrow. This much I promise you. And, I will enjoy making him one.'

Ajiva couldn't see the guard's face, as the brace prevented him from looking up. But the guard's voice sounded slurry, like a man with a few broken teeth and a swollen face. It was the guard Ajiva had punched on the chin.

Ajiva smiled to himself and thought, *I wish I had punched him harder.*

A shower of spittle hit his face.

'Don't smile, you idiot,' said the guard. 'Your friend won't live beyond tonight, given the hospitality he got from us. On second thoughts, I am going to leave you with a torch, so that you can see what awaits you tomorrow,' the guard said and stepped out of the dungeon.

He carried the torch back into the room and stuck it in a hole in the wall. The room became bathed with the yellow light of the flame. The walls were a tapestry of pain. Men had clawed and punched at the wall in their pain. Nails, clumps of hair and clotted blood were glued in uneven patches on the wall.

The guard loosened the brace around Ajiva's neck.

'Enjoy watching the freak die tonight. It's going to be your last,' said the guard. The door slammed shut and Ajiva heard locks click in place.

He closed his eyes, started counting his breaths again, and eventually drifted into a dreamless, fitful sleep.

'… is it a sin?'

The voice floated into the dark slumber like a whisper. Ajiva opened his eyes. The scarred man was slumped on the floor, exactly where the guards had left him. A thick, sticky drool of blood and spit flowed down from the corner of his lipless mouth. In the golden halo of the torch, the scars on his face and body appeared even more grotesque. His only eyelid was swollen and red.

For a moment, Ajiva thought he had imagined the voice and then, the man's mouth moved.

'I-Is it a sin?' the man asked.

'Is what a sin?' asked Ajiva.

'Looking ugly,' said the man with the scars, and coughed. A thin spray of dark blood flew out of his mouth. A few drops hit the muddy floor of the prison. A swarm of flies suddenly came alive, buzzing and feasting on the blood. Some of them made it to the man's face, who did not have the strength to wave them away.

'Being different? Having a skin which is the colour of pale milk or charred wood … do you think one is a blessing and the other a sin?' said the man. 'Once upon a time, I believed that being born in a tribe of hunters and fishermen was a blessing. We lived in the mountains and forests, far from the cities, kings and their unending greed for land. We worshipped the air and the water, where the birds and fish lived. We worshipped the beasts, the lord who protected the beasts, the lord who lives in graveyards … the one who protected our bulls and saved us from the mountain cats. Then, the kings came with their horses, their steel, their chariots, their priests and magical incantations. They saw us as an accursed people, those whom the gods had shunned.'

'They saw my people and judged us on the colour of our skin, the curls in our hair. Even then, I thought I was fortunate. Unlike most others in my tribe, I was tall and my skin was paler … not the colour of milk but the colour of rice husk. I came to this cursed walled city, learned their language and told nobody who I really was … I did not want them to see me as just another savage. I became a guard for the caravans, a hunter who kept vigil at night, the one who kept the merchants safe from mountain cats and bears while they slept in their oxcarts full of grain and furs …'

'But I was destined to suffer. One night, I was asleep on the edge of a caravan, away from the fires. I woke up to a smell. The breath of a great beast with hair and teeth. The beast savaged me brutally and left me for what I am now—an ugly bag of scars and tissue, forever in pain and shunned by all. I went back to the mountains, back to my people and all they saw was a traitor. So, here I am, an outcast, shunned by all, someone children are afraid to look at,' said the man.

After finishing his tale, the man closed his eyes and lay immobile. For a moment, Ajiva thought life had, indeed, ebbed out of the man. But then, the scarred man's chest heaved and he coughed again. The flies on his face took off as a fresh mist of blood sprayed out from his mouth.

Ajiva studied the scarred man carefully. The skin around his ribs was black and blue. His ribs were clearly broken, which explained the dark blood the man was spitting.

*He will not see the morning sun rise,* thought Ajiva. *All he has are a few more hours of pain.*

Ajiva closed his eyes and started counting his breaths again.

And then, he started dreaming. He was hiding in the bush, staring at a thicket in the jungle. Everything was green and lush. The sun was high in the sky. His skin felt warm. His mouth was dry. And then a voice whispered in his ear.

'Now, do it … now,' said the voice. It sounded calm, soothing.

The arrow flew into the air, its metal tip shining in the afternoon sun. Ajiva's eyes saw the target move. A tall deer with dark eyes and glistening dotted skin, its ears perked up. It sensed danger and leapt.

And just like that, it was gone. In its place was now a fawn. A young deer, barely a few days old. Its body was thin, its small tail wagging, unaware of the coming danger.

The arrow was still cutting through the air.

Ajiva screamed. The scream sounded different from his usual voice. He sounded like a boy. The fawn turned but it was too late by now. The arrow ripped through the deer's tender skin and burst through its neck. Blood gushed out from the wound. The fawn fell to the ground.

The fawn's mother turned and saw her child die. It stared at Ajiva as he burst through the bush where he had been hiding. And then, it turned and fled into the jungle—leaving its child to die alone.

Ajiva started sobbing, holding the dying fawn's head on his lap. Tears obscured his view.

'It's okay,' said the soothing voice. 'We are dying from the moment we are born. This poor thing is in pain. You know what you have to do.'

Ajiva held the fawn's neck and twisted it. He heard the deer's neck snap and saw its eyes turn dark. Ajiva dipped his finger into the pool of blood and drew a sign on the deer's neck—two snakes curled into each other.

'What is born will go back into this soil. You can neither kill nor can you die. For, we are all one,' said the soothing voice.

Ajiva snapped out of his sleep. He could sense eyes on him. The scarred man was staring at him curiously.

'What did you say?' he asked.

'Did I say something?' asked Ajiva.

'Yes … you said … what is born will go back into this soil—' began the man with the scars.

'—you can neither kill, nor can you die. For, we are all one,' said Ajiva, surprised at his clear recollection of the words from his dreams.

The scarred man's face seemed to light up at the words. Then, he closed his eye and whispered what sounded like a prayer.

'Hand and flesh,
Arm and leg,
Stem and root,
Wings and feathers,
Hair and teeth,
Worms and birds,
Master and slave,
Hunter and prey,
Man and God
... we are all one.'

The eye opened again. 'What do you see in your dreams, brother?' asked the man. His voice sounded weak.

Using the thumb of his foot, Ajiva drew the symbol of the two snakes on the floor.

The man stared at the symbol, and then at Ajiva.

'Do you know what that is?' asked the man. 'It is the sign of my people. The ones who live in the mountains ... once upon a time, we were known as the Ajivika. Who are you, brother?'

'I-I don't know,' said Ajiva. 'I don't remember who I am. I just see this sign a lot in my dreams.'

'Come closer. Show me your face,' said the scarred man. Ajiva realised that the dying torch in the dark dungeon was pegged in a hole in the wall just above the scarred man, which is why he could clearly see the scarred man but that man could not see Ajiva. For the scarred man, Ajiva was just a voice in the dark.

Ajiva moved a few steps closer but the chain held him back, just a yard short of the light.

'I can't come any closer,' said Ajiva. 'I am chained to the wall.'

With every ounce of strength left in his body, the scarred man crawled across the room on his fours, leaving a trail of blood on the floor. Ajiva could hear his breath wheeze in and out with every move he made.

When the man was just a yard away from Ajiva, he looked up and stared at Ajiva's face for a long time.

'You are …' he said and paused, as though he was straining at the dying leash of his memory, '… the man from the market. The one with the boy.'

Saying that, he continued to stare at Ajiva. He coughed again; his face so close to Ajiva's that droplets of blood spraying out of his mouth covered Ajiva's face.

Suddenly, the bearded man started laughing. He laughed, despite the pain it caused him, till tears rolled from his one eye and down his mangled face.

'Fate plays jokes that we take a lifetime to understand, brother,' said the scarred man. 'I have only one thing to tell you … go to the same place from where this poor girl … this Miracle of Kampilya has come from … a village called Soumyapur,' said the scarred man.

He then turned around and crawled away from Ajiva. When he reached right below the flaming torch, he held the wall with both hands and raised himself. He groaned in pain, blood oozed from the wounds on his face and back. The flies buzzed and danced around him, feeding off the blood and pus.

When he was on his feet, he leaned back against the wall. His tattered clothes and his bleeding wounds made him look more like a scarecrow made of flesh and blood than a human being.

'Behold, brother,' said the man. 'For the only act of kindness, I have received in a long, long time … for that boy, for your son … I set you free,' said the scarred man.

With his broken wrist, he held the flaming torch, brought it close to his torn rags and set himself on fire.

'No … no … no,' screamed Ajiva, straining against his chains.

But the scarred man was already one fire. The flame licked at his scarred skin and the hair on his body. He smiled for a moment, and then blood began to ooze out from his mouth. He had bitten hard on his own tongue, to stop himself from screaming.

As he watched the flames turn the scarred man into a human torch, Ajiva heard a voice in his head whisper calmly.

*For, we are one.*
*Hand and flesh,*
*Arm and leg,*
*Stem and root,*
*Wings and feathers,*
*Hair and teeth,*
*Worms and birds …*

The guard smelled the smoke before he heard the screams. He was fast asleep on the floor, his belly full of soma and his head full of dreams.

He opened his groggy eyelids and sniffed the air like a rat sticking its head out of a hole. Something was on fire. It was the smell of flesh and hair burning. Then he saw wisps of smoke curling out from under the door.

Something was on fire in the dungeon. Something human. There were five cells. Two of them were empty. One of the cells had two prisoners—the scarred freak who had scared the girl from Soumyapur and his companion. They were in the cell at the far end of the dungeon.

The three other cells held only one prisoner each—a cow thief, a rapist and a drunkard. They could wait. He picked up a pot of water, and walked towards the door, throwing it open.

Smoke billowed out. The men in the cells were screaming with fear, banging the doors with their bare hands, rattling their chains. The guard ignored their hollering and kept wiping his tearing eyes with the back of his hands. He placed the pot on the floor, untied his turban and dipped it in the water in the pot. He, then, tied the wet cloth around his mouth and nose and walked past the empty cells.

The smoke was coming from the last cell. The one which held the scarred freak and his friend. He pulled the key for the shackles from his waist, sucked a quick lungful of the acrid air around him and threw the door open.

A body was burning in one corner of the cell. The skin and hair were completely gone, the flesh was cooking now. He could not make out who it was. In the far end of the room, he saw a second man passed out on the floor, chained to the wall.

The guard crossed the room in three brisk strides. Holding his breath, and struggling to keep his burning eyes open, he struggled with the shackles behind the man's back. Eventually, he heard a click.

The man's eyes opened. Their eyes met.

Ajiva alone walked out of the cell, rubbing his chaffed wrists. As he crossed each cell, he opened the latches on the doors. Men rushed out of their cells, not even nodding or looking at the man who had freed them. Ajiva climbed up the stairs and went into the room, where the guard had been asleep a few moments ago. He picked up the guard's garments and a coat of armour that was resting against the wall. He was almost out of the room when he saw a small door on the side. He walked up to it and threw the door open. It was the armoury. A neat row of swords was lined up against the wall. He picked one up, checked its weight and balance, and then discarded it. He tried another. This one felt right. Thrusting the sword into a leather sheath, he tied it around his waist. At the far end of the room lay a couple of bows. They were made of fine wood. He picked one up and pulled its taut string. The twang that bounced off the walls sounded like music. He slung two quivers full of arrows on his shoulder and stepped out into the cool night.

Jeeva was on the floor outside the courtyard, shrivelled in the cold, fast asleep, unaware of the body burning in the dungeon, unaware of the rapist and drunkards who had fled past him, unaware of the guard with the broken neck slowly breathing his last in the cell. Ajiva shook the boy awake and gestured to him to follow quietly.

An hour later, just as the drawbridges around Kampilya were being lowered, a commander and his son trotted up on their fine horses. The guards manning the outpost waved them through.

'Where to, sire?' asked one soldier.

'To Soumyapur,' said the commander who, for some strange reason, was carrying two quivers full of arrows on his shoulders.

'May Agni guide your path,' said the guard and waved them along.

## 20. The Rules of the Jungle

The jungle lives.

Its breath is fragrant and cool; the air smells of wet grass one moment and of wildflowers the next. The jungle is always astir even when it is still. Beasts, small and large, skulk in the shadows. Snakes crawl over the moist soil, worms swarm under it. The jungle breathes and sighs; breeze shakes the leaves and flattens the waters of flowing blue streams. Twigs snap when stealthy paws step on them, however gently.

The jungle has no friends or foes. Its dwellers get shade and nourishment. Those who disrespect it, die—like the ones who can't see in the dark and yet choose to walk in the gloom.

For in the jungle there are only hunters and the hunted. And there are hunters who prey on the hunters. Life and death are constantly battling each other in the jungle.

The moon brother called Eka watched the battle unfolding in the sky with curious eyes. The snake writhed and struggled as the eagle holding it in its claws soared higher. Just a few moments ago, it was the snake who had been the hunter—a silent crawling killer with venomous fangs gliding over the grass. A voracious devourer of rats and frogs, and a stealer of unhatched eggs. Now, the same naga was moments away from its death. The eagle had dived down from the sky and picked up the snake in one fell swoop. Most likely, the eagle would soar higher and higher, before dropping the snake on a rock or a boulder. The bones would break, perhaps the fangs would snap too. The eagle would then swoop down to peck and claw away at what little life remained in the snake.

*The jungle ensures that every hunter is hunted too,* thought Eka.

Up in the sky, the snake writhed and lashed. It was a young snake, only a few weeks old. In a few days, it would have become fatter and heavier. Then the eagle would have struggled to carry the snake this high. But now, the battle was almost over. A few more flaps of its wings and the eagle would be high enough for the drop.

All of a sudden, the game of death turned on its head.

A bird, much smaller than the eagle, a kite perhaps, flew in from nowhere and darted towards the eagle. And then, another bird joined in. And then, another. The kites were trying to snatch the snake from the eagle. Claws and beaks came at the eagle from all directions.

It was now a three-way fight, between the snake, the eagle and a kettle of kites.

'One of our moon brothers has just returned from Kampilya, brother,' said Jwa, who had no interest in watching the fight.

'Uh-hmm,' said Eka, still engrossed in the battle. Jwa could only see the unburnt part of Eka's face and for that, he was happy.

'The girl who survived has slipped back into silence, brother,' said Jwa.

Eka turned around to look at him. Jwa fought the overwhelming desire to look away from the scarred face. Perhaps Eka read his expression, for he turned back to look at the battle in the sky again.

'How did that happen?' asked Eka.

'She saw a person in the crowd who … resembled you, brother. She screamed for a while and then fainted,' said Jwa.

'Resembled me? How so, brother?' asked Eka.

'Pardon me, brother … he had a scarred face, they say,' said Jwa.

Eka mulled on Jwa's words for a few moments, even as his eyes stayed glued to the battle taking place above them. The kites were now giving the eagle a hard time. The eagle wasn't letting the snake go, so it was slower. The snake continued with its frantic writhing.

'The people in the plains now have a new name for you, brother. One that scares them,' said Jwa.

'What is it?' asked Eka.

'They call you Ardhamukha, the half faced one,' said Jwa.

'I like the name,' said Eka. 'It sounds scary.'

Jwa saw Eka's lip curl at the corner. *Was he smiling?*

'Brother, how long can we go on like this? We don't have homes. We live in caves. We have neither armies nor war horses. Mithila has both. Do you think we can win?' Jwa asked.

Eka took his time before answering.

'Do you see that eagle above us? That's Mithila … proud, strong and a supreme hunter. Do you see that pack of kites? They are smaller and slower. Yet, they peck and claw and fight together. That's us. Who do you think will win, brother?' asked Eka.

Jwa looked up. The eagle had started tiring. That very moment, the eagle let the snake go. The snake fell down curling and twisting from the sky. The kites swooped down. Defeated and tired, the eagle swirled around, watching the kites tear the snake apart.

'Together, we will triumph, moon brother,' said Eka. 'Together, we will tear Mithila apart. Keep an eye on that girl. I had meant her no harm but now she might just be of some use to us.'

# 21. The Caravan

The novelty of the caravan wore off in just four days for Ajitha. Now it was just a humdrum, endless succession of small villages, green fields, muddy streams and small forests that got over before they even began.

Unlike a royal procession that had decked up elephants, soldiers in armour, drummers and trumpeters and enthusiastic crowds showering flowers, a merchant's caravan was a dull affair. It wasn't much to look at either, just a long row of oxcarts, one after the other, trundling down muddy, winding roads.

The bells around the oxen tinkled, horses snorted as they marched, mosquitoes and flies buzzed and hummed irritatingly around the ears of men. The wooden wheels of the carts groaned and creaked as they strained under the weight of the goods. Hour after hour of the monotonous sounds coming from the caravan put the merchants, soldiers, cooks and drivers into a stupor.

Occasionally, a merchant or a soldier would hum a song about home or an old lover, just to stay awake. The heat and sweat of the plains added to the stupor. The only relief came when a soldier, usually one who'd had too much to drink the night before, fell off a horse. Everybody laughed like they had never laughed before, except the ones who fell off their horses.

At first, Ajitha had stared at the sight of the little villages, fascinated, as they passed by, with their waterlogged rice fields, plough-wielding farmers and grazing buffaloes that gazed back with watering eyes. But then, village after village, the same sights greeted him. When the caravan entered the first jungle, thirty kosas away from Kampilya, Ajitha's breath quickened.

But then he realised that he wasn't out on a royal hunt. On this trip, he was a merchant's son, not a kshatriya looking for blood sport.

For a moment, he eyed the bow slung around Avanti's horse and had a fleeting image of her letting him use it.

'Don't even think of it, *little* brother,' said Avanti watching his gaze on her bow. After that, the jungle was as exciting as one of the boring dances in the palace that his dear brother Trivikrama was so fond of.

The daily routine of the caravan was mind numbingly predictable. Wake up before dawn, bathe in a stream or a pond nearby, eat a fruit or two, mount your horse or oxcart and keep going. And yes, Trivikrama had been right about having to shit behind the bushes.

'Keep an eye out for scorpions and snakes. They don't know the difference between a prince's backside and a commoner's,' Avanti had said grinning, clearly relishing Ajitha's discomfiture. He had hoped she wouldn't follow him as he slipped into the bushes. Avanti's watchful eyes seldom missed anything and she never let him go out of her sight.

The routine for the rest of the day wasn't fun and games either. One sat on the horse, back stiff, thighs chafing and buttocks turning into balls of iron. In the afternoon, when the sun was high in the sky, they stopped at either a shelter or in the courtyard of a temple and ate lunch cooked on an open fire. The menu, like the north star in the night sky, remained the same: boiled rice, pickles and vegetable stew with either too much salt or too little spice.

On the second day, a soldier had spotted a deer and killed it with one clean shot. By the time lunch was over, even the marrow in its bones had been sucked clean. Even Ajitha had shamelessly licked his fingers. For the rest of the day, he had sniffed his palms and fingers that smelled deliciously of spices and cooked meat.

After lunch, it was more riding till the sun turned into a red orb in the horizon. Then, they would set up camp. The oxen would be unyoked, fed with water and giant balls of gram and jaggery the size of elephant dung. The cooks would prepare the only decent meal of the day. A few pots of soma would be opened. Guards would crack obscene jokes and laugh till late in the night. Some of the drunk ones would eye Avanti surreptitiously, which would make Ajitha want to stab them with a dagger. And then, they would all go to sleep.

The next morning, they would wake up with the sun and the same routine would follow. Despite that, life on the caravan was not without its charms. Or for that matter, without its perils. Sometimes, the soldier leading the caravan would suddenly stop and raise a hand. The caravan would grind to a halt behind him. A herd of elephants would cross the caravan path, slowly, taking their time. Because of the increased threat of beasts and predators, at night, soldiers would keep the fires burning at the edge of the camp and take turns staying awake.

Avanti and Ajitha slept inside a tent in separate beds.

In the darkness, both stayed awake. Avanti, listening to the sounds of the forests. Ajitha, listening to the sound of her breath, lost in love and in a world of what-ifs.

This routine continued day after day, night after night. Until the fifth day, when things began to change.

At first, slowly. And then, suddenly.

Vishnupada couldn't wait for this stupid journey to end. He craved a warm oil massage and a steaming hot bath to soothe his aching back. He missed holding his wife's soft belly when they slept, pinching his son's chubby cheeks and even the quacking of the ducks in his backyard. Most of all, he really missed the familiar contours of his soft bed and fluffy pillows back home in Mithila. He was sick of the boiled vegetables, the overcooked rice and the cramped confines of the oxcart which stank of spices and his own sweat.

It had been six years since Vishnupada had travelled with a caravan and he had forgotten how monotonous and exhausting these journeys were. He had never intended to be on this caravan either, until that beautiful lady riding on a horse had turned up in Mithila and whispered into his ears.

'Do not react to what I am about to tell you. Don't jump off your horse, or fold your hands, or salute … nothing, understand? Nod your head if you understand me,' Avanti had whispered.

Vishnupada had wanted to shoo her away but something about her companion, the young boy on the horse, had seemed familiar. Oh, so familiar. Also, the woman had the air of someone who was used to passing orders and seeing them obeyed.

So, Vishnupada had nodded his head meekly.

'The boy you are staring at is Prince Ajitha,' Avanti had said, slowly. At which point of time, despite all the warnings he had just received, Vishnupada had greeted the prince with folded hands.

'I asked you not to do that, you idiot,' Avanti had snapped. The instructions had come in a fast and furious torrent after that. She had told him that the prince was travelling incognito and that no one, absolutely no one in the caravan, except Vishnupada, was to be told about his true identity. The prince would be just another merchant's son travelling back to his hometown, Kampilya, and Avanti would be his elder sister, promised to another man.

He was told that the prince was not to be treated any differently, at any point of time during the journey. He would eat what others ate. Travel by horseback. He wouldn't bear any arms, nor would he be allotted a caretaker or a servant. If by any chance the caravan came under attack from jungle bandits or wild beasts, only Avanti would be responsible for his safety. If, by chance, all of them got captured, Vishnupada was never to reveal the prince's true identity. If he did, he would lose his head, Avanti had warned him.

'Nod if you understand,' Avanti had whispered. Something about the girl had scared Vishnupada. He had bobbed his head, up and down, like a lamb.

'Now, turn around and tell the soldiers in the caravan that you have two additional guests, the son and daughter of a merchant from Kampilya,' Avanti had said.

Vishnupada had meekly made the announcement. After which, Avanti had spurred her horse and trotted along with Ajitha to the back of the caravan.

It was right then that he had made his first error.

'Bhima,' Vishnupada had said, addressing his favourite servant. 'I am going to Kampilya. And, so are you.'

'Forgive me, master, but why the sudden change of plans? You have not even packed your clothes,' Bhima had said, not trying to disguise his surprise from his master who was known to be a predictable man, in his personal life and especially, in his business life. 'Also, sire, your oxcart is not ready.'

Vishnupada had known what Bhima had been trying to tell him, with as much finesse as a man of his upbringing could summon—that Vishnupada's journey with the caravan, without due preparations, would be pure, unalloyed hell. Vishnupada would have to wear the same clothes he was wearing right now or borrow coarse clothes from others. That he would have to rest his back and bottom on a common oxcart, not one furnished with silk cushions and a soft bed. And that with no time to make special provisions, the merchant would have to eat the same food that servants and soldiers managed with. No fine meats, no special fruits.

Bhima knew his master of eleven years well. He knew about his love for rice soaked in ghee and of peacock meat flavoured with seven different spices. He knew that only the most succulent boar meat would meet the approval of the richest man in Mithila.

'I know what I am doing, fool,' Vishnupada had said, with gritted teeth. 'Send a rider home right now and ask him to bring a bagful of my clothes. Inform my wife that I am going away to Kampilya and won't be back for a month.'

Bhima had dispatched the rider with the instructions, pitying the welcome the poor man would get after he had informed his master's wife about the change in plans.

'Who *really* are the woman and the boy, sire? Are they the reason you have changed your mind?' Bhima had whispered.

*Clever little guy*, Vishnupada had thought. *Sometimes a little too clever.*

Vishnupada was tempted for a moment to spill the truth. He wanted to boast to Bhima that the Prince of Mithila had chosen to travel with their caravan. That if all went well, the king of Mithila would owe him one more favour—one Vishnupada planned to milk to its fullest potential someday. That there was a strong probability that the Prince of Mithila might reminisce later in life over the joy he had experienced travelling in a caravan owned by a very generous merchant from Mithila called Vishnupada. That maybe, someday, the prince might even appoint him as the chief revenue collector or the head of all trade guilds of Mithila. Or give him a thousand villages as a reward. *Maybe, maybe …*

He saw Bhima staring at him, eagerly awaiting an answer. At that moment, Vishnupada broke out of his reverie

'They are important people. But I can't say anything more,' Vishnupada had said, a little pompously. Standing behind Bhima, feeding a handful of grains to one of the horses, was one of the servants Bhima had hired. The tall one without any eyebrows.

*Was he listening in? But, what difference would that make*, Vishnupada had thought then.

Now, as he sat inside the oxcart, nursing his hurting back, all these thoughts came back to him. Suddenly, the oxcart came to a halt.

'It's almost time for lunch, master,' announced Bhima, poking his head into the cart. Vishnupada thought of the menu and groaned. Boiled beans, rice and the same old mango pickle.

*For the fourth damned day in a row.*

He staggered out of the oxcart and stretched. The archer woman was there too stretching her back. The prince was standing a few yards behind her, staring at her like he always did.

*A fine pair of brother and sister they make,* he thought. *Wonder what happens in their tent when the flaps are sealed tight.*

Right behind the prince was the tall servant without the eyebrows, lighting a fire. The fresh recruit, the one Bhima had hired the day before the caravan left Mithila. The one who had come at a bargain.

*What was his name again?* thought Vishnupada.

Something about the whole scene felt odd to Vishnupada. Something gnawed at the pit of his stomach.

But before he could give it further thought, his stomach growled with hunger. And all other concerns were forgotten.

It was time for lunch.

Resting under the cool shade of a peepal tree, Bhima watched the dozen men sitting in a circle, wolfing down rice and boiled vegetables, unmindful of the searing heat of the afternoon sun. The peanuts intrigued Bhima. That's what he called the men he had hired at the last minute in Mithila, though never to their faces.

Peanuts—nothing else described them better.

They were bald, clean-shaven hard men with no fat on their bodies. Each one of them looked like the other, just as one peanut was indistinguishable from the other. What made them all look so alike? Was it the complete absence of hair? Not even one of them had a wisp of hair on his chest, his back, or even on his eyebrows. Was it their shiny skin which was the colour of old rust? Was it the absence of fat on their bodies that made their bones, ears and noses stick out of their cheek-less faces?

*What made them look so alike?* wondered Bhima. Perhaps, it was the expression on their faces, their vacuous pleasant smiles and the look of servile obedience that made them look so alike. Like peas in a pod.

*It was as though they were not just happy to serve but born to serve,* thought Bhima, with a smirk. *Slaves by birth.*

For eight years, Bhima had run caravans for his master Vishnupada. And before that, for three years, he had done the same for his father. In all these years, he had mastered the art of extracting work from servants.

Treat them like bulls. Fill their bellies, massage their egos sometimes, and on the rare occasion give them a taste of the whip. Also, keep your expectations low. Irrespective of how well you paid them or how devoted they pretended to be, hired help invariably fell short of what they were paid to do.

*Unlike the peanuts.*

Ask them to cut down a mountain and they were likely to reply, 'Just one, master?' Pass a command and it was done before the words rolled off the tongue.

They woke up before everyone else and toiled gladly even after the sun died in the western sky. They yoked the bulls, fed and massaged the horses, cleaned the oxcarts—all of it with smiles on their faces. Every night, they even washed the caked dirt off the wheels of oxcarts, something they were not even paid for. The peanuts were glad to cook an extra meal for a hungry person in the middle of the night or massage a soldier's aching back, without expecting an extra coin or even a word of appreciation. At times, Bhima wondered if they ever slept.

*Just for a few bags of rice and a journey back to Kampilya.*

Yet, for all their hard work and dedication, they were a queer bunch. They did small things, everyday things, so differently. They never slept inside a tent. Even on nights when the skies opened or when the wind turned cold, they would sleep under the open skies, staring at the moon and stars above, with their large unblinking eyes.

*It was as though they were in love with the skies … as though the stars spoke to them.*

They weren't afraid of the dark or of the terrors it held. Most others, even the armed soldiers, rarely ventured out of the camp after sunset and stayed close to the safety of the fires, till daylight. They held their bursting bladders and soma-induced vomit all night, until the first rays of the sun hit the top of trees.

Not the peanuts. Bhima had seen them venture into the dark woods even when the owls screeched in the dead of the night, without even a torch in their hands. For a while, he had even wondered if they could see in the dark. But the peanuts did not possess eyes that glowed like flying foxes and mountain cats, creatures to whom the depths of the night seemed like daylight.

But the peanuts shared something else with the mountain cats. They walked around as stealthily as cats. More than once, Bhima had been startled out of his wits when one of them had sneaked up behind him, only to serve him a tumbler of soma. It was almost as though they had padded feet.

*Strange, strange men,* Bhima had thought.

Off all the freakish folks Bhima had seen in his life while leading caravans across the sixteen mahajanapadas, the peanuts were amongst the strangest. He had seen tribes in the valleys beyond Takshashila where men bedded their mothers-in-law as well as their daughters. He had met men who ate fried worms and snake head pickles in the hills south of Tamralipti. He knew of kingdoms that sacrificed their entire stable of horses when their chieftain died. And yet the peanuts had to be amongst the strangest.

*Not the strangest, but amongst the strangest.*

Which is why, on the fifth day, resting under the leafy shade of that peepal tree in the outskirts of a village called Balabara, Bhima wondered how the peanuts would behave once the caravan entered the ancient forest of Naimisha.

Even the sanest of men went a little batty in the woods of Naimisha. Bhima remembered the tales his grandmother had told him about the forest—of men getting lost and becoming delirious, of there being strange birds and beasts few men had seen before and of the first men who had lived in the mountains of the forest.

Naimisha spooked Bhima. The trees of Naimisha were tall and grew so close to each other that sunlight rarely touched the moist, moss-covered soil. Two moody rivers crisscrossed the jungle, changing path so often and so fast that few knew where they would be flowing the next day.

But unlike any other jungle, the strangest part about Naimisha was the silence. A brooding, everlasting silence. It was the kind of silence that played games with the minds of men. The laughter of a man would echo and bounce around the forest, only to sound like the vile snigger of an evil giant. A twig snapping would sound like the crack of a whip. A screech of an owl would sound like the laughter of an evil witch. Even the oxen and horses seemed to sense the unease of the woods and became quieter. Naimisha was the stealer of sleep and destroyer of sanity.

*And I am going into the forest with the strangest of men*, thought Bhima, staring at one of the peanuts whispering into the ear of an ox, stroking its neck. The ox seemed to like it and shook its neck vigorously. The bell around its neck tinkled.

Perhaps the peanut felt someone's gaze on him, because he turned around and met Bhima's gaze. Then he smiled. It was a broad smile, and Bhima shivered.

*What is it about these freaks?*

The peanut bowed low again and continued stroking the ox, whispering in its ear.

Vishnupada made his second mistake that very evening.

It happened in the village Balabara, located at the edge of the silent forest of Naimisha. Once upon a time, Balabara had been a part of the jungle, a small settlement of the first men. What life in this ancient settlement had been like or who those first men were, nobody knew. It was all a long, long time ago.

All that anyone knew about the history of this place was that about fifty summers ago, Simhamukha the Conqueror had arrived here with his archers, spearmen and elephants, and razed the woods down to establish the village. He had named it Balabara, after a friend of his who had died in battle. Nobody knew what happened to the first men who had lived there. Perhaps they had moved deeper into the forest, perhaps they had been slaughtered. They had just melted away from time and history, like dew drops in the sunlight.

Either way, the village of Balabara was the last outpost where caravans usually camped before entering the eerie desolation of Naimisha. They all knew that in Naimisha, they would have to face a heavy silence that would last three days and nights, a silence that would seep into the minds of men and oxen alike, one they would have to endure before they could reach the outskirts of Kampilya. So, Balabara was the one place where all rules of the caravan were usually broken. Men drank and ate to their heart's fill. They gambled, fought and whored around for one night. It was almost as if they did not expect to come out alive at the other end of the forest. As a result, Balabara was outrageously prosperous, for a village on the edge of a forest.

It had two small inns and one large brothel. The men of Balabara were fat and perfumed, the women thick-thighed and buxom. The village's wine, brewed from honey and flowers, was sweet. Not as sweet as the wine that was sold in the markets of Mithila or Kashi or Takshashila, but better than the sour, spoiling hooch that the caravans carried in their sealed pots.

But before the drinking and whoring began, the men of the caravan had one last thing to do—one last prayer, one last propitiation, one last sacrifice.

At the northern end of Balabara lay its only spiritual attraction. A temple of Agni with a pond in its courtyard. The temple itself wasn't much to look at. A flat solid structure with two dozen stone pillars that supported a thatched roof over the courtyard. The courtyard led to a small, smoky sanctum where a fire burnt day and night. It was like every other Agni temple in the sixteen kingdoms.

The pond was unlike any other. It bubbled and boiled. Strange odours emanated from its frothing waters. Once upon a time, the first men had believed that a dip in the pond could cure men of their aches and pains. But not the brahmans of Balabara. For them, the boiling water had always been sacred, a testament to the power of the god of fire, Agni, who was worshipped inside the sanctum.

A brahman sat at the edge of the pond, chanting mantras and tossing flowers. Vishnupada stood next to him, hands folded, eyes closed, as always praying deeply for the priest to end his rituals soon. His stiff back was killing him and he couldn't wait to sleep on a soft bed in the inn that Bhima had arranged for the night.

Vishnupada opened his eyes and looked at his fellow travellers. Beside him sat the three aged brahmans, bent and wrinkled, who had joined the caravan from Mithila. They were headed to Kampilya and from there on to the grammar school in Takshashila in another caravan. As usual, they hadn't paid for their journey in either copper or kind.

Behind the brahmans sat a dozen merchants, who seemed to be in as much agony as Vishnupada. Some of them were boys, too young to have a beard, barely four or five years older than his son. This was their first caravan journey. Vishnupada was willing to wager half of his wealth that they knew all about the famous brothel of Balabara and its buxom courtesans.

*The things that make the young feel alive!*

The thought made him smile. Seated among these merchants was the prince. Despite his best attempts to look like a merchant, Ajitha stood out. Everything about him, from the way he walked to the ease with which he mounted a horse, screamed out that he was a warrior. Then, there was the way the prince held his head. The chin rarely pointed towards the earth and his eyes looked right above the heads of men. That gaze, if nothing else, screamed of his noble birth.

Warrior. Royalty. Prince.

Vishnupada wondered if others had observed as much as he had.

*So much for travelling incognito.*

Vishnupada had badly wanted to talk to the prince during their travels. To make sure he had slept well, eaten well, bathed well. To make sure that the prince remembered him and his hospitality for years to come. But that wretched woman was always with the prince, circling around him like a vulture circling around a dying animal. For three weeks, he had waited for an opportunity to talk to the prince alone and he hadn't been given one yet. Vishnupada scanned the crowd behind him, for the girl. He couldn't spot her. Maybe she was hanging around with the soldiers outside the temple guarding the caravan.

This was his opportunity. He had to find a way. But it would be an inauspicious omen if he got up in the middle of a sacrifice. Not to mention extremely conspicuous. Everyone would notice, and they would gossip. That girl would hear about it too. A trickle of sweat ran down Vishnupada's forehead.

*Feisty little fox*, thought Vishnupada. He did not like the way she spoke to him. Or looked at him. It was as though she thought he was a servant or a shudra, not one of the richest men in Mithila.

The brahman droned on with his incantations. More flowers were tossed into the boiling pond. Vishnupada closed his eyes and time slipped by like the ghee the brahman was pouring into the fire.

'Let the master of the sacrifice, the owner of the ritual, the one to whom all benefits shall accrue step forward,' the priest said eventually.

Vishnupada opened his eyes, realising that he had fallen asleep for a while, standing. The priest was looking at him.

And, then, a thought struck him. He looked at the crowd again. The prince was there, the girl wasn't.

Vishnupada bent down and whispered into the brahman's ear. 'I want that boy to be the master of this sacrifice,' said Vishnupada, pointing a finger at Ajitha.

The priest looked surprised. This was unusual.

'Is he your son?' the priest whispered.

'No, just do what I say,' whispered Vishnupada. 'I will pay you more.'

For a moment, the brahman's eyes had flashed as if he were angry at that suggestion. But then greed had triumphed, as Vishnupada knew it would.

The brahman whispered back again, 'Which boy? The one who looks like a warrior?'

*So, they all suspect.*

'He is a merchant, not a warrior. Call him forward,' said Vishnupada.

The brahman straightened and waved his hand at Ajitha. 'You … yes, you boy. The one next to the pillar. Come here.'

Vishnupada wanted to pinch the stupid priest's ears.

*That is not the way you address the Prince of Mithila.*

Everyone in the crowd turned around to look at Ajitha, their eyes widening in surprise. A murmur ran through them. Ajitha got up and walked hesitantly towards the sacrificial fire. Vishnupada scanned the crowd nervously. The girl still wasn't there. He welcomed Ajitha with folded hands.

'Now, what's your name, boy?' asked the priest.

Ajitha paused for a moment. He could hear Aacharya Gurukripa's voice in his head.

*A man who lies in the presence of gods or his parents is no man at all.*

And yet, he could not tell the priest his name.

*He needn't mention his full name Ajitha Vikrama Shaurya,* he thought.

'Ajitha,' said the prince.

'Your father's name?'

'Simha.'

'Your gotra?'

'Kashyapa.'

The priest began saying the mantras again. He handed Ajitha a fistful of rice and a cup of ghee. Ajitha opened his fist over the fire, which crackled and burnt when the rice fell in it. Then, he poured the ghee.

Vishnupada grinned at the prince. Ajitha stared back at him, stony-faced.

Outside the temple, a bald man with no eyebrows watched the ceremony with interest. When it was over, he walked over to the stream outside Balabara where his brothers were bathing the oxen. He looked around to make sure there was nobody listening, and said, 'Moon brothers! Something strange has happened. I think we have a very interesting travelling companion.'

# 22. Naimisha

Avanti watched as the bald, hairless men sat in a circle, animatedly talking to each other. For three weeks, she had observed them with mounting curiosity. They were unusual men. Some might even say strange. They bowed, smiled, served and aimed to please all the time. And yet, there was something odd about them that she couldn't quite put a finger on. Like an itch in the middle of one's back that one can't quite reach, the feeling rankled her.

'Strange men, aren't they?' asked Ajitha. The prince was standing behind her, leaning against the wooden door of the temple.

The sun had almost set and the last rays of the sun shone on the temple, painting everything around them in a bright shade of orange. In the dying light of the sun, the boy looked different. The softness of his cheeks had blurred, while his soulful eyes looked sunken and deep-set. He looked like the man he would become in a few more years.

*Rugged and almost handsome,* thought Avanti.

'What's that garland around your neck?' she asked. A small handwoven garland of red-petalled flowers rested around the boy's neck.

'Well, the merchant asked me to participate in the ritual,' said Ajitha.

'Why aren't the others wearing it?' asked Avanti.

Ajitha stayed silent for a moment. He did not like where this conversation was going.

'Because I was singled out,' he finally said.

'Idiot,' spat Avanti, her eyes turning dark with anger. 'I turn my eyes away for one minute and he does this. I should chop off his fingers for this.'

'Don't. He is just trying to be nice,' said Ajitha.

'I know kings and princelings love flattery. But flatterers can get you killed,' said Avanti. 'And it's my duty to ensure that you don't end up with a knife in your back.'

'I can take care of myself,' said Ajitha, blood rushing to his face.

'Oh. Like you did just now, by revealing to everybody that you are not one of them?' asked Avanti, bitterly. 'I turn my attention away for one moment ... just one moment and you do this—'

Ajitha felt his temper rising.

'If you care so much about your duty, my lady ...' said Ajitha, '... you should have been with me inside the temple, instead of enjoying the breeze outside.'

They stared at each other for a few moments, eyes locked, nostrils flaring. Much later, Avanti would always think of this moment with a pang of regret.

'Yes, my prince,' she hissed. 'You are right. I should have been there. I forgot I was protecting a boy *not a man*.'

She knew she had crossed a line, the moment the words came out of her mouth. Ajitha turned away from her and stormed towards the village where a large tent was being set up for the evening's festivities.

Avanti sighed and followed the prince. They did not speak till the moon rose high in the sky, when they eventually went back to their tent.

The moon hung low over the village, a large white orb with a dark spot in the middle, like a large pearl with a stain at its heart. They lay in their beds, close enough to hear each other breath but far enough that they couldn't touch each other even with outstretched arms. A deep chasm of silence divided them.

The sounds of festivities coming from the village—peals

of drunken laughter, the steady thumping of a drum, the occasional sound of a man retching, the giggle of a woman—trickled in through the open flap of their tent. A gentle breeze wafted in and toyed with the flame of the lantern kept at the corner of the tent. The flame threatened to die but resolutely held on.

They hadn't spoken a word all night. Avanti had followed the prince all around the village. But he had refused to acknowledge her presence, much less look in her direction. He had gone from one tent to another, watching the festivities with expressionless eyes, till he entered the one where soma was being sold. From the face he had made while he swallowing the drink, Avanti could tell that the prince wasn't too fond of soma.

But a broken young heart and a bruised ego craves for the madness and solace that only soma can induce. So, the prince drank glass after glass till his eyes turned red and his purse became empty. An ageing courtesan, a large woman whose pendulous breasts looked like they had fed several infants, approached the prince and sat on his lap.

That was the first time that evening that Prince Ajitha looked at Avanti. He gazed across the room, straight at her, as though he had always been aware of her watchful gaze. He smiled, a drunken slobbering smile that was full of sadness, before he waved the courtesan away. The courtesan walked away, her large hips swinging, but not before she grabbed at the prince's crotch and whispered something in his ear.

The prince had laughed, risen from his chair unsteadily and staggered out of the tent. Avanti followed him back to their tent where he had collapsed into his bed.

And now, they lay in the darkness, listening to each other breath.

'Y-you dislike me, don't you?' asked Ajitha.

Avanti did not answer, pretending to be asleep.

'I know you are awake. So, answer me, woman!' he said. 'W-why? Why do you dislike me?'

'I don't dislike you.'

'But you don't like me either.'

For a moment, she thought of telling the boy about the night she had spent with his brother in that brothel in Mithila. But she knew he was drunk and hurting already.

*He is just a boy, in love for the first time. I should be kind to him,* Avanti thought.

'I am here to do my duty. How I feel about you doesn't matter,' she said flatly, hoping that the conversation would end there, and that he would go to sleep and let her sleep too.

Instead, Ajitha laughed, a low chuckle.

'And people think we have it all … kings and princes. Look at us, my mother is a widow who never speaks. My brother is a widower who drinks to drown the memories of his dead wife. And me, the good boy, struggling to woo the woman I love—'

Ajitha stopped abruptly. Outside, the thumping of the drum had also stopped. A woman laughed raucously. A man shushed her to silence. She giggled.

The silence inside the tent seemed to drag on and last forever, like the memory of a long-gone friend.

'My prince, your time for love will come,' said Avanti softly. 'I am just not the one.'

'And, why is that, Avanti?' asked Ajitha.

'That is a story for another time, my prince. We have a long and perilous journey starting tomorrow morning. And you need to rest,' said Avanti, before turning down the wick of the lantern next to her and dousing the room in inky darkness.

The courtesan had a delicious mouth. A warm tasty mouth that reeked of cloves and soma. Bhima wanted to bury his cold nose into her mouth and leave it there.

'Can you … suck my nose, dear?' Bhima asked, rubbing on his nose. Then, he burst out laughing at the absurdity of his own question. His laughter sounded distant and alien to him.

'I can suck on something else,' said the courtesan coquettishly, wrapping her arms around his chest, pressing her big lumpy warm breasts against his face.

She was a whole hand taller than him and built like an oak tree. Bhima had always liked his women tall and wholesome. This one was big breasted, round bellied with hips that had rings of flesh that ran around the body like serpents crawling up a tree. The rings were nice to hold on to while making love and kept you warm in bed while you slept.

They made their way to an oxcart, laughing, kneading and prodding each other. Once inside, more giggling and prodding followed. After they were done, they slept for an hour in a tight embrace, drenched in sweat, inside the cramped confines of an oxcart. When he opened his eyes next, she was already awake. He gave her one silver coin which was the bargain they had struck and an extra one as a reward for her pleasing nature.

She pressed the coin to her lips and then, kissed him on his chest. They made promises to see each other whenever he passed through Balabara next. Both knew that the promises, like most made after vigorous love making, were empty.

Perhaps they would meet again. Perhaps, they would not. No guarantees.

*Even if we met again, would we remember this cool night with the large moon in the sky?* Bhima thought, as he watched the woman waddle away, her ample buttocks swinging from side to side.

He tied his dhoti and staggered towards the camp where the tents were pitched. A few soldiers had passed out around the dying fires, which glowed dully in the dark. Most of the soldiers were inside their tents, fast asleep.

He stood there for a second, taking in the scene. A dozen tents, pale and glowing in the moonlight, flapped and moved in the cool breeze blowing from the jungle. He turned around to stare at the forest.

*Naimisha.*

Tall trees stood in the dark, so close to each other that he wondered if even air could pass in between. The forest seemed to be still, absolutely still, as though it were a boulder or a corpse.

*Naimisha. The killer of sanity. The enemy of life. Or was it the other way around?*

A shiver ran down his spine. Bhima spat on the ground and walked towards the tent he shared with a dozen other men. Dew was starting to fall and the grass under his feet was wet, cold and soggy.

His tent lay ahead, beyond the tents of his master and the other merchants who had all paid extra for their exclusive living quarters. He walked past them silently, like a ghost in the darkness.

In the next moment, his heart stopped. Something moved. Something crawled. On its fours. In the darkness. Then, he caught its silhouette in the moonlight. It turned. And looked right at him.

The eyes gleamed. It wasn't a creature. It was a man. A man with no hair on his face. A man at the edge of a tent, a tent in which the young merchant and the woman from Mithila slept.

*It is one of the peanuts.*

Bhima opened his mouth to shout. But suddenly, he heard the grass rustle behind him. Instinctively, he felt the hair on the back of his neck rise. Just as he turned his head to look behind him, a hand snaked around his neck. It was a thin hand, almost muscle-less, but strong. It was choking him, slowly breaking his neck. He kicked, struggled and tried to scream. But not a sound came from his throat. Just a croak, like a frog being swallowed whole by a snake.

Bhima was now on the ground, his feet kicking desperately on the wet soil. His eyesight was blurring. The last thing he saw while he was being dragged away was the crawling man with gleaming eyes ahead of him, crouched on the ground next to the tent.

The peanut was smiling while he listened to what was happening inside.

Dawn broke over the camp abruptly. One moment it was dark. Crickets chirped, dew fell lazily and fireflies glowed. And then, it was light. Birds sang. The dew on the leaves dried. And the sun appeared from behind the clouds as though it was an errant boy revealing himself in a game of hide and seek.

The first to wake up were the industrious and the sober, the only ones who had not consumed soma the night before. The peanuts—as Bhima called them, or Moon Brothers, as they called themselves—woke up first and began their daily labours in earnest. They bathed the oxen, brushed and fed them before yoking them.

A few soldiers woke up next, stirred by the smell of their own vomit and stale breath. Some rushed out of their tents and threw up some more. A few emptied the tumblers lying next to their beds for the last dregs of soma, hoping to silence the painful throbbing that echoed inside their heads.

The brahmans of the caravan made their way to the pond at the far end of Balabara for a bath and to offer their morning prayers at the temple of Agni.

Vishnupada woke up well after dawn. He stared at the undulating roof of his tent for a while, before it struck him that it was pale, the colour of wheat. It was bright outside.

*So much time wasted!*

He threw back the sheets he had covered himself with and cursed Bhima. He knew the fool was fond of whores and soma. Who wasn't? But Bhima was an early riser and it was his job to wake his master up.

*The fool must be fast asleep, his face buried between the thighs of some flea infested whore,* thought Vishnupada. *Servants are like bulls. Sometimes you have to stroke their ego, other times you have to whip them.*

Vishnupada stomped out of his tent, cursing under his breath. One of the bald, hairless men was waiting outside.

'Sire,' he said.

'Not now,' snapped Vishnupada and walked away.

The bald man followed him.

'Sire, I have bad news.'

Vishnupada stopped and looked at the bald man.

'What is it?'

'Sire, one of the oxcarts is … missing.'

Vishnupada shook his head from side to side, in disbelief.

'Missing … missing? What do you mean *missing*?'

'It's gone, sire.'

'What do you mean … *gone*?'

'Sire, as you know we have fifty carts. And a hundred and ten oxen. Two for each cart. That's a hundred oxen. And ten spare oxen, just in case some of the others fall ill.'

'I know that, you fool. It's my caravan. Tell me what has happened!'

The bald man looked worried, almost afraid. He wiped at his forehead which was drenched in sweat.

'I was yoking the oxen to the carts when I noticed that we had only eight extra bulls, instead of ten. And one cart was missing when I checked. It seems someone has driven away with one cart and an extra pair of oxen.'

'Which cart is missing? Do you know?'

'I don't, master.'

'Call Bhima right now. You know him, don't you? The one with the curly hair who makes my food.'

'Sire, that is the other thing. Master Bhima is missing too.'

For a moment, Vishnupada gaped at the bald man, his mouth wide open.

*That ungrateful wretch. The worm has stolen from me after all these years. The bastard*—thought Vishnupada.

'Get me four soldiers, preferably those whose eyes are not blood red with soma,' said Vishnupada. 'NOW!' he yelled. The bald man ran towards the tents where the soldiers lived.

Vishnupada stared at the running man with mounting fury.

*I am going to get that thief Bhima. I am going to drag him in chains through Naimisha and when I get to Mithila, I am going to bribe an official to get his hand chopped off.*

It was then that the thought struck him. He had only twenty soldiers accompanying the caravan. If he set four of those hounds after Bhima, he would have to enter Naimisha a few soldiers short. That was a bad idea, especially since the prince was also with him.

What if bandits attacked? What if the caravan encountered a herd of mad elephants?

The thought sobered Vishnupada. But, in the next moment, anger seized him again. He couldn't let that wretch Bhima get away. What sort of a world would it be if servants got away scot-free after stealing from their masters? No, he would have to do something. He would make an example of Bhima. Treachery has a price. Bhima would have to pay for his sins.

*I will dip the ungrateful wretch's hands in boiling oil before chopping them off myself. No, I will whip his back till his skin comes off and then rub salt on it. I will bribe the judge in the nearest town to blind him and throw him off a cliff.*

Vishnupada paced up and down chewing on his fingernails till they turned raw and bloody. When the soldiers arrived with the bald man, Vishnupada told them what had happened and gave them a purse full of coins.

'Hunt this thief down,' said Vishnupada. 'And hold him here until I come back in a fortnight. I want him alive. He couldn't have gone far.'

An hour later, the caravan started on its journey through Naimisha. It was four soldiers short.

That was Vishnupada's third mistake.

But it was not his biggest error. That was yet to come.

The caravan entered Naimisha a few hours after daybreak, a long slow line of oxcarts, trundling one after the other. From a distance, the caravan resembled a line of ants, scurrying along, hauling morsels of food on their heads. Each ant sticking close to another.

Naimisha did that to men and caravans. Men and oxcarts stuck close to each other as a general feeling of unease and fear hung over the caravan. Nobody knew why. Perhaps it was all the bedtime stories the men and the women in the caravan had heard in their childhoods. Of the first men who had lived in the jungle and of their strange customs and gods, of beasts that roamed freely feasting on the flesh of men and children. Perhaps it was the famed silence of Naimisha, the quiet forest, the breaker of sanity, the feaster of souls.

For the next two nights and three days, the caravan would have to endure the silence of Naimisha until it reached the safe refuge of Kampilya. To get there, the caravan would have to travel along the greatest road in the sixteen mahajanapadas. A road that was made with rock and limestone but watered with the blood of men slaughtered by Simhamukha the Conqueror.

When the road had been built forty summers ago, countless men died of snakebites and scorpion stings. Tigers had become fat and slow, feasting on the flesh of soldiers and stone breakers. And so, even though the maps of Mithila called the road, Simhamukha's Path, the caravans had another name for it, Rakhta Marga—the blood-soaked road.

Vishnupada sat on his horse, sour faced, looking at the curving road that led into Naimisha. Ahead of him, were two soldiers on horseback. Both had their swords unsheathed. Behind Vishnupada came the long line of carts. Soldiers rode on horseback up and down the length of the caravan, keeping their eyes peeled.

The smiles and the laughter were gone. All Vishnupada could see were tense faces, clenched jaws and unsheathed swords. He turned around to scan the length of the caravan for the two faces he wanted to see. The girl and the prince.

Their faces were gaunt and sullen. The girl caught his gaze and held it. It had the same steely expression as before. Vishnupada hated her, from the bottom of his heart. At that moment, he really wished he had never gone to the palace, never met either the prince or this angry girl or undertaken this silly journey with them.

All he longed for was the comfort of his home, for the reassurance that counting his coins gave him, for the familiar stench of the markets of Mithila, for the sight of his chubby son, for the squawking of ducks at his home, for the familiar sight of Bhima waiting for him outside his home ...

*Bhima, you bastard,* thought Vishnupada.

The girl was still staring at Vishnupada. He turned his eyes away and looked at the road ahead.

Avanti watched as the merchant broke eye contact with her. Something was wrong. She could feel it in the way the merchant had looked at her. It wasn't his usual look of dislike mixed with fear. That was a feeling she was used to. Weak men often felt that way about her. This was something else. This was *regret.*

Beside her, Ajitha sat on his horse, still recovering from his soma-drinking session of last night. He looked up and down the caravan as if something wasn't right.

'What's wrong?' asked Avanti.

'How many soldiers did we have in the caravan when we left Mithila?'

'About 20,' said Avanti.

'I can see only sixteen right now,' said Ajitha.

'That's strange,' said Avanti. 'Perhaps some of them are still asleep inside the oxcarts, recovering from soma ... just like you, my prince.'

'Perhaps,' said Ajitha and smiled.

# 23. Nila

Trivikrama sat on his throne and watched as king after king, chieftain after chieftain, general after general, courtier after courtier, bowed low, mouthed insincere words of praise, showed off their exotic gifts, received theirs in return, bowed again and walked away.

It was his coronation day. The twelfth one. As was custom, it was an apt occasion to remind everyone who the Lord of Mithila and the most powerful man in the sixteen mahajanapadas was. And so, the procession of the ruled over and the vanquished began in the grand hall of Mithila. The kings and chieftains whom his father had defeated bowed their heads low. The generals bowed even lower. The courtiers couldn't have bowed any lower, even if they had tried.

And yet, despite all this bowing and flowery flow of flattery, Trivikrama felt alone in the great hall of Mithila. He missed his brother, especially his brashness, his insolence, his sarcasm. More than anything else, he missed his brother's lopsided smile that mocked, taunted and on occasion, even infuriated Trivikrama. Right then, Trivikrama missed that smile a lot. He was tired of being around men in the palace who scraped, crawled, fawned and praised him for no reason at all. None of them, with the exception of his brother and Aacharya Gurukripa, ever looked him in the eye. And Aacharya Gurukripa, God bless his soul, was not his friend. He was his teacher.

*The palace feels like … a basket full of snakes*, thought Trivikrama. The thought brought back an old memory.

Back when he had been a boy, Trivikrama had seen a trickster from Vanga perform a ruse in the great hall. He had opened a basket and dropped one venomous snake after the other into it. The snakes had writhed and lashed at each other as they were being put into the basket. The trickster had closed the basket and shaken it hard. The angry hisses of the snakes had filled the hall.

The trickster had made a long speech about how dangerous the snakes could be and how angry they were. Then, with great ceremony, he had carved a small hole in the basket, rolled up his sleeves and thrust his hand inside. He kept it there for a moment or two. The audience gasped. Women averted their eyes in terror. But the trickster had kept his hand inside and had talked to the crowd effortlessly.

Eventually, he had pulled his hand out. In his hand was a cobra, the most dangerous of all snakes. He tapped on it. It hissed and spat. The trickster laughed and deposited the cobra into another basket. Then, one by one, he pulled each snake out of the basket through that hole, much to the delight and horror of the court, who had clapped and cheered.

Later that night, Trivikrama had called the trickster to his chambers for an audience. After giving the trickster a purse of silver, Trivikrama had asked him what the secret to the trick was.

'Was that some kind of mind trick you played on all of us?' Trivikrama had asked. 'Did you dull our collective minds to make us see only what you wanted us to see?'

'No, my king. I did no such thing,' said the trickster. 'I did not sedate your minds. I sedated the snakes. The basket had herbs that put them to sleep. Why sedate men when you can sedate the snakes?'

*The problem is,* thought Trivikrama now, looking at the assembly of fawning courtiers, with their disingenuous smiles, *that these snakes are not sedated. They are writhing, crawling, waiting to bite, eager to pump their venom into my flesh and draw blood.*

Trivikrama was the one who seemed to be sedated, he was the one in a stupor, and he knew it. A few months ago, he would drink sometimes to remember his wife and sometimes to forget her. Now, he did not even know why he drank soma. It was as though soma was his only friend. His last friend. The only one that listened to the echoes of his lonely heart.

Sitting on his throne, the king of Mithila was well aware of who he was.

King. Ruler of sixteen kingdoms. Mourning widower. Addict.

His throat felt parched and he longed for the sour taste of soma, for the numbness it brought along with it, for the warm feeling it filled his body with, and for the temporary lust for life it gave him with each dreg.

After the court was done, he retired to the ivory chamber and poured himself a glass of soma. By the time Aacharya Gurukripa walked in, he had finished his third tumbler. Gurukripa looked pointedly at the tumbler but said nothing.

'How are the courtiers dealing with Ajitha's absence at the ceremony?' asked Trivikrama, toying with his glass.

'There is some gossip. But most are buying the story that the prince is unwell and has been advised by Chavuka to be confined to his chambers,' said Gurukripa. 'Chavuka, of course, has been sworn to secrecy. I think he is holding up his end of the promise.'

'What else? Any word about my brother?'

'I got a pigeon that Avanti dispatched from a town called Samhira. It was sent two days ago. All is well. The prince has taken well to the caravan. He is hale and hearty. Maybe a little bored,' said Gurukripa, with a smile.

'I warned him,' said Trivikrama, smiling. *I hope he is enjoying squatting behind bushes.* 'Where would they be now, Aacharya-ji?'

'The last leg of their journey, my king,' said Gurukripa. 'The most perilous stretch of it all. This morning they would have entered the forest of Naimisha.'

Trivikrama said nothing, just downed his glass and then filled it again to the brim.

Nila walked into the Queen Mother's chamber and knew immediately that the queen was in a bad mood.

*A mood most foul.*

The queen was at her usual station, behind a low table, seated cross-legged on the floor, doing what she usually did. She silently scribbled away on a piece of parchment. Nothing about the scene was unusual. Everything was where it was supposed to be. The inkpot sat on a table on the right-hand side of the queen. The quill was being worked furiously, scratching away on the surface of the dried palmyra parchment.

The queen's head was bowed, eyebrows drawn together and back bent. As always, she hadn't said a word when Nila had entered. So, how did the eunuch know the queen was in a mood most foul?

The eunuch chewed on the question as she bowed low before the queen. The answer dropped like a spreading bloodstain on a white cotton cloth.

It was the lack of an acknowledgement. Usually, when Nila entered the room, the queen gently nodded her head at her, never looking up from her precious parchments. The nod was the queen's way of acknowledging the presence of another human being in front of her. A gentle bob of the head, which most people wouldn't catch. But Nila had seen it several times and understood its significance.

Today, the queen hadn't nodded. Hence, a mood most foul.

Nila straightened and waited for the queen to finish her writing. For some reason, the queen kept on writing. She wrote more furiously than usual. Her knuckles had turned white as if she was gripping the quill with a feral anger. In the dead silence of the room, the quill's rasping sound, as it tore its way into the parchment, sounded deafeningly loud.

*What does she write about?*

The queen had become even more withdrawn since Prince Ajitha's departure. She ate even more sparsely, her eyes looked gaunt and the cheekbones on her emaciated face stuck out like knobs of mushrooms.

At that moment, Nila, half man, half woman, felt nothing but pity for the Queen Mother. What horrors or secrets did this lady of noble birth have in her head that prevented her from talking to any other human being, including her own sons? What made her live like a hermit when everything around her was full of richness and opulence? What had made Madhusmita, once the most beautiful woman in the sixteen kingdoms, whose beauty poets sang about and whose voluptuous body sculptors loved carving, become this pitiable bag of bones?

What makes a woman stick to a vow of silence even when her elder son, mad with grief at the funeral of his wife and child, weeps like a baby? Madhusmita hadn't shed a tear or even observed a period of mourning. How could she have mourned? She lived like a vagabond. After the funeral, she had just come back to the chambers and continued scribbling.

And yet, here she is. In a foul mood, because her youngest child was venturing into a jungle that was full of peril and stalking death.

Nila was so lost in her contemplation that she did not realise the queen had finished writing and was now staring at her with hollow eyes.

'Forgive me, my queen,' said Nila, bowing again. 'The prince and the caravan would have entered the forest of Naimisha by now. In three more days, they will be in Kampilya.'

*Safely,* Nila wanted to add but kept quiet.

'Also, my queen. There is a rumour spreading across the provinces. About a creature they call Ardhamukha. Stories of his terror are spreading. Some call him the slayer of brahmans. Some of the stories seem to be entirely made up. But, either way, mobs of men are beating up cripples and men with deformed faces. I heard that in Kasi, a man who had served in the army of Mithila, whose face had been disfigured in battle, was beaten to death. The king has called for strict punishment for his killers, but how does one punish a mob, a crowd? Who does he punish?'

The queen waved her hand impatiently, as though she did not want to hear any more of this.

Nila kept quiet. The queen picked up her stack of parchments and tied them together. She got up slowly, using her thin arms to lift the weight of her frail body off the ground.

A parchment which was loose fell away from the stack she was carrying under her armpits. A cool gust of wind blowing in from the courtyard outside, made the parchment fly across the room, twirling like a falling leaf, making it land at Nila's feet. The eunuch looked towards the queen for a moment before bending down to pick up the parchment. The parchment was face down but Nila could see the red ink that the queen used seeping onto the back of the parchment.

For a moment, curiosity overtook Nila. All the eunuch wanted to do was flip the parchment and read what was written on the other side. What did the queen write about? What was written on the other side? Was it the name of some god? Was it the name of the queen's dead husband whom she had loved so dearly?

*One quick glance. One moment.*

Nila picked up the parchment with her fingers and was about to turn it over, when she felt the hands of the queen on her wrist. The fingers were cold, thin and bony. But the grip was vice-like.

A grip that said only one word: *Don't.*

Nila looked up and saw the queen's eyes burning into hers. The eunuch let go of the parchment. The queen bent down, picked it up and without a word, walked away.

Nila stood there for a while, her body trembling, before she bowed again to the gaunt disappearing figure of the Queen Mother.

# 24. Naimisha's Mysteries

With every passing day, Ajiva's dreams were growing stranger. But he was no longer afraid of them. He did not toss and turn the way he used to; he no longer woke up bathed in cold sweat. He just observed them like a man watching a snake charmer play a strange tune, making a cobra dance.

They were no longer nightmares; they were just dreams—strange dreams.

Tonight, he dreamt of the twin snakes again. They were

writhing and crawling. It seemed as if they were becoming stronger. He could feel the black venom coursing through their blood. Their fangs were growing too. They crawled over each other, enjoying the pleasure of the cold scales on each other's body.

And then, one of them turned and looked straight at Ajiva. The dark beady eyes of the snake felt like blazing embers of fire burning into his consciousness. He did not look away. He stared back. The snake hissed, its fangs bared. The forked tongue quivered.

For a moment, Ajiva felt fear. Then, his eyes opened.

It was dark. The fire had died. The boy was fast asleep. The jungle was quiet. So quiet he could hear his heart thumping against his chest. So quiet that if he stopped breathing, he was sure he would be able to hear his blood move through his veins.

A twig snapped nearby. He heard the deep-throated growl before he saw the beast. Thick fur, a little taller than a dog. Its eyes glowed in the dark.

*Wolf.*

Ajiva knew wolves didn't hunt alone. They were always in a pack, part of a family. More of them were around, he just couldn't see them. It was dark and the bushes around him were thick. But they were there, he could sense them. Waiting, sniffing in the dark, smelling their prey.

Ajiva glanced at the bow and quiver of arrows lying next to him. He placed his arm on the bow. And then, he heard another growl. This one had come from right behind him. The boy stirred and mumbled, still lost in deep slumber.

*If I shoot an arrow at one, the others will go for the boy.*

The wolf right ahead of him stepped out of the bush. The tongue was lolling. Saliva dripped from its pink mouth. He was clearly the leader of the pack. The one who would pounce first. The she-wolf.

The wolf took a step forward and crouched.

*Any moment now.*

Ajiva slowly rose to his feet, bow in hand, arrow placed on the string, his breathing dead even. From the corner of his eye, he spotted another wolf emerge from the darkness. They were waiting for the cue from their leader.

The next moment, the sash around his stomach fell away, exposing his wound. Blood, pus and maggots.

The she-wolf stared at the gaping wound, eyes burning like dark coals, tongue lolling. Then, as suddenly as she had appeared, she turned and walked away into the darkness of the night.

One by one, the wolves melted away into the night. Ajiva walked up to the fire and prodded it with an arrow tip. Embers flew in the darkness. The fire came to life again.

The boy stirred. 'You have to sleep,' he mumbled to Ajiva. 'No point staying awake all night,' he said sleepily, before covering himself and falling asleep again.

It had been two days since they had fled from Kampilya. Once they were outside the walled city, Ajiva had led them to the pier on the banks of River Ganga. A dozen longboats made of timber were tied to stakes that had been nailed to the ground. A boatman, drunk on palm liquor, was snoring in one of the boats, swaddled in blankets.

Quietly, Ajiva had untied one of the other boats from the stakes and gestured to the boy to stay quiet. Together they had waded into the waters, dragging the boat behind them. The water was cold and muddy. When they were far enough from the tied boats and the snoring boatman, Ajiva jumped onto the boat and helped the boy in. They quietly paddled away even as the sun slowly rose in the distance, turning the sky crimson.

Jeeva turned to look back at the first city he had visited in his life. From a distance, bathed in the ochre rays of the morning sun, Kampilya looked like the great city it once had been. Its mighty walls looked tall and stout. The guards walking the turrets of the wall resembled ants scurrying on an anthill. Right then, Jeeva thought of the ruined palace, the princess' statue, the overflowing drains in the market and the poor girl who screamed all the time, and he did not miss the city anymore.

The current in the river was strong and it dragged the boat away from the shores furiously. Halfway down the river, the sun broke from behind the clouds and that's when Jeeva realised how broad the river they were crossing was. It looked more like an ocean than a river. In the distance, shoals of dark, fat fish jumped out of the water.

Jeeva dipped his hand into the cold, rushing water.

'Don't put your hand in, Jeeva,' Ajiva had warned. 'The water is full of crocodiles.'

'What are they?' the boy had asked puzzled.

Ajiva realised that the boy, having grown up in the mountains, had probably never seen one.

'Have you seen a lizard?'

'Yes.'

'Well, imagine a really long lizard. One big as this boat but with really sharp teeth.'

'Are you trying to fool me?' the boy had asked, eyes wide with horror.

'No,' Ajiva had said, smiling at the boy's expression.

Jeeva pulled his hand back in and for the rest of the river

crossing, he stayed in middle of the boat. He turned his eyes away from the shores of Kampilya to the other side.

Even from a distance, the boy could see that the two shores couldn't have been more different. The walled city was on a flatland. The other shore looked more rugged. On it, the riverbank rose and led to a thick forest, packed with trees so tall that some of them seemed to touch the clouds. A thin white cloud of mist shrouded the trees.

'Are we going there?' Jeeva asked, with a tremble in his voice.

Ajiva nodded.

'Why?'

'We can't go back to the city,' said Ajiva. *Not after what I did last night.*

'Where are we going then?' Jeeva had asked.

'To a place called Soumyapur, where this girl … the Miracle of Kampilya comes from.'

'But why?'

Ajiva did not reply.

'Do you know where it is?' the boy asked.

'I think I do. It's in the heart of that jungle. On a mountain in the middle of that jungle,' Ajiva had said pointing towards the other shore.

'Does this jungle have a name?' the boy had asked when they had disembarked on the other shore.

'Naimisha,' Ajiva had replied.

He had shot an arrow into the ground and tied the boat with rope to the arrow and lifted the boy out from the boat.

For a moment, they had stared at the thick jungle and the mist that hung around it. Then, wordlessly, they had walked into the forest of Naimisha.

The day after the encounter with the wolves, Ajiva and Jeeva continued their journey through the forest. The forest was quiet, still and unmoving. If it wasn't for the occasional breeze that rustled the dead brown leaves on the forest floor and caressed the canopy of green above them, the forest would have seemed dead. Streams ebbed and flowed but with a stillness that seemed unnatural. Birds cooed and cawed, but in hushed undertones, as though they were whispering dark secrets to each other.

*Were they afraid of waking up some force that slept deep within the jungle?* thought Jeeva.

If the forest were a human being, it would have been the jogi, the wordless man in the cave who had lived, but had barely moved or breathed.

In this deep womb of silence, Jeeva felt as if a thousand eyes were watching him constantly. Eyes that were embedded in the heads of creatures that walked, crawled, climbed and stalked in the forest. Occasionally, he would hear a twig snap nearby or the sound of scurrying feet but he was yet to catch sight of a single beast.

The thought made Jeeva shiver. He quickened his pace and caught up with Ajiva, who walked a couple of steps ahead of him, straight-backed, bow held loosely in one arm, taking long purposeful strides. It was as though he knew exactly where he was going and what he was doing.

Jeeva could never understand how a man who did not remember his own name or who he was or what he did a few years ago, remembered roads, paths, tongue-twisting names of kingdoms and their confusing histories, and strange facts about roots and shoots that grew in every kingdom? How could he shoot and set an ancient pillar on fire and yet struggle to remember who his own kith and kin were?

Was he a fraud? A trickster who lured young boys away to sell them as slaves or a magician who would sacrifice him at the altar of some primitive god in the jungle? The thought had crossed his mind several times but then again, he knew that Ajiva had never asked for company. At every given occasion, the quiet man had taken care of him—hunted for him, skinned the creatures, cooked them, fed him, watched over him while he slept.

*And, yet, who was he?*

'How far away are we, Ajiva?' the boy asked. His feet were calloused and beginning to swell. Even for someone who had grown up in the mountains, the incessant walking was beginning to tire him.

Ajiva paused and turned around to look at the boy.

'Do you want to sit for a while?' he asked.

'That would be nice,' said the boy. They sat down, staring at the green canopy above them in which a family of squirrels silently jumped from branch to branch, again and again. Ajiva opened the satchel slung on his back and pulled out a wood-apple he had plucked the day before. He wiped it with a piece of cloth and tossed it to the boy, who caught it and bit into it ravenously.

The wood-apple was still fresh and juicy and a thick line of juice ran down the side of Jeeva's mouth.

'So, how far are we from this place ... Soumyapur?' Jeeva asked.

'I don't know exactly where Soumyapur is but I know the mountain on which it is located ... the Langur Peak. Once we get there, I am sure we can find this village,' said Ajiva.

'Have you been to this Langur Peak?'

'I am not sure but ...' said Ajiva, but then he became lost in thought, as though he was trying to remember something from a past life.

'But what?'

'I know what it looks like. The face of the mountain looks like a langur, a snarling angry one ...'

'Which means you have seen it, right?' asked the boy, taking another bite of the apple.

'Maybe ... maybe.'

'And, yet you don't remember anything about this village on this Langur Peak ... this Soumyapur?'

'No, I don't.'

'That's strange, is it not?' said the boy, tossing the apple's core into the bushes. 'Look around you ... we have been walking for almost three days now and we have not met a single human being till now. Yet, there is a mountain in the middle of this soulless jungle and on top of it, there is a village. If you have been to this jungle and to this mountain, then what are the odds that you have not been to this village? And if you have been there, why can't you even remember the name of the village? I find that surprising because you remember so many places and strange things about those places. And yet, you don't remember this village?'

Ajiva frowned for a while. The wood-apple he had taken out for himself was still untouched. Then he smiled, a big broad smile.

'You sound grown up ... almost like one of the boys in the city,' Ajiva said. 'Come, let's go. I can eat this apple while we're walking. Let's get to Langur Peak before it gets dark.'

'One more thing,' said the boy, as he rose, dusting himself. 'What if that man in Kampilya was wrong? What if he was just another madman sending you down some crazy path?'

'Sometimes, Jeeva ...' said the man who once the boy had thought was a jogi, '... sometimes, you just have to follow the path. Keep walking. Take one step after another. Keep walking. The answers will come. I may not remember my name but this I know. Besides, what do I have to lose? Not so long ago, I was a half-dead man rotting inside a cave.'

## 25. The Long Night

The moon brother left a trail as he hacked his way through the jungle. A trail of dripping blood and pain marked his route.

His feet were raw and bloody with blisters. The skin on his face, arms and legs was a hideous patchwork of a thousand tiny cuts, each one of them becoming deeper as he tore through the prickly, thick foliage of the jungle. Occasionally, he grunted in pain and bit his lips hard to keep moving forward.

*Don't stop. Don't stop,* he told himself repeatedly like a mantra.

And stop he did not. Not during the day; not even at night, when the jungle turned dark and was full of luminous, hungry eyes. He stayed clear of the main road that cut through the forest and instead chose the perilous, thick-jungled track that the first men had used for centuries before it had gone to waste. Now, only the hunters of men—tigers, leopards and wolves—used this path.

He was bleeding profusely. They could smell him. In the dark, they could see him as well. And a hungry belly does not care. But, as long as he kept moving fast—really, really fast—he knew he had a chance. If he stopped, exhaustion would take over, making it difficult for him to move forward. Sleep that had been playing hide and seek with him for days would not take too long in overcoming him if he stopped.

So, he kept going, pausing only at the fickle streams of Naimisha that forever changed their paths. He splashed his bare skin with the cold water and resisted the urge to scream out aloud each time. Each wound spoke its own language of pain and he understood what each one of them was telling him: sit down for a while, rest, sleep.

*No, no, no. I can't sleep.*

The moon brothers, who were a part of the caravan, had made the decision together that very night. The same night he had sneaked up to the tent and heard the archer woman and the boy speaking. He had told the others what he had overheard. And they had decided that one of them should go back and inform the council. One of them would have to take a chance and make the journey across the jungle alone. That too in very little time. One of them would have to be prepared to die.

He had insisted that that the honour should be his. After all, he had overheard the conversation. Conveying it to Eka should be his good fortune. His privilege. The others had nodded in agreement.

So, squatting over the shallow grave of Bhima whom they had murdered and buried, the moon brothers had plotted and planned. Did they need to steal a horse? No, that would get the attention of the caravan leader, of the soldiers and more importantly, of the archer woman.

Should they steal an oxcart instead? No, oxcarts were slow and time was of the essence. The message would have to get to the council and to Eka with enough time to spare.

Should they mount an attack right now? No, they were few in number and the soldiers, despite their lack of fitness and incessant drinking, were better armed. Also, there was the archer lady who seemed to know what she was doing.

Then, there was the boy. If he was who they thought he was, he would know how to wield weapons. They would be outmatched and this opportunity would slip.

So, it was decided. One of them would have to do it the hard way. One of them would have to cut through the jungle, and get to the council as soon as possible to tell them about their discovery.

He had packed a cloth satchel with fruits and some dried meat, armed himself with a sword and bid his moon brothers goodbye. They had kissed him on his forehead and wished him luck.

'Look up, brother,' one of the moon brothers had said. 'The moon is almost full. You won't be running into pitch darkness. Fortune is with you.'

And so, the moon brother's journey of pain had begun. He had run, walked and dragged himself through the jungle. He had ranted and raved inside his head. He had cursed his fate and his weak body. But he had kept going.

Fourteen hours later, he saw his destination. It loomed ahead in the darkness.

With one last curse, he mustered all his strength and ran up the slope. He was almost home.

Inside the cave, which had once been a tiger's den, Eka lay on the cold floor stroking the scars on his face with a finger. He saw a moon brother stare at him curiously.

'It doesn't hurt, brother,' said Eka. 'It just looks terrible.'

The moon brother looked embarrassed. 'I am sorry, Eka,' he said.

'No, I don't like that name anymore,' said Eka. 'I like the other one … the one that my enemies fear!'

'Ardhamukha?'

'Yes,' said Eka. 'Ardhamukha. Half face.'

Eka smiled. Only one half of his face did. The other half remained the way it was, a mess of fissures and scars that resembled parched land.

'Do you want to touch it?' asked Eka seeing the moon brother still staring at his face.

The moon brother shook his head politely.

'I know you want to,' said Eka. 'Come here, touch it.'

The moon brother crawled towards Eka, who held him by the wrist and placed the man's palm on the scarred side of his face. The moon brother shuddered.

'Feels dead, right? Like a cold piece of stone,' said Eka and laughed. The laugh was hollow and bitter. It went on for a while, echoing off the low roof of the cave till it died abruptly. 'This is the greatest gift the rulers of Mithila gave me. Others might forget what happened to us, the injustice, the shame, the loss and the cruelty but not I. For me, every day is a reminder. A call to revenge. I don't have to look any further. The reminder is etched on my face,' said Eka, and laughed again.

The moon brother stared at Eka's face and caressed it gently with his fingers. For a moment, Eka closed his eyes savouring the touch and then, he held the moon brother's hand and pushed it away.

'No pity, brother,' said Eka. 'No pity, no mercy.'

As soon as the moon brother who had started running from the caravan made it to the top of the mountain, he collapsed. He lay face down on the cold soil for a while, gasping for breath. For a moment, darkness threatened to overpower him. He did not know if it was sleep or death.

He screamed aloud, knowing fully well that his other moon brothers were close by. Within earshot. The sound that came out of his mouth was more a groan than a scream, like the croak of a frog when a snake swallows it. Every limb in his body was sore and begging for the darkness, whose power grew stronger.

He clawed at the wet soil with his hands and screamed again. This time it sounded like a roar. This time, when the velvety darkness poured over him, smothering him in its hug, the moon brother let it wash over him, drowning in its inky embrace.

Later, when he awoke, he realised he was warm. His arms and legs were covered with a tiger's hide. A moon brother was wiping his face with a wet rag. Another was massaging his sore feet. A fire crackled in the cave. From the roof of the cave, a lizard stared at him with dark pearl-like eyes. He looked around the cave. Around him, the men of the council sat staring at him, waiting to hear whatever he had to say.

*This was what the struggle had been all about.*

Standing behind them in the shadows was the man who led the council. The one with the burnt face. The one who would be king. The one who would reclaim their lost pride and glory.

*Eka.*

'Brother,' said Eka, taking a step towards the moon brother. 'Ideally, I would have wanted you to rest, feast and sleep tonight. But this is not an ideal world. I see you have put your life at great risk, broken every rule of the jungle to get here. I am sure you wouldn't have done that if it was not something that required our immediate attention. So, brother, tell us what is it? What do you know that made you care so little about your life?'

The moon brother closed his eyes for a moment, gathering his strength and his thoughts.

*Choose your words well.*

'My fellow moon brothers …' he began, his voice a whisper, '… the Prince of Mithila is on his way to Kampilya … He is in a caravan. He is unguarded except for sixteen guards, who don't know who he is and a woman archer, who guards him night and day …'

The effort of speaking the words seemed to take a toll on the moon brother because he closed his eyes and stayed silent for a few minutes.

The members of the moon council stayed silent too, waiting for him to say something more. Then they all began talking to each other animatedly.

Eka stared at the burning fire for a long time. And then, he began speaking. The instructions were precise, the plan was daring. Every moon brother had a role to play. Tonight, the moon brothers would rest. Tomorrow, when the moon would be full again, they would start hunting.

For a few moon brothers, this would be their last night of sleep. But they did not care. Some stayed up all night plotting and discussing the plan to the last detail. Others slept like babies.

Eka stood outside the cave staring at the almost full moon, listening to the silent jungle. He knew what the people from the cities called the jungle—Naimisha—the stealer of sanity.

The forest was far from that. For the people who loved being surrounded by noise, greed and dirt, Naimisha was indeed a foe. A threat to their sanity. But not for Eka. For him, Naimisha's silence was a boon. A balm to all the pain and anger in his mind.

*It was home. Now and forever.*

The thought made him smile.

*If tomorrow went well, things would change. Mithila would pay the wages of its sins with the blood of its kings.*

# 26. Avanti's Favour

The caravan had been inside the silent forest of Naimisha for just two days and a night. Yet, for the men of the caravan, it already felt like a lifetime.

In the first hour of the first day, those first-timers who had never been to the forest but had only heard bedtime tales of it from their grandmothers, laughed nervously as though they wanted to test the silence of the forest. Almost, mocking it. Their laughter had echoed in the forest, again and again, like a coin spinning inside an iron vessel, till it had sounded like the mirthful cackle of a demon. When the sound of their own joy had scared them, the men had stopped laughing and started speaking to each other in hushed voices.

And then, the silence had won. It had enveloped them like the grief one experiences at the passing of a loved one. Laughing or even smiling had felt wrong. And so, the caravan had trundled deeper into the jungle, joyless and noiseless. Even the oxen had seemed to sense the stillness of the jungle and rarely made the bells around their necks jingle. The wooden wheels of the oxcarts had creaked and groaned. The brahmans had prayed under their breath, constantly fiddling with their prayer beads.

On the first night, the soldiers had set up a perimeter of fire around the camp, bonfires were lit. Soldiers had walked all night from one bonfire to another, poking the fires with wooden logs, keeping them alive. The last thing they had needed were the twin enemies of darkness and silence. Inside the camp, the men had tried to sleep, with little success.

Silence, usually a balm for soothing sleep, was the problem now. The cloying quietness of Naimisha seemed to stoke their worst fears. They imagined eyes peering at them from the darkness beyond the camp. Some slept fitfully, dreaming of their worst memories from childhood. The soldiers had destroyed the last jars of soma at Balabara, knowing fully well that intoxicated men would surely go mad in the forest.

The men of the caravan, sleepless through the first night, were bone-tired and red-eyed on the second day. The caravan trundled along the narrow path, which twisted and turned like an unending maze, as they went deeper and deeper into the belly of Naimisha. With every passing moment, the trees around them grew stouter and shorter, while the canopy of green above them grew thicker. The sun which had played hide and seek for the last few hours, slowly began to disappear. With every passing moment, the road became narrower as wild creepers and bushes began to claw their way into the road. It was as though the forest did not want the road to exist. As if it wanted to swallow up the road and anybody else who travelled on it.

In the afternoon of the second day, the mist descended. At first, it was just wisps of puffy white cool vapour, like the smoke from the wick of a lamp that had just been extinguished. Then, it wrapped around the wheels of the caravan and the legs of the horses. By early evening, the mounted soldiers could barely see the ground their horses trotted on. Sometimes, a little gust of wind would sweep the mist around and the men would be able to get a glimpse of the forest floor. Some claimed they could see crawling snakes and scorpions. Others claimed to see wet masses of worms. Most dared not look at the forest floor, afraid of what they would see.

*Naimisha is beginning to take its toll*, Avanti thought to herself, as she saw fear dance in the eyes of men. She looked at the prince riding next to her. He had been silent for a while but fear was yet to seep into his soul—just like it was yet to seep into hers.

Avanti had travelled through the forest before and it did not scare her. Not, at least, in the way the forest scared other men. Silence had long been her friend, a companion who whispered to her words of solace on long, dark nights. What she was truly worried about was the fear of other men. Men who are afraid, see things that don't exist. And delusion is the first step into the house of madness.

'You hate the gods, don't you?' Ajitha asked, leaning towards Avanti, interrupting her flow of thoughts.

They had been riding at the back of the caravan for several hours now, largely silent, staring mutely at a line of oxcarts navigating the winding road ahead of them, like a noiseless line of ants. So, the question, when it came, startled Avanti. She tugged at the reins of her mount, which snorted and came to a halt. Ajitha did the same.

'What makes you think so?' she asked.

'When we stopped at that village, the one before the forest … ah, Balabara, all of us went into the temple of Agni for prayers and sacrifices. But you stayed out. That is probably the only time you did not follow me like a shadow. I wondered what could be strong enough to keep you away from your duty? What could stop you from entering a place of worship? It cannot just be a lack of belief but a much stronger feeling, hence, hate,' stated Ajitha.

Avanti patted the neck of her horse and smiled. A big dazzling smile which made Ajitha stagger and sway like an elephant drunk on fermented soma. For the first time, he noticed that a dimple, the size of a thumbnail, showed up on her right cheek when she smiled. He resisted the urge to touch it and instead stroked the mane of his horse, making him purr with pleasure.

'I don't hate the gods. I just don't believe they can hear us and if they can hear us, I don't think they want to help us at all. They are deaf and they are dumb like the stones they are made of. And I do not see the point of going to a place where men pretend to hear their voices and sing praises of beings who are not interested in hearing their praises,' she said.

'But you believe in the gods? Which ones do you believe in the old tree, river and mountain gods that the first men believed in? Or the new gods we worship like Agni, the god of fire, Indra, the sacker of cities?' asked Ajitha, his curiosity piqued.

'What difference does it make, Ajitha?' she said, smiling. 'I believe in the existence of a god or a force because who else could have created this forest and the fire that warms our skins? Who is the owner of this breath that flows in and out of our body and where does it go? Who really gives birth to us and who really claims us when we are gone? So, I think there must be a god.' Saying that, Avanti tugged at the reins, as though she wanted this conversation to end. Her horse broke into a slow trot. Ajitha followed her.

'So, then why not worship him, thank him for everything he has created?' asked Ajitha.

'Who said it is a *he*? What if it is a *she*? What if *it* is neither a he nor a she?' Avanti asked, without smiling. 'What if we are just playthings for that entity? What if our sadness or happiness doesn't matter at all to this god or these gods? That would explain why some children are born deformed or good people die young. Or why a madman with half a face would slaughter an entire village and leave their bodies for crows and jackals to feed on? Wouldn't a benevolent god listen to the prayers and pleas of the innocent?'

'Aacharya Gurukripa has taught you well, Avanti. I have seen you wield the sword as well as any warrior but you have a way with words too,' said Ajitha. 'You are his true daughter.'

'That's an honour I have not had in this lifetime. But I pray—' she began, and then smiled, at Ajitha's surprised expression.

'You are not his child?' asked Ajitha.

'Your teacher is a rare and noble man who loved his wife and son. He raised me as his daughter but I am not his flesh and blood. I pray that I have that good fortune in my next birth. That's another reason to believe in the gods. I hope they are not as deaf and dumb as I think they are,' she said, and kicked the horse on its side.

Ajitha sat on his mount, digesting what he had just heard. *If she wasn't Gurukripa's child, who was she? And why had Aacharya-ji not told him and Trivikrama the whole truth?* thought Ajitha, before patting the back of his horse, setting it to a brisk trot. Soon, the two mounts galloped side to side. They raced along the side of the caravan, overtaking one oxcart after another. But then, they stopped. The road had ended abruptly. A small shallow stream, about knee deep, flowed across the road. It was a little wider than an oxcart.

It wasn't the sight of this stream that had made them stop. Across the stream, for a moment, they had caught sight of the setting sun, which had played hide and seek all day long behind the green canopy of the jungle. The red, burning sun was now disappearing behind a large, dark form. A mountain and an ugly one at that. Out of the face of the mountain a massive waterfall dropped, milky and thick. A mist hung around the neck of the mountain like a ghostly hand.

Ajitha stared at the mountain rising out of the jungle with awe. On it was a face that the forces of nature had carved—an angry snarling face. A face that resembled a beast, one with sharp teeth and bulbous eyes.

'Langur Peak,' announced Avanti.

Looking at the peak, Ajitha felt the hair on the back of his neck rise. He said a quiet prayer to the gods, and hoped they were listening.

*One more night. Just one more night,* Vishnupada had told himself all day long. Now, that night was here—cold, silent and discomfiting—he lay in his makeshift tent, eyes wide open, listening to the sounds of the forest. The forest was silent. Vishnupada breathed in and the sound of his breath was deafeningly loud. No crickets chirped, no frogs croaked, no jackals howled in the distance. It was as though the forest was devoid of life.

If that were the case, why did he always feel like there were a thousand eyes on him? Vishnupada pulled his blanket closer. His mouth was dry. He wasn't embarrassed to say that he was afraid. He was afraid to step out of his tent, afraid to stare at the dark forest around him, afraid of that cursed milky mist that clung to his feet wherever he walked. Every sound, even a man coughing, made him jump.

*Naimisha, stealer of sanity.*

He missed Bhima. He missed his big smile, his stupid sense of humour and his unquestioning obedience. The anger at his betrayal had ebbed. Now, he wished Bhima was in the tent with him, sleeping on the floor, with that stout staff next to him. Instead, here he was, all alone, staring at the flap of the tent, straining to hear the sounds of the forest.

*I am going mad, slowly but surely. Just one more night.*

When the sun rose tomorrow morning, they would move again. By noon, they would be at the river. By the time the sun set tomorrow evening, he would be in a soft comfortable bed in the palatial house of his cousin who lived in Kampilya. But before that, he would take a warm bath, get his body oiled and massaged by the servants of the household—the young, nubile girls who had little hands and soft skin. He closed his eyes and breathed in, savouring that thought.

Suddenly, he heard a rustle. He opened his eyes and saw a shadow move behind the flap of the tent.

'Who goes there?' Vishnupada asked. He hoped that his voice had sounded commanding. Instead, it had come out as a squeak, a scared entreaty from a boy who had yet to attain puberty.

'Reveal yourself, right now,' he said, sitting up on his bed.

One of the bald men entered. He folded his hands and bowed low. Vishnupada sighed in relief. He wanted to scream at the man for scaring him but did not have the energy. All he felt deep down was relief at having the company of another human being.

'What is it?' he asked.

'Master, dinner is ready. Will you have it here or outside?' asked the bald man.

On any other day, he would have had it in his tent, a quiet

dinner alone, one with extra helpings and delicacies made just for him. But, right now, he needed to see a few friendly faces, hear a few jokes, crack a few himself, laugh hard and slap a friend's back in mirth. He missed Bhima.

'I shall have it outside with the others,' he said. 'Have the lady and that boy had their dinner?'

The bald man's expression changed.

*What is he smiling about?*

'Yes, master,' he said. 'In their tent.'

'Good, give me a little time to get ready,' said Vishnupada, waving his hand to dismiss the man.

The bald man stood where he was.

'Anything else?' asked Vishnupada.

'Yes, master,' the bald man began hesitantly. 'The men of the caravan look tired … some of them look ill. They need a good night's sleep or else they might be slow on the move tomorrow. And, if we slow down, we might have to spend another night in this jungle.'

Vishnupada stared at the bald man, mouth wide open. The last thing he wanted was to spend one more night in this cursed forest. Even if Indra and all the apsaras of heaven promised him their company, he would not stay any longer than he had to in this silent burial ground of a forest.

'I don't want to spend one more night here. Not one more moment than necessary,' said Vishnupada, his voice quavering. 'What do you suggest we do?'

'Master, as is custom, we have one large cask of soma left unopened. One that we would have opened in celebration at the end of the journey. I suggest we open the cask right away. Give the men a glass each. Nothing more. It might help them sleep well,' said the bald man.

Vishnupada considered it. He liked the idea. He would

like to have a glass of soma too. The thought of the warmth of the drink as it coursed down his throat, and the sweet sleep that would follow comforted him. Anything, that would take his mind off the god-awful silence of this forest, was welcome.

'Just one glass for each of the men,' said Vishnupada. 'Not one glass more.'

'What about the soldiers, sire?'

'Give them a glass each, once their shift ends, not before,' said Vishnupada.

'Yes, master. A glass each for everyone then,' said the bald man, who bowed and turned to leave.

Vishnupada got up from his bed and threw on a silk scarf. The taste of soma, which he was yet to drink, had already filled his mouth. He combed his hair with his hands. It had become muddy and knotted. With a grunt of disgust, he wiped his hands on the tent's cloth. A long, warm bath, followed by a shave tomorrow, he promised himself.

He walked out of the tent and looked around. A bonfire had been lit at the centre of the camp. A dozen men sat around it, staring at it glumly. A couple of guards slept on the ground with their swords and shields next to them. At the far end of the camp, another fire burnt where the bald men were cooking broths and curries. In the distance, he could see the dark form of the flowing stream. It flowed silently.

*How could a stream flow silently? How could water flowing over rocks and boulders be noiseless?*

Vishnupada shuddered. He knew what lay beyond the stream. The mountain—Langur Peak.

He had ensured that the opening of his tent did not face the mountain. That way, he wouldn't have to set eyes on the dark, ugly mountain. But now, thinking about the mountain made him want to look at it once—like the moth that knows better than to get too close to the enticing flame and yet, flies towards its fiery death.

Vishnupada turned to look at the mountain. The black, towering edifice rose above him, dwarfing everything around it. The tall trees around the mountain looked like grass, the clouds up above looked like a milky necklace around its neck. He stared at that grotesque face that the gods had carved on the facade of the mountain. The protruding rocks that looked like eyes, the gaping hole halfway down the face which looked like a snarling mouth and the sharp jutting rocks that looked like teeth.

From that mouth, fell a waterfall of great height. Yet, the cascade fell onto earth noiselessly or so Vishnupada thought. Perhaps, they couldn't hear it since they were far away from the base of the mountain.

Vishnupada had hated the sight of the mountain the very first time he had seen it fifteen summers ago. And he hated it just as much right now. He averted his eyes from the gaping mouth and looked up towards the peak of the mountain, the summit, where few men had ever reached. The silhouette of the peak stuck out in the dark night like the jagged edge of a dagger. As Vishnupada continued to stare at the peak, a gentle breeze rolled down from the mountain. The clouds parted for just a moment and the moon emerged, a large silvery ball of light in the inky, black night. It was then that a movement caught his eye.

It was right at the edge of the peak. Something or someone stood there right now. There was no mistaking it.

It was a man.

His silhouette, framed by the rising moon, was clear. Perhaps, he was looking down at the fires of the camp below. Perhaps, he was just staring down at where the waterfall fell to the ground. Perhaps he was looking right at Vishnupada. But who could possibly live atop that hideous mountain, thought Vishnupada. The one village that had been up there, Soumyapur, had been completely wiped out by the man with the half face, from what Vishnupada had heard.

*Then who was the man up there.* Vishnupada shivered. *Was it him?*

The breeze blew again. The clouds drifted and the moon was hidden again. The peak was once again engulfed in darkness. Vishnupada rubbed his eyes and squinted towards the peak.

The man was no longer there. Perhaps he had imagined the whole thing, Vishnupada thought.

*This jungle is driving me mad.*

He needed that glass of soma. Or perhaps, he needed two of them. Vishnupada turned his gaze away from the Langur Peak and started walking towards the campfire, his footsteps crunching on the dead, dry leaves that lay on the forest ground.

❧

The two tumblers of soma lay untouched in front of them, spoiling slowly in the dark. Neither of them had felt like drinking. They could smell the drink though, the sweet smell of fermented honey. The bald man who had carried their drinks to them had insisted that the soma was fresh, that the cask had just been broken open.

But neither Ajitha nor Avanti had been tempted. Instead, they had gone to lay in their beds in the darkness of the tent, their ears straining for any sounds emerging from the forest. But there were none, just an all-encompassing silence.

Ajitha turned in his bed to looked at Avanti. From the

way she lay, like a philosopher gazing at the stars—one foot crossed over the other, her head resting on one palm—he knew she was wide awake.

'So, what happens tomorrow?' he asked.

'Tomorrow, my prince,' she said. 'We reach Kampilya.'

'I know that,' said Ajitha 'What after that?'

'I am sure Aacharya Gurukripa has sent instructions that would have reached the commander of Kampilya by now. For my part, I will hand you over to the military commander of Kampilya. They will welcome you with flowers and garlands. And, then you will meet … no, grant an audience to the girl they call the Miracle of Kampilya and escort her back to Vaishali. This time, it will be with a lot more fanfare, with a small army to escort you back,' said Avanti.

'And what will you do?'

'My duty,' she said. 'In a couple of days, I will come back to exactly where we are right now. Back to this jungle, at the base of this mountain. I will then go up the mountain to find out exactly what happened in that village Soumyapur … why all the brahmans of that village were killed and why their bodies were left for vultures to feast on?'

In his mind's eye, Ajitha could see Avanti riding alone on a horse, heading back to this silent forest—unafraid of man or beast or of any other danger that lurked in the solitude of Naimisha. For a moment, he considered telling her that he wanted to go with her, to ride alongside her, to watch her as her dark flowing hair swayed from side to side, to match the rhythm of his horse with hers as it laboured up the mountain.

But he knew it was pointless. Their story was destined to be one of unrequited love—a sad saga for poets to write about.

'So, what happens to us … you and me?' he asked. 'Do we meet again?'

In the dark, he could hear the sheets of her bed rustle. Had she turned to look towards him? Or had she turned away from him, wondered Ajitha.

'If the gods will it so, my prince, we will meet again. Or if you or the king or Aacharya Gurukripa commands me so, we will meet,' she said.

'Then I shall pray to the gods that we meet again,' Ajitha said. 'Will you?'

'I don't pray to them, my prince.'

'So, what's that about? Why don't you pray to the gods? Who are you if not Aacharya Gurukripa's daughter? What is this great secret you hide in your heart?'

'It's a story I would rather not tell, my prince.'

'What if I commanded you to?' said Ajitha, only half joking.

'I could lie,' said Avanti.

'But you won't. So, consider this a gift, a parting gift from you to me,' said Ajitha. 'Tell me why you don't pray to the gods … who are you?'

She was quiet for a while and then sat up on her bed. 'For that story, I will need to have some soma,' she said, before gulping down half of the tumbler in one go.

'The city we are going to … that's the one where I was born,' Avanti began.

'Kampilya?' asked Ajitha.

'Yes … Kampilya,' she said, almost spitting out the name of the city as though it was distasteful to her. 'I grew up listening to stories on my grandfather's knee about how it had once been the city of Panchali, the princess of Panchala, the one who had married the five Pandava brothers and, in whose name, a great war had been fought. To avenge the dishonour of that princess, thousands had died. That was the golden age of Panchala. But then that era had ended. Kings changed, banners changed, dynasties fell and new bloodlines rose, the morals of rulers and citizens also changed. The pride of men became more precious than the honour of women. Panchala grew less in influence, even as newer kingdoms like Mithila shone,' she said.

She paused to take another sip of the soma.

'The bald man was lying,' she said making a face. 'The soma is bitter, spoilt.'

'Uh-huh,' said Ajitha. 'Go on!'

'Ah, the story, my prince,' she said. 'I owe you that. Twenty-eight summers before I was born in a royal household, Kampilya was a rich city but one in decline. We did not have one raja who ruled the city, rather a hundred rajas—'

'A gana-sabha like Vrijji,' interrupted Ajitha.

'Yes, a hundred rulers, who came together in a sabha and ruled the city,' she said. 'My father was an elder in the sabha. An old, respected man. A man of values, they said of him. A man who claimed lineage from King Drupada and Panchali himself. Even then, Kampilya was prosperous. Poets have said its streets were lined with gold … though, all I remember is the way the markets smelled when I was a child … of flowers, and fresh vegetables, and spices from beyond the Vindhyas and sometimes … of clogged drains,' she chuckled at the memory and choked on the soma.

She sat up, hugged her chest and continued to cough. Ajitha rose from his bed, walked up to her and sat next to her, close enough that he could smell the soma on her breath. He gently thumped her back till the coughing subsided.

Her skin was cool and soft. 'Maybe, you can tell me the rest of the story some other time,' he said tenderly. 'Rest now, Avanti.'

'No, my prince,' she said, her voice slurring. 'A story … I owe you one. And, I always repay my debts!'

*The sura is hitting her already,* thought Ajitha. *Must have been really potent.*

'So, where was I? Ah, my story … the story of how one of the hundred princesses of Kampilya became a spy, a warrior and sometimes, even a whore. So, when I was about eight years old, the king of Mithila, your father, Simhamukha the Conqueror, turned his eyes towards Kampilya. I don't remember much about the war or the siege that followed. I was too lost playing kings and soldiers in my garden with my two younger brothers, Surya and Vijaya. But then, Kampilya fell. Most of the hundred rajas fled the city but three elders stayed back to work out a truce. It would turn out to be a costly truce. A truce that would change my life,' she said.

Avanti brought her tumbler to her mouth and found it empty.

'Can I take a sip from yours?' she asked, but did not wait for his approval.

'That's the first time I learnt what strength and weakness was all about. We were called to the great hall. Your father sat on a throne, raised on a pedestal, resplendent in gold and red silk, surrounded by ivory tusks. Below him, on the ground, sat the three elders in bare white linen, in mourning for their loss. One of them was my father. One by one, they washed your father's feet. And then, the new king of Kampilya demanded a gift from them. A gift of kinship in return for their right to administer their kingdoms. The elders could go back to administering their kingdoms, collecting taxes on behalf of

Mithila, provided they each gave one of their sons to the king to become his wards. The other two elders offered their firstborn sons as soldiers in the army of Mithila. My father, the one educated in scriptures, struggled to offer his young sons to the king. Instead, he offered something else,' she stopped the story, and took a deep drink from her cup.

'Me,' Avanti said. 'He offered me. I was eight years old, still playing with wooden horses and flowers. And he offered me. Not in marriage, for everyone knew the king was devoted to his wife, not as a ward to be raised as an equal in the royal household but as a slave girl, one to wait on and bow and scrape in the royal household. I will always remember the words he said to your father, "Sire, I offer my firstborn as your dasi." I was offered like a bag of grain or a piece of wasteland or a pair of cows after a yagna. I was given away as daan, just charity.'

'Were you there?' Ajitha asked.

'Yes,' she said.

In the dark, Ajitha wished he could see her face. But he wasn't sure he wanted to see the pain on her face right now.

'A week later, I was packed off to Mithila. My mother was distraught. My brothers stayed away from me and so did my father, the man who claimed to be from the race of Draupadi. On the last morning, just before the royal caravan was about to leave for Mithila, he came to me and hugged me. I did not shed a single tear and neither did he. Maybe he had wept all night before, like I had. All I remember now are his last words to me,' she said, downing the rest of the cup in one swift gulp and getting up from her bed.

Her gait was unsteady. She walked across the tent and threw open the tent flap just a bit. Moonlight lit her face. It was the saddest, yet the most beautiful face Ajitha had ever seen.

She turned to look at him. 'Do you know what that learned man said to his daughter?' she asked. 'He said "True love is letting go of the things you love the most. Someday, you—my daughter—will understand this."'

She closed the flap, staggered towards her bed and slumped on it. Ajitha got up and covered her with a sheet. From her deep breathing, he knew she was asleep.

Ajitha bent down and kissed her tenderly on the forehead.

*Good night, sweet princess! Sleep well.*

Outside their tent, a form moved in the dark. A thin man with a bald head. He walked carefully, away from the camp, keeping his eyes peeled for any movement.

He crossed the band of soldiers sleeping around the campfire. He pinched one of them gently on his forearm. The soldier did not move. Then he pinched harder, till the soldier's skin turned deep purple. The soldier stirred, but just a little. His eyes fluttered open, trying to fight the thick haze that the sura had induced. Then, his body gave up the fight. He mumbled something and slipped back into deep sleep.

One by one, the bald man repeated the same procedure on every one of the soldiers. Then, he walked towards the perimeter of the camp, where soldiers sat slumped at their outposts. Their spears lay next to them, on the ground. The bald man picked them up, one by one. For a moment, he considered pulling out the daggers from their waists too.

*Risky*, he thought. *What if they woke up.*

He let them keep their bows and arrows too.

*Can't shoot straight if you can't see straight.*

He walked to the edge of the camp, where the other moon brothers were waiting.

'Is it done, brother?' asked the moon brother they called Swa.

'Yes, they are sleeping like babies,' said the moon brother, handing them the spears. 'The seeds we mixed in the sura have done their work. They will be in deep sleep for a few hours. Even when they wake up, they will remain dazed for a while.'

'Will they be able to fight?' asked Swa.

'Unlikely,' said the moon brother.

'So, we just have to fight the woman archer now?' asked Swa, who had noticed that the woman had never had sura even once during the journey.

'Ah, moon brothers,' said the other one. 'That's where we got lucky. She had a glass, maybe even two. Now we just have the boy prince of Mithila to handle. And, he *is* just a boy.'

'Wait for an hour and then give the signal to Eka,' said Swa. 'We attack just before dawn.'

## 27. Langur Peak

The sign from his dreams was everywhere. It was chiselled onto the face of the ancient weather-beaten boulders which had once been mountains. It was carved on the barks of the old, dying trees in the forest. He saw it painted with dye on the walls of the caves they took shelter in at night.

At first, Ajiva thought the sign was merely a figment of his imagination, an extension of his dreams. He saw it almost every night in his dreams: the two wobbly lines entwined with each other. They could be earthworms, or snakes. Somehow, he knew they were snakes. Two snakes that crawled, stung and gnawed at each other.

The signs were everywhere, and yet not everyone could see them. Whoever carved these signs wanted only the ones looking out for the signs to see them, but not the others. Only the seekers would be able to spot the signs, all others would be blind to them.

While Ajiva could see them everywhere, the boy was blissfully unaware of them. The deeper they went into the forest, the more signs Ajiva was able to see.

*What were these signs? Had they been carved out randomly or were they signposts leading to some place?*

This sign wasn't the only thing that seemed familiar to Ajiva. He would look at the rotting trunk of an ancient tree and suddenly, a vision of the same tree would flash before him. Only in his mind's eye, the tree would be alive, green, flowering and full of birds.

During the day, he seldom had to look at the sun to plot his way through the dense jungle. He seemed to know exactly where he was going. Sometimes, he would look at a mossy lake and know that after an hour's walk from there eastwards, he would reach a clearing in the forest where there would be an old conical-shaped rock. And sure enough, the rock would be there, with the sign carved on it.

Other times, he was able to remember narrow trails and tracks in the jungle that were once well used by men but which were now covered with shrubs and plants. It was as though the jungle had reclaimed them. And yet, in some parts, the trails were alive—perhaps a few men had used the path recently.

Ajiva also remembered the trails that he knew he should avoid, ones that herds of wild elephants used, and he stayed clear of them. He knew where the watering holes that they used were—the empty caves in the hillocks which were once home to tigers.

The deep silence of the jungle did not haunt him. The jungle felt familiar and comforting.

It felt like home.

The boy, on the other hand, seemed ill at ease. He kept humming most of the day and sometimes, even talked to himself. It was as though the silence was his enemy, a foe to constantly break.

'What is that?' said the boy, pointing at something in the horizon as they walked uphill. The boy had wanted to lead the walk up to the trail and Ajiva had let him. The boy was two dozen paces ahead and almost at the top of the hillock they were trying to climb, Ajiva was well behind him.

The boy's finger was pointing upwards. Ajiva knew that they were walking up one of the tallest mountains in the forest. Only one mountain was taller than the one they were on.

'Langur Peak,' said Ajiva, as he walked past the boy, who was gaping at the dark, black hill that towered above them, mouth wide open.

Jeeva stared at the face of the angry, snarling monkey carved on the face of the mountain. The dark rocks that looked like bulging eyes, the massive outcropping of rock that looked like the snout of a langur and the waterfall that cleaved its way through that feral face.

He decided he did not like the Langur Peak. For once, he wished he were back home, in the little village below the mountain, in his warm bed covered by woollen rugs, watching his grandfather sleep.

Ajiva was ahead of him by now, taking long strides. The boy ran after him, gasping. An hour later, they were almost at the foot of the mountain called Langur Peak. The face of the langur looked gigantic as they looked up the mountain—the eyes were now covered by puffy, white clouds that moved lazily.

The jungle path had, suddenly, disappeared. Ajiva was now leading the way, hacking his way through the dense outgrowth. Halfway up the mountain, he paused and raised an arm.

The boy froze and slowly walked up to Ajiva, who was squatting on his haunches. They hid behind a bush with red blossoms.

'There,' said Ajiva, pointing through the bush. 'Down below in the valley.'

The ugly peak was there, the waterfall that fell off its face was flowing as a small stream at the base. The boy looked at it and did not spot anything unusual.

'Look at the clearing on the right of that small stream at the base,' said Ajiva, whispering. 'Can you see it now?'

Jeeva could see it. From where he sat, it looked as if a cluster of small pale pebbles lay scattered around the base of Langur's Peak, at a little distance from the stream. As he looked harder, he realised they were oxcarts, not pebbles.

It was a camp.

'Who are they?' asked Jeeva.

'Most likely a merchant's caravan headed to Kampilya,' said Ajiva.

From their vantage point, they stared at it for a while, wondering what to do next.

'Should we join them?' asked Jeeva, who was a little tired of the same diet of fruits and boiled roots. 'They might have some food.'

'I am not sure,' said Ajiva. 'Look at the flag that is flying on that tent. From here, it looks like the crimson flag of Mithila. And we are fugitives from the law.'

'So, what do we do?' said the boy, his voice heavy with disappointment.

'Let's go down this mountain once it's a little darker. And make camp near the stream, so that I can get some fresh water ... maybe even hunt some fish, even though it might be difficult to do that in the dark,' said Ajiva. 'We can look at the camp from closer once we are down there and make up our minds on what to do. For now, let's just hide here.'

Jeeva sat down and stared at the mountain. Ajiva sniffed the air and looked up at the skies.

'We might have a rough night,' he said flatly. 'It might rain.'

## 28. Trivikrama's Epiphany

The play was coming to an end. The protagonist, a king in exile, had just taken a sip of the magic potion. Soon, the memory of his past life would come back. He would remember who he really was. King, killer and above all, kshatriya.

As the actor clumsily swayed around on the stage, holding his head in his hands, pretending to be overwhelmed by a flood of old memories, Trivikrama wondered how a man in that situation would react. Would he sway around like a drunkard or would the weight of memories rushing in crush him and make him faint?

On one corner of the stage, the actress with dishevelled hair and tear-streaked cheeks lay on the floor, looking at the swaying man. She was playing the role of a potter's widow who finds the king, who has lost his memory after a battle, lying half dead next to a river. She takes care of him, helps him heal and then falls in love with him.

For many years, they live happily in the forest like husband

and wife, except for one pinch of sadness: they cannot have any children. Life goes on, he crafts pots, she cooks and cleans for him, till a wandering all-knowing saint comes to their house. Good woman that the wife is, she feeds the rishi.

Pleased, the rishi offers her a boon, just one boon. Dutifully, she passes on the boon to her husband. The saint tells him to ask for whatever he wants, silently, in his heart. The king closes his eyes and prays: 'God, give me a son and give me my memory back.'

'You asked for two boons,' says the rishi. 'Ask for one and ask it aloud this time.'

The man looks confused; and this was the moment Trivikrama liked the most in the play. The pivotal moment, when choices are made, when destiny takes a strange, unexpected road—when actors become the characters they play. Or not.

The man closes his eyes and repeats his wish aloud.

'Give me my memory back.'

The woman falls to the ground, broken. She cries not only for having lost the chance to have progeny, but also because she knows their life would never be the same again. Their love would be tainted, irrespective of who he had been in the past. For she had always known he was a man beyond her reach, her social stature.

She cries and wails. The man staggers around as his memories rush back.

Trivikrama knew that from here on the play would go downhill. It would get preachy. The man would remember that he was a king, he would remember his duty and more importantly his social standing, that he was a kshatriya. He would see his wife for the potter woman that she was, a shudra. He would offer her a place in his palace, a room where he would occasionally consort with her, but not the role of his wife.

That belonged to another woman. A woman of his own standing. The play was a tragedy, unless of course the playwright had put a twist in the end where it would be revealed that she too was of noble birth.

*Unlikely.*

Trivikrama wondered what he would do if he was in the place of the king with no memory. What if the shudra woman was his wife, Savitri? Would he abandon her for his kingdom and the silly courtiers who came along with it? Would he put duty over love?

*What I would do to spend even a moment with her, hold her hands once again? To walk with her again ... to hear her laugh, and see her eyes flash when she got angry with him.*

He noticed that the stage was starting to swim. Tears in his eyes were blurring his vision. These were the first tears he had shed since she had died a year ago. The first tears he had shed since he had watched her burn on a pyre. The tears he had never shed in mourning, having locked them away instead, deep in the chambers of his heart as he had whored and drowned his grief in soma.

The actors on the stage were done. Trivikrama wiped his face with his palms, not caring if anyone saw their king crying. It felt good. He wanted to laugh, to live again.

The brahman who had written the play came on stage. This was the part that Trivikrama liked least. The part where the brahman delivered a monologue about God, duty and social order. The moral of the story would be spelled out to the audience, in no uncertain words.

The brahman was a short man with a large stomach and pudgy arms and legs. He bowed low to Trivikrama and launched into the monologue, in a raspy voice.

'Thus, the shastras say:

When they divided Purusa,
how many portions did they make?
What do they call his mouth, his arms?
What do they call his thighs and feet?
The Brahman was his mouth,
of both his arms was the Rājanya made.
His thighs became the Vaiśya,
from his feet the Śūdra was produced.'

The brahman paused and looked at the audience. Trivikrama resisted the urge to get up and leave. He knew this homily was going to be long and he was in no mood for it. He had bedded women across every varna. He had tasted their bodies, drank along with them, kissed them and all of them had tasted alike. They had laughed and cried alike. Their mouths had smelled different but not because of their varna, but because of what they had eaten or had to drink before kissing him.

His own great grandfather had been born to a kshatriya man and a shudra woman, and he had been the greatest empire builder of them all. The great Yadava king, Vasudeva, the one who some worshipped and called Krishna, had been a cowherd. Satyakam Jabal, the great rishi, did not know who his father was, yet he was a saint. The folks in the mountains worshipped another god whom they called Mahadeva. Some called him Shiva. No one knew anything about his parentage, and that he had slain the great king Daksha, who was a brahman.

And here, this silly brahman was prattling on about accidents of birth deciding love, fate and the basic nature of people. Born from the foot, born from the thighs, born from the mouth ...

*Born from the mouth, born from the mouth.*

And, suddenly, just like that it all came to Trivikrama. The brahman was still droning on and on. But Trivikrama jumped to his feet. He had no time to waste. He pulled off a gold chain from his neck, threw it on stage and walked out of the theatre, unmindful of the startled actors, the guards who followed him or the courtiers who seemed convinced that their king had gone mad.

When Gurukripa caught up with him, Trivikrama's face was pale.

'We are in great danger, Aacharya,' said Trivikrama. 'I know what Ardhamukha wants. I finally know what his game is all about.'

She stood with him by the edge of the cliff. The valley below was foggy, covered in mist. Her skin felt cold, his arm rested on her tender shoulder.

She smiled. This is the moment she wanted to be in, for the rest of her life. With him, here on the edge of this cliff, looking at all the beauty below them. He turned to look at her and smiled, that broad, rakish smile of his. She leaned on him and held his arm, her fingers tracing the battle scars that ran on them like thick vines.

She loved touching them, once he had fallen asleep, after making love.

A breeze blew. At first gentle and then, a stiff angry breeze. It blew upwards from the valley and drove the mist up from down below. The mist was now a moving, howling wall of white that blew fast and hard from the valley below.

Her heart started racing. She turned to look at him. The

love of his life. He looked different, older. There was sadness in his dark eyes now.

He freed himself from her grip, took a step backwards and fell into the wall of mist, into the valley below.

She watched him drop into the abyss. She screamed. The wind howled in answer, drowning out her scream of agony.

He was gone. She had done something wrong. The wall of mist had now changed colour. It was no longer white. She stuck a finger in and touched the mist. It was moist and smelled of rusted iron.

She looked at her finger. A drop of liquid hung from it. It was red. She licked it. It was blood. Her own blood.

Rani Madhusmita woke up, screaming. She had to do something. She had to find Nila. She knew it in her gut, in the burning insides of her heart—something was wrong, something bad was about to happen.

## 29. The Hunt Begins

The bat is the hunter supreme.

He is prey in daylight, hunted and vulnerable. Crows, in packs, hunt him when the sun is up. So, he hides and waits—in caves, dank corners and black crevices that feel like home.

When the sun sets, when darkness reigns, the bat flutters back to life. The night is his friend, the inky depths his ally.

He is now hunter supreme. The lord of the skies. The master of the dark. He hears everything, sees every move, every rustle, every breath, every wing flap, every falling leaf as it snaps from the branch and hits the ground.

It is his time to hunt.

Eka smiled as he stood at the edge of the cliff, watching the campfires down below in the valley sputter in the darkness. He raised his head and stared at the moon playing hide and seek with the clouds.

Darkness was his ally, his old loyal friend. It was his time to hunt. Mithila was asleep. Its men were asleep.

He was now hunter supreme.

Eka closed his eyes, took a deep breath, filling his lungs with air. He bunched his palms into fists and thumped his chest, till his fists hurt and his chest turned red.

And then, he screamed. It was not a scream of pain.

It was a declaration of war.

At first, it sounded like a distant wail of an animal in pain. Then, it echoed off the walls of the Langur Peak and became louder as it bounced down the valley.

Kanakadasa was curled up, deep in slumber, when he heard it. Even before he opened his eyes, his hand reached out for his sword he always kept next to him, whether he was at home in Mithila or guarding a caravan inside the jungle. He patted the ground beside him for the sword.

The sword was not there.

His eyes opened fully now. Had he heard a scream? Or was it the scream of one of the men he had killed in battle a long time ago?

It was dark, pitch dark. *It shouldn't be this dark*, he thought to himself. And where was his sword?

He shook his head and looked around. The men around the dead campfire were fast asleep. Some were snoring, all of them were lying motionless. A plume of acrid smoke was rising from the fire near. How had the fire died so soon? It should have burned all night long. He had poured a quart of oil into it himself before settling down to sleep.

He looked up at the sky. The moon was right above him. It was not yet midnight. How had the fire died out?

He stood up, walked towards the firepit and poked at it with a twig. Nothing. No embers flew out of the pit. Just a wisp of smoke. It was as though the fire had just died on its own.

*Fires like these don't die unless they are put out.*

The thought made the hair on the back of his neck stand. He dropped to the ground and crawled on all fours in the darkness to the nearest soldier who seemed fast asleep.

The soldier was deep in slumber. Kanakadasa held the soldier by his shoulders and shook him. The man mumbled something incoherent but did not wake up. His foul breath reeked of sura. A thin line of drool ran from his wide-open mouth.

Kanakadasa placed two fingers under the sleeping soldier's nostril and checked for his breath. It was deep and ragged, like that of an old, dying man. He patted the ground around the sleeping soldier for his sword or spear. There was none.

Panic rose within Kanakadasa like a river in spate. The fires in the camp were dead. The soldiers were fast asleep. No, passed out, not asleep. Their weapons were missing.

*They had been drugged. But, how and by whom? And why am I still awake?*

The answer came to him like a flash of lightning in the dark sky. It was the sura, the last cask that had been opened the night before. Kanakadasa had not had a single drop of sura for sixteen years. As always, he had taken the glass handed over to him and then given it away to another soldier. That is why he was still awake.

*An attack is eminent.*

Vomit rose to his mouth. He was alone and unarmed, in a camp full of half-dead people. Still on his fours, he crawled in the darkness until he reached the edge of the camp, where the forest began. The skin on his arms was raw and burning. He crawled into the darkness of the jungle until he reached a stout tree.

He took one last look around. The camp behind him was dark. Nothing moved in the darkness. He waited to catch his breath and then, quietly climbed the tree and sat in the dark, not knowing what to do next.

Then, he heard the scream again. Only this time, it was followed by more voices echoing off the jungle.

Kanakadasa bit into his fingers, fighting the urge to scream in terror. He knew he had no option but to hide here and watch his friends in the camp die.

Vishnupada had heard the scream too. But it had sounded different to him. Like a babble of voices whispering in the dark. Something deep within him urged him to open his eyes and talk to them.

But he felt warm and comforted. He was dreaming of Mithila. Of his home where white ducks with their soft feathers swam around in the pond, of the soft palms of his wife who massaged his feet when he came back home tired after a long day at work, of his luxurious bed and of the smile of his chubby son who sometimes sneaked into his bed in the middle of the night.

Vishnupada knew he was dreaming. He knew he was in the middle of this cursed jungle and yet, the dream was so pleasant that he was afraid of losing it. So, he fought the voice in his head that told him to open his eyes.

Then, he heard the scream again. His eyes opened, just a little, before they flopped close again.

He wanted to sleep—just sleep, embrace the memories of home, bask in its warmth even though he knew it was all just an illusion.

❧

Ajitha sat on his bed, eyes wide open, heart pounding hard as though it would tear itself out from his chest.

The scream had woken him up. Across the tent, Avanti lay motionless. He jumped out of his bed, grabbed his sword and walked over to Avanti's bed. He tapped her on the shoulder. She did not stir.

The cups of sura lay next to her, empty.

'Avanti ... Avanti, wake up!' he whispered, as he shook her harder. She did not stir, not one bit. He held her wrist and felt a throb. She was alive.

Then, he heard another scream. He knew it for what it was. A cry of anger, a challenge to war—a battle cry.

And yet, the camp remained silent. The soldiers outside did not roar back at the voices in the dark. There was no call to arms in return. No torches were lit. Nobody came to their tent to wake them up. Not a soul stirred.

For a moment, Ajitha wished he was back in the palace in Mithila, surrounded by the king's guards and with his brother, Trivikrama, just a scream away. He wished he had taken his brother's advice and stayed back in Mithila. His mouth felt dry and his feet unsteady.

'Coward!' he said, once, and then slapped himself across the face—once, twice, thrice.

Tears of humiliation sprung and blurred his vision. He wiped them quickly with the back of his hand. He saw Avanti lying in her bed, senseless. He had to save her.

He bent down and picked up her bow and quiver of arrows and slung it around his shoulder. Sword in hand, he walked towards the flap of his tent.

*What if they are waiting outside?* he thought. *But who were they?*

So, he turned around and walked instead towards the back of the tent, which faced the jungle. He stuck the sword into the fabric and gently ran the sword down. A cold breeze wafted in.

Ajitha stuck his head outside the tent and peered into the darkness. A hundred yards from the tent, the forest lay waiting.

A hundred yards of open ground before safety. There was no cover. If he ran for it, he could make it even if he had to shoot an arrow or two to give himself cover.

But he was not alone. He had to get Avanti there too.

The moon brother smiled. He knew the boy would do this. Three moon brothers were waiting at the front of the tent, swords drawn, lying down on the ground, eyes half closed, pretending to be unconscious.

If the boy or the archer woman were stupid enough to exit the tent from the front, they would walk into a trap.

But the moon brother knew the boy wasn't stupid. He would not walk out of the tent from the front. He knew the boy would try and sneak out through the back of the tent. And that's why he was here—the best archer among the moon brothers, one who could shoot a hawk's eye even as it swooped down from the skies to grab its prey. He just had to wait and watch.

He heard it clearly—the muffled scraping sound as the sword slowly tore through the fabric of the tent.

Slowly, he placed an arrow on his bowstring, pulled it back and took aim.

The boy's head was sticking out of the tent. He was looking at the jungle, a hundred yards away. The moon brother waited in the darkness, waiting for the boy to come at him.

If he wanted, he could shoot an arrow at the boy right now and watch his head explode like a ripe pumpkin. He could feel the tautness of the bow string and the pressure on his shoulders and fingers build up.

But he had his instructions.

*Wait and watch. Don't kill the boy. Maim him if needed but capture him alive.*

Thc boy withdrew his head back into the tent. The moon brother exhaled and lowered his bow and arrow.

*Wait and watch.*

The war cry was coming closer. Eka would be here soon.

Ajitha scooped up some water in his cupped palm and sprinkled it over Avanti's face. She did not wince or startle awake, as he had hoped she would. He shook her shoulder once again, this time crudely.

When there was no change, he slapped her across her face hard with his wet hand. She moaned but went back to sleep. The drug, whatever it was, must be quite potent.

He gently kissed her on her forehead, steeled his will and slapped her again, this time so hard that his palm hurt.

Avanti awoke, her eyes squinting, searching in the darkness, trying to fight sleep. He shook her shoulder again.

'Stay awake, Avanti. Don't sleep,' he whispered, panic rising. He knew she would slip back into oblivion soon. He had to do something fast.

And then, he heard someone call out his name.

'Prince Ajitha Shaurya of Mithila,' said the voice from outside the tent. 'Step out and I might spare your life.'

Kanakadasa saw them coming from a distance. At first, they had looked beautiful, like a procession of fireflies coming down the mountain. But logic had spoiled the moment for him. Fireflies don't move in straight lines. They danced and swayed in the dark. This procession was moving in a straight line, taking its time.

As they came closer, Kanakadasa realised it was a line of men holding flaming torches in their hands. And, then, he heard their cries. One after another, the men beat their chests with fists and screamed. They screamed to announce their arrival, for they knew that nobody would be there to challenge them.

Once they were closer, Kanakadasa knew who had betrayed them—the bald, scrawny slaves who had joined the caravan at Mithila. He knew that because the men in the procession looked exactly like them.

Bald, thin and hard ... like peanuts.

All of them were on foot, armed with spears and swords. All of them except one. Their leader, their king. A man wearing a turban. Most of his face was covered. He sat on a horse, straight and proud. Slung on his shoulder was a longbow, very much like the one that the warriors of Mithila carried.

The procession came closer and closer, till they passed under the very tree he sat on. If one of them looked up by chance, he would be immediately spotted. He stopped breathing, afraid that they would hear him.

They bellowed and screamed their war cries, one after the other and marched towards the centre of the camp. At the end of the line were two men sweating and dragging a crude cart on wheels made of wood that creaked loudly as it was pulled along. Despite the high branch that Kanakadasa sat on, he could hear the strange sounds that were coming from within the cart.

The leader who sat on the horse was now entering the village. Much to Kanakadasa's surprise, he did not even pause to look at the oxcarts packed with furs, gold and silks.

*If he is not a bandit, who is he?* thought Kanakadasa.

Instead, the man on the horse trotted over to the tent at the corner of the camp, the one where the boy and the archer woman slept. And then, the man uttered a few words that made Kanakadasa's blood run cold.

'Prince Ajitha Shaurya of Mithila,' the man on the horse screamed. 'Step out and I might spare your life.'

In that moment, which seemed to last a lifetime, Kanakadasa knew that his children would not grow up like him—ashamed and branded as the sons of a deserter. That he would get a chance to wipe the dishonour that he had lived with all his life. God was giving him a shot at redemption. A chance to reclaim his own destiny. A chance to die like a hero.

A veera marana.

'For Mithila,' said Kanakadasa to himself, and scampered down from the tree.

Across the camp, beyond the stream that flowed silently, Jeeva and Ajiva watched what was happening with disbelieving eyes.

Earlier in the day, as dusk had turned into darkness and the bats had come out of their hiding places in caves and treetops, they had seen the camp come to life. The oxen had been unyoked, washed at the stream and fed with dry grass. Fires had been lit, and food had been cooked over open fires.

By the time the sky had turned into a carpet of twinkling stars, the soldiers had set up a perimeter around the camp. They had sat around in small groups of three around the burning fires, eating the food that had been served to them by slaves. Even from the distance, Ajiva had been able to make out that the mood in the camp was sombre, almost glum. There had been no singing, no raucous laughter or brotherly banter that was the hallmark of fighting men when they got together in the evening. The men had just sat there like statues carved out of stone, staring at the burning fires or at the stars far above them.

It was as though the silence of Naimisha had smothered their camaraderie, turned them into individual islands of loneliness and reflection.

*Perhaps they missed home,* Ajiva had thought.

It was then that the bald men came bearing earthen pots of wine. That had got the soldiers excited for a while. They'd had a glass each and for a while, it had seemed that it was only a matter of time before someone would burst into a song or dance.

But much to Ajiva's surprise, one by one, the soldiers around the campfires had started falling asleep. A few had held onto their spears and slept, while others had just stretched out on the bare ground and fallen asleep.

It was then that Ajiva noticed that the only men bustling

around were the bald men, who had earlier done all the menial work in the camp. They had bathed the oxen, lit the fires, cooked the food and then, given the soldiers their drinks.

'What is that man doing?' the boy whispered, pointing at one bald man.

'Which one?' asked Ajiva.

'That one,' said the boy, pointing at one of the bald men, who was at the far end of the camp. Ajiva had squinted into the darkness to see him. The bald man was bent over a soldier passed out next to a fire. Looped around his shoulder were half a dozen bows. He was now bending over the soldier, tugging at something.

*Was he cutting his throat?*

In the next moment, the bald man straightened. In his hand was the sword that had belonged to the unconscious soldier. The bald man tucked the sword into his waistband and moved to the next fire.

'He is relieving the soldiers of their weapons,' said Ajiva.

'Why would he do that? What if the animals attack the caravan at night?' asked the boy.

Ajika knew the answer. Four-legged beasts did not relieve men of their weapons before attacking them. That kind of treachery was unique to men. An attack was coming alright, but first the men of the caravan were being stabbed in the back.

'An attack is coming in the night. These men in the camp are going to die,' said Ajiva flatly. 'Let us get out of here. Come on. We have seen enough.'

Even in the darkness of the bush they were hiding behind, Ajiva could sense the boy's shock and anger.

'How can we do that?' said the boy. 'These poor people are unarmed and asleep. We must help them. We can't leave them to die. It doesn't matter if it's a jungle or … a cave in the mountains!'

The last words stung Ajiva, especially because he knew the boy was right. But he also knew that their cause was hopeless. He knew the bald men were not robbers. They had not put the men to sleep and relieved them of their weapons only to steal the precious goods from the caravan or the oxen. That could have been done far more easily. The bald men were the advance party for an impending massacre—an advance of well trained and armed men, who would get here soon.

He and the boy would be no match—

'Ahhhhhhhhhhhhh!'

The war cry cut across the forest and bounced around in the valley. Ajiva stared at the camp. The bald men were still busy gathering swords, spears and bows and piling them up at the centre of the camp like firewood for a bonfire.

And then, he saw a procession of torches coming down the valley.

'Wait here,' Ajiva told the boy. 'Don't move, irrespective of what happens or what you see. Promise me that.'

The boy nodded.

'If I don't come back by dawn, take the same route we took while getting here and head back to Kampilya. Don't wait for me,' said Ajiva, before handing the boy a sword.

Before the boy could reply, Ajiva had melted into the darkness, a shadow in the dark silent jungle.

'Ahhhhhhhhhhhh!' the voice in the jungle screamed again. The boy shuddered and tried to hide further into the bush.

The prince's tent was just three hundred footfalls away from the tree Kanakadasa had hidden in. At first, he thought he would run for it but how would that help? He was unarmed and not as fast as he had been a few years ago. If one of those bald treacherous bastards saw him, they could cut him down with an arrow in an instant.

Even if he made it to the tent alive, how would he be able to help the prince? He would be just another loyal idiot who would have delayed the prince's capture by a mere few moments. He needed a weapon. A sword, a spear or a bow. Something that would give him time to create enough of a distraction for the prince to escape.

*Indra, god of gods, conqueror of conquerors, help me,* he prayed. *Help me, Agni, o purifier of souls, O destroyer of ego and bodies.*

The gods answered with a breeze that rolled down Langur's Peak. Silence followed. Kanakadasa cursed the gods. He did not want to die a craven coward like his father. He wanted a death that the gods would remember—even if they refused to help.

He bunched his fists and looked up at the sky to vent his anger at the gods. The sky was beautiful, dark and spotted with a million lights, countless worlds where other men worshipped other gods. He folded his hands and prayed once again.

When his eyes opened, he saw something twinkle across the treeline. He stared into the darkness. Nothing.

There it was again. A faint dull glow. A ray of moonlight hitting something that nature had not made. Something that men had made and polished with their cursed hands.

The tip of an arrow. From his hiding place, below the tree, Kanakadasa stared into the darkness till his eyes became used to it. He could see a man sitting on a tree. He had a bow with an arrow strung on it, pointing towards the tent. He was waiting for the prince to come out of the back of the tent. If the prince came out, he would surely die.

Kanakadasa would not let that happen. He looked up at the sky, thanked the gods, got down on all fours, and began crawling towards the tree on which he had seen the archer.

The moon brother's shoulder was beginning to cramp. This was taking longer than he thought it would. He knew that the prince had only two options. One, walk out of the camp and surrender to Eka. Two, try to sneak out of his tent from the back and get slaughtered at his hands.

*Do it, little boy* thought the moon brother. *Come out, come out.*

The moon brother wanted to be the one who shot an arrow at the Prince of Mithila. The man who captured him. As much as he loved and adored Eka, he wanted this honour for himself. He eased the pressure on the bowstring a little, hoping the searing pain in his shoulder would ease up.

For a moment, he considered giving his shoulder a break, lowering the bow and giving his shoulder a quick rub. Anything to ease the pressure, to get the blood going again. But what if the prince tore through the tent right at that moment and made a dash into the darkness of the jungle. The forest was just twenty footfalls away from the tent and the boy seemed fit.

*Endure the pain,* he told himself. Behind him, a twig snapped. The moon brother turned sharply for a moment. Was there someone there? What had moved? Was it a tiger? He scanned the darkness behind him.

Nothing. Just darkness. Clearly, the pain in his shoulder was driving him mad. He was imagining things like an idiot.

He turned his attention back to the tent.

*Come out, come out, young boy.*

This time, he heard it clearly … a clear snapping of a dry piece of wood. A piece thick enough that no small creature like a jackal or a rat could have broken it. Something bigger and heavier had stepped on it.

A hunter. Something was stalking him, watching him in the dark while he was waiting for the prince. Something was creeping up behind him. Either a tiger or a wolf. Or maybe even a man. In an instant, he swivelled around, the arrow pointing into the darkness, ready to let it fly. But it was too late.

Kanakadasa resisted the urge to scream as the arrow pierced through the left side of his chest, slicing through muscle, bone and tendon. He bit his lip so deeply that a stream of blood poured down his chin and spilled onto his chest, mingling with the dark blood oozing out of the wound in his chest.

But Kanakadasa's other arm, his stronger right, was moving through the air with every ounce of energy that his will could muster. When his fist met the bald man's head, a spray of blood blinded the wounded soldier.

The bald man fell to the ground like a dead horse, falling on a marshy field. Kanakadasa dropped to his knees and let the rock in his hand fall too. It was sticky with the warm blood and tissue from the bald man's skull.

'For Mithila,' whispered Kanakadasa under his breath. He held the arrow that stuck out of his chest like a flagpole. He considered yanking it out of his flesh, but he knew doing that would make him scream in pain. The enemy was close by and the forest was silent. He couldn't make a noise.

Kanakadasa prised the bow from the dead man's stiff fingers and slung the quiver of arrows around his shoulders.

Then, he stumbled towards the prince's tent, leaving a thick trail of blood on the forest floor.

His vision was blurred and his feet felt unsteady.

*So, this is what being drunk feels like … not bad, not bad at all,* he thought and smiled despite his burning shoulder and the taste of blood in his mouth.

## 30. The Coward's Sacrifice

Ajitha watched through the slit in the tent as a soldier bludgeoned one of the bald ones to death with a stone. The soldier staggered towards the tent, an arrow sticking out of his chest.

Ajitha waved at the soldier asking him to come in. The soldier stepped into the tent and collapsed on the ground. His breathing was heavy.

*He won't see the sun rise again,* thought Ajitha. *But, neither will I.*

'Prince of Mithila,' said the voice from outside the tent. 'For the last time, come out and I will spare your life.'

The soldier looked up at Ajitha. The prince recognised him. He was the one they called coward.

'Speak to him, my prince' whispered the soldier, between breaths. 'Buy me time. On the souls of all my ancestors, I will get you out of this tent alive.'

Ajitha nodded his head.

'I am Ajitha, Prince of Mithila, son of Simhamukha the Conqueror,' he yelled back. His voice sounded shaky and like a child's. 'Harm me, and my brother, Trivikrama, king of kings, will make sure that you and your people will not be safe in this world or in any other.'

The men from outside the tent laughed, a derisive, mocking laugh that the prince had never heard before.

'Come out, boy,' said the voice. 'And I will spare your hide. Else, I will skin that girl with you first and make you watch. Then, I will peel the skin off your body while you are still alive.'

The soldier grasped the prince's hand. For a grievously wounded man, he had a strong grip.

'Leave now,' he gasped. 'Take the girl … run to the jungle … hide for a few days. I will keep these traitors engaged.'

The soldier picked up an arrow, stuck it into the ground and used its support to get up. Blood dripped from his mouth.

'Go, my prince,' he whispered to Ajitha. 'And tell my sons that Kanakadasa was no coward,' he said, waving a limp hand towards the back of the tent.

Eka waited patiently. Around him, the moon brothers were busy working. The soldiers of Mithila were fast asleep, like newborns who had just feasted at their mother's breasts. He watched as the moon brothers bound their hands and legs with rope. Two tight knots, just to be sure.

A few soldiers stirred and mumbled as they were being tied, but the drug in the sura was so strong, that none of them woke up. The moon brother, who had prepared the dark concoction which was mixed in the sura, had joked that even the oxen wouldn't wake up if they had it to drink. But then, oxen, like most animals, don't drink what's not good for them. They can smell something and instantly know when something is wrong. It is a skill that men had once possessed but a lifetime of soft beds and easy food in the cities, away from the perils of the forests, had dulled their senses.

He could see the two moon brothers next to him getting restless. They held a torch in one hand and a sword in the other. They wanted the prince to come out, and for the ritual to begin.

He could see it in their eyes. The anticipation, the bloodlust.

Eka did not want to charge into the tent. Nobody could predict what could happen in a confined space. In the heat of the fight and the darkness of the tent, swords would fly and blood would be spilt. One wrong move and the Prince of Mithila would be lying on the floor, leaking blood and life.

He wanted the prince alive. So, he waited, patiently. Eka knew the prince would not come out through the front entrance of the tent. For all their talk of bravery, he knew these men of war from the cities well. They would sneak away like jackals after a feast, at the first given opportunity.

He knew the prince would try and leave from rear end of the tent. A moon brother was waiting for him there, the best archer amongst all of them. His instructions were clear. Do not kill the prince. If needed, maim him, but get him alive.

'Let's go in and get the boy,' said Jwa, keeping his voice low. 'What if the boy gets beyond our archer, Eka?'

Eka smiled. 'If that happens ...' he said, '... he will have only one way to go. Up the Langur Peak, and that's our home ... it's been a long time since I hunted and I have never hunted a prince. I look forward to it.'

Eka looked up at the moon. The night was dark and still young. A couple of bats swirled and flew in the night sky.

He was the supreme hunter.

Across the stream, Ajiva watched, bewildered, as the bald men went to work. He was still on high ground and from there, he could see most of the camp and even beyond it. Soldiers were being tied up, the comatose merchants were being carried out of their tents and made to lie inside oxcarts. The two brahmans who had been asleep in their own tent were also dragged out and tied with ropes to horses.

Neither the merchants nor the brahmans stirred. They had to be carried around like sleeping children and deposited on horses and oxcarts. In one corner of the camp, he could see a band of men waiting outside one of the tents.

One of the men, a thin tall man with most of his face covered by the folds of a turban, yelled something. From this distance, Ajiva couldn't make out what the man was saying but he could guess. Perhaps, the people inside the tent were awake, and this man wanted them to surrender.

There was something different about the man on the horse. He was straight backed and had a poise only leaders of men have. The other bald men kept some distance from him, as though they respected and, perhaps, even feared him. None of the others wore turbans, except this man whose face was covered.

*Why would a man keep his face covered even in the middle of the night? Especially when he is with his own men? And why is he getting all the soldiers and merchants tied to their horses and oxcarts?*

The answer came to him in a flash. The man in the mask was Ardhamukha, the bandit who had killed the family of that poor girl in Kampilya. The man who had slaughtered a village of brahmans, mutilated their bodies and left them be feasted on by crows and vultures.

Clearly, the men of the caravan were being prepared for a ritual sacrifice, a blood ceremony of pain, death and mutilation. To his horror, Ajiva realised there was little he could do to stop it. He was outnumbered badly. There were about fifty of those savages armed with spears, swords and bows. He had a sword, a bow and about twenty arrows.

Yet, he knew he had to do something. Perhaps he could help the men in the tent get away. Perhaps, he could kill a few of these savages. One of them dead now, meant one life saved in the future. But, if they came after him, he would have little time to escape into the woods, take the boy and run for their lives.

He turned back and looked at the mountain behind him. The tallest tree under the mountain, that's the one they were camped under. That's where the boy was hiding, watching all that was going on, not in the least comprehending the horrors that the night held. In his innocent mind, this was a game of soldiers and bandits. One where bandits just robbed people and let them be. In his mind, Ajiva was a hero and for once, he wished the boy didn't think of him as a hero.

But he had to be one now, a reluctant one, a saviour who had no other choice. He cursed and silently climbed down the mountain getting closer to the camp, where blood was about to flow like water.

Avanti knew she was stuck in a dream. No, in a never-ending nightmare. Again and again, it played out in her mind, continuously, repetitively, like the wheels of a chariot rushing downhill. She wanted to scream and snap out of this nightmare. She tried time and again, each time she failed. And each time, the nightmare came back with more clarity, more vivid than the last time.

She was nine years old, playing with her brothers in the

grove next to the lake behind the palace. Without realising, she had reached the edge of the lake. Suddenly, she lost her balance and fell into the water. When the water hit her, it knocked the breath out of her. She realised she couldn't swim. She struggled, her thin arms and legs flailing. She screamed and icy cold water filled her mouth, choking her throat, flooding her lungs. It was strangling her from the inside, killing her one painful moment after another.

Then, she saw a figure swimming towards her. A man with strong arms, his chest knifing through the water. It was her father. He had dived into the water—to save her. His saintly face was full of love and compassion. He smiled at her and extended his arm. She grasped it. He pulled her out of the water. Outside, he held her in his arms. The sky above was blue and clear. She breathed in relief and smiled.

Out of nowhere, the expression on her father's face changed. The benevolence was gone. It became cruel and hard. The jawline taut, his eyes cold.

'True love is letting go of the things you love the most, my daughter,' he said and let go of her. She fell back into the cold water of the lake next to the grove behind the palace.

The nightmare kept playing in her mind over and over again.

'Avanti,' a voice whispered to her.

She was stumbling through the dark woods now. Thick branches and trees surrounded her. They all seemed to reach out to her, to claw at her arms and legs like an army of demons pecking at her. The disembodied faces of men she had slain in combat stared at her from the darkness. They glowed in the dark.

They stared at her with pale, unblinking eyes. Some had scars on their faces, others had sores on their skins from which worms crawled out. She felt her heart pound, as though it would tear away from her chest. What was that feeling? She was afraid and ashamed. She wanted to die. Tears stung her eyes.

'Come, my love,' said a kind and loving voice. A hand held hers and she felt reassured. She took one step after another and went deeper into the darkness.

Ajitha turned around and looked at the tent, one last time. Inside it was a man, a soldier waiting for his death. A man, the world had branded a coward. But he was the bravest man Ajitha had known in his entire life. Ajitha knew he had to live to tell the story of Kanakadasa.

So, he held on to Avanti's hand and plunged into the silent night with her. Above him, the clouds parted suddenly and the forest became lit with the silvery moonlight.

Kanakadasa had once heard a sage speak about dying. 'When you die, the soul escapes through the top of your head like a spark of fire,' the bearded man wearing beads around his neck had said.

Kanakadasa knew right now that he was dying, yet he saw no spark of light. He was dying one drop at a time, as the blood leaked out from his chest and mouth. He knew the prince and the woman would have reached the jungle by now. It was just some time ago that he had smashed the bald man's head with a stone and yet it felt like he had lived a lifetime since then.

*Pain does that*, he thought.

He had done his duty. Now, it was time to end his misery. He picked up the lantern kept in one corner of the tent, and turned the wick up. The tent lit up in golden light. He could hear the men outside the room talking to each other, excitedly. They were expecting the prince to surrender any moment now.

*Not in this lifetime, wretches!*

He picked up an arrow and with all his might pulled the metal arrow tip apart. The arrow tip sliced into his hand, but the pain did not bother him anymore. The arrow now had a blunt wooden tip. He thrust it into the flame of the lantern, till it sputtered and caught fire. He set the arrow on the string, pulled it back and shot the arrow upward towards the roof of the tent. The arrow tore through the cloth on top and stayed there.

Kanakadasa looked up towards the top of the tent, his head swimming. For a moment, he thought the flame had died out. And then, he saw a small red flame. Slowly, the flame spread as the tent caught fire.

Kanakadasa picked up the sword that the prince had left him with and screamed with all the strength he had in his dying body, 'Mithila' he yelled.

The men outside saw the tent on fire and rushed in. Kanakadasa was waiting. He swung his sword, catching one of the rushing moon brothers on his head. The head split apart, spraying Kanakadasa's face with blood. Another moon brother rushed behind him. Kanakadasa had an arrow in his other hand, which he thrust into the man's face. It bounced off his cheek and into his eye socket. Kanakadasa yanked the arrow back and the man's eyeball came with it.

Kanakadasa felt a searing pain in his abdomen, as though a thousand burning pieces of coal had been thrust inside him. The screaming man with one eye had thrust a sword into Kanakadasa.

Kanakadasa staggered back and fell. Above him, the roof

was still on fire. It had made a gaping hole, through which he could see the sky. Stars shined above.

*It is a sign.*

The heavens were opening up to welcome him. He was dying a hero. Kanakadasa closed his eyes and let the darkness envelope him.

Deeper and deeper, they plunged into the murky forest to the echoes of their stumbling footsteps and ragged breath. With all the might in his body, Ajitha dragged Avanti into the darkness. With one of her arms wrapped around his shoulder, Avanti was nothing like the fierce warrior he had met in Mithila a few weeks ago. She was now a ragdoll consumed by feverish nightmares and exhaustion. She stared at him with bloodshot, horror-filled eyes which rolled around in their sockets. She mumbled incoherently, slurring, repeating one word again and again: Father! Father!

He knew the drug, whatever they had given her, would take time to wear off. Suddenly, she collapsed on the forest floor. Ajitha paused for a moment to gather his breath.

Behind him, in the distance, where the camp was, a bright flame was burning. Their tent was on fire. The soldier had done his part. It was time for Ajitha to do his.

*Get her to safety.*

He dragged Avanti into the darkness. He did not know where he was going but he knew he had to run. Run till the sun came up—run and hide.

Up ahead, the forest seemed to change. The moonlight, which had till now occasionally streaked through the treeline above, seemed to have given up hope and died here. The darkness got deeper, inkier. Ajitha found that strange, and yet he kept rushing towards this impenetrable wall of darkness. What else could he do? Where else could he go?

And then, they hit the wall of darkness.

Only, the wall was real, made of solid rock that ran so high and firm, he couldn't see the sky above. Ajitha knew he had run right into the straight wall of Langur Peak.

Behind them was the enemy, ahead of them was the impenetrable face of the mountain. Ajitha knew there was no way he could hide here. The enemy would come straight at them, with their torches and swords. He had to keep on running.

*But, where?*

The smooth curving wall of the mountain ran as far as his eyes could spot, like the arms of gigantic monsters, welcoming them in an embrace of darkness.

For the first time in his life, darkness scared him. It was no longer his friend. It was his foe. It was smothering him, slowly locking him in its steely embrace, squeezing the light out of him.

It was in this moment of extreme despair and failure that he heard a voice in his head. It was barely a whisper and yet, it was louder and clearer than any war cry that Ajitha had heard in his life.

*'Darkness is not the absence of light, Ajitha. It is an illusion that the light is gone. Light is always there. Look for it within you and then around you.'*

Ajitha laid Avanti down on the forest floor gently. He sat down next to her, cross-legged, and placed his palms one over the other, in his lap. He slowed his breath down, ignoring the whoops of celebration coming from the camp, ignoring the fear coursing through his brain that was telling him to keep on running.

He closed his eyes and for a moment, everything became quiet and calm. He was back in the thousand pillared hall of the palace, walking around in the silence. The lamps were dim and everything around him was awash in a pale-yellow light. He was home and happy.

But that wasn't enough. He closed his eyes and went deeper—into the darkness of his mind. There, everything was perfect, still and calm like a flowing stream. He savoured the moment. He wanted to stay there forever.

Ajitha opened his eyes. The silence of Naimisha was now his friend. He was one with the forest. The darkness was now his ally.

He looked across the wall of the mountain. The same inky darkness all around. But what was that in the distance? A faint beam of silvery moonlight seemed to battle the gloom like a family of fireflies defiantly lighting up the night.

Ajitha knew he had to get there. He got up, dragged Avanti to her feet and started running towards the light.

'The prince is not there, Eka,' said one of the moon brothers.

The cloth of the tent had entirely burnt down. Only the wooden pole at the centre, which had held the tent together, was standing, still on fire like a solitary torch. The bodies of the soldier and the three moon brothers who had rushed inside were still on fire. The smell of cooking flesh and burning hair filled the air.

Eka stared at the scene, his dark eyes resembling burning coals as they stared at the fire eating into the burning bodies, turning them into shapeless pieces of flesh and tissue. The moon brothers waited impatiently, calming the horses, stroking their necks, waiting for Eka's command, waiting for the hunt to begin.

'Brave man ... this soldier,' said Eka, eventually, pointing to the only burning body that wore an armour. 'Let their bodies burn to ashes.'

'What now?' asked Jwa.

'We wait,' replied Eka. 'The boy has only one way to go ... and we know where that path ends.'

## 31. Eka's Message

The entrance to the cave yawned open like the mouth of a dead man. A single beam of moonlight speared down from the sky illuminating a shallow pool of still water which glimmered in the darkness. Ajitha stared at the pool transfixed, enchanted by its shimmering beauty, before he stepped into the cave.

His bare feet scrunched against the fine wet sand on the floor and the sound bounced off the walls of the cave, before it died a silent, ominous death. Ajitha looked up. For a moment, he thought he was standing under the body of a coiled serpent. Concentric whorls of glistening smooth rock curled upwards, getting smaller and smaller, until a narrow hole at a great height sliced an eye into the roof of the cave. It was from this opening that moonlight streaked into the cave and onto the pool, lighting it up like a lamp. Ajitha realised it was the reflection of this light that he had spotted in the darkness of the forest.

Ajitha closed his eyes again for a moment, and opened it, hoping his eyes could see better in the cave. He stared at the concentric curves of smooth rock and spotted something—an aberration. The curves were not without blemish, after all. There were lumpy little protrusions jutting out of the walls. But what were they? He ran his eyes downwards, and looked at the walls of the cave around him.

There it was! A small piece of rock jutting out, at the height of his chest. And just above it, to the right, another rock. And, then another.

*A stairwell. Perhaps an ancient one built by the first men who were long dead and gone.*

Ajitha's eyes followed the primitive stairwell as it ran up the wall of the cave. It spiralled up and above, till it ended abruptly, about halfway to the roof.

*Why would anyone build half a stairwell? Unless, unless … there was an exit there.*

Ajitha stared at the spot where the stairs ended. Nothing, no beam of light came in from there. And then, something moved in the darkness. Something flew in. A flying fox. It screeched once, flying in mad circles, before it flew into the shining moonbeam and out of the cave.

So, there was an opening at the end of the stairs, an opening wide enough for a big bat to fly in. But was it wide enough for him and Avanti to squeeze through?

*What choice do I have?*

Ajitha dragged Avanti's limp body towards the pool in the middle of the cave and put her to rest carefully on the floor of the cave. His mouth was parched and his arms and shoulders ached from the effort of carrying her through the forest. Despite the coolness of the cave, he was bathed in sweat.

He lay down on the soft sand and dipped his face into the pool of water. The water was cool and refreshing. Ajitha again closed his eyes and dunked his face into the water. Like a thirsty dog, he began drinking the water, lapping it up with his tongue.

When Ajitha had had his fill, he opened his eyes. He screamed—a noiseless cry muffled by the water. Staring back at him from under the depths of the water were faces of dead men. They did not have skin or tissue or eyes. Just skulls, one lined up above another. The bottom of the lake was a burial ground.

Ajitha pulled his head out of the lake and forced himself to heave out all the water he had drunk.

He had to run.

*Run and hide.*

Eka could sense the restlessness of the moon brothers. They said nothing and yet, he could sense their unease. The moon brothers had done their bit, now they wanted the action to begin, for blood to be spilt, for vengeance to be savoured.

'How much longer, Eka?' whispered Jwa, stroking the neck of Eka's mount.

'Anytime now,' said Eka, eyes firmly fixed on the mountain. 'We've waited twelve years. What do we lose in a few more moments?'

'How about livening things up a bit? Let's begin the hunt,' said Jwa.

Eka continued staring at the mountain. The moon was shining brightly. The night was perfect.

'We will hunt tonight, I promise. But I have something to show to our moon brothers first. Something that they will remember the night by,' said Eka.

'Show them what, Eka?'

'You will see, moon brother,' said Eka. He dismounted from his horse and waved his hand. Two moon brothers carried a long box made of wood. The others whispered amongst themselves.

Eka opened the box with a kick of his foot. The moon brothers gasped. Inside the box, lay a longbow unlike any the moon brothers had seen before. The bow was unusual in shape and carving. It was as tall as a man and thicker than a giant's fist. A quiver of arrows rested next to the bow—each arrow the length of a man's arm. Even in the darkness of the camp, the arrowheads made of polished metal gleamed.

Eka bent down and lifted the bow, seemingly unaffected by its weight. He plonked the bow, which was a head taller than him, into the moist mud, and plucked on the string. A twang echoed through the camp. Some felt the vibration of the string course through their flesh and sinews.

The men stared at Eka, mouths agape.

Eka picked up the quiver and slung it around his shoulder. For a moment, he bowed his head, as though lost in prayer to the old gods. But the moon brothers knew Eka did not pray to any god.

And then, he spoke.

'For twelve years, we have bided our time and watched Mithila grow. We have seen them become giants, men who stride around the world with no care for the people they walk on. For them, the rest of the world and its people are nothing more than ants, worms and creatures, whose life, pain or death does not matter. But, tonight that changes. Starting tonight, we will no longer be creatures to be trampled underfoot. Starting now, we are the hunters. We will hunt and we will kill, without mercy or thought. Tonight, we will declare war on Mithila,' said Eka.

'Watch me now, moon brothers,' said Eka, stringing an arrow onto the bow. 'Our vengeance begins here.'

The stupor was starting to wear off. Her vision was still blurred and she had problems standing on her feet without support, but the nightmares were almost gone, distant memories like flashes of lightning in a dark sky. Lying on the floor of the cave, Avanti stared at everything around her, with the large curious eyes of a newborn, even as Ajitha splashed her face with water from the pond.

As she wiped the water off her eyes with the back of her hand, she looked up at the opening in the roof of the cave and was transfixed by what she saw. The full moon, with its dark spots and blemishes, was shining like a pearl, playing hide and seek, as wisps of passing clouds, stirred by the breeze covered it every now and then.

'W-water,' she croaked out, when she realised that her throat was parched. Her tongue snaked out to lick at the rivulets of water running down her face.

Ajitha ignored her cry for water and kept splashing her face, with his cupped hands.

'W-water … I am t-thirsty,' she said, and realised that her voice sounded feeble. 'Please … please.'

'Not this water,' Ajitha said. He did not want to tell her what he had seen at the bottom of the pond, for she had seen enough horrors in her dreams.

'Please …' she begged again. 'Just one mouthful.'

Ajitha thought about it for a moment and then, scooping up a handful of water from the pond, poured it into her open mouth. She coughed as the water hit the back of her dry throat. He poured one more fistful of water, trying to block out the vision of what he had seen at the bottom of the pond … the watery grave … a procession of hollow eyes.

'Now, we have to go, Avanti,' he said. 'We have to keep running.'

For a moment, she looked confused. He could imagine her feverish mind throwing up a thousand questions, but mercifully she did not ask any. Avanti dug one elbow into the soft sand of the cave floor and tried propping herself up. But she wasn't strong enough yet, her arm gave out and she collapsed back onto the ground.

Ajitha stood up and holding her under her armpits, helped her onto her feet. She staggered around, weak-kneed like a drunkard, but she gripped his shoulders and steadied herself.

'Where to, Ajitha?' she asked.

If she could have seen his face in the darkness, Avanti would have realised that, despite the fear of looming death, the prince of Vaishali had smiled—for this was the first time that Avanti had called him by his name in all the time he had known her. The way friends and lovers did.

Ajitha led her to the foot of the stairwell.

'One step at a time,' he said, calmly. 'You hold onto the wall. I will be by your side. Always. Trust me.'

The stairs were crude and misshapen like the rotting teeth of an old man. Each stair jutting out of the wall of the cave, was of unequal size and of a different form. It was as though whoever had carved out the stairs in the wall had been in a hurry, in a race against time.

The gaps between the stairs varied too. Sometimes, two

stairs were separated from each other by the length of a newborn infant; other times, Ajitha had to stretch to his full height to grab the stair right above him.

Avanti held on to the wall, still reeling from the after-effects of the drug. Ajitha held her by her shoulders, every time she took a step on the stairwell. And so, higher and higher they went up the stairwell, till the pond was just a shining little orb at the bottom of the cave.

Ajitha looked up and realised that they were almost at the end of the stairwell, and, yet, he couldn't see any sign of the opening from where the bat must have entered. No gleam of moonlight, no gust of breeze gushed down from the walls of the cave.

'Where are we going?' Avanti asked.

'Up,' said Ajitha, for he could think of nothing else to say.

The stairwell ended abruptly—the last stair jutting out of the wall like the gnarled broken finger of an old giant. Ajitha stepped on it and stared at the wall beside it. A hole big enough to allow a small man crawl in was carved into the wall.

Inside the hole was darkness.

'Wait here,' said Ajitha to Avanti, who was one stair below him.

'Where else can I go?' said Avanti, a faint smile playing on her lips as she held onto the cave wall.

Ajitha stuck his head into the hole. It was deep, and so he crawled inside and looked up. He could see a patch of the night sky, with the stars shining above. The hole was a tunnel.

Ajitha smiled, only for the second time that night. He crawled out of the hole, and carefully placed his feet back on the stairwell. The last thing he wanted was to fall to his death or worse be captured with a broken foot.

*That won't look good when the court poets write this part of my story,* thought Ajitha.

'What's there?' asked Avanti.

'Freedom,' said Ajitha and held out his hand.

Pain snapped Vishnupada out of his stupor—a white hot pain that seared its way from his shoulder and flowed down every muscle and sinew of his body.

He screamed—but no sound came from his mouth. Just a gagging sound. The taste of something burnt and metallic filled his mouth. It was the taste of blood, his own blood.

Vishnupada opened his eyes. His eyelids felt as if balls of iron had been tied to them. They opened slowly but slumped back shut almost instantly. In that one moment that they had been open, Vishnupada had seen hell.

Something was on fire—a tent. He saw that his oxcarts were lined up in a circle. His merchants—seasoned veterans of the road as well as the young apprentices—were seated on the carts. But something was amiss. They were all smiling, terrible smiles with their teeth bared and blood dripping from the corners of their mouths.

*It could not be. It had to be a nightmare.*

Vishnupada willed his eyes to open. This time, he saw it all, clear as daylight. The merchants and their apprentices were seated on the carts and tied up, their mouths had been tied with rags so firmly that their lips had sliced open and bled. Some of the men had slumped on the carts, eyes closed, lost in their nightmares of pain. The few that had their eyes open stared at the world in terror, tears of unbearable pain streaming down their cheeks.

The soldiers were there too, bound with ropes to the yokes of oxcarts, along with oxen. The four brahmans had been singled out, their insensate bodies tied to the wheels of the oxcarts.

Nothing made sense. Nothing at all. The bald men were going around with knives in their hand, waiting for something.

*What is happening?*

Through his half-open eyes, Vishnupada looked at his arms. They were bound too. Why had these bald slaves tied him up? Were they bandits? If yes, why had they seated them on the oxcarts? Why hadn't they just stolen from them and melted away into the darkness?

With great effort, Vishnupada opened his eyes again. He turned his head around and saw a strange sight. A man, thin like the other slaves, was standing next to a horse. Unlike the others, this man wore a turban on his head and most of his face was covered with a cloth.

In his hand was a gigantic bow, so tall it stood a head above the man.

He was saying something to the bald men, who seemed to be in awe of this man. And then, he pulled out an arrow from a quiver. It was unlike any arrow that Vishnupada had ever seen in his life. It was longer than a man's arm and thinner than a finger—yet, it looked strong. Nobody could shoot an arrow that long, not even with a bow like that.

*Who could wield a bow like that? Not even the gods,* thought Vishnupada.

The man turned towards the mountain, and most of the bald slaves turned along with him. It was as though they were waiting for something to happen there. But, what?

It was then that one of the bald men dragged a cart towards the centre of the camp. On the cart was a cage made of bamboo. Inside the cage, was an angry mass of fur, snarling teeth, claws and eyes that glowed in the dark. At that very instant, one of the bald men looked straight at Vishnupada. He stopped in his tracks and slowly walked towards him, taking his time, probably savouring the fear in Vishnupada's eyes with each step he took.

'Are you afraid, master?' he mocked Vishnupada.

Vishnupada closed his eyes. The next moment, he felt a hard slap on his cheeks.

'Wake up,' said the bald slave, rubbing his stinging palm. 'The show has just begun.'

The walls of the tunnel were damp and smelly. The loose mud stuck to Ajitha's skin as he wriggled on it. When most of his body was inside the tunnel, he turned around, lay on his back and looked up. Above him, the night sky shone bright with carelessly strewn stars. From there, the tunnel ran straight upwards, the length of three men standing one above the other's shoulders.

Whoever had burrowed the tunnel had badly wanted to get out of the cave in a hurry, perhaps. But, why had they tunnelled vertically upwards in a straight line, instead of creating a gradual slope upwards? Ajitha pushed his body further into the tunnel using his hands and feet, when the crown of his head bumped hard into the wall of the tunnel.

He cried out. Tears of agony sprang to his eyes. Waves of pain ran down from his head to every inch of his body. He rubbed his head. It felt hot and sticky. He was bleeding. His scalp had opened.

His head had hit solid rock.

Now, he knew why the men who had dug this tunnel had gone upwards, instead of sideways. It was because, like him, they too had hit rock. So, they had dug whichever way they could to find freedom.

Now, came the hard part. The tunnel was shaped like an elephant's trunk bending upwards—a straight line with a curve at the bottom. He was now lying at the curve staring up at the straight passage above him. He now had to stand on his feet, before he could start clawing his way up the tunnel. But there wasn't enough space for him to bend his knees and stand on his feet.

Ajitha knew that the only way out would be to crawl his way through. He knew it would be tiring but he had no choice. He stared at the stars above again and breathed in, filling his lungs with as much air as he could. Then, he bent his neck and rested it on the wall of the cave, just where the tunnel curved upwards. He exhaled and, at the same time, bent his knees as much as he could and pushed his body upwards. His neck was clear of the bend but his chest was now crushed against the bend of the tunnel.

He tried to breathe in again and realised he couldn't, for his ribs were being crushed by the wall of the tunnel. Using his legs, he pushed again. Nothing happened. His body remained stuck in the same position—his head and neck in the straight trunk of the elephant, and the rest of him in the curve.

Fear fogged his mind. What if he was stuck here forever—unable to move, unable to breathe. He would run out of breath, choke and die like a fish out of water. In his mind's eye, he saw the pond at the bottom of the tunnel and the skulls of the men, with their toothy smiles and hollow sockets, inviting him to join them.

*Push, you idiot. Don't die in this hideous tunnel,* Ajitha yelled at himself.

Using all the might in his legs, he pushed again, hard. As

if by miracle, most of his upper body went into the straight trunk of the tunnel. It was then that he realised that a large part of the turn in the tunnel had broken free and fallen onto his lap as a heap of clay.

Ajitha opened his mouth and sucked in as much air as he could. He squeezed the damp clay on his lap and it broke into smaller lumps. Clearly, the tunnel diggers had dug a broader tunnel but rainwater had dumped mud and sand and made the tunnel narrower. Ajitha smiled, when he realised that Avanti wouldn't have to struggle like him to navigate the bend.

When his breath steadied, Ajitha stood on his feet and began feeling the walls of the tunnel with his hands.

There, they were—mud had covered them but not fully—two cavities, separated by an arm's distance, hollow enough for hands to hold them and feet to get stuck into. The men who had dug this tunnel had done well. They had carved footholds and hand grips.

Ajitha dug his hand into the cavities and pulled his body up. Freedom was just a few footholds away.

Ajiva watched the unfolding scene with the morbid curiosity of a child hypnotised by the sway of a dancing cobra. He knew something terrible was about to happen and yet, he was paralysed by the sheer curiosity of what was happening in the camp. He had scampered down the mountain, making sure he stayed hidden behind the tall trees. Where the treeline had ended at the foot of the hillock, he had hesitated.

Up ahead was an open riverbed, beyond which was a narrow stream and then lay the camp. A few large boulders lay strewn on the sandy riverbed like marbles on a child's playfield. If he had to get closer to what was happening, he would have to make a run for one of the boulders, preferably one closer to the stream. But, even if he managed that, what would he do? There were just too many bandits.

Also, the full moon was shining brightly right behind Langur Peak. If he ran across the open riverbed, he might be spotted. So, he waited and watched.

From his hiding place at the end of the treeline, he looked back at the hillock from where he had come down. He hoped the boy was still hiding there, not watching the goings-on in the camp. Ajiva turned his eyes back to the camp and stared at the strange thin men, who continued to toil like ants.

They kept the campfires alive by stoking the fires, yoked the oxen to the carts, and even lined up the oxcarts one after the other as though they were preparing for the caravan to resume the next morning. A few of them had tied up the drugged soldiers, priests and merchants to the oxcarts. But most of them were standing around expectantly beside the man whose face was wrapped in a cloth, their chieftain, the man who wielded the largest and longest bow Ajiva had ever seen.

*No man could wield a bow like that. No man dead or alive.*

The men standing around the chieftain were staring at the bow. He said something to them, and the men turned towards Langur Peak.

*They were waiting for something to happen. But, what?*

Ajiva stared at the mountain. Nothing happened. The moon was resplendent, like a large pearl. A cool breeze was blowing. Trees swayed; the stream gurgled on. Just then, a dark cloud drifted across the night sky and enveloped the moon in its embrace.

The riverbed turned dark. Ajiva saw his opportunity and ran towards a boulder at the edge of the stream. When he got there, he peeped out again. Nobody from the camp was looking at him. They were still staring at the Langur Peak.

It was cool and dark by the time Ajitha came out of the tunnel. He sat on the soft dew-drenched grass and dusted the mud off his skin, which fell off in clumps. He looked around. Above him, a narrow winding path, well used, and shaded by trees led up the hill to probably the pinnacle of Langur Peak. Where else could it lead?

Below, at the foot of the mountain, he could see the fire burning in the camp. Around it stood a band of men, staring up, their faces turned towards the mountain.

For a moment, he thought that they were looking right at him. He felt their gaze on him. Fear froze his blood cold.

*Would they just stand and stare if they could see me?*

Also, the moon was not visible anywhere. They were in the brightness of the camp and he was in the dark. There was no way they could see him. Even if they could, what could they do from that distance? But what were they staring at and what were they waiting for?

He did not have too much time to ponder on this. It was time to run. He bent down into the hole and called out to Avanti. In the darkness, he could see her silhouette as she struggled up the tunnel. Her strength was coming back but she was nowhere close to being herself yet.

'Come on, Avanti,' he said. 'Faster.'

She was almost there, just beyond his arm's reach. He lay on the ground and stretched into the tunnel. When his palms touched her wrists, he pulled her up. For a moment, he almost slipped back into the hole but he dug his feet into the ground and pulled her up.

They lay on the wet grass, gasping for breath.

'Let's go,' he told her. 'We don't have time to pause.'

She shook her head and sat up. In the darkness, he stared at her forlorn form. Her hair was muddy and drenched with sweat, her skin was covered in dirt. She looked nothing like the fierce goddess whom he had met in the courtyard of Mithila a few weeks ago. And, yet, at this moment, in the depths of fear and despair, he was in love with her more than ever before.

'Avanti,' he began, watching her as she swayed on her feet. 'Now, more than ever before—'

The sky behind her cleared. The dark cloud moved and the full moon emerged in all her pristine glory. Suddenly, the forest was bathed in silvery light. He realised right then that the men in the camp would be able to see her now. And, then, he heard an unmistakable sound he could have recognised in his sleep. A sound that Aacharya Gurukripa had made him hear so many times that he even dreamt of it when he was asleep. A sound produced only when a tight string unleashed all its wound-up tension and let an arrow fly.

Someone had fired an arrow from a bow so strong that he had heard it from so far away. From the confused expression on Avanti's face, he knew that she had heard it too and recognised the sound. But she was still drugged and slow. And, still on her feet when she should have been lying down on the grass.

That instant, Ajitha made his choice. He leapt up and pushed her down with all his might. Avanti staggered back and fell in a heap. Ajitha spun around and looked at the camp.

Perhaps, he had been mistaken. For nothing happened, no arrow pierced his chest and the men in the camp continued to stare at the peak—right where Ajitha was standing.

Ajitha heard the arrow before he felt it. A whoosh as the

missile tore through the sky and towards him. He looked at it and saw it heading right at his body. He leapt but even as he did, he knew it was too late.

The arrowhead tore through his calf muscle and embedded itself on the soft grass with a dull thump, pinning him to the ground. A spray of blood splashed out from the wound, blinding him for an instant and drenching the grass.

Ajitha heard a pitiful high-pitched scream of pain. He turned to look at Avanti. Had she been hit too? Avanti was crawling towards him on all fours, eyes wide open in terror, but she seemed unhurt.

Ajitha realised that it wasn't her who was screaming but him.

The moon brothers knelt around Eka, heads bowed, as he held the pose. He stared at the mountain, holding the bow steady even as the string kept vibrating. No man, dead or alive, could shoot an arrow that far, halfway up a mountain, against the wind, in the darkness of the night—not the greatest of legends. Perhaps the gods could do it, but who had ever met them? Today the moon brothers had seen the Prince of Mithila fall and a god rise among them.

Eka turned to the men.

'Let the hunt begin,' he said, in almost a whisper.

One of the moon brothers opened the cage placed on a cart at the centre of the camp. Four feral hounds leapt out, snarling and snapping. A moon brother bought a piece of cloth from the prince's tent that had burned down and threw it in front of the hounds.

The hounds circled the cloth, sniffing and growling, before

turning around and leaping into the darkness of the forest. From the depths of the jungle, one of the hounds howled—a long wail that woke up the even the men in the camp who were in the deepest of stupors.

They stared at the scene around them with bewildered expressions. Some tried to scream and realised they were gagged. A few saw the horror around them and pinched their own tied arms, as if trying to dispel a terrible nightmare. When they realised that this was no ghastly apparition that their minds had conjured up, they struggled against their bonds and prayed to the gods for mercy. Tears of rage, frustration and self-pity streamed down their cheeks when the truth, about their helplessness and the misery and pain coming their way, hit home.

The moon brothers looked at them with mocking grins on their faces.

'Begin the ritual, moon brothers,' said Eka. 'The night is young and the hunt has just begun.'

The moon brothers advanced towards their prisoners with unsheathed swords. One by one, they undid the gags of their prisoners. They let them beg and plead for mercy. The merchants offered all their gold in exchange for their lives. The brahmans appealed to the inner goodness in the hearts of the moon brothers and warned them of judgement that lay beyond this life. Some soldiers spat at the moon brothers, knowing fully well that their fate was already sealed. Others offered to dedicate their lives to whatever cause the moon brothers were dedicated to.

The moon brothers heard them out, calmly, before taking their lives, one after one, by slashing their necks in one clean stroke. Blood spilt on the mud, the gurgling sounds of men choking on their own blood filled the camp.

And just like that, all the prisoners were dead—except one.

Vishnupada was beyond tears or entreaties. He stared numbly at the dead and dying bodies of his men strewn around the camp, as though they were ragdolls that a child had carelessly discarded.

When a moon brother removed the gag from his mouth, Vishnupada looked at him with hollow, expressionless eyes.

'Master,' said the moon brother. 'You are the chosen one.'

Vishnupada nodded, even though he did not know what he had been chosen for.

'Rise,' said the moon brother. Vishnupada rose and followed the moon brother, who walked towards the edge of the camp.

Eka stood there, his face swaddled in the turban, waiting. The bow lay on the ground.

'Now, merchant,' said Eka. 'You have been spared for one reason and one reason alone. You will be my messenger. You have one message to deliver to only one person. This is my message.'

Eka leaned over and whispered something in Vishnupada's ear. When he was done, he patted the merchant on his shoulder. Vishnupada stood like a statue for a few moments before asking 'Who should I deliver this message to?'

Before he answered, Eka held his turban with both hands and slowly removed it. As the turban came off and revealed Eka's face, Vishnupada averted his gaze from the mangled mass of tissue and bone.

'Look at me, merchant,' said Eka, smiling. The lipless rictus grin showed off burned gums and misshapen teeth. 'You are privileged. You will deliver that message from one king to another. That message is meant for the King of Mithila, Raja Trivikrama. Tell him that it is a message from the king of the free lands, the ruler of Naimisha, Eka. If he doesn't recognise me yet, tell him that the message comes from Ardhamukha, the slayer of his brother, Prince Ajitha. That's something he won't forget.'

The massacre was swift and gruesome. One by one, the bodies fell and the soil slowly turned red. Hidden behind the boulder, Ajiva felt helpless. He knew he couldn't stop the killings. He was only one man with a bow and the bandits were one too many.

Yet, he had to do something. How else could he go back to the boy? He hoped the boy wasn't watching what was happening, that he was too far away to hear the muffled screams of the men choking on their own blood.

Ajiva peeped out from behind the boulder. The chieftain of the bandits was now talking to one of the men in the caravan. Even in the dark, Ajiva could make out by the silks the man wore and the girth of his stomach that he was a prosperous merchant, probably the owner of the caravan. The bandit chief leaned towards the merchant, and took off his turban, unveiling his face.

Ajiva felt his pulse quicken.

*What a hideous face!*

A wave of pity engulfed Ajiva—and, it reminded Ajiva of something. Of the man in the dungeon, who had sacrificed his life for Ajiva, the freak who had been mauled by a bear. Looking at the bandit's face from a distance, a strange concoction of feelings overwhelmed Ajiva: sadness at his plight, revulsion and something else he couldn't quite place.

And then, the feeling went away, just like a wave receding

from the rocks on a seashore. The bandit was a cold-blooded killer, a slayer of men, men who had wives waiting for them at home, children who slept in their laps, aged parents who would grieve the death of their sons every day for the rest of their lives. Those men bleeding to death on the other side of the riverbed would soon be just memories in the minds of their loved ones.

Had the same bandit not slaughtered a whole village of brahmans including women and children? Had he not terrorised that poor child in Kampilya to such an extent that the poor girl woke up screaming every night? Justice needed to be served.

*The bandit must die. Now. Even if he were the only one Ajiva could kill.*

Ajiva knew he had one shot. Just one shot. If he missed, he wouldn't get another. He pulled an arrow out of his quiver and rested it on the string. He couldn't hide behind the boulder and shoot at him. He had to stand up, reveal himself and let the arrow fly.

He had one shot.

Ajiva closed his eyes, breathed in and out. The sounds from the camp receded, becoming distant. The gurgling of the stream became quieter. All he could hear was his own breath—in and out, in and out. In a moment, that stopped too.

Ajiva opened his eyes and stood. The whole camp could see him now—the bandits, the dying men and the bandit chief. But no one was looking his way. They were all staring at the bandit chief mesmerised, who had a crude staff in his hand. On top of the staff was a white flag, which hung limply.

Ajiva aimed for the bandit chief's chest and pulled the string back to his ear. He breathed out and felt the pressure ease on his fingertips that held the arrow. In a moment, the arrow would fly. It would tear through the night air, fight the breeze and hit the chest of the bandit chief. The arrow tip would tear through the skin, rupturing tissue and bone, making his heart explode.

At that very moment, a cold breeze blew in from the mountains. The flag on the mast fluttered. Ajiva saw the flag unfurl. The emblem on the flag was not the hawk of Mithila. It was an emblem he had seen before—a sign he saw almost every day in his dreams and nightmares. Two snakes curled against each other.

Ajiva felt his breath quicken and his fingers loosen. The arrow was free. It cut through the night and whizzed above the stream, above the bodies of the dead and hit the bandit chief in the chest.

Only, it was off the mark. It did not pierce the centre of his heart; the arrowhead cut through skin and tissue and shattered bone but was a few inches off from where it was supposed to be.

The bandit king slumped for a moment, and held onto the arrow, which had pierced him just below the shoulder. Blood dripped from the arrowhead, which now stuck out from the bandit's back.

Ajiva stood on the other side of the riverbed, staring at the twin snakes on the flag, oblivious to the fact that the entire camp was staring back at him.

Eka pulled the arrow out of his chest with one quick yank. Blood flowed out of the wound like a gushing river. He stared at the archer who had fired an arrow at him. The men around him were staring at him too, bewildered, still in shock at what had happened.

'I want him … alive!' screamed Eka.

Ajiva watched the bandits charge towards him. He turned

around and ran, as fast as his feet could carry, towards the treeline. In his mind, all he could see was the flag with the twin snakes.

They stumbled up the path, leaving a trail of blood with each step they took. He was losing blood and his strength with each step. Everything was a blur. In the distance, a wolf howled.

The hunt was on and they were the hunted. They were after him. They did not care about her—just him, and he was slowing them down. He couldn't run, he could barely walk. And, he was slowing her down.

Avanti kept whispering something to him. He couldn't hear what she said anymore. He was tired and he needed to sit, rest, catch his breath. His heart was beating against his chest like a galloping horse.

'I-I need to rest,' he said, surprised at how weak his voice sounded.

'No, no, my prince, we need to keep going,' Avanti pleaded.

'Rest … rest,' he mumbled. His mouth felt dry, he was drenched in sweat and yet, he felt cold.

She rested his back against a tree and examined the wound on his leg. She had ripped a piece of her blouse and tied the wound, hoping it would stop the bleeding. The cloth was drenched by now and the blood continued to seep down his foot. She looked at the path they had just walked on. A black trail of blood glowed in the dark moonlight—a ghostly marker of death.

The wolf howled again. The hunters were close.

'Avanti,' said Ajitha. 'What did your father say to you the last time he met you?'

Avanti stared at Ajitha's face. It was pale, as though all the life within him had drained out. She ignored the question and tied the cloth around the wound tighter.

'Tell me, Avanti,' Ajitha said again.

'I am not letting go of you, my prince,' she said.

'Tell me, what did he say?' Ajitha insisted.

'He said … true love is letting go of the things that you care for the most,' she said. 'That someday I, his daughter, would be able to understand this. That's what he told me.'

Ajitha laughed, a soft delirious chuckle.

'Well, my love, he was wrong … I am about to prove him wrong,' said Ajitha, smiling. 'Give me a hug, Avanti.'

She leaned towards him and hugged him gently. Ajitha sniffed her hair. It was damp and yet, he could smell nothing. He embraced her tightly, feeling the curve of her chest against his shoulder. Tears welled up in his eyes. He smiled and hugged her tighter, savouring the moment, before turning her around deftly. Suddenly, her back was against his chest, their faces next to each other. His arms were around her neck now. With his free arm, he pushed her neck down, choking her, with all his strength.

'No … no … no,' she screamed as she struggled to break his stranglehold but hours of wrestling with his brother had taught him well.

*The python's grip never fails.*

In a moment, she would slip into darkness. The drug would hasten it. He just had to stop at the right time.

'True love is fighting for the things you care for the most, Avanti,' he whispered into her ear, as she slowly stopped struggling.

He laid her down gently on the grass and kissed her on her lips. He placed a finger under her nose to check her breathing. It was uneven but it was there. It would be a few hours before she woke up again.

Ajitha stood up and stared at Avanti, one last time. The wolf howled again. They were closing in. Death waited downhill. The Prince of Mithila turned around and walked towards it.

## 32. The Two Snakes

Ajiva walked uphill in the darkness, slowly and carefully. He knew his destination, they did not. The tallest tree in the mountain lay straight ahead. If he did not stray off the path or lose his way in the darkness, he would get there eventually. So, he took his time, and stealthily kept going, careful not to disturb the creatures of the night who occasionally stared at him with startled luminous eyes. Occasionally, an owl would screech and his pursuers would look in his direction but they couldn't spot him because Ajiva was one with the darkness—unlike them.

They were a band and they hunted in a pack. Like a wolf pack, they spread out in broad arc and slowly walked into the forest, a sword in one hand and a flaming torch in the other. He turned around and saw them walking up the hill, a collection of bright flames that lit up their faces and their upper bodies. They looked like ghosts, with their bony bodies, hairless faces and red flaming eyes that reflected the fire of the torches.

Ajiva considered reducing the number of his pursuers. All he had to do was crouch in the darkness and fire an arrow. He could take all the time in the world to aim at them. They wouldn't even see it coming. *Just like that, one lesser*. But, he did not. He told himself that it would be cowardly of him to do so but he knew that was not the real reason. Perhaps he was afraid that it would give away his position. Though deep in his heart, he knew that was not the reason, either. These men knew something about his past, they knew something about the twin snakes that troubled him in his dreams and he had to find out what that was. Dead men do not talk and he had to get one of them to talk to him.

But, how? Could he take one of them prisoner and beat the truth out of him? No, that would not be wise. There were too many of them right now. And Jeeva was hiding under that tree right now. Ajiva had to get uphill first and get the boy to safety. Then, he would stalk these bandits and find out more about them.

Ajiva smiled. That sounded like a plan. And, then he heard the howl of a wolf. He had heard it all night. But it had always come from the direction of the camp and beyond it. This howl was different. There was no mistaking it. This came from up the hill—from where Jeeva was hiding.

Ajiva broke into a run and the forest suddenly came to life. Langurs who were sleeping on top of their trees woke up and screeched, owls and bats flew helter-skelter, branches snapped under his feet and arrows hissed past his head. But none of that mattered right now.

The boy was in trouble. The sky was starting to lighten and in an hour, it would be dawn. Daylight was his enemy. He had to find the boy before the sun came out.

Behind him, the men shot arrows in his direction but Ajiva cut through the jungle, ignoring them, his eyes searching for one thing: the tallest tree on the mountain. And then he saw it, a few hundred yards away, a tree so tall and broad that it would take three men standing next to each other to hug it all around. He would be there any moment.

Just a few paces away from the tree, he saw it. The stupid shepherd boy had lit a fire. He had lit it behind the tree but on a night like this one, a fire like that and the smoke coming from it could be seen for miles.

But the boy wasn't there. Instead, there sat a wolf with shaggy grey hair, eyes that glowed in the dark and a long tongue from which a small stream of saliva dripped. Next to the wolf sat a man, just like the ones who were chasing him. He was thin, bald and tall. His right hand was buried inside the shaggy hair at the wolf's neck, stroking it. The wolf purred. When the bald man saw Ajiva, he pulled his hand out from the wolf's hair and smiled at Ajiva. It was a confident smile—the smile of a victor, of a man who knew what he was doing.

'Ah. I have been waiting for you. We have the boy,' he said in a tribal tongue that Ajiva recognised, and raised both his hands in a placatory gesture. Ajiva noticed that his left hand was missing; only a stump remained at the end of the wrist.

Behind Ajiva, the rest of the pack was coming closer too. He could hear them running uphill, the twigs breaking under their feet, the rustle of the leaves on the forest floor.

'If you come with us …' said the man calmly, still smiling. '… nothing will happen to the boy. On the other hand, if you don't …'

'You have the boy and I have you, don't I?' said Ajiva, and pulled out an arrow from the quiver in one swift, effortless movement, aiming it at the man's chest.

The wolf snarled, baring its teeth. Ajiva shifted to aim the arrow at the wolf instead.

'Don't shoot the wolf,' said the man and whispered something in the wolf's ear, who whimpered and melted away into the darkness.

'What about your men?' asked Ajiva.

The bald man yelled an order into the night. It was a single word in the ancient tribal tongue: 'Go.'

The pursuers stopped and the forest became silent.

'What now?' asked Ajiva.

'It will be dawn soon. With sunrise, a new world begins,' said the man, poking the fire with a stick. Embers flew in the dark.

'I meant how do I get the boy back?'

'You will see. Let's wait till dawn together, shall we?'

Ajiva sat on the floor and looked downhill. His pursuers were withdrawing. Their torches seemed to be moving farther and farther away, till they became just pin pricks of flame in the distance.

In the camp below, the oxcarts began to move, one after the other, in a straight line. Ajiva wondered who was driving the carts because the men who had got the caravan here were all dead. Perhaps, it was the bandits.

Ajiva watched the strange sight as the caravan moved beyond the river and into the forest that lay past it. One by one, the carts entered the forest and disappeared.

'Look,' said the bald man pointing towards the horizon. 'It's almost dawn. Day is about to break. A new dawn. Everything will make sense to you soon, my friend,' said the bald man.

Ajiva stared in the direction where the man was pointing. Behind Langur Peak, the night sky was lightening. Streaks of red scarred the sky, paying tribute to the blood that had flowed in the night. The sun would rise soon. Ajiva wondered what the boy was up to and silently hoped for his well-being. He would have prayed, had he known which gods he worshipped, the old gods of the forest and the mountains or the new ones of the cities. He couldn't think of any, so he gripped his bow tightly and stared at the auburn sky.

Ajiva sat down next to the tree. A few minutes later, without realising what he was doing, Ajiva fell into a deep, dreamless slumber of calm—in sharp contrast to all that had happened the night before. A sleep so calming and peaceful, the kind of sleep he had not experienced since he had woken up in that cold cave, on top of that ice-covered mountain just two months ago.

The persistent chirping of sparrows woke him up. Two plump birds bounced around on the moist grass, chittering and pecking the ground, an arm's reach away from Ajiva. The sun had just risen and its golden rays filled the world with such warmth and comfort as Ajiva had never felt before—or at least, he did not remember having felt it before. Above him, the canopy of green treetops swayed hypnotically to a gentle breeze.

For a moment, he was a boy, a child, lying in the same place, under the tallest tree on the mountain, staring at this beautiful sight. Everything was as it should be. Everything was beautiful and perfect.

The very next instant, the illusion of peace was gone, like mist evaporating under the burning rays of the sun. Dark memories of the night gone by rushed in—of wanton slaughter, of a relentless pursuit, of a man with a deformed face, of the missing shepherd boy and the man who had taken him—a man with a big smile and one hand missing who had sat right next to him stoking the fire.

Ajiva jumped to his feet, looking for the man even as

his hands reached out for his bow. The man was not there, neither was his bow. The fire had been doused. He touched the stones around the fire. They were cold.

A few yards up the hill, something shone brightly in the morning light. It was a sword that had been left there stuck into the soil.

Whoever the man was, he had taken his bow and arrow and left him a sword.

*Why?*

None of it made sense. Why had he simply not slit his throat while he lay asleep? Where was the boy now? And how was Ajiva going to find him in the middle of this great forest that sprawled as far as his eyes could see and, in whose breadth, caravans had gotten lost before, never to emerge again?

Ajiva walked up the slope and wrenched the sword out of the ground. A big clod of soil came along with it. The sword was heavy and beautifully balanced. It was unlike any other sword he had wielded before—and yet, it felt like it was an extension of his arm. Why would the man leave a magnificent sword like this behind? Was he a numbskull?

And then he saw the mount. A tall horse—a wild one with a black mane and glistening dark shiny skin—was tied to a tree. It snorted, exhaling vapour, in the cool morning air. Ajiva walked towards the horse, swinging the sword, savouring the strength of the magnificent weapon.

He stroked the beast's neck and the horse snorted again in approval. He untied the horse and jumped on the saddle. The horse broke into a gentle trot downhill, as though it knew exactly where he was supposed to go. Further downhill, they stopped at a clearing and he saw the campsite. The tents still stood there—empty and flapping in the breeze like abandoned orphans—but, the oxcarts were gone and so were the bodies of the men.

The blue stream flowed tranquilly next to the campsite, unmindful of all the ugliness and pain of the events of last night. Beyond that, the Langur Peak stood majestic and foreboding. The milky waterfall fell from its mouth and hit the ground at a place beyond the trees, from where a great white foam flew upwards.

On another day, Ajiva would have sat there wondering at the stern beauty of the peak. But, not today. He had to find the boy.

Something caught his eye. A speck. A movement at the top of the peak. He could see two dots moving—a man and a boy. The man was dragging the boy by his long hair, a boy with a frail body, a boy barely fourteen or fifteen years old. The boy had been stripped off his clothes, his mouth was covered with a piece of cloth and his hands tied behind his back. He only wore a thin garment around his waist. The man dragging him along was dressed in black and wore a turban; most of his face was covered.

Despite the narrow valley between them, Ajiva knew who the man and the boy were. It was the man with the deformed face. The lord of the bandits, the one who had massacred innocent men in the valley the night before.

*The boy is Jeeva,* thought Ajiva.

A band of men followed the boy and their chief.

They all stopped at the edge of the peak. The man with the deformed face kicked the boy behind his knees. The boy slumped to the ground. And then the man opened his mouth and said something. His voice bounced across the valley and Ajiva heard him.

'This is how the revolution begins, brothers,' the voice said. 'With blood and sacrifice!'

He then drew out a gleaming dagger and ran it across the boy's neck, even as he held the boy's hair. He raised his arm skywards holding the head up, while the boy's headless body dropped like a falling leaf down the peak and into the raging waters of the fall before disappearing into the foam below.

Ajiva screamed like a wounded animal. It was a scream of rage and anger. Hot tears flowed down his cheeks. He raised the sword up in the air—making his own declaration of war. In that moment, he did not care who he was, or what his past life had been like, or that he was alone and outnumbered. All he wanted was revenge. He would not stop till he beheaded every single one of those savages and drank their blood out of their skulls. He tugged at the reins of his mount and slapped its rump with the blunt edge of his sword.

The horse charged forward. It tore down the mountain path, into the valley, through the riverbed and towards the foreboding form of the Langur Peak.

Avanti ran through the jungle bush, stumbling and falling and crying. The words of that freak had woken her up and then, she saw the sight. The man with a deformed face was standing at the edge of the peak, holding a boy by his hair.

In the next moment, only the head remained in the air held up by the man like a trophy. The body had fallen into the waterfall. She could not see the face and yet, she knew who it was. It was Ajitha. The Prince of Mithila.

She had failed and now, the prince's body lay at the bottom of the mountain, broken by rocks, to be feasted upon by beasts and fishes. She stumbled into the thick forest, ignoring the thorny shrubs that tore into her skin, unaware that the blouse that covered her breasts was torn and hung in bits, unmindful of the rivers of blood that ran down her back, ignoring the trail of shredded skin and tissue she left in her path.

She had failed in her duty to Mithila, to the man who had raised her as a father, Aacharya Gurukripa, and most of all to the boy who was the Prince of Mithila. A boy who had loved her, one she had scorned time and again. A boy who had given up his life to save hers.

All she could hear in her head, again and again like drops of water dripping into a pot, were his last words whispered into her ear: 'Love is fighting for things you care for the most.'

Wiping the welling tears with the back of her palm, Avanti plunged deeper into the forest.

The steed was fast, faster than the wind, lighter than any other mount that Ajiva had ever sat on. It galloped up the winding mountain path that the first men of the forest had carved out of the jungle a thousand years ago. The horse followed the path as though it knew every turn and every corner.

Ajiva realised that the horse had probably taken this route a thousand times before. He knew the horse was following its instincts. He knew it was going home, back to the men who had tamed it, raised it and fed it.

It was a trap. But Ajiva was beyond caring or thinking. All he wanted was blood and vengeance. And he wanted it now. He felt the desire for it course through his body like an alchemist's potion. And, yet, he felt strangely detached, as though he was just an observer watching whatever was happening.

The heavy sword was in his hand, gleaming, ready to be stained. The breeze was blowing down the mountain, cooling him, parting his beard, mashing it against his chest.

Ahead, the mountain path turned and coiled like a serpent—and suddenly, he had a vision.

A vision of a large leafy tree, a tree with a thousand hanging shoots and countless branches and a woman with the smile of an angel, laughing and swinging on a swing suspended from the tree. She was swinging, in and out over the edge of a cliff and yet, she wasn't afraid. She was laughing, amused and enjoying the danger as tears rolled down her eyes. Tears of blood that streamed and mixed with each other like mating snakes.

The vision was gone as quickly as it had come. But as the path turned right, ahead of him he could see the tree he had seen in his vision—a broad tree with a thousand shoots hanging from it. A swing hung from one of the branches but no woman was there. The tree was brown, bare and leafless, as though all life had been sucked out of it.

*Am I going mad?*

The horse kept galloping hard, heaving and gasping, even as the slope got steeper. The tree was now behind them. Ajiva knew what would come next. A massive yellow rock, a rock so ancient that the first men had worshipped it as the preserver of the beasts of the jungle. A rock that was the sign of fertility, regeneration and rebirth.

The rock was there, tall and covered with a fresh paste of ground turmeric roots that the men of the forest used to cure sores and infections of the body. And so, as Ajiva kept going further up the mountain path, a queer sense of familiarity overwhelmed him. The crevasses of the boulders, the peculiar turn of the path, a withered dying tree, a pond filled with moss, an abandoned cave—all of it seemed familiar.

And, then, he saw it—something that seemed alien and strange in the simple, primal beauty of the jungle—an arch made of stone and rock, carved by hammer and chisel like the ones used in distant cities. On top of the arch was an inscription in the language of the plains: Soumyapur.

Ajiva tugged at the reins and the horse stopped in its tracks. The bald men were waiting ahead beyond the arch, lined on the sides of the mountain path, staring at him with curious eyes, waiting for him. There were over a hundred of them and he was alone.

If he went ahead, he would surely die. He looked up at the sky—a hawk was circling above him in the blue sky. It screeched.

'For Jeeva,' he screamed, raising his sword towards the heaven and charged at them.

They did not attack him all at once, like he thought they would. Instead, they parted and ducked and made way as he swung and slashed his sword at them. They blocked his thrusts with crude wooden shields and danced away from his path. Even when his sword pierced the bodies of men, they chose to fall, bleeding instead of thrusting a spear or sword in return. Not a single archer fired an arrow at him.

And then, his mount went down. Ajiva landed on his back, sprawled in the mud. He got back on his feet and kept swinging the sword around him, keeping the circle of men around him at a distance. The men watched him with eager eyes, but kept their distance, like hungry jackals waiting for a wounded lion to tire and die. The sword felt heavy and he began to tire and yet, he kept swinging it.

Eventually, exhausted and out of breath, Ajiva stopped. He stood unsteadily on his feet, and thrust the sword into the ground. He rested his palms on it, leaning on it like an old cripple leans on a walking stick.

From the corner of his eye, he saw the crowd parting slowly.

The bandit chieftain, Ardhamukha, walked towards Ajiva. His face was still swathed with his turban. In his hand was a sword as heavy and as impressive as the one Ajiva had. It was stained with blood.

Ajiva felt rage bubbling in his heart. He spat on the ground, pulled his sword out of the mud and ran towards Ardhamukha. The bandit moved away and clapped Ajiva on the back with the blunt end of his sword. Ajiva stumbled and landed face down on the wet soil.

'Tie him up,' said Ardhamukha.

Half a dozen hands grabbed Ajiva and bound his hands behind his back with ropes. The man he knew as Ardhamukha stood still for a long time, studying Ajiva with a curious expression on his face, an expression that Ajiva couldn't understand.

'Go ahead, wretch,' said Ajiva. 'What are you looking at? End it. Kill me now!'

'Kneel,' ordered Ardhamukha.

Ajiva kept standing. A man behind him kicked him on the back of his heel and his knees buckled.

Ardhamukha walked up to him, his sword swinging by his side.

Ajiva closed his eyes for a moment—he thought of his life or what he could remember of it—waking up in the cold cave in the mountains, being nursed to life by the boy, the strange journey down the hills and now this. He realised he would die without really knowing anything about his past. He had been reborn a stranger to himself and he would die a stranger.

When he opened his eyes, he saw Ardhamukha kneeling right in front of him. The bandit's terribly deformed face, masked by his turban, was a few inches from his.

'Look at me,' said Ardhamukha. 'Even if it's the last thing you might see in this life.'

Slowly and methodically, the bandit put one hand behind his turban and opened the knot that held the cloth which covered his deformed face. A horrible patchwork of burnt tissue and scars ran down one side of his face, even as the other side was pristinely well-preserved. As the veil fell away from the bandit's face, Ajiva screamed once, before falling into a deep, dead faint.

In that one moment, all that he had forgotten about his old life came back in a spate of memories. He realised who he was, how he had landed up in the cave of a far-away mountain and why everything on this mountain path—the boulders, the tree with the swing and even the whole forest—had seemed so familiar. In that moment, Ajiva realised that after all those years of wilderness and darkness, he had finally come home. In that instant, he also realised why the girl they called the Miracle of Kampilya had screamed when she had seen the man with the scars standing beside him at the window.

The girl hadn't been horrified by the tribal's face. She had been terrified by Ajiva's face.

For when Ardhamukha's veil had fallen, the face that was revealed, at least one half of the face, the well-preserved half of the face, was an exact mirror image of Ajiva's face.

'Welcome back, my brother,' said Ardhamukha, eyes brimming with tears. 'I have waited for this moment for so long.'

Darkness enveloped Ajiva and for once, he was grateful for it.

Avanti scratched and clawed and pulled at the wet soil with bare hands till her nails came off and fingers bled. Like a mongrel digging a hole, she kept at it, ignoring the agony, till all of her was covered in dirt.

The tears had stopped an hour ago. The sense of shame was gone too. All she felt was a hollow numbness. The sun was high in the sky and she had been digging for a few hours now, without stopping for even a sip of water, even though she could hear the roar of the waterfall nearby.

She had found the headless body bobbing up and down in the water, stuck between two boulders. It was a pitiful wreck—a white bloodless mass of strange misshapen lumps of broken bones and dark bruises. When she had spotted the body, she had fallen to the ground and howled and beaten her chest, like a widow at a funeral. She had kept her distance, afraid to touch it as though the coldness of its skin would seep into her and leave her with an unbearable sense of loss and failure.

So, she wept like a child from a distance, mourning for the Prince of Mithila. When the tears had finally stopped, she had dragged the body out of the water. The loincloth had been washed away and the body was naked. This was no way for anybody to die, definitely not a boy and surely not a prince.

Avanti stared at the body, a few tendrils and leaves wrapped around it. Gently, she cleaned the body with water, trying not to look at the neck. When she was done, she paused for a moment. She couldn't carry the body back to Mithila. She considered cremating it but she knew a fire would attract attention. And she would need a big fire, one that would consume the whole body. She did not want the boy to be half burnt, a feast for the creatures of the night.

So, she decided to dig a grave.

When the hole was large enough, she stepped outside it, slowly dragging the body inside. She stepped out and stared at the naked body. She could not bury him without giving him a shred of his dignity back. With one swift tug, Avanti tore the tattered blouse off her chest and used it to cover the boy's torso. She looked around the silent forest and then, unwrapped the garment around her waist. She looked at the body one last time and then lay her garment over it.

Ajitha Shaurya, the Prince of Mithila, would be buried in an unknown grave, covered with a shroud made of a slave girl's tattered skirt. All because he had been courageous enough to sacrifice his life for a girl he had loved.

She wanted to cry but her tears had run out. All she felt instead was a cold deep anger. She kneeled on the ground and began to drag the heaps of mud that she had dug out of the ground, back into the shallow grave.

By the time she was done, the sun was low in the horizon. Soon, it would be dark and the creatures of the night would come out to hunt. Avanti looked at the grave one last time and walked towards the waterfall.

She bathed under its cold water, unmindful of the burning pain in her fingers. She walked out of the water naked and trekked towards the campsite. The campsite was bare except for a few empty tents, that looked like ghosts in a children's play.

She scoured the camp carefully. She found a half-eaten fruit and devoured it in two bites. She found a blunt dagger in one of the tents. She used it to tear into the tent cloth. When she found a piece of discarded rope that had been used to hoist the tent up, she used it as a sash to wrap the tent cloth around her naked body.

And, then, she headed out to the one place in the camp

she had resisted looking at so far—the tent in which she had spent the night before. She and Ajitha. There was nothing left of the tent, except for a pole with a piece of cloth on it. The body of a man lay there, almost burnt to cinders. An animal, most likely a lone wolf, had tried to feast on its bones and had left a mess behind.

She sat down next to the defiled body, put the dagger on the floor next to her and closed her eyes. She did not realise how long she sat there—for she relived every moment that had happened the night before: arriving at the camp, drinking the sura, the attack on the camp, the stupor, the nightmares, the flight for life and eventually, Ajitha whispering something in her ears even as he strangled her: 'Love is fighting for ...'

She relived the whole chain of events again and again, till each moment was burnt into her consciousness like a flaming wound.

She would never forget. She would never forgive.

When Avanti opened her eyes, the sun had set in the distance. It was almost dark. Avanti held the handle of the dagger in one hand and rested its blade on her scalp. With one deliberate stroke, she moved it backwards. A clump of her long curly locks fell on her lap—the locks that Ajitha had so loved to look at. The dagger was blunt and along with locks, her skin came off and blood oozed down her forehead and face, blinding her.

Avanti did not wipe her blood away. She let it flow. She placed the dagger on her scalp again and shaved her locks again.

She would not forget. She would not forgive.

Avanti, the Princess of Panchala, swore a blood oath at that moment. That till the time she breathed and walked the face of the earth, she would have only one mission, one purpose. She would not rest till she had killed every last one of those bandits. She would not grow her locks till she had severed the head of that king of bandits, that cruel tyrant who had killed the love of her life, Ajitha.

The dagger continued to move in swift strokes in the dark, and Avanti bathed in her own blood.

## 33. Brahma Hathya

It was yet another quiet morning at Balabara. Over a week had passed since the last caravan had departed from the village at the fringes of Naimisha towards the city of Kampilya. All summer long, the caravans passing through the village had become thinner and thinner—fewer oxcarts, fewer men. But, since the last one had left after a night of raucous merrymaking and drinking, not a single caravan had come to the village.

Instead, bands of armed soldiers mounted on horses had passed through the village and into the jungle. From the armour they wore and their battle-scarred bodies, the villagers knew that these were not the highway guards who kept bandits at bay but seasoned, unsmiling men of war. These soldiers did not stop at the village to enjoy its fine honey-flavoured sura or bed its buxom prostitutes, they just rode right into the forest as though the village did not exist.

Since the caravans had stopped, life in the village had changed. It had become quieter. In the past, the elders in the village would often talk about missing the old days when silence had reigned supreme in the village, when you could hear the squawking of wild parrots and the mating calls of peacocks from the woods of Naimisha. But, as trade had flourished and the caravans had started to pass through Balabara, the village had become noisy, drowning out the sounds of nature.

But, now, the silence was back and nobody liked it, not even the elders. For, there was something unnatural and cloying about this silence. It felt like the desolation and darkness of Naimisha had seeped into the village.

*What bleak times we live in,* thought Devasukha, the priest at the temple of Agni, as he stepped out of the pond, drenched to the bone. As was the norm these days, the village was quiet. He could not hear the usual hubbub of daily activities: the incessant pounding of iron from the blacksmith's workshop on the outskirts of the village, women singing songs as they went to fetch water from the pond, the neighing of the horses, the tinkling of the bells around the cows' necks as the farmers dragged them to the fields. Devasukha shuddered at the quiet, and changed into his ochre prayer clothes. He stood outside the temple, with his eyes closed, and said a silent prayer to the god of fire for purity, brightness and the welfare of all.

He heard the sound as soon as he opened his eyes—the steady thumping of hoofs on hard ground. At first, he thought it was another band of grim-faced soldiers passing through towards Naimisha. But then, he realised the sound was coming from the east, from Naimisha.

He turned around and immediately began rubbing his eyes, in disbelief. Were his eyes failing him? After all, his father had gone blind as a bat in his later years. No, he was seeing just fine.

A caravan was slowly emerging from the woods of Naimisha. No caravan was expected to come out from the forest … and yet, one oxcart followed another.

The caravan kept coming closer. That's when the brahman spotted the man leading the caravan. He sat there holding the reins of the horses, staring ahead, glassy-eyed, seeing everything, comprehending nothing.

And then, Devasukha spotted the birds. They circled above the caravan and some even swooped down and flew away with something soft and pink in their beaks.

*It can't be … it can't be,* thought Devasukha, shaking his head in disbelief. The birds had bald heads and long necks.

They were vultures. This was a caravan of the dead.

One by one, the oxcarts rolled past the temple of Agni. The priest stood transfixed, mouth agape, staring at the macabre tableau on display, while the bells around the necks of the oxen jingled.

On each of the oxcarts were the bodies of men, mutilated and cut open by careful design but beyond human imagination. On the first cart sat the fat merchant from Vaishali, the only alive human in the entire caravan—wordless and zombie-like, staring ahead, unblinking and unflinching.

In the oxcart behind him, sat three brahmans nailed to the floor of the oxcart, their faces a hideous sculpture from which lips had been cut off and whose teeth had been bashed in. The vultures had done the rest—they had feasted on the eyes and flesh of the cheeks, and even picked on the bones. Streaks of dried blood, black and sticky, stained their chests and swarms of flies buzzed over them.

In the next ten oxcarts were the bodies of the soldiers, the kshatriyas, wearing their armours and breastplates, immaculately preserved except for their arms which had been sawed off. The vultures had fed on the bones that stuck out of the shoulders till all that remained were hollow sockets. Worms and maggots stuck out of these sockets dripping down the slippery armours which were stained in dark blood and tissue.

Then came the oxcarts bearing the merchants, the vaisyas, the men of sharp intellect and trade. Their thighs had been cut open with knives and daggers. The birds had gnawed the flesh to the bone, and feasted on the soft flesh below the torso.

On and on the procession went, till the last oxcart reached the temple of Agni. Devasukha did not know what prodded him into action. Was it the stench coming from the carts? Was it the buzzing of swarms of flies? Or was it the clacking sounds of the vultures feasting on the bodies of men?

But the brahman couldn't just stand there staring anymore. He walked to the last oxcart and tugged at the reins. The oxen stopped. The bells around its neck stopped jangling.

Perhaps the oxen ahead heard one of its brethren stopping. One by one, all the oxcarts came to a stop, till all the bells stopped ringing.

The buzzing of flies filled the air. The birds of prey flapped their wings and continued pecking: *clack, clack, clack.*

Devasukha threw up, vomiting everything he had ever eaten. The birds of prey paused, turned and looked at him with eager eyes.

The brahman screamed. In the distance, the village had started stirring up. But he couldn't wait for help to come. Ahead of him, on the first cart, sat the only man alive, the merchant from Vaishali.

The brahman walked to the first oxcart slowly, averting his eyes from the gruesome spectacle of death. He knew he would remember this till his last breath—and perhaps, even beyond.

By the time he reached the first cart, a few villagers had already joined him. They kept their distance from the oxcarts, horrified by what they saw. And yet, they did not run in terror—for the sight was too maddening, too methodical for their minds to solve or understand.

Eventually, when Devasukha got to the first cart, he tapped the merchant gently on the shoulder.

The merchant turned his neck and stared at the brahman with unblinking eyes. They were red-rimmed and dry as though they had shed all the tears of a lifetime in one go.

'Are you Trivikrama, the king of Vaishali?' asked Vishnupada.

The brahman shook his head. Clearly, the merchant was beyond the reaches of sanity.

'Are you Trivikrama, the king of Vaishali?' Vishnupada repeated the question, again.

The brahman paused for a moment, before he nodded. For the rest of his living days, he would wonder why he did not shake his head again to say no.

'I have a message from Eka, king of the free men, the ruler of Naimisha and all the forest tribes,' said Vishnupada. 'Here it is.'

For a moment, Vishnupada stayed silent. And then, with a strength that made the brahman step back, he screamed the words that the brahman said everyday as he sat in front of the immortal fire in the temple of Agni.

'When they divided Purusa,<br>
how many portions did they make?<br>
What do they call his mouth, his arms?<br>
What do they call his thighs and feet?

The Brahman was his mouth,<br>
of both his arms was the Rājanya made.<br>
His thighs became the Vaiśya,<br>
from his feet the Śūdra was produced.'

At that moment, everything about this grotesque procession made sense to Devasukha. He fell to the ground and began crying like an orphaned child, who had witnessed the death of everything he held dear.

## 34. Madhusmita's Parchment

In the great palace of Vaishali, time dragged its feet slowly. The lord of Mithila was in a dark mood and it spread around the palace like an angry plague, killing one smile at a time, touching everyone and sparing none. Soldiers, nobles and servants avoided Trivikrama's gaze and conversations stopped abruptly wherever he went.

Trivikrama felt a thousand eyes on him all the time. They stared at him, waiting for him to say something, do something—swing into action, declare war or take a dramatic oath that rivers of blood and vengeance would engulf the enemies of the great kingdom.

But Trivikrama was frozen. For the first time in his life, he did not know how to command. Something was paralysing him, something so deep and primitive that he could not recognise it. Was it fear?

It had been three days since the caravan of the dead, as the people of Mithila called it, had been spotted at that cursed village of Balabara. The story of the caravan and its horrors had spread across the sixteen kingdoms like wildfire. And slim tendrils of fear had spread like poison, paralysing everything, except the rumours.

From the farthest edges of the empire, spies relayed strange messages. Farmers had stopped tilling and harvesting their fields. Brahmans had closed the temples down. The famed flower markets of Vaishali were empty and the granaries that fed the cities were running low.

Caravans had stopped moving between most of the sixteen kingdoms. Neither offers of bountiful gold nor threats of flogging could get the merchants to move the produce from one city to another. And, then the news came that the soldiers had begun to rebel. Young conscripts had begun deserting their camps when they were ordered to march into the forests. The commander of Kashi had beheaded a few runaway soldiers the evening before, only to discover that more soldiers had vanished in the middle of the night.

Everything had begun to fall apart. The empire had stopped in its tracks.

Diseased men with sores and pus-filled wounds streamed into the cities of all sixteen kingdoms, as the men guarding the gates disappeared. People saw ghosts and goblins where none existed and lynched mendicants and beggars to death. Charlatans with miracle cures and promises of heaven made more gold than all the merchants of Vaishali put together.

The only places of business in Mithila that still prospered were the taverns and the whorehouses, where men found comfort in drink and in the pleasures of the flesh. Trivikrama thought of going to one of these houses himself, but guilt stopped him.

His brother, the only one in the whole world who had playfully mocked, taunted and toyed with him, was unaccounted for. And here he was thinking of romping with strange women. So, the lord of Vaishali, chastising himself, stood on his balcony and stared gloomily at the black clouds gathering in the horizon, nursing a half empty glass of sura.

The monsoons were almost here. In a few days, the skies

would open up, the rivers would swell up and the forests of Naimisha would become almost impossible to navigate. His brother, if he was alive, would remain a prisoner of these savages for a few months. God only knew what horrors he would have to experience. The poor boy!

*I should have never let him go!*

The savages wouldn't be stupid enough to kill him—after all, if they did, what would they bargain with? What would they do when the rains ended? Where would they hide from the fury of Vaishali?

Or would they?

'Aacharya-ji,' said Trivikrama, turning around, a little too fast. The world swam in front of his eyes. 'Why would this king of bandits hold my brother hostage and not kill him?'

Trivikrama could see the irritation on his teacher's face. He had asked the same question several times during the day and Aacharya Gurukripa had patiently answered each time, for he knew the questions came not from a king but from a brother whose heart struggled with the fear of unbearable personal loss.

This time, however, the aacharya did not answer. Instead, he picked up the cask of sura and poured himself a drink. He downed the drink in one gulp.

Trivikrama stared at Gurukripa in surprise, who, much to his own surprise, smiled.

'My dear Vikrama, it's not just your brother who is in danger but my daughter Avanti too,' said Gurukripa. 'She may not be my flesh and blood but I have raised her for years as my own. However, you and I are more than just a brother and a father right now. We have a duty to this kingdom and its people. Ponder on that, my king.'

'But I don't know what to do, Aacharya-ji. This enemy is

new. He doesn't have a kingdom I can lay siege to. He doesn't have an army I can wage war with. He doesn't use chariots and swords and elephants to fight us. He uses fear. He breaks us from within. Why else would he slaughter men of birth by their caste? The vaisyas' thighs were cut off. The warriors' arms were amputated. The brahmans' faces were mutilated. He is not worried about committing brahma hathya, the gravest of sins or of the consequences of his actions in this world and beyond. How do I fight an enemy like this—one without a moral code, one who I cannot see?' said Trivikrama.

'You are wrong, my king. This man … this Ardhamukha has a code. He has a plan and he wants to be seen,' said Gurukripa. 'Why else would he send that one merchant alive? Why else would he set up an elaborate trap? Send one of his men disguised as a brahman to our court and then send his severed hand to us. Don't look surprised. That was his plan all along. Send a learned man into our court, allow him to make a public prediction and then make him disappear. All this madness began with that single incident, did it not?' asked Gurukripa.

Trivikrama shook his head in disbelief and then nodded. 'But, if all this is true, how did this savage predict the dhumaketu, the fire pouring from the skies? Something that even the learned men of this court could not predict.'

'Knowledge is not the preserve of only the civilised, my king,' said Gurukripa. 'If there is anything our scriptures have taught us, it is that thieves can become saints and even gods can sin.'

'So, what do I do now, Aacharya-ji?' asked Trivikrama.

'Wait, my king, be patient. As painful as it might sound, patience is often the greatest action,' said his teacher. 'Let him make his move. I am sure you will hear from him soon. Till then, let me take care of this sura,' said Gurukripa, who picked up the cask, bowed and left Trivikrama alone in the room.

The sound of thunder boomed in the distance as the dark clouds continued to roll in.

An hour later, the desire for distraction triumphed over guilt and virtue. The taverns and the whorehouses beckoned. Trivikrama was in no mood to play hide and seek. The tunnel be damned. The king walked down the empty palace courtyard towards the stables. The sky above was dark and gloomy. A ball of dry grass swirled and danced in the cool wind blowing down from the riverfront.

The king stopped and sniffed the air. It was about to rain. Two guards snapped to their attention when they saw him walk unsteadily towards the stable. He waved a bored, limp hand at them.

He mounted his favourite steed clumsily and almost fell off it. If only Ajitha could see him right now, the barbs he would throw at him! Trivikrama chuckled at the thought and felt a sting of pain in his heart.

*Brother, where are you?*

The guards were staring at him curiously. Trivikrama realised that tears were rolling down his face. He pulled the reins hard and the horse galloped forward. A bolt of lightning lit up the yard and through the corner of his eyes, Trivikrama spotted something.

Something unusual, something out of place.

Big drops of rain had begun to fall. He tugged at the reins and the horse stopped. To his right, at the far end of the archery yard, where his brother would shoot arrows at strawmen, was a strange figure.

Something that looked like a giant matchstick. Trivikrama dismounted from his horse and walked towards it. The skies had opened up by now, and the rain was so thick that he could barely see anything. His turban was drenched and weighed heavy on his head. He threw it away and kept walking towards the alien object, his feet splashing in the wet puddles of mud and water.

Darkness was all around him when he got to the object. A bolt of lightning lit up the yard.

It was a long spear, twice as tall as Trivikrama, embedded in the ground. He looked up and on it was mounted a head—the head of the Prince of Vaishali.

Trivikrama sank to the ground. From a distance, the guards watched as the king tore at his hair, beat his chest and beat the ground in front of him like a madman.

No one came to offer solace, for the insane are capable of anything. And there was no human being more dangerous than a man who has lost everything he loved.

From the terrace above, the Queen Mother watched her son grieve. She did not cry or mourn. She went back to her low desk on the floor and sat down, stone-faced. She dipped her quill into the inkpot. She was out of ink. Madhusmita picked up the dagger lying under her desk and in one neat motion ran it over her bony forearm. A thin sliver of blood trickled out and ran over the countless other scars on her arm. She did not wince or cry out in pain.

She let the blood run down her arm and into the inkpot. When it was full, she pressed on the cut with a coarse cotton cloth and wiped it dry.

She dipped the quill into the inkpot again and wrote on the parchment. As always, she wrote only one line again and again.

*I have sinned. I have sinned. I have sinned.*

When she was done with her sheaf of parchments, the Queen Mother rang the bell lying next to her. Despite the sound of the booming thunder outside, Nila the eunuch heard it and her burly form appeared in the room.

'My queen,' said Nila, staring at the parchment, waiting for orders from the Queen Mother.

'Summon my son,' said Queen Madhusmita in a clear voice, much to the eunuch's surprise, for she had never heard the queen speak before. 'When he is done grieving, I have a story to tell him.'

THE END

# Epilogue

'Spinner of yarns,
teller of tales,
tell me a story, tell me a story,
a story of kings and queens,
of princes and commoners,
of a time before Gautama & Chandaka,
a time after the great war,
when Agni was an old god,
when Vishnu was a young god …'

The storyteller replied:

'Hear this story, old friend
Be warned,
The land of Bharata was unlike any you know today,
Darkness and light reigned in equal measure,
A land fertile,
Watered with blood and honey in equal parts,
This is not a tale for the feeble hearted,
So, hear me with care and lightness,
Suspend your thoughts,
And hear this tale from your heart,
The tale of men gone by,
Of a boy,
Of brothers and blood …'

# About the Author

Journalist, technophile, communications expert, cricket enthusiast, T.V. Mahalingam was all those things, but above all he liked to tell a good story. An avid reader, he could talk for hours about mythology, science, history and a million other things. As someone who loved fiction and fantasy, it comes as no surprise that he authored his first novel *Brahma Hathya* on Indian mythology and fantasy.

## Brothers Forever

Thirty nine years! That's how long I knew T.V. Mahalingam (Arvind). Ever since I opened my eyes, I've known him as my brother. I'm told that he was the first one in the family to hold me in his arms.

We were born about three and a half years apart and so growing up, our interests, likes, hobbies were similar. Of course, every family has an intellectual one and another who's more studious. In our case, he turned out to be the bright, curious child who read novels at a very young age. Whilst not being bothered about his own grades in class, he would be particularly concerned about mine.

If he was the one who could engage in a discussion or an intellectual debate with my father, I was his shadow. Siblings do that often. You look upto the elder one. What made our relationship special was that we were best friends. I would spend more time ogling at the girls in his class whilst he laughed about it.

We studied in the same schools, played cricket together, bunked classes whenever India was playing a match, and watched movies back to back till our eyes turned red and we both had headaches. During lunch breaks, we would share jokes and revel in each other's company.

His career took him to journalism, his work ethic and amiable nature made him quite the man to be around.

Through the years, one thing remained constant—we would talk almost every morning while traveling to work. Most calls were three-way chats between him, my parents and me. If there's something called love—it's what we felt for each other.

We always knew he could write well. We would discuss books and movie scripts, and analyze what could be better in them. The COVID-19 days took something from everyone. We lost him at that time. It took me a year and a half to muster up the courage to read his book. And when I finally read *Brahma Hathya*, his first novel on Indian fantasy and fiction, I realised I had found my new favourite author. Call it a brother's bias. But irrespective, the book is a riveting read, its characters outstanding and the plot unforgettable. The beauty of any good writer is that their stories become legends and folklore long after the ink has dried and the parchment has crumpled. In *Brahma Hathya*, I hope the reader finds exactly that.

He completed his masterpiece days before Mahadeva claimed him, and here I am continuing his journey of publishing his book so that this story finds its audiences and the scale that it deserves.

To you, my brother Arvind, all I can say is that the feeling of void will remain forever but thirty nine years of memories will last a lifetime. Until we meet again.

Love from your brother
Naarayan T.V.

PS: Amma and Appa are proud parents. I can't wait for your nieces to grow up and read your novel.

# A Note of Endearment

T.V. Mahalingam or Arvind as his loved ones called him has been the light of my life. He was my husband, my partner, my friend, philosopher and guide. He was the Northstar of my life.

Every day with him was an adventure, each moment magical, something right out of celluloid. What started as an exchange of notes at a Global Nasscom Leadership Summit in February 2008 between two media professionals led to a soulful romance between two kindred souls and an exhilarating courtship with labyrinthine twists and turns. It ultimately culminated in our marriage at an Arya Samaj temple in July 2009.

Our bond was ethereal, our connect deep, soulful and passionate despite our different geographical backgrounds—me, a Kashmiri pandit and he from Palakkad in Kerala. Arvind was multi-lingual having lived in seven different cities. He was quick witted with an amiable disposition and a colloquial sense of humour.

He was naturally drawn to supporting philanthropic causes especially around education, economic empowerment and environment. He was an evolving individual with a balanced blend of the temporal and the spiritual, and a beacon light of inspiration for me for the road ahead.

*Brahma Hathya*, his first book reflects his unbounded imagination, aesthetic sense and total dedication. I trust the reader will savour and relish his flowing and descriptive narrative style, the detailed construction of diverse characters and the overall gripping storyline as much as I did.

To put it in the form of one of his favourite quotes by Walt Disney: 'We keep moving forward, opening new doors, and doing new things, because we're curious and curiosity keeps leading us down new paths.'

Ruchi C. Mahalingam

# Acknowledgements

I can imagine vicariously that writing a book involves imagination, passion and above all the endurance to stick to the task and time to dedicate to the endeavour. That credit for all this, of course, goes to the author T.V. Mahalingam.

*Brahma Hathya* is T.V. Mahalingam's creation. I can only imagine him typing away on his laptop early in the morning before his work commitments for the day began and late into the night when he had solitude for company. However, every good piece of work comes to life only through the good wishes and blessings of people. In this regard, I have to thank Ruchi, T.V. Mahalingam's wife for trusting me to get the job done. I didn't know how to begin. But then there were friends who volunteered to help. If not for a gentleman called Navroze who constantly coaxed me to move faster, I can't imagine where we would be.

Help came from places I never expected. But when Mahadeva and Mahamaya will it, who am I to question it? Amit Doshi, probably one of the best conversationalists I've met in my life introduced me to Karthika V.K., Publisher at Westland Books. I remember my first conversation with her after she'd read the book. I'm forever obliged to her for having the faith. You're one of a kind.

The brilliant team at Westland who've been patient with me—Amrita Talwar, Ipshita and Pallavi Mohan. I am grateful that I have friends and colleagues like Harshad, Krunal and Mihir who've supported me every day.

Above all, my father T.M. Viswanathan whose grit is second to none. You pushed me to read the book at a time when I thought I wasn't emotionally ready. And to my mother Seetha Viswanathan who has sacrificed for the family and stood like a pillar of strength every day. If not for them, I wouldn't have progressed at all. I would be remiss if I didn't mention my wife Deepa for bearing with me through long hours and weekends, although it doesn't surprise me given her affection for my brother.

I must confess that finding the time and energy for publishing this book, even during the midnight hours, in the midst of demanding professional commitments would not have been possible if not for the love of my brother and the waft of his sweet memory. At the end of it, there is only a sense of relief that the book of a worthy author will be in the hands of book lovers and followers of mythology-based fiction. I can confidently state this piece of creative work is eminently readable and deserving of appreciation from all quarters, a rare gift to all lovers of mythological fiction. Thank you to everyone who has been instrumental in publishing this book. Now onward to Kedar, Mithila and Naimisha where a world of love, fantasy and courage beckons us.